.I328628-001 9781982193041 TX 36.0 260

BAEN BOOKS
by JOELLE PRESBY

The Dabare Snake Launcher

The Road to Hell (with David Weber)

To purchase any of these titles in e-book form,
please go to www.baen.com.

THE DABARE SNAKE LAUNCHER

JOELLE PRESBY

THE DABARE SNAKE LAUNCHER

Copyright © 2022 by Joelle Presby

All rights reserved, including the right to reproduce this book or portions thereof in any form.

A Baen Books Original

Baen Publishing Enterprises
P.O. Box 1403
Riverdale, NY 10471
www.baen.com

ISBN: 978-1-9821-9304-1

Cover art by Kurt Miller

First printing, November 2022
First paperback printing, November 2023

Distributed by Simon & Schuster
1230 Avenue of the Americas
New York, NY 10020

Library of Congress Control Number: 2022035880

Printed in the United States of America
10 9 8 7 6 5 4 3 2 1

THE DABARE SNAKE LAUNCHER

Part I

dabare \ da-ba-RAY \

an engineering construction made with repurposed parts and extreme technical know-how, which either works flawlessly or not at all

origin: West African Fulani

Definition from *The Cassini-Sadou Dictionary*, 3rd ed.

CHAPTER ONE

SADOU MAURIE'S GUTS COILED AS IF THEY WERE living snakes trying to work their way out of her body through sheer boa power. The misery had a familiar taste. Dry mouth, exhaustion so great even her tongue wanted to lie flat rather than help with a wet swallow. The fine dust standing in the air longer than any reasonable breeze should allow finally triggered recognition.

It was Africa, West Africa. And from the taste of the air, it was somewhere near home. She felt too hot, even for dry season, and wanted to sleep and dream of air-conditioning. She forced her eyes to focus on details.

A good metal roof slanted down overhead and met solid cement-block walls with large windows bringing in the light to save on electricity.

This latest mistake had landed her somewhere with a few resources. Had they finished fixing the well system? She couldn't remember.

A chart hung at the foot of her cot. Tightly squinted

eyes let her read it: schistosomiasis, fever, and complications. What was *schisto* again? A vague memory from grade school health class dragged up a cartoon diagram of blood flukes infesting a liver. With luck the horrid medicine had killed off the microscopic beasties. If not, well, it wasn't like a woman needed her kidneys, liver, or other internal organs. Maurie squinted at the chart to see if she could make out the names of the medicines she'd been dosed with.

A machine roar from overhead rattled the cement-block clinic building. Not quite the quiet bushlands where she'd been working last week, but still home. Of course, the nonprofit hadn't considered flight paths when they picked the spot for this clinic. Foreigners forgot that when locals could afford it, they used supersonic air travel to get to their destinations too.

If Maurie could just stop breathing and let her intestines have whatever they wanted, she would have given up days ago. But the treacherous gut wasn't stopping and besides this was home—no quitting without permission. And absolutely no surrendering to a mere snail-borne river sickness.

The orderlies were not allowing any such cowardice. Maurie searched the room for her attendant. She remembered powerful arms and tightly braided no-nonsense hair framing an expressionless dark face. Ah, there she was.

Ms. Oumarou regarded her with a posture that indicated a faint disdain as if Maurie's illnesses were too mundane to be worth much effort. Maurie let her eyes drift close.

Ms. Oumarou, who certainly didn't have a nursing degree or any sort of medical license, shook Maurie awake at least once every five minutes. The small woman should have been overwhelmed by the number of patients, but Maurie suspected this was a slow day. Ms. Oumarou's forcefulness might also be why Maurie hadn't been able to give up. Yesterday, she'd tried to say thank you and been repeatedly ignored. Today, Maurie was too exhausted to be a good patient.

"*Mange.*" Eat. It was an order, not a suggestion. Maurie took the spoon and filled her mouth.

She hated this stuff. Sweet yams with the life boiled out of them mashed to nothing but soft pulp. There was too much in the bowl, she wanted to complain, but she was too tired. So Maurie ate exhausting spoonful after exhausting spoonful. When the bowl was empty she dropped the spoon, letting it clatter on the floor.

Ms. Oumarou scooped it up and favored her with a scowl. Maurie managed the faintest smile. She had done it on purpose. It had taken extra energy to make the spoon land on the floor instead of the bowl.

"*Bete.*" Ms. Oumarou tapped her lightly on the head and tucked the sheet up over her shoulders. "Beast," she added in case Maurie hadn't understood. The woman did have some English. Maurie was pleased to hear it. Her own French was execrable.

So, she was sick. Wasn't everyone?

Maurie was grateful to be too old for American boarding school intake physicals. She could imagine the horror on the clinicians' faces if she'd had to report this one to the medical office. "Um, yeah, I had a high fever, no, not 101°F, an actually high fever, 108°F, the kind treated in the field with ice baths when you can get the generator working long enough to make ice. A cool stream seems to work okay too. And yeah, so I think it was probably malaria because chloroquine fifteen seemed to work, but then I got *schisto* or something like it from the stream..." They'd look things up on their tropical diseases wiki and argue with her about her symptoms and how infectious she might be to other students. They never did want her blood donations. Not a great loss when Maurie didn't particularly want to get extra needle pokes, but such was life.

The fever broke.

Maurie woke soaking in sweat with too many sheets wrapped one on top the other over her. She pushed them off, and Ms. Oumarou was there to catch and bundle them up.

"Stand up then," the orderly said.

Maurie glared. She did not want to stand. Where was her bowl? Her stomach growled and she'd willingly eat without even the threat of constant wake-ups, but that wasn't Ms. Oumarou's plan for her.

"*Mange*. Eat!" Maurie demanded.

The woman responded with a flow of French that Maurie caught barely enough of to recognize that she was being chastised in rather low form and compared to all manner of animals, most quite poorly bathed. "*Leve toi*. Up. Up." Ms. Oumarou clapped her hands.

Maurie looked pointedly at her tray.

"*Toilette premiere*," Ms. Oumarou insisted. *Clean first.*

No wonder they were called orderlies. All they did was order you about. Maurie stood. Bare feet on cool concrete, she was tempted to lie down and attempt to suck the coolness out of the silk-smooth floor. She straightened her knees against temptation.

The world shifted uncomfortably, but Ms. Oumarou's strong arm held her up while the other stripped off the hospital gown and sponged her off.

Moderately cleaner and with a new gown wrapped around herself, Maurie was placed on a fresh hospital bed with the back lifted high up. There was a bowl on the left side. Ms. Oumarou took the lid off.

Rice this time, with a meaty broth poured over top. Ms. Oumarou stuck a spoon into the bowl and left it sticking straight up.

No Japanese cultural sensitivity training had reached this clinic. Or maybe it had, and the orderly was fighting back against foreign rules. Maurie felt a surge of sympathy for her. She imagined the woman had enough of a struggle with strange foreign patients and entirely too many native diseases. Maurie hoped Ms. Oumarou had been spared corporate rule makers.

"*Mange*," Ms. Oumarou said again, and she left to tend another patient.

Maurie's eyelids let her know they wouldn't mind if she wanted to take just a brief rest before struggling to lift the spoon as many times as necessary to empty the bowl. Maurie met Ms. Oumarou's glare from across the ward.

Those other patients were entirely too compliant. They didn't distract the woman at all.

Maurie ate. She considered dribbling some of the broth down her front in toddler-like obstinacy. Her stomach rumbled in objection. She carefully cleaned the bowl with the slightly bent old aluminum spoon.

When Ms. Oumarou wasn't looking, Maurie straightened the spoon to fix the odd half twist some past patient had applied to it.

Fixing things was what Maurie did. It didn't always get her hospitalized. She hadn't known that the clogged well had been filled intentionally to keep people away. When Grandpere had asked her to fix that village's water problem, she hadn't thought to ask why they hadn't already done it themselves.

Pascaline, the sour cousin always ready to point out problems, also hadn't asked. "People say there's a curse on the well," she'd said and kept her distance, managing the work crew's food needs rather than get involved with troubleshooting the barely half-functional digging gear or minding their finicky portable generator. Maurie had ignored it but now she wondered. Probably just the fever confusing her thoughts, but Pascaline had a talent for avoiding injury, illness, and pain.

Except of course for the thing that had happened to her parents. It had happened to Maurie's dad too, of course, but losing one parent wasn't really the same as losing both. And it helped that her dad hadn't been at fault. One giant kaboom neither Maurie nor Pascaline had seen for themselves, and everything changed.

Grandpere'd held everything together after. Both sons gone, he'd had to resume the director position while still managing the extended family, which was a harder job than even maintaining profit margins in a declining industry.

Oil and natural gas, crude energy sources from a poor nation, piped and shipped to companies too rich to be national at all. One of their biggest buyers, TCG, had done something important recently. If Maurie were less tired she was sure she could remember. It had something to do with them not being such a big buyer in the future. But Uncle Fabrice had some kind of plan. If it worked, the TCG thing was also going to improve the Sadou family money situation and make this poor country rich enough to fund their own bush country clinics without foreigner-led nongovernmental organizations involved.

Her eyelids betrayed her, closing. The spoon stayed clutched in her hand.

Maurie woke next to the treacherous utensil being tapped on her forehead as a makeshift cattle prod.

"So. You lived." Pascaline, her younger cousin with the permanent crease between her eyebrows and the always glaring deep brown eyes, seemed annoyed. "I bet against you, you know." Pascaline's parentage was the same general muddle of ancestors connected to a half dozen tribes as Maurie's was, but on her cousin those genetics looked good. Maurie didn't need a mirror to know that the clinic staff would've assumed she was a vagrant who'd stolen the tailored field gear if queenly Pascaline hadn't been the one to bring her in. Pascaline's expression was assessing, and she'd taken the time to have her braids redone with gold beads.

Maurie closed her eyes again, hoping Ms. Oumarou would rid her of the annoying visitor.

Pascaline's stolen flatware whacked her forehead again in a fast double tap. Where had she gotten two spoons?

"Stop that!" Maurie pulled away.

Pascaline chortled. "I knew you were awake. And to be quite honest, I won more on you than I lost. I just had to get it going by being the one to bet you'd die so the others would get over the horror of being negative about it all. Get out of bed today, and I'll cut you in for a share."

That was Pascaline, always focused on the bottom line.

"How much?" Maurie croaked out. Her voice came out annoyingly healthy sounding. No coughing lung infection component with this latest super bug apparently.

"Ten percent," Pascaline said. "I was prepared to go to twenty if you got up before noon, but that pretty *Médecins Sans Culottes* kid wanted a drink and to chat about Switzerland, so I was late getting in here."

"It's *Sans Frontières*. *Sans Culottes* would be without underclothes. Sort of. In slang, though, unless you meant to make a reference to that group of French revolutionaries who—" Maurie narrowed her eyes at her cousin. It was hard to know what Pascaline would do with any information you inadvertently gave her. "Old slang. It probably doesn't mean a thing to anyone under twenty."

"Says the ancient thirty-eight-year-old." Pascaline grinned too broadly for someone also in her thirties. "Brain works too. Another win for me. Ha." She let out a satisfied sigh. "We did get you pumped full of meds and into that stream fast enough after all."

Maurie groaned. She didn't feel like her brain had escaped being boiled. Maybe it was only lightly sautéed instead. So the local Doctors Without Borders MD was cute, huh? Wait. There was a doctor? Why hadn't the patient ever seen the doctor? Her bladder was beating its own insistent demands. It felt even more unhappy than her intestines did at the moment, so she was probably minutes away from wetting herself.

"Fifteen percent," Pascaline countered, misinterpreting the grimace. "But that's my final offer. I won't go any higher than that."

"Liar." Maurie swung her legs off the side of the bed. "Help me to the outhouse. Or I'm staying in bed."

Pascaline pulled back about a meter. "Walk first. I can't carry you and claim it."

Maurie looked around for shoes. There didn't seem to be any.

The polished cement floor gleamed with a cleanliness any Western European hospital would be proud of. It also felt pleasantly cool under her feet. She balanced and carefully shifted her weight from the bed onto her own feet. They held her. And no spike of fever or nausea wiped her out.

Maurie walked around the bed to Pascaline and punched her in the stomach. The blow didn't quite have her usual force behind it; too many days in a hospital bed would do that, but her cousin doubled over nicely.

Ms. Oumarou was holding up another patient and paying her no attention at all when Maurie made her way to the outhouse behind the clinic. A line of visitors' inexpensive plastic flip-flop shoes lined the back porch. Maurie slid her feet into an orange-and-purple pair for the trip to the outhouse and back. The smell of the outhouse was reasonably well contained by a makeshift metal door set into a wood frame, and woven-grass matting gave the hole a bit of privacy. Maurie held her gown carefully out of the dirt and squatted.

Her bladder thanked her.

Pascaline banged on the door.

"I've got toilet paper."

"I still hate you." Maurie cracked the door and accepted the peace offering. It was hard to stay mad at Pascaline when she was so annoyingly useful. Maurie finished up and came out.

Her cousin held a bottle of hand sanitizer at the ready. Maurie accepted a large dollop. "Do we truly not have running water here?"

"They've got it," Pascaline acknowledged. "But they can't boil all of it, and some shitheads keep letting their cattle take dumps upstream of the town's water intake system. I wouldn't risk it, if I were you." The woman shrugged. "I had a water truck sent to supply the ward when I found out where you'd been admitted. They've been using it for your baths and for all the cooking."

"I still dislike you," Maurie amended. "They use contaminated water for cooking?" The mind boggled.

"Heat does kill most of the microbes. And nobody local picked this site for the clinic." Pascaline lifted an eyebrow to let her know she expected better of her usually sharp cousin. "And didn't I say I sent you a water truck? Some people." She shook her head. "You want me to get the doctor to get you released, or you just want to walk out of here yourself?"

Maurie sighed. "Do you have another bet riding on that?"

"Nope. But other people do. I don't care."

Maurie looked back at the clinic building. It had her bed in it. "I don't have shoes. These belong to someone else. Go buy me some and I'll check myself out." She could take a nap in the hospital bed while she waited.

Except that Ms. Oumarou stood on the porch with her hands on her hips.

Maurie slipped off the stolen flip-flops and tried

to act like she wasn't embarrassed. She stepped onto the clean concrete, careful to leave the shoes in the precise position where she'd found them. Pascaline, the coward, had vanished. Presumably she was going off to buy shoes, but Maurie thought she'd have found a reason to go even if there wasn't a convenient errand.

"I'm up." Maurie smiled brightly. "I suppose I'll just go lie back down now and rest until the doctor can see me."

Ms. Oumarou scowled and blocked the door back into the ward. Maurie peeked over the woman's head. Her bed was now occupied by someone else. They may or may not have had time to change the sheets first. She sighed.

"How about a chair?" Maurie said, "I'm only just starting to recover. Do you think I can have a chair?"

Ms. Oumarou pointed. A scattering of small stools hand-carved from tree trunks lined the side of the porch against the cement clinic wall. Tourists would pay outlandish amounts for even the smallest of them and put it on a display shelf. But this place didn't have tourists, so people sat on them. The largest was about eight inches in diameter and not much taller than that. If she could get back indoors, she might be able to sit on the edge of someone's hospital bed instead.

"I can just step inside and lean against the wall." Maurie tried to brush past. It was an attempt doomed before she started, but there was something about Ms. Oumarou that made Maurie want to try her.

"*Assis toi.*" The orderly put her hands around Maurie and lifted. One moment Maurie's toes were grazing the concrete and the next her butt was on a stool. Not forcefully but not with any extra gentleness, and there she was. *Sit down*, the woman had said, and sitting Maurie now was.

Ms. Oumarou smiled and turned back to her patients inside the clinic, satisfied that her troublesome charge had been dealt with.

Maurie leaned against the wall of the clinic and closed her eyes. Pascaline would be back later.

But Pascaline wasn't back. The porch shade's coolness lulled Maurie into dreamland with a bare touch of breeze brushing her skin. Someone else waited.

A swath of vapor in a woman's shape with a serpentine thing trailing after her mounted the single step onto the cement porch. The water power, Mami-Wata, twitched an algae-mossed skirt hem, and the snake spirit untangled itself from around her feet to curl up out of sight. Wet comfort breathed over Maurie better than any air-conditioning. The rank scent of river mire settled in after. And Maurie started to drown.

"Not yet!" Mami-Wata yanked a spirit coil from Maurie's face and shook it, so the snake head attached bobbled back and forth. "No drowning my acolytes."

The snake spirit hissed unwilling acceptance and huddled in an angry pile of coils at its mistress's muddy feet.

"Where was I?" The water woman swayed side to side as if she were part snake herself. "Scrawny. If there were more offspring, I'd swallow you whole and tell the ghosts to quit their clamoring until a better one was born."

That sounds painful, Maurie thought.

"Oh, yes, yes, it is." Mami-Wata spat and venomous fangs drove into Maurie's face. "You are mine now."

The bite spread agony and bitter cold at the speed of a panicked heart. Maurie grabbed her cheek to claw open the wound and attempt to bleed out some of the venom, but Mami-Wata slapped her hand down. And then the spreading chill held her numb.

Maurie wanted to vomit but couldn't move her constricting throat enough to let the rising bile out. Shivers alternated with burning heat, and she forgot about the old wooden stool and the solid cement porch.

Instead Maurie struggled in river mud on the edge of a not yet dry stream bed. Heat beat down on her. Too late, she could move, but nothing stopped the searing pain spreading from the bite.

Not fair, she thought. A reasonable dream should at least include her feeling somewhat better while she endured the weirdness her subconscious chose to inflict on her.

Heat and sweat boiled over her body. *A fever dream*, Maurie decided.

Mami-Wata writhed back as snake, woman, and steam all at once. But she smelled of that almost dry, more mud than water, stream bed next to the last bush camp Maurie's team had used. It was the same one she was fairly sure that Pascaline had used to dunk her in when the fever got bad, and the rest of the team had scattered across the countryside searching for the nearest clinic.

"A *mami-wata* is a river spirit," Maurie said, "and I don't believe in spirits."

"A Maurie girl," the spirit snapped back, "is a noble one, and I don't believe in nobility no matter what silly colonialist names the living are calling their young these days."

"That makes no sense."

Maurie tried to force her mind to other things.

There were other problems to think of. She pushed her subconscious to fixate on anything else in hopes of redirecting fever anxiety in a more rational manner. Her cousin Reuben was still in prison last she'd heard, or at least jail awaiting trial. The bail set too high, he hadn't asked for help early enough, and—

"I'm not done," Mami-Wata interrupted. "But I can curse him too if you don't pay attention properly."

The spot on her left cheek where the fangs had hit throbbed in a fiery pulse, and Maurie screamed.

"That's more like it." Mami-Wata slid an arm or coil onto a bit of dream space turned riverbank. "And since you weren't my preferred sycophant, I'll have to be more blunt than usual. I really don't believe in nobility. That wasn't just me mocking you, much though you richly deserve it."

Maurie curled tight in a ball and focused on breathing as the pain ebbed. She really should not have let Pascaline help her to the outhouse. There must have been chamber pots to use. Ms. Oumarou would notice soon that Maurie was unconscious on the clinic porch, wouldn't she?

But she didn't wake up. "Okay. I accept responsibility. Tell me what I've done," Maurie said, hoping to rattle her subconscious into a giving her some hints that might at least partially explain this bizarre self-torture. The Reuben thing was very wrong, but it was a lot more Uncle Benoit's fault than hers. Perhaps if she'd stayed in closer contact with her cousins, she could have known about Reuben's situation sooner and helped him get a lawyer immediately when her own funds could've been enough?

"Enough!" Mami-Wata slapped her. The sky spat hard drops of rain that sizzled when they hit the parched ground.

Another spirit, snake shaped, lifted from the water and slid a calming caress around the spirit woman's arm.

"This is why I wanted the other one," she said to the snake. It tasted the air and lunged upward to wrap a coil around its mistress's neck.

Mami-Wata caught the snake just behind the eyes. She lifted it to her face and hissed at it. Then gently unwound the coils and released it into the water. An imprint of tire tracks mottled a tattoo pattern on the snake's skin a few feet beyond the head and again about a car width's later on the long snake's body.

Maurie's pain eased as if Mami-Wata's momentary distraction thinned the intensity of the fever dream.

Maurie uncurled from her fetal position and slapped her arms and legs to return feeling to them in case the snake spirit decided to slither in her direction, and she needed to run for her dream life. The size of the monster snake gave Maurie a disturbing pang of empathy for a field mouse at dusk who could hear the sounds of soft scales rustling against the grass between her and her burrow.

Mami-Wata petted the passing length of the snake with affection as it disappeared into the dream fog.

"That one was a boa before," Mami-Wata said offhand, "hasn't got a handle on spirit life yet."

"Aren't you supposed to have water snake familiars? Or be a water snake yourself or some nebulous spirit of the water thing?" Maurie's aching face wasn't helping her think.

"Are you trying to talk me into murdering you?"

Mami-Wata flicked out a forked tongue and then made a very human expression of disgust. "I could still swallow you. You might wake up after, but you wouldn't enjoy it."

The impression of fire flared around Mami-Wata's form. The pain howled back.

Maurie curled into a tighter ball. She forced out an objection through teeth chattering with renewed fever chills. "Do whatever you have to, delusion."

"I hate unbelievers," Mami-Wata replied.

Wet splattered Maurie's head and arms. Drips ran down her spine. The venom tingled but didn't burn like the bite had. "And my subconscious hates me," she translated to herself. "That and it does not understand snakes at all. Since when do water snakes spit cobra venom?"

Mami-Wata grabbed Maurie by the back of the neck and shook her. "What kind of idiot meets a spirit creature in a fever dream and thinks physical laws have any power here?" Her snake tongue flicked out.

"Point," Maurie acknowledged.

Mami-Wata shook her again in exasperation. She dragged Maurie down the embankment.

"This doesn't seem like much of a spirit world." Her trailing foot caught on a root in the mud, and Mami-Wata had to yank her up higher to free her from it.

"Yes, well, it's your subconscious," Mami-Wata said. "And besides this isn't the spirit world. You're dreaming, remember?"

The spirit woman dunked her. Water, murky and deep, surrounded her. Mami-Wata's strong arm dragged Maurie up to the surface.

The spirit woman laughed. "Finally, she's speechless."

Mami-Wata brushed the water out of Maurie's eyes. "Bitten, blinded, drowned. Three times cursed. Or blessed, perhaps. You are one of mine now."

She pushed Maurie backwards. Maurie's feet slid on a smooth cement porch, and a solid concrete clinic wall broke her backwards tumble. She slid down to a seat on an old wood-carved stool.

"No other spirits can claim you. Much as they'll want to, you're mine."

Maurie ran a hand over her feet. They weren't muddy at all, though she was dripping. "I'm already baptized."

"Yeah, well, maybe the regular angels were busy." Mami-Wata tapped her on the nose. "God works through all things, blah, blah, blah." She stepped off the clinic's porch but paused to turn back and add, "Though even devils can quote scripture."

"Which are you?" Maurie asked.

"Haven't decided yet," Mami-Wata replied. "You figure it out."

CHAPTER TWO

ETHAN SCHMIDT-LI HID THE PHOTOS HIS WIFE kept sending from the fiftieth birthday party. He'd managed to intercept the invitations in time to prevent any of his colleagues from coming. Officially, his company TCG had a policy decrying ageism, but Ethan had no faith in that sort of document.

A glance at the mirrored floor-to-ceiling office building windows confirmed his light brown hair still appeared almost as thick as it had been in his twenties. He still looked thirty-five thanks to expertly applied hair care and even more careful use of male makeup.

Male use of everything from concealer to eye shadow was a fad exclusive to a part of China he never visited but which had gotten lots of special interest news coverage in North America. Beijing, Berlin, and Atlanta were the company's three main offices, so affectations that had cultural ties to the other parts of the corporation served him well. And more importantly it helped hide his scowl lines.

Ethan was only Assistant Director for the Sciences,

North American Division, and he badly wanted a vice president position one day, preferably in operations, but he'd take sales or marketing if that's what he could get. He'd had a slow start and hadn't gotten his MBA until he was nearly forty, but he'd let his classmates think he'd been twenty-eight like most of them. So long as he didn't mention his real age or let anyone meet his wife—who, darling though she was, had an exceptionally naive view of humanity—he had a real shot at breaking into the million-dollars-a-year pay bracket, and more importantly finally getting a job where he controlled the company instead of the company controlling him.

The last six months he had dedicated himself to working through the company's internal promotion process, and he'd succeeded. The fat packet on his desk held a detailed position description with pay and benefits on the right side and had all the forms for moving out of his current position on the left. Legal wanted him to sign the more detailed version of the nondisclosure agreement as if he'd have access to scientific research when he went back into sales management.

Ethan laughed and flipped pages, initialing all the paragraphs. He'd sign a blank check if that's what it took to get back into the revenue-generating side of the business.

The next job was going to be great. He'd been interviewing for Sales Director, North America, and had almost been blindsided by the goofballs at the Nairobi University Kilimanjaro Campus. Ethan's NUKCs, they called themselves. They were technically working with Ivy League–designated research grant money, but good old Chummy had talked him into twisting the rules and funding a small team of researchers in East Africa.

After surviving that first round of interviews he'd hauled in a few of the researchers who'd rotated out of Kilimanjaro recently and listened to their excited babble. Carbon nanofiber gobbledygook speak had poured out, and he'd sent them over to a few level-headed engineers who came back with shining eyes saying things like "industrial lengths" and "space elevator." Then marketing got involved and rebranded it DiamondWire™. Legal reminded everyone of corporate's nondisclosure policy, and some market analytics types suggested not selling the tech at all but keeping it solely for TCG's use.

A space elevator! Ethan had had a great laugh in his private office over that idea. The engineers seemed certain it could be done. There had been notional designs for one for ages and even some prototype ideas for placing one on the Moon. But Earth-to-orbit was where humanity really needed a space elevator. The limiting construction challenge was finding a material that could serve as the central tether. If it could truly be made, a carbon nanotube fiber around twenty-two thousand miles long would do it. The TCG scientists at Kilimanjaro insisted that DiamondWire™ could be made in *any* length, including that one. If actually true, then TCG had just gotten the final component necessary to build the first planet-based space elevator.

A few previous experiences of being stung by discoveries that didn't pan out had kept Ethan's smile superficial. He'd made his arrangements. And he'd continued the interview rounds for a transition back into sales. They'd hate him when this was over, but he didn't care.

Two pages stuck together and he had to break his concentration to flip back and check that he hadn't missed any other pages. It reminded him to check on a few more things. Transitioning out of sciences needed to go just right.

Ethan sent his assistant, Jax, a query to look up who was at Kilimanjaro now. Before the breakthrough, he'd assumed the scientists were running around the Kilimanjaro garden and parks facility run by TCG's small entertainment division. Taking a relaxed sabbatical like that was certainly what he would have done if he weren't working on climbing to corporate power. It wasn't like the scientists were really expected to make breakthroughs. Sure, he'd always told them he expected results, but they weren't fired if they didn't find anything.

Ethan had only shifted over from sales to sciences because it had let him jump up to assistant director without waiting for Cory Aanderson to die first. Good thing he had, too. Far from dying, Cory kept rising through the sales ranks. The corporate ladder was more of a scaffold than a straight line, but as long as Ethan kept climbing, many paths led to the C-suite.

The next page was an acknowledgement of his responsibility as a manager to follow each country's laws relating to human resources management. He rolled his eyes.

Ethan paged Chummy. It was rude and impolite to summon him with the ancient in-house propriety comms system, but the man had almost lost him the promotion. There was absolutely no call for questions that pointed when speaking to a senior executive in your own company. Ethan was going to make certain Chummy knew how pissed off he was.

The buzzy noise sounded from right outside. Ethan gritted his teeth in annoyance.

"Go right in, Mr. Tchami," Ethan heard Jax say from the outer office. The door stood open. Jax's gut pressed out the button-down shirt even when he sucked it in hard to make a good impression, as he was trying to do now. His assistant treated TCG's head of human resources like someone who mattered. Ethan gave a mental shrug. It didn't hurt.

"None of that," Fabrice Tchami said. Ethan muttered under his breath in unison with the man, "Just call me Chummy."

Ethan then schooled his features to calm blankness.

Chummy rattled the door frame with his powerful knock and strode in flashing those bright white teeth in an ear-to-ear grin. He loomed over Ethan's desk, took Ethan's right hand, and pumped it in a two-fisted handshake.

"Congratulations!" Chummy said. "Well deserved. I couldn't believe it when I heard you were interviewing for sales. I put a word in Jeffy and Zhou's ears, and I'm so glad they listened."

Ethan's mouth fell open, and he closed it again before forming words to reply.

Chummy gave him a sly wink. "I went to school with Jeffy," he added as if that explained everything, and in a way it did.

The entirely too pleased man in front of him was, yes, technically, a vice president since the head of human resources for the conglomerate did rate a boardroom seat with the C-level officers. But HR on all levels made the same or less than any profit center position three levels below. They weren't actually important or in control in any way. Or shouldn't be.

The blood ran out of Ethan's face. Chummy flashed a dimple.

Except, of course, when they'd managed to parley their shoulder-rubbing positions into personal friendships with the people who did control the company's direction.

Ethan stole a look at the screen in front of him where he'd been composing a scathing input for Chummy's annual report to be submitted after he transitioned back into sales. All the profit center directors were asked to contribute to the reviews for the non-profit-generating colleagues. The profit rainmakers controlled the trickle-down to the admin bloat, was the usual way everyone said it.

Ethan switched screens to hide it from Chummy, and the goofy picture of him grinning over the cake with that giant "50" scrawled in frosting filled the screen instead.

He almost switched it back, but Chummy had already seen that he was hiding something. Something in the twitch of the man's eyebrows warned Ethan that he'd noticed and was now interested.

Chummy's smile grew even bigger. "And it's your birthday too?"

"Uh, just passed." Ethan swallowed hard and used the distraction. "I took a few days off. Had to fly the wife to the Caicos, but I don't like to make a big deal about it. The company is more important, though I was grateful to have the few days off, of course."

"Of course, of course." Chummy patted him on the back.

He'd come around to Ethan's side of the desk and was looking closely at the photo on the screen, leaning in to expand one corner. Ethan closed his eyes. The glaring number on the cake required no closer inspection.

"What a beautiful woman." Chummy whistled appreciatively. "I'm starting to understand why you never bring her along to the office get-togethers."

"Oh, she doesn't really do social gatherings much," Ethan lied.

Chummy nodded along, some pleasant memory flickering across his rich brown face. "My last boyfriend was the same way. Couldn't stand crowds." Chummy sighed with a theatrical flair Ethan suspected wasn't studied at all. "Probably why that relationship didn't last. Though the hours make it hard to meet anyone and, well, I couldn't date anyone at work. Can't break the rules I set up. Should have thought more carefully before I wrote those." He turned his bright smile back on Ethan. "Wise of you to find your love first and then jump into the work."

Ethan blinked. He wasn't going to say anything. None of the harsh words he'd planned seemed safe to say. Ethan just nodded, thinking as fast as he could.

"Say, Chummy, let me know if you ever need anything, okay?" he said, after what he hoped wasn't too long of a pause.

"Sure." Chummy nodded right back. "There is this one thing. You'd want it anyway, but it's best to get this sort of deal top-level support. I'll send your assistant a subsidiary contract; you'll want to approve; it'll help you out with the elevator." He patted Ethan on the back. "Just brilliant giving the researchers free rein like that. And congratulations again on Sciences Worldwide. I can't wait to see what you do with the elevator project. The scientists all adore you, of course, and wanted to revolt when operations was going to run the big build, but I floated your name." Chummy paused to give him another wink. "Not that anyone needed much convincing. Ops loves a sales guy, and the scientists all know you have their backs, so we made a new position, and you're the go-to guy to make this all happen."

Chummy tapped on the door frame again as he let himself back out. "Knock 'em dead, champ."

Ethan stared after the man, appalled, and then with growing horror looked back more carefully through his new position description. Chummy was exactly right. Ethan Schmidt-Li's promotion had not been to North American Sales Director.

He was now Chief of Sciences, Worldwide. A job that hadn't existed before. Maybe not even a profit center position.

Ethan started to sweat. He didn't have the luxury of spending another five years off track if he was ever going to enter the C-suite. And space elevator! Sure, he'd approved that research field for the team at the Nairobi University affiliate campus, but it was like cold fusion or faster-than-light travel. Bits and pieces of useful science came from side discoveries made while studying it, but a working one wasn't ever going to be built. Was it?

He leaned back in his chair. The ergonomic smart system started a back and rump massage as the soft chime reminded him to lean back his neck to let it work the kinks out of his upper spine and shoulders. His mind raced and he set his fingers on the keyboard to type as fast as thought.

He needed the chief scientists to conduct thorough second checks of material properties. He needed the company's engineering teams to give him their absolute best for the design phase. Hell if he'd let them go forward using a hundred-year-old concept design! Absolutely not.

This thing was going on his résumé. He didn't trust any of the director-level managers in engineering.

Jax's dossier on all the employees currently at the Kilimanjaro site arrived in his files with a chime. A check of the document size showed his assistant had been thorough. As if someone had warned him not to expect a move with his boss over to the sales building.

Ethan closed his eyes and focused on the horrible situation immediately in front of him. One did not turn down a promotion at this level and hope to ever rise in the company again. He was simply going to have to take this crackpot space elevator project idea and make it work.

He remembered bits and pieces of the suddenly no longer irrelevant debate from the glorious past few months when he'd been sure his replacement would have to handle the mess. The engineering management dweebs had been irate about not having one of their own in overall control of this project.

Ethan sent Jax a note: "Order gift baskets." He tagged the contact files for all the spouses of the five chief engineers he'd need. His assistant had all their preferences on file. Flowers, fruit, artisanal cheeses, specialty bacon—they'd get whatever they really liked.

A certain Zen feeling overcame him. Ethan was good at this, and he knew it. He might be a late bloomer, but he'd paid rapt attention to office political dynamics, and he knew exactly how and when to cheat to get what he needed.

Ethan composed personal letters and wrote them out by hand on actual paper. There were known high achievers in TCG who got hard jobs done again and again. Their bosses would try to destroy anyone who poached them. Ethan was past caring.

He composed a list and selected a core team. He sent them all invitations to Kilimanjaro and asked them to bring their families. He expanded the list. There were more people he'd need. The spouses for that group were added to the list too. For the two single guys he wanted from engineering, he suggested one bring his golf buddies and the other treat his current lady friend. The Kilimanjaro amusement park was truly top-notch. Ethan had never been, but his wife and her friends had gone several times.

Chummy's human resources minions had a myriad of regulations that prevented exactly this sort of behind-the-scenes maneuvering, but all those rules had one core weakness. Ethan could do anything he wanted as long as he used his own money. And since he'd always wanted power and not cash, he had built up a sizable nest egg, which let him afford things exactly like this.

When it really mattered, Ethan would liquidate everything to turn money into power.

"That idiot can't make a consistent profit selling energy! And you think he can manage a project of

this scale? This is a classic *dabare*! You need the sort
of people who can take a solar-powered hot plate, two
bicycles, a shipping crate, a boat engine, and mound
of rubber ties and build a market day food truck that
not only runs but looks beautiful. That's the level of
dabare skill you need here. Instead, you have Sadou
Moussa. He might have lots of friends and locally
powerful connections, but that's just not enough. You
do realize the kids Maurie and Pascaline have been
his problem solvers since their teens and been running
the whole technical side of the family business for the
last fifteen years, right?" She paused a moment as if
doing a calculation. "Make that twenty-five years. I
can't believe I'm that old."

Chummy winced at her words. "Aunt Mami, listen..."

"No, you listen." The woman on the screen of his
car's built-in phone glared from kohl-rimmed eyes
with a not entirely angelic halo of white frizzed hair
around her brown face. "You want this to work, you
need to get your butt over here and run it."

"I'm just a human resources guy," Chummy said.
"Sadou has all the energy right there ready to tap, a
workable location and a mass of great technical talent.
Sadou Moussa can handle this."

"Bullshit you're just an HR anything. This isn't
coddling whiners to protect a company from lawsuits.
This is what people outside business think HR is!
You read people and you pick the ones so eager to
bleed for a cause that they'll do it for just a company.
Sometimes you can even take rational people and turn
them into that."

"And I'm picking Sadou," he said.

"For all the wrong reasons!" Aunt Mami rolled

her eyes and continued the argument. "Oil, gas, and related mechanical engineering is one thing, but space systems engineering is a whole 'nother level. I read your summary. You need hypersonics people, maglev experts, and don't get me started on the civil engineering side of this! You need to quit your job and come run things over here if you want Sadou Corp to be able to build this thing."

"I can't quit!" The light changed. The visual blinked off because he had the car in driver operator mode, and corporate car insurance rates didn't allow distractions while driving. The call dropped a few moments later.

Chummy hit a button on the dashboard of his car to reconnect. He left his thumb on the dash an extra moment to have his fingerprint scanned to make the call personal and link the charge to his own account rather than the company's.

"Okay, you can't quit." Aunt Mami tilted her head to the side. "And why can't you quit? Might it be because this plan of yours to give the family some work that pays in this century and has potential to keep paying isn't exactly the most ethical choice?"

"It's a gray zone, but the family needs it."

"Just gray." Aunt Mami sighed and shook her head. "Fine. How long do you think you can get away with it?"

Chummy shrugged even though he knew she couldn't see him. Even if it had been on, the camera for the built-in phone system pointed at the comfortable back seat where anyone using the automatic drive system would sit. Out loud he said, "As long as I can. See what you can do to make it long enough, okay?"

"I'll use all my very best curses," she assured him.

Chummy acknowledged that with a snort. "No one believes that shit about you being possessed by a water spirit."

"Yeah, well, the nickname sure has stuck hard for nobody believing it, hasn't it?" Her expression turned bleak. "One snake bite changed my life."

"One underfunded hospital," Chummy corrected.

"You mean poor."

Chummy shrugged again. He mashed a button to switch the car over to autodrive even though the routing system would take an extra five minutes to reach the airport. It had a glitch. The thing always stopped for a recharge at the North Central exit instead of using Charles W Grant Parkway and the recharge stations at the airport itself.

He shifted his seat back to where the camera could see him.

"This is exactly the problem, Aunt Mami. It wasn't about the snakes. Antivenom treatments were well understood even then. If the hospital hadn't been nearly broke, they would have had a few more doctors and not needed to wait for one to be woken up to come treat you. What happened should never have happened."

"And sending Michel out in the dark to try to find the snake and bring back its body to confirm they'd used the right antivenom was foolish, and that sweet man was foolish to have agreed to do it." Aunt Mami waved a hand. "I shouldn't have brought it up."

Chummy gave his relative a tired smile. "You can bring it up anytime you want."

"I like being Mami," she said.

"I know."

"Okay." Aunt Mami shook her head. "I don't think

they can do it without you, but I'll help as much as I can. And I will happily curse anyone who gets in the way."

"Curses have a way of turning on us," Chummy cautioned. Aunt Mami's affectations bothered him sometimes.

"Yeah, maybe. They've never worked before, but then neither have the prayers of blessing, so why not try something new?"

"I'm almost at the airport and I need to call—"

"Grandpere Moussa, the great patriarch of the Sadou family, my dead husband's cousin who will adore you forever for this." Aunt Mami held up a finger in admonishment. "Do not let him manage the funds for it himself. He hasn't got the willpower."

"Yes, Aunt Mami. I don't need spiritual inspiration to know that." Chummy cut off the call and started the next one.

The name Sadou Moussa popped up on the contact screen with video declined.

"Hello?" Grandpere himself answered. "Who is this?"

The man had answered an unknown number without an assistant screening the call. Not the way to manage the valuable time of a senior executive, but maybe he had better managers these days and could afford to be less careful with his time?

"It's Fabrice," he said using his first name, and then when he didn't get an immediate response, Chummy provided his full name with the family name first as was normal back in the home country. "Tchami Fabrice. How are you, my old friend?" Chummy didn't let his concern show. He waited a few beats for the image to turn on. It didn't.

"Oh Fabrice, my brother! It's been a long time!" The video stayed off while Grandpere meandered through greetings extending through every board member Chummy worked with and wishes for everyone's continued good health before giving him a chance to bring up the reason he'd called.

This was the man who many years ago had arranged for the care of a younger cousin by marriage who was barely even related to the family heirs. Chummy had had his schooling paid for and had received a fat stipend provided in addition. It had let him prove himself and make the contacts that he'd used to build his career. It had been a generous gift even decades ago when the family's wealth had seemed both vast and secure. But years of executive search experience were forming a lead lump in Chummy's belly. Sadou Moussa wasn't the man he needed.

"How are you looking today, my brother?" Chummy hinted. Maybe looking in the eyes of the man he was trying to make very rich would help him see a way to push things. Some people could be shaped.

"Well, I'm well. Cut all the hair off ages ago when it started to make me look old. You remember. We saw each other ten years, no, twelve years back at that graduation party for Reuben in Boston."

Chummy did remember. The Sadou patriarch had complained of more aches and pains then and had started to use a cane. Chummy recalled trying to get the patriarch to hire a promising physical therapist who could've had him walking easily again and being rebuffed. He returned his focus to the present. "You could turn on the video?"

"Oh, I don't know how. It's a new system Pascaline

and Maurie put in a while back. You know how it is. People keep discontinuing support for things as soon as you get to understanding them."

Chummy froze his own video feed before the horror could show. Aunt Mami was right. But still, Sadou Moussa was the man they had.

Grandpere's face suddenly appeared on the screen. Not so many age lines etched the familiar face, but he sat with a slump.

A young woman's voice in the background said, "There you go, Mr. Sadou. Let me know if there's anything else I can do."

"Isn't it wonderful to have staff?" Grandpere smiled pleasantly and turned the conversation back to Chummy's health.

The man did have aides, and he trusted them. Chummy took comfort in those observations. The Sadou patriarch could be turned into an excellent delegator, perhaps. Chummy nodded to himself. He might be able to make this work. And besides, he had to now.

Ethan Schmidt-Li, another imperfect choice who'd been the best he could do under the circumstances, had signed off on the contract already.

"I'm well," Chummy finally summed up. Now he could get to the good part. "Turn off any transcription programs you've got." He paused a moment while the man conferred with his staff to confirm that indeed the automated transcript program that came with his business communications program suite had never been installed. Then Chummy continued, "Never mind that. I have some things to tell you. I'm sending work your way. I'm paying the family back for all you've done." There would be the engineering design proposal, and the contract details to follow later. First, he needed to sell it.

Chummy himself wasn't much of a salesman, but whatever his other limitations, Sadou Moussa did understand how to be an excellent buyer.

The output from installed and heavily used transcription programs waited for Chummy on the jet. John-Philip Jeffy used every new business efficiency tool as soon as he could arrange to acquire a prototype. And as CEO of TCG, Jeffy could arrange quite a lot.

Some of them didn't really work, which is why Chummy had DeeDee. She fed him the transcripts, so he didn't have to spend time learning the system-of-the-week. Chummy cringed internally at the similarity between Sadou Moussa and himself and resolved to get DeeDee to teach him how she did it.

Jeffy's comments boiled down to one overall sentiment.

"Ethan Schmidt-Li is an asshole," DeeDee summarized. "And Mr. Jeffy would rather work with someone who isn't."

Chummy considered the stories he'd been told about the man. It wasn't untrue.

"He's our asshole," Chummy agreed. He settled down into a generous seat and stretched out his legs for the flight. "Has he done anything nasty yet?"

"Well, sort of. We've got a problem."

Chummy's gut clenched. Then relaxed. DeeDee would not be frowning at her screen and ignoring his rules about practicing eye contact if it were something truly serious. Like, just as a random example, if a newly appointed Chief of Sciences, Worldwide, had realized the contract the Vice President for Human Resources had asked him to approve without bid was one that benefited his own extended family. Not a thing strictly forbidden, but Chummy was certain that Jeffy would have his job and ensure he never worked again if he learned Chummy had done something to risk the elevator.

"Sorry, boss." DeeDee Nelson blinked blue eyes through stringy blonde hair and did remember to turn her pale face toward him and to speak out loud. "It's Mr. Schmidt-Li. He's using actual mail, so I almost didn't notice. But he used the company printer for the mailing addresses." She made a grabbing hand gesture with a wire-mesh glove and scowled at her screen. "I think he's going to poach a whole lot of people. How do you want to stop him?"

"I don't." Chummy thought about Jeffy's message. "See what you can do to help him. Let the team know to start some search efforts for filling in the kinds of people he isn't recruiting. Did he get a public relations director?"

DeeDee's brow rumpled as she searched. "No. Or at least not deliberately. There's a mass of interns I don't think he had anything to do with directly who just got stipends approved. Doesn't seem like he rejected anyone and looks like the lead scientists asked to hire everyone who applied. Not following policy." Her scowl deepened. She disliked rule-breaking.

"Hmm, Pascaline Tchami, same family name as yours."

Chummy froze.

"She has three months of 'Assistant Communications Director for Sadou Corporation' on her résumé. They should be rescinding that internship offer if they have time to do background checks. Her college dates at MIT came back unverified."

DeeDee looked up at Chummy. "So, no. No real PR types. How many should we get him?"

"A full team," he said. Pascaline would hate him if she ever found out, but he had to do it. "And scrub those internship applications. Make sure the unqualified get notified that we wish them the best of luck finding positions elsewhere."

"And don't lie on your résumé." DeeDee added, "I can't believe she thought she could get away with it."

The internship cancellations took an extra day to process, because DeeDee followed rules. And the corporate policy said legal got to review all personnel changes after a formal offer had been made.

CHAPTER THREE

SADOU MAURIE LIVED. PASCALINE GOT TO COL-
lect on her bets. And while she was at it, she also
downloaded her mail. And then threw her own private
celebration. The internship didn't start for two weeks.

The limited connectivity in the bush country had
delayed her getting the message, but she finally had
work! TCG had accepted her application to join the
space elevator build crew. Yes, it was only as an intern,
but she was going to take the job.

Ha! Take that, university administrators. The most
important work on the planet, and she, Tchami-Sadou
Pascaline Magdalene Awa, was going to be a part of it.
Or rather Pascaline M. Tchami would, with her name
shortened down and westernized to fit in corporate
forms just like it had been for that attempt at college
all those years ago.

With nothing else better to do, Pascaline went
home to tell the world. She hoped it would rip Uncle
Benoit's heart out. No more minute little controls
about where she'd go and what she'd do. No more

spending weeks as Aunt Julienne's shopping compan-
ion to carry her things while being threatened with
involuntary makeovers by Aunt Fatime. The excuse of
academic scheduling conflicts was growing more and
more thin, but Pascaline wasn't going to need any of
that anymore. She reveled in anticipation.

The way the baked heat of the helicopter cabin
flash-dried any attempt at sweat heightened her old
anger. The thin blast of cool air from the overworked
air conditioner added dust to the already unpleasant
ride. A cabin air filter at least needed to be cleaned,
a corner of Pascaline's mind noted. She better sic
her cousin on them to nice them to death and get
the maintenance caught back up before they started
killing people.

Pascaline logged it.

The corner of her phone showed her location was
being tracked by one of the aunts or uncles. She rolled
her eyes. Where were they when she'd had Maurie
burning up with a sudden onset fever and no clear
idea which of the nearest clinics had a capable staff?

Maurie was her only regret. If Grandpere had to
keep sending her out into bush country to fix broken
stuff, someone needed to watch out for her.

If Grandpere had ever listened to Pascaline's opinion,
they'd have a team of devoted animal haters conducting
biological warfare against all the slithering, skittering,
and flying disease carriers living next to family business holdings. But he ignored her, and this last time
it had nearly killed Maurie. She thought about warning
Grandpere but gave it up as impossible to get through
to him. She always argued, and he never listened.

This, along with a general disinclination to do

anything other people would label charity work, was why Maurie and not Pascaline was always the one Grandpere called when he had a mission of mercy. Some of the people in Sadou's employ had to be from cities and major towns. But the ones with extended family in need invariably lived somewhere inaccessible and inhospitable. He'd send Maurie to get their dry well re-dug, their electricity restored, or their access roads repaved. And Pascaline went with.

Pascaline let herself imagine the luxury of Kilimanjaro. They did research there. It was private land owned by a corporation. They probably made regular gifts to important people in Tanzania and other important people in Kenya to keep it free of interference, but Pascaline didn't really care about that part. Uncle Fabrice—no, Uncle Chummy, she needed to start calling him the name he went by outside the family—he would have arranged something stable.

That beautiful new private city-state had the planned ground station for the space elevator. They had electricity that didn't brownout. Houses without compound walls around them. New streets with top-of-the-line traffic controls and automated trash removal. Even the public restrooms were clean. She'd seen the documentaries and noticed the things the people being interviewed hadn't even thought to mention, because it hadn't occurred to them that those things might be unusual. It was a rich place where everyone got richer just by being there.

The parent company was TCG and Uncle Chummy worked for them, so naturally she'd used Tchami as her last name instead of Sadou in hopes that someone would recognize a relative of an important man.

Forms rarely had room for all the names a person collected. And for once, family might help her instead of getting in the way.

But whatever—the important thing was that this job was away. She'd seen the stunning views of the wildlife refuge the company ran through an entertainment division. If they could afford that much care for beasts, the human living conditions were going to be amazing.

Pascaline couldn't wait.

No more irritating bowing and scraping to aunts and uncles to keep the trust payments coming into her meager bank account. The bets on Maurie had plumped her account balance up again, but even better was the news that had finally set her free to tell everyone exactly what she thought of them.

Other less important messages had also waited for her. Her cousin Reuben needed more money. This part-request, part-demand came from his mother Aunt Julienne. Something about jail and lawyer fees. Delete.

Pascaline skimmed and junked the pile of increasingly irate messages from Uncle Benoit. She could have gone to Yaoundé and found some unnecessary make-work from Grandpere, but Uncle Benoit's tone had changed. Intrafamily trouble, and she didn't have to care. Not that she would have cared per se, but she'd have had to pay attention to know who was gaining power or losing it and who she had to be polite to this week or risk losing her welcome.

Large expenditures and embezzlement, Uncle Benoit mentioned. And Grandpere. He didn't say it directly in the messages, but the words had a copy-and-paste generic feel to them, like he'd been sending almost the same thing to a lot of people and Pascaline's youth hadn't earned her much in the way of personalization.

Something came from Great Aunt Mami too. And that was odd.

"I found a boy you'll like." That's how she started the message. No introduction, no greetings. The time stamp was recent unlike the rest of the mess, so Pascaline responded.

"Aren't we passed arranged marriages?" she typed.

"No. And the correct usage is past, not passed."

Pascaline sighed. Her comm device showed the little bubbles that Great Aunt Mami was composing something more.

"And don't blame autocorrect. You have a top-of-the-line device, which I know, because I paid for it."

"Yes, Great Aunt." Pascaline flexed her fingers and prepared to really enjoy herself. *"And I'll be returning it. I'm paying for all my own things from now on."*

An image appeared on the screen making a raspberry. *"You and what lottery?"* Showers of bills falling from the sky replaced the face and were followed by a line of trees sprouting cash instead of leaves.

Mock me, old woman. You and your "paid for" doctoral education and resulting prosperous career. Pascaline typed, *"There's this space elevator. I've got work."*

"Of course."

Pascaline startled. Maybe Uncle Chummy had noticed her application, and he had needed to help it along to get her the position, and then he'd mentioned it to Great Aunt Mami? She'd hoped to get the spot without help. She pushed down a pang of hurt.

"Did Uncle Chummy tell you?"

"No, the spirit world has a deep sensitivity for multination corporations and financial windfalls." Pascaline reread that twice before Great Aunt Mami added to it. "You're supposed to either agree with my amazing psychic powers or point out that Fabrice is my father's second wife's youngest."

"Yes, Great Aunt." Pascaline reconsidered. If Great Aunt Mami was representative, then the rest of the family wasn't going to even notice her grand escape.

"Yes, Great Aunt? Yes, Great Aunt?!? You're starting to sound too much like Maurie. So boring. I hope you haven't changed that much or this boy won't be a good match. He's coming north and you can meet him and accept the engagement tomorrow. Give you time after you land to settle in and freshen up."

"No, Great Aunt."

"That's my girl!" A grinning snake emoji punctuated the sentence. "Oh, and watch yourself, Little Benoit is up to something, like usual. A lot of family members have checked in at WuroMahobe last few days."

Pascaline stopped answering. Whatever Uncle Benoit did was no longer any of her concern.

"But don't you worry, Pascaline. I've got plans for you. Big plans, and I won't do you the indignity of telling you about them. So be prepared to be surprised. My Fabrice might have told you some of it, but I'm quite sure he's left most of it still to your grandpere to announce."

Great Aunt Mami sent a final video short of herself leaning in and winking. "You are going to work harder than you've ever worked in your life. Believe it."

Pascaline did not dignify that with an answer. The internship's details specified a forty-hour workweek, free meals at the deluxe cafeteria, and full access to several gyms including one with an Olympic-sized pool.

The pilot noticed when Pascaline's head came up after ending the conversation with Great Aunt Mami. He waved at her, clearly unaware of her report on the helicopter's maintenance status. She gave him a nod. He'd probably be pissed, but if she proved to be right about the cabin air filter not being the only thing in need of checking, she might have saved his life. Or not. Sometimes aircraft did malfunction on the ground instead of in midair. She took comfort in the imagined annoyance all the aircraft maintenance people would be directing her way.

Helicopter blades thunder far too loudly for the pilot to make conversation, so she arrived almost happy.

They circled over WuroMahobe. Ant lines of dump trucks streamed from the limestone quarry road to the plant. The mountains of extra silica and iron oxide seemed in good supply. The primary and secondary crushers for the low and high calcium carbonate limestone lines were running smoothly. No glitches in the loaders or trucks stalled on the side of the road waited for her to save them.

Over a rise, upwind, the workers' town spread out with the Sadou family compound rising first and highest. All the houses here were constructed of quality concrete block well fitted with cement mortar, but the owner's compound had a bit extra. A fifteen-foot wall enclosed a large courtyard with the rooms of the house encircling it and wide windows appearing only on the second floor. The first-level rooms did have windows but only on the interior. The rear of the mansion-sized house shot up to a third story with more rooms and windows streaming in light. The greenery of the interior courtyard flowed up trellises to an open-air patio on the roof on the front house.

During some weeks this or that department from the cement plant or the quarry would be hosted for a celebration here, but in the dry season heat, nothing seemed planned for the coming weekend.

The helicopter set down on a mowed landing pad outside the family compound and promptly lifted off again as soon as she was out. Dry yellow-brown grass crunched under her shoes. The takeoff blast whipped Pascaline's clothes against her with hot air even the rotor's speed couldn't turn cool. The sensation of slowly baking to death wrapped Pascaline in a smothering hug before she'd dragged her bag the few steps to the front door.

A jumble of parked vehicles surrounded the few trees tall enough to provide meaningful shade in the empty savannah. The drivers had ignored the orderly painted parking lines in favor of cramming as many vehicles as possible into the limited shade. Great Aunt Mami had been right. There were a lot of family members here.

Alone in the full blazing sun, Great Aunt Mami's ten-year-old compact car with faded red paint sat in prim alignment with the parking lines. The two bumper stickers on the car read, "Payback and Pay Forward" and "Cheat me and I'll hex your ass." PPF was her one-woman microbank. The threats and semi-spiritual mumbo jumbo were pure Great Aunt Mami.

Uncle Benoit had no car here in the paltry shade, but that luxe golf cart right next to the largest tree trunk was so out of place it could only belong to him. Some of the assistant plant managers' houses had garages. She'd bet her last centime one of them had evicted his own vehicle to make a space for Uncle Benoit's and that this golf cart was the way her uncle went to pick it up.

The lure of air-conditioning inside stopped Pascaline from turning and flagging down the pilot to beg a trip back out to some larger town.

That and the fact that she didn't even know the pilot's name. Maurie would have known something like that, and if Maurie flapped her arms up and down and looked beseechingly at the sky, any helicopter pilot who'd just spent a trip being charmed and delighted by her cousin would happily turn right around and land again to take her back onboard.

Pascaline had no such delusions about herself. The helicopter soared overhead and landed again a quick hop away, dipping out of Pascaline's sight behind some single-story roofs. In this factory town, it would be at the garage and hangar area on the other side of the workers' homes where some of those who kept the plant's machinery running also maintained a supply of helicopter parts and fuel.

Pascaline could hear the yelling before she stepped up to the door.

She held the front door open with a shoulder and dragged in her bag. The rush of coolness would dissipate if she stayed in the doorway, so Pascaline stepped inside.

The spacious foyer had the interior patio-side windows clamped shut against the heat, but the streaming light made the cool tile floor sparkle. A welcoming space in spite of the people occupying it, she looked up to greet the family.

Uncle Benoit, Aunt Fatime with her husband Uncle Moise, his brother Uncle Jacques, and Aunt Julienne, cousin to Uncle Benoit's first wife, waited just inside. Great Aunt Mami stood off in the corner by the coffee carafe. She held onto the little pushcart like a walker and glared at the whole room.

"Good afternoon, Great Aunt," Pascaline said.

Uncle Benoit shook his head at her. "Now is not a good time, Pascaline. We can see you a bit later."

"Now is fine," Great Aunt Mami snapped back. "Because we are done here. Not another centime from me! Do you hear me?" Her voice rose and cracked, but there was still fury behind it.

The old woman abandoned the coffee cart and stalked through the circle of seated family members. She held up a finger and shook it at Pascaline.

"You should have told me about this." Great Aunt Mami shook with a whole-body tremor. Rage.

She thinks Uncle Benoit told me whatever his newest scheme is and I kept it secret from her. As if anyone tells me their plans voluntarily. Pascaline moved out of her way, but the woman adjusted her path to come nose to breast and glare up at Pascaline.

"Don't you ever trust these jackals." Great Aunt Mami turned her head and spat on the floor. Then she stumbled, and Pascaline had to catch her or let the old woman fall on the floor.

The fight went out of her great aunt. She seemed to shrivel in on herself. "Open the courtyard door. I need to go get my things."

Pascaline complied, and Great Aunt Mami left through the courtyard.

Uncle Jacques coughed awkwardly to fill the silence

and quiet conversation started up about coffee and who needed refills. Aunt Fatime accepted another cup.

"What just happened?" Pascaline said.

Uncle Benoit took a long sip from his coffee before answering. "A woman who has been pretending to be part of this family for a long time without making a contribution was finally spoken to about it. She'll come around."

"Great Aunt?" Pascaline wasn't able to keep the incredulity out of her voice. "Are you sure that's a good idea?"

Uncle Benoit rolled his eyes, and Pascaline's already low opinion of the man dropped even further. This man was going to be eviscerated. Lions would eat his flesh and carrion birds would scatter his bones. And yet Great Aunt Mami had been the one wobbling out with tears in her eyes, not him.

Pascaline swallowed hard and said nothing.

"My brother." Uncle Jacques cleared his throat and made a deferential nod at Uncle Benoit. "Old Aunt Mami is one issue. But, about the other, I still say it's a bad idea."

Aunt Julienne nodded along and continued an argument from before their joint attack on Great Aunt Mami, "Grandpere knows his business, and he'll step down himself when it's time. Don't go pushing things!"

The courtyard door hinge gave a loud squeak as it reopened.

Great Aunt Mami stood there, letting the heat rush in and the cool air slip out.

"I've decided to cut my funding of all estates at the end of the month. If you don't appreciate what I do for the family, you can do without. But I'm staying and making use of all this mess I've paid for until then. If you try to have the staff remove me, remember who pays them when the budgets don't close." She motioned to the maid holding the door who'd turned still as a statue. "You can close the door now."

"And enjoy being the latest victim." Great Aunt Mami gave Pascaline a bitter smile, and the focus of the room turned to Pascaline.

The door closed.

"I've been out with Maurie working on Grand-pere's bushland projects. I don't know what's going on," Pascaline said, using her blank not-understanding face. It worked occasionally, even with family, though never with Great Aunt Mami. But her oldest living female relative was no longer in the room. "I'm sure you have many things to do, so I'll go as soon as you let me know what you needed." The deflection and acquiescence had been automatic. She'd forgotten she could burn all these relationships now.

"That's not the way we do things in this family," Aunt Julienne said with a long-suffering tone. Something twitched in Uncle Benoit's face, and Pascaline felt inspiration hit. It would be more fun if she didn't tell them straight out that their hold on her was gone.

"Oh, is Reuben out of that Luxembourg jail? I had meant to send him a care package, but..." Pascaline let the question trail off using gestures to convey uncertainty about his current status. She'd had no such intention, and they'd all realize that if they thought for another moment about her instead of themselves. But if at least two of them fell for the same misdi-rection... Bingo.

"It wasn't his fault," Julienne snapped back at the

same time as Aunt Fatime said, "Well, he's not from my side." The squabble broke out instantly.

Pascaline made her escape.

Only Uncle Benoit caught her eye long enough to deliver a stern glare.

She did agree, actually, that Reuben hadn't done much wrong which was why he'd been sitting in jail awaiting trial for six months instead of laughing it up as a free, much less ethical, man.

He'd have not been charged at all if he'd been willing to give evidence, but that wasn't going to happen with that cousin. He had too much respect for people who shouldn't be respected.

When a man gave him work, he supported him. When he later discovered the work wasn't completely pure, well, he'd blame himself, saying, as he had in a long apologetic message to the extended family, that he should have figured it out before he linked himself to the organization.

Loyalty sucked.

Pascaline wouldn't let herself be taken in like that. Not even for family. She stepped out to the interior courtyard and firmly closed the door behind her.

They could figure out she was gone after she'd left. Telling anyone in advance would be a waste of breath.

Pascaline ducked behind a large bush immediately on entering the courtyard. She wasn't getting called back in there until she'd had time to check her messages in detail and find out what had exploded while she'd been in the bush with Maurie.

"Idiot family." It would be good to be free of them. But Great Aunt Mami with all her money had looked destroyed, not elated. Uncle Benoit could be nasty when he chose to be, but the end of the strange conflict she'd witnessed bothered Pascaline. She didn't know what was going on and hated it.

She found the maid who'd been holding the door for Great Aunt Mami not too long ago. Pascaline made a grunt to get her attention and pushed her bag at the woman with a small bill. The woman accepted it with as much delight as if Pascaline had said something polite and known her name.

"Which room, Ms. Sadou?" she asked.

"Wherever my aunts and uncles are least likely to find me."

"First floor, left corner suite. The interior hall is being retiled, so it's only accessible from the garden entrance."

"Perfect."

"But the air-conditioning is shut off for that section of the house, since it's not in use."

"Because the people laying the tile don't count," Pascaline noted.

"Yes, ma'am." The maid shrugged, her face carefully expressionless, but her tone held wry understanding. "And the ones cleaning up, but we don't count either."

"It's still perfect."

The woman nodded and led off with Pascaline's bag.

A new arrangement of pots and hanging vines divided the courtyard into alcoves. Greenery abounded in greater quantity than her parents had tolerated during the couple years Pascaline had lived here as a kid. But unless they'd changed the masonry, she still knew the place.

Any of the doors to the back part of the house

would serve, but with a staff member to follow, she wouldn't have to guess her way through the plantings. If the current family member managing the plant hadn't knocked out too many walls, any of the further doors would open into suites of rooms for family visitors. She could hide out in one at random and call the helicopter hangar to get out of here. The dusty orange tinge of today's sunset threatened dangerous flying weather, but tomorrow might dawn clear.

Pascaline stumbled upon an occupied alcove before she reached the room. The maid murmured an apology and sped through the neat collection of wicker chairs to a break in the planters. A few doors to the lower-floor private apartments were visible just beyond.

Great Aunt Mami reclined in the closer lounge chair with her tough-cased business laptop and a drink on the table beside her. Pascaline had asked for a place her aunts and uncles wouldn't immediately look.

The maid had neglected to mention her great aunt. Pascaline considered demanding a return of her tip.

Great Aunt Mami seemed as much a queen at her leisure as she'd always been until she turned her head to see who'd come and showed puffy red-rimmed eyes.

"Okay, good," she said. "Close it, please."

A gardener working on some trailing vines pushed closed a window, picked up his shears, and left for another part of the courtyard garden.

"Jacques likes to see plants rather than more cement when he's off work," Great Aunt Mami pointed out.

Pascaline suppressed a groan. "He had them make it into a puzzle garden?" The window just closed was the front living room's furthest west window. And it opened into the same room where she'd left her uncles and aunts some time ago. Turned completely in the opposite direction, a straight line had been cut through the oversized planters by shifting a few this way and that to allow the staff a reasonable access to the first-floor visitor apartments. With the window shut, no one inside the room could hear them, and Great Aunt Mami sat too low for them to see her. But Pascaline had a clear view of the group.

"There are worse hobbies than gardening," Great Aunt Mami pointed out. Her glare implied she was thinking something like, *He could enjoy ruining other people's lives like your dear Uncle Benoit.*

"And you don't mind the annoying path shapes because it lets you listen in on their conversations," Pascaline said.

"So ridiculous." Great Aunt Mami shook her head. "Can you believe I actually thought they were planning to push your grandpere out?"

"Sounds like they are." Pascaline pointed out.

Great Aunt Mami shook her head more violently. "Fabrice can't allow that. Not now. But me..." She opened her hands. "There's nothing he'll be able to do about that."

"Why do you even care?" Pascaline asked. Great Aunt Mami could sometimes be induced to explain if asked the obvious questions with enough bluntness.

"You are such a stupid little girl." Tears, again, ran down her great aunt's face, so Pascaline didn't try to retaliate for the insult. Not that fighting with Great Aunt Mami ever seemed wise. Uncle Benoit and the others still sat inside the room drinking coffee and talking about things with big gestures and frequent smiles.

Great Aunt Mami shifted the computer off the table and onto her lap. "Might as well save what I can." She glared at the keys.

"Everything I've done." Great Aunt Mami paused her typing to waggle her right hand at the glass bottle on her table as an example. It was a mango juice blend from an orchard further south, a product of one of the little business she'd funded. Pascaline had seen the bottles in European airports sometimes. "Even the little ventures that were really doing well. This will erase it all."

"Uncle Benoit is not going to drain your bank account."

"Will he not?" Great Aunt Mami's red-rimmed eyes stared into hers. "He won't have to. My businesses will merely start having troubles. The shipping service I have them using belongs to a second cousin of your Aunt Julienne's. More things are going to fall off the back of trucks. When sales people need to travel to ensure good relationships with buyers, the Sadou friend at the visa office will not waive the fees anymore and may well insist on double payment for the times they've traveled before without paying. These aren't fat-margin businesses. They are small independent enterprises that can make enough profit to support one smallish family or maybe two, if everyone works at it consistently."

"You could hex him," Pascaline suggested. That had been Great Aunt Mami's thing. Even her bumper sticker, produced by yet another small print-on-demand business, said so.

Her great aunt sat up and focused fully on Pascaline. "You know better than that."

"They say you gave Uncle Chummy a blessing, and it made him rich."

"Yes. I did." Great Aunt Mami finally acknowledged it, and then proceeded to shatter Pascaline's perspective on family history. "I introduced him to your grandpere back when we were all a lot younger, and Fabrice impressed the family with his smarts, and they sent him off to school in Germany where he made a lot of good friends with other very talented people. Fabrice did it all entirely on his own after that start. But it was a very good start. Your grandpere's uncle ran the family then, and he felt very guilty about me, so when your grandpere and I went to him about helping Fabrice get an education, he was more than generous."

I could've used a blessing like that, she thought. Pascaline pushed the bitterness away. The powerful great aunt sat hunched and uncomfortable in a chair designed for relaxation.

"That's still a blessing for Uncle Fabrice," Pascaline said and sat down next to her great aunt. "I'm leaving, so you should really go ahead and do whatever you want to my aunts and uncles."

Her great aunt squinted at her. "The coast isn't that far away."

Sometimes it took effort to follow her great aunt's comments. Aunt Julienne did have that yacht in Douala, and Uncle Benoit and other extended family members did like to cruise together. So she supposed they might go farther than the usual Mediterranean route if there were something interesting to see. She supposed they could just head south and sail around the Horn of Africa. Or they could extend a Med tour and go through the Suez. Over on the African east coast they might pull in at some port like Mombasa in Kenya and then take a train or private aircraft inland to see a niece working on the space elevator construction project.

"Uh, I haven't actually been to Kilimanjaro, but the map is pretty clear that it's not particularly coastal. And I'm no angel investor with small businesses they could destroy, so I won't be risking my job to take time off and give guided tours to unauthorized family visitors." Pascaline paused and added, "And I still don't understand why you haven't cursed any of them yet."

"You don't really believe... And how could you think... You aren't really... Huh." A look of pure bafflement washed across her great aunt's face. "Oh. Okay." Great Aunt Mami fixed Pascaline with a level look. "I don't care if anyone else thinks we're blood or not. You need to understand some things." She held up a hand. When Pascaline flinched at the beginning of the curse gesture, Great Aunt Mami rolled her eyes and turned her palm inward before flaring her fingers to begin ticking off points one finger at a time.

"One. The contract is for a launcher here, or sort of here. Definitely not at Kilimanjaro. They don't have room to do supply launches from there at the same time as they're constructing the ground station and figuring out how to get the tether line set up. Lifted from Earth to orbit could be done, but it's much more efficient to build at geosynchronous orbit and drop it down. But that requires a lot of carbon in near Earth space where it's not very plentiful. So that's where we come in. We'll have to find a mountain of our own that works."

Pascaline didn't interrupt even though she was only partially following Great Aunt Mami's explanations.

These were not aspects of the space elevator's construction plan that had been publicly available, and Pascaline had been reading every single TCG press release.

"I figured your grandpere's engineers would work something out with one of the more stable mountains on the coast so the payloads have a lot of our country to fly over before anyone has to deal with other nations' airspace," she continued.

"Two. Curses and blessings are only as useful as the superstition of the person being afflicted. Fabrice is sweet but suggestible, especially back when he was young and needed a bit of confidence to go out and do his thing. Benoit and the others of his generation are far too jaded to care one bit what I say.

"Three. You have far more to lose than you think you do."

Great Aunt Mami twitched the last two fingers on her hand. "I don't remember what the last two points are. Maybe your ancestor spirits hid them from me for your own protection." Great Aunt Mami arched an eyebrow. "Or perhaps there aren't any such creatures at all."

Pascaline squirmed internally at the pitying expression on the old woman's face. "My internship contract is for a position at Kilimanjaro." *And I'll be leaving just a soon as possible,* she promised herself.

Great Aunt Mami didn't believe in spirits and yet she invoked them all the time. Pascaline was glad she hadn't leaned back in the chair. It had felt almost safe to have some kind of witch queen in the family, but now she half expected the sky to open up and drop lightning on the woman.

Great Aunt Mami laughed, a look that fit her far better than the earlier tears.

"You should see your face," Great Aunt Mami said. "It's like I just told you outer space is a colonialist myth."

Something scuttled behind the front leg over the wicker table closest to Great Aunt Mami. It darted across to hide under a large planter. A roach of some kind maybe, but no, it waved a stinger. Pascaline jerked her feet away from the scorpion. She still wore her tightly laced bush country boots, but...

Great Aunt Mami wore red plastic sandals. Comfortable things in the dry season heat, if you expected to be indoors or in a well-maintained courtyard.

The scorpion with its sting tail held high darted from the planter's shadow under Great Aunt Mami's chair to another planter behind her. It dodged around Great Aunt Mami's heel when the older woman shifted it back. The old woman nearly crushed it with her exposed foot, and the scorpion scurried on, unconcerned.

Pascaline's warning died on her lips.

Great Aunt Mami peered at Pascaline and shook her head. "Just so you know, I think your uncle and the rest of them will still go through with that engagement I put together for you. And"—she held up a hand—"you should seriously consider it. Get married a few times and you'll have a lot more families to fall back on if one of them turns out to have idiots in the younger generation eager to run people out."

The bitter twist on Great Aunt Mami's face eased and her usual laugh lines deepened. "And I do know there's no way Grandpere Moussa, Little Benoit, or even Baby Maurie will let you go off to try to take another outside job now. With the education you've gotten, they'll expect you to pay back. You are the only credentialed engineer in the extended family, you know." Great Aunt Mami's eyes twinkled. "So you'll be managing this project no matter what. Oh, and even if they did let you skip out, I do still have plans for you."

Pascaline opened her mouth and snapped it shut again.

None of that was true, or rather it might be almost true, and she couldn't let it be. Pascaline stood back up, careful to avoid stepping on anything with a stinger. It was time to flee. But politely.

How do you tell a woman you think she's a witch when she's just confessed to not believing in her own power?

You don't. And you try to make sure she doesn't curse you accidentally.

"May I get you anything, Great Aunt?" Pascaline slowed her exit for a few moments. The old woman wasn't one to make idle threats and something about being in her plans didn't sound particularly pleasant to Pascaline.

Great Aunt Mami flapped a hand in dismissal. "Don't worry about all that." She pointed at the window and Pascaline's aunts and uncles. "I can fix them. They just surprised me, and..." She nodded to herself as if assessing something private but important. "It hurts."

She focused intently at Pascaline. "I have everything I need. Have had for a while." Great Aunt Mami considered Pascaline with an expression the younger woman couldn't read. "You, though. Not so much."

Not what Pascaline had expected to hear, but maybe another hint might come if she pressed. She cast a glance over Great Aunt Mami's head at the window into the front of the compound. Uncle Benoit had taken a position in the middle of the circle, about where her stool had been, and seemed engaged in calming the group down. She figured she had a few more minutes before they'd send someone out after her, and that only if she was even on Uncle Benoit's agenda for the evening at all.

"That lot is trying their very best to ruin us." Great Aunt Mami's expression of disgust and the eye roll she directed at the group inside shocked Pascaline with its familiarity. She'd seen that look in her own mirror far too many times.

Great Aunt Mami winked. "I will have to select some fine curses for everyone, so don't worry. I'll get mine back."

Pascaline suppressed a shudder and changed the subject. "So about that not having everything I want thing..." Pascaline rolled her shoulders to show what she hoped would come across as honest inquiry. "Do you have any suggestions?"

"Need. Not want. You do already tend to get what you want, which is likely why you don't have what you need." Great Aunt Mami's familiar enigmatic grin flashed across the old woman's face. "And absolutely, I do have a suggestion. Why don't you go meet your future husband?" Great Aunt Mami's expression was pure satisfaction. "Not that I care one way or another," she added with a sly look at Pascaline.

"Wait." Pascaline backed away. "You'd said engagement before. Possible engagement, right?"

Uncle Benoit made a gesture out the window toward her. Not good. She'd stood in the wrong place where they could all see her. She didn't want their attention just yet. If the family was trying the semi-arranged-marriage route again so soon she needed time to plan. And to find out what contract Great Aunt Mami was talking about.

Whatever this was, it wasn't something she was ready for. Dealing with family required careful planning because they didn't just go away forever afterwards. She could quite easily offend everyone. Had in fact.

Time to do some research and make plans.

Pascaline fled.

CHAPTER FOUR

THE SADOU FAMILY COMPOUND MIGHT BE THE largest home, but the workers' village boasted several respectably sized buildings and a mass of them had grown along the quarry road and outwards toward the plant itself into almost a second entire town. The solidly built residences were single story with durable metal roofs and wide windows, but many of them had those windows tightly closed, which meant central air and prosperity. No mud huts or woven grass walls for Sadou employees or their families. At least not while that plant stayed in business.

And those pesky details were things Pascaline had to care about again. Overnight she'd learned absolutely nothing about this supposed contract Grandpere might or might not have. But she had received new mail.

"We appreciate your interest in our internship program. Further assessment indicates your application is not right for us at this time. We wish you the best..."

Pascaline could wish them quite a lot of things too, and none of those involved a best anything. Great

Aunt Mami's car was missing from the lot outside the Sadou family compound. Pascaline didn't bother to call the helicopter hangar and attempt to arrange a flight. She didn't have anywhere else to be, and it would be too easy for that would-be suitor to find her if she put her escape from WuroMahobe on a printed flight schedule.

Pascaline could enter any one of those employee's houses at random and whatever child, caregiver, or elderly person remained home at this hour would meet her and probably even make her a lunch. But they would give her a full greeting: they'd ask about her health, and ask about her extended family, and each of her relative's health statuses, and about the pleasantness of her travels, and her thoughts on the weather, and... Pascaline shuddered.

She took refuge in the cement plant itself. The lime-stone crushing made a pleasant racket, and the comfort of heavy machinery drowned out other problems.

The factory supervisors messaged each other, and everyone she normally bothered went into hiding.

Her usual visits included inspections and complaints which made this stroll through the work zone a perfect way to hide. When nobody wanted to see her, she could be invisible with very little effort. She didn't have the energy to dig anyone out and settled for walking the plant looking for things that were wrong. The effort was unrewarding.

They were doing fine. The right machinery was greasy, and the right machinery was clean. She found nitnoid things but nothing egregious.

A framed photo of Uncle Jacques hung on the wall. A metal tag engraved with "General Manager" had been tacked to the bottom of the frame. Someone else had been in charge of operations last time. Pascaline couldn't remember the name. A hard knot in her belly worked tighter. She hadn't realized Uncle Jacques was somebody who took thankless jobs and did them well when she'd decided to rile up the aunts and make her escape last night. Aunt Julienne and Aunt Fatime would be Sadous forever, but if their dispute got bitter enough, Uncle Jacques, as a mere brother of Aunt Fatime's husband, might be discarded, and the plant would get another—probably less capable—manager.

Unable to find either distraction or insight inside the plant, Pascaline drafted a team of workers and attacked the outside. Beyond the plant and the houses which clustered near it, a rolling savannah stretched to the horizons. The always encroaching grasses teemed with sharp-toothed venomous creatures.

Too many snakes and not enough concrete summed up the situation nicely, in Pascaline's opinion. She'd pave it all if she could, but the plant couldn't waste inventory on that large of a personal project. She considered the double-width concrete sidewalk between the factory and the houses. It'd been laid down so long ago that grass poked up in enough cracks that the whole thing was closer to a gravel walk than any proper paving.

The plant could give her one day for a patch solution. She found the announcing system and summoned the on-shift manager. The foreman appeared and accepted her orders with a warmth which made Pascaline uncomfortable. She made up for it by picking an easy job for herself. The family's cement plant shaded the slight rise in the broad expanse of grasslands. After assigning the workers to separate patches where they had enough room to swing machetes without hurting each other, she took that shady spot for herself. A few others working on either side of her would also get shade, but she couldn't think of a way to deny them and make her preferential positioning more obvious. The ones in the sun weren't even complaining. She did need a solid line of people attacking the brush so the creepy crawlies would know to slither in the opposite direction. And for the ones who'd rather stay and attack, she needed people on hand to correctly identify the snake and run for the appropriate antivenom.

If a few decades earlier, Great Aunt Mami'd been bitten and had had no treatment, she'd've been dead. Instead, she'd gotten a delayed injection of not quite the correct medicines and had to live with a lifetime of nasty side effects. Pascaline much preferred an immediate correct treatment with no long-term infirmities.

She made sure her closest workers were locals who could be counted on to properly identify any snakes that came out of the brush at them. She didn't expect it to be her, but someone would probably be bitten today.

The rustle of dry stalks in the slight breeze hid the sounds of creatures moving in the brush. The plant's assistant managers under Uncle Jacques had ignored it all through rainy season, and now in mid dry season, grasses topping over even Pascaline's five-foot-ten-inch frame encroached on everything. The employee's parking lot, filled mostly with motorbikes, had lost a third of its space to the overgrowth.

She hadn't asked how many people had snakebites this year, but she didn't have to.

The foreman complained of the snakes on the path between his house and the factory as if the devil had put them there instead of his own inaction. But maybe he hadn't the authority to stop work for a day to clear brush or to hire ground crews. He'd let her take workers for her grass-clearing party with a cheerfulness that made her suspicious. If she had time, she'd check up on how their on-time delivery rate was going. He might be planning to blame her grass clearing for a slew of late deliveries.

Or maybe he was tired of his people getting bitten.

Antivenom worked. But only if it were applied in time with the right variety for that snake and the person wasn't bitten too many times. Had there been deaths lately?

Pascaline eyed the cement plant employees working the grass line with her. She didn't know any of their names.

The one beside her to her left kicked a rock and jumped back with practiced caution. A scorpion brandished its arched tail. A painful threat but not a deadly one. Usually.

Pascaline ignored it and focused on the back-and-forth sweep of her machete. Tall grasses fell. The slither and scamper of small things in the brush made their usual ominous rustling whenever she slowed enough to listen.

Professional courtesy seemed to require she give the creatures a chance to scurry back into the remaining grasses. The idiots who'd let the grass grow so close should have known field mice and insects would move in and snakes and scorpions would follow.

If there were farms nearby, they could rent a

machine to do this work instead of risking people. Or if anyone could spare the cost, the plant could buy a machine to do this regularly and then rent it out to plant employees' families who wanted to try a bit of farming on the side.

If Great Aunt Mami were still on speaking terms with Uncle Jacques, this problem could have become yet another profitable little business. Though maybe not. Great Aunt Mami had an already established business that sold antivenom.

Pascaline snorted.

The workers on either side glanced at her but didn't comment or slow their back-and-forth attack on the grasses.

Most of the noises moved away, but something poisonous coiling to strike would make much the same sounds. Another workman had been bitten yesterday, she heard a man further down the row mention it between swings. Pascaline had been away or her rages would have kept the grasses safely back from the paths and roads.

Sometimes the snake bites you; sometimes your machete bites the snake.

"Pretty lady, pretty lady!"

That wasn't a snake's voice. Snakes only talked in fire stories. Pascaline kept her back-and-forth machete swings low and even. If she didn't stand up ever again, would he fail to recognize her in the workers who'd been drafted to come out with her to help tame the brush?

"Pascaline!" He'd found her, more's the pity, but he had switched to plain speaking, which was a definite plus.

She wondered how annoyed his family was going to be when she turned him down, and he reported it back to them. Aunt Julienne and Aunt Fatime had tracked her down last night in a rare moment of unity to let her know in no uncertain terms that they expected her to go through with this engagement.

Pascaline reluctantly stood and turned to look at her prospective fiancé, Endeley Adamou.

He was reasonably attractive in a bush chieftain's son sort of way, with a strong body and laughing deep brown eyes fringed with thicker eyelashes than a man should have. Though she vaguely recalled Aunt Fatime's mention of his background implying that his people weren't really from the grassland area. She didn't pay attention to details that didn't matter. No one ever wanted to pair her up with men who had top-tier laboratories in need of a lead researcher or a giant failing business for her to reorganize. If those sorts of people existed, they either weren't single or weren't considered eligible by the extended Sadou family. Possibly they didn't know they needed Pascaline to rescue them, she mused.

Adamou's warm hand closed over her machete hand.

She jerked back in annoyance, and he released her hand but not before twisting it to make the sharpened flat of metal slip from her hand into the grass. Rude.

But not unwise. She allotted him two points for thinking of his own safety and deducted one for not considering the things that might come out of the grass. But she couldn't let him know he'd been judged positively or he'd get annoying.

Pascaline whirled on him wearing a mask of irritation. She was going to annihilate him now to make sure he knew it was a bad idea to touch her. So what if she never really set any of the men down gently? This one she was going to hurt.

But Adamou leapt back with a twinkle in his eyes and grin.

"I just wanted to make sure you were unarmed first." He spread his hands open showing their own emptiness. "Didn't want to be hacked into pieces without you having at least a moment to think about it first."

Worse, he held himself with an easy muscled calm, and laugh lines creased the corners of a mouth set in a handsome warm face. Adamou was beautiful.

As if I need a machete to hack you apart. Pascaline glared.

"Would you like to go inside? My guys refilled the gas for the freezer's pilot light in the factory break room, so we have ice for the drinks now." He crinkled his eyes at her, smiling without moving his mouth.

"No." Pascaline did pace back a few meters from the edge of the grass line, though. The people hacking back the tall grass might still disturb something venomous, and it wasn't reasonable to stand with her back to it for too long. Adamou walked back with her. His eyes stopped roving the grass line and examined her chest instead.

"This isn't going to work out for us," Adamou said, looking back into her eyes with a sadness that was entirely false.

Pascaline gaped. That was her line. She was the one who said that. Of course, not those words exactly, because she'd never bothered to be quite so generous about it, but had he really just said that?

"You what?"

Adamou shrugged elaborately. "I met this woman and although my family would really like me to marry someone that they picked out, this other woman is really nice, and I don't think it would be fair to you if I pretended..."

Pascaline felt her eyes narrow. "You did not."

"No, really," Adamou insisted. "She's amazing with languages and has been sending my uncle chocolates and coffee to try to warm the family up to her."

"You aren't in love with anybody." Pascaline was sure of that much. "You just checked out my boobs."

"They are magnificent," Adamou acknowledged with a grin, "but Hadjara does exist."

"And how many others?" Pascaline watched him and the twitch of his lips confirmed her guess. She found herself liking him in spite of herself, and unfortunately for her reputation he seemed aware of what she really thought.

"Let's not get into how many," Adamou said. "You aren't really wanting to settle down at all either, so what if you just go back to the family compound and tell your aunts and uncles that we don't suit?"

"Why should I be the one to take all the blame?" Pascaline glared at him.

He recoiled.

She hid a smile. She still had the upper hand.

He definitely didn't want to be the one remembered as the reason for calling off the almost final engagement. She wasn't quite sure why, cross-tribe politics wasn't one of the things she bothered to study, but something about how he was maneuvering the conversation implied he'd used up too much of his social capital on appeasing some of those "let's not get into how many" women and their families. The Sadous lacked a single core tribal affiliation and thus would always be new rich—until such a point as they lapsed into middle class—but they had family connections to the leaders of most of the influential tribes in West Africa, if you went enough generations back. Adamou smacked of old money and a familiarity with power.

He didn't seem like the type to have intentionally sought out vulnerable women with no recourse if the breakups went poorly. And Great Aunt Mami would have known if he were.

"So if I were to take the blame"—Pascaline regarded him levelly, well aware that the men hacking at grass behind them were making too much noise to overhear— "what would it be worth to you?"

Adamou had opened his mouth to speak, but now nothing came out.

Out of his league. Pascaline decided she was enjoying this after all. She was always out of their league, but few of them realized it quite so quickly. It was almost a pity he didn't suit.

"Um…" Adamou wasn't letting himself be distracted by breasts now. "What did you have in mind?"

Pascaline considered the sky. "What have you got?"

"The family must have shared the financial statements with you." Adamou was stalling.

"That's what your family has. What can you offer?" Pascaline looked at him closely. He wore nice clothing, locally purchased but in good repair instead of brand-new. He probably didn't have access to a trust fund of the size her uncles and aunts had.

"I'm getting the impression that I'm probably going to give you whatever you want," Adamou said.

Oh, you get what you want. Might be why you don't have what you need, Great Aunt Mami's words echoed.

"Don't cave so quickly." Pascaline was annoyed. "You really need to make me work for it or it isn't much fun."

"I don't even do my own bartering in the market," Adamou objected. "I'm not allowed after I sold my birthright at age six for two fried *makala*, and my nanny had to go bargain for it back."

"You did no such thing." Pascaline shook her head, but she did like the renewed effort he was making. It wasn't her fault if she had a reputation as the sort of person it was easier to give into than to fight. She did still like a fight. She almost regretted some of the times she'd made people who tried to fight dirty with her pay for it. "Tell me what really happened."

"I didn't have any coins, so I gave them a really expensive watch that had belonged to my chief's grandfather."

"Okay." Pascaline acknowledged. "Close enough to a birthright. I'll accept the substitution."

"So what's my damage?" Adamou looked over at her, still trying to use his attractiveness to edge some kind of concession out of her. He was probably used to women giving him pretty much whatever he wanted. Maybe even needed. "I'd suggest a kiss, but I'd rather not get a busted-up face."

Pascaline might have liked to kiss him, but now that he'd said that her face heated.

"I'm sorry," he said immediately. "I shouldn't have brought it up. I'm sure that guy must have deserved it."

Pascaline was confused for a moment, and then she

remembered. Several years ago she'd been accused of giving a man a black eye, a broken arm, and more. It hadn't been her. It had been the on-and-off boyfriend of the man who he'd been having a secret relationship with, and the whole thing had been really complicated and awkward for the guy, so she'd let Aunt Julienne think she'd done it. And when the family hadn't argued for her, people had believed it. For almost a full year it had stymied her family's attempt to marry her off, so from her perspective, it had been more than worth it.

"Not a problem," Pascaline said, "but I want something more useful. A favor later. A big one. I'll let you know when I think of something. In the meantime, you can call me up if you hear about something you could do to help me that I might be willing to accept as the favor."

Adamou gave her a side-eye. "Help you what?"

Pascaline loved that look. It meant she was going to get a very eager helper who couldn't wait to clear the favor off his record. "I want out. I'm looking for a job, an internship, maybe a fellowship. Anything outside the country with reasonable pay or room and board plus some kind of stipend. Ideally working with rich and powerful people."

"You could have any of that here," he said.

He didn't get it. Few people did. "Yeah, and here I'll be Little Pascaline until the day I die. Somewhere else I might one day get to be someone. Help me get out. I'll call it all off. Say it's all my fault, once again. And you can enjoy Hadjara and all the rest of your lovely woman friends."

"You're an angel." Adamou gave her a bow. "I think Hadjara might know someone. I'll give you a call soon."

"Better do it quick," Pascaline said. "My family won't accept my refusal for very long if they have to keep living with me."

Adamou stumbled. He hadn't expected bluntness. For reasons unclear to Pascaline, most strangers expected her not to know her own reputation and especially not to understand other people's motivations. If he needed it spelled out for him, she could spell it out.

"My whole family finds me irritating. They'll push hard to get someone else to take me in if you don't find me a job out of the country that can let them let me go without losing too much face."

"Then"—Adamou was clearly processing this—"why don't you just stop being, er, irritating." His tone made it sound like he considered the term irritating not to be the most appropriate descriptor. Pascaline ignored it and answered the question asked.

"I don't stop, because I shouldn't have to. They have unreasonable expectations, and besides, if they were right, they'd have to change first. I find them even more irritating. And I like leaving the country. There are far more interesting jobs out there."

"Out there," he repeated. "Any hints on what sort of thing would be a good fit for you?"

"I'll take any lead," Pascaline said. "No need to go to extremes to meet the terms of the favor." She didn't want to seem overbearing.

"But as I understand the situation, your family is going to keep looking for a way to marry you off until you get out of the house, and if my leads don't work out, they'll keep making the rounds of eligibles, and this plan isn't going to get them to cross me off the target list for very long."

"So Hadjara isn't going to marry you, then? Oh, you can keep your secrets." Pascaline smiled. He was a quick study. "I don't think I'd mind terribly much if things didn't work out."

"Mmm," he said in response. "Something long-term, perhaps you'd like a nonprofit where you can help people?" He read her expression correctly. "Or not."

"I like helping myself," Pascaline agreed. "Just room and board is fine as long as there's long-term profit sharing. Maybe a management training program as long there's no strong hierarchical corporate policy. I'd hate to be penalized for subordinate failures."

"Right. Lots of power, ideally with lots of money, no more interpersonal contact than absolutely necessary."

"Exactly right." Pascaline almost wanted to back out of the deal. This guy really did get her. "Just so you know, I'm not convinced I'd mind being married to you."

He didn't answer.

"So you might want to be quick about those job leads." Pascaline drove the hint in harder. No matter how much she liked individuals, they never liked her back, so this kind of pressure always worked.

"Yes." He opened the door for her. "I believe I understand you perfectly."

Pascaline considered Adamou for a long moment before stepping through the door. He had, according to Aunt Julienne, a new doctorate from Yaoundé and a good position waiting for him in his family's business. Aunt Julienne didn't remember what either the degree field or the business were exactly. She'd said maybe it was palm oil and clearly remembered no details. A grocery store chain supplier, possibly? Pascaline hadn't wasted time on reading his background files herself.

In person, though, wow. Adamou was well-built with the sort of gym muscles an actor might envy and had a nice face to go with the whole package. It wasn't that he was unlovable. It was that the life that went with a marriage to him or anyone like him was.

Her family wasn't going to believe her if she went with the truth, but since they never accepted the first reason she gave, Pascaline decided that she'd start with the truth this time. When the grandchildren's grandchildren were gone, she didn't want to be the one with the greatest number of descendants remaining. She wanted to be the one that everyone lied about having been distantly related to.

Endeley Adamou arranged a flight home from the north country as quickly as possible. Pascaline's two aunts were starting to act interested in arranging a more direct family connection, and one jealous uncle had hinted he might drop Adamou into the limestone grinder if he stayed too much longer. Admaou had handled unwanted female interest frequently enough to be both unsurprised and adept at avoiding it. But he'd done what he was sent to do, and it was time to go.

A very large mountain waited for him, and he wanted to get back to it. The palm plantations down the slopes near sea level would continue their regular cycles of growth and harvest, but his uncle, the chief, required a report. And in exchange, Adamou could return to his private studies with only a few of the tribe members coming up to pester him now and again to ensure he was still alive.

The note he was expecting arrived. Hadjara appreciated his "kind assistance" getting the introduction to his uncle. "But considering," blah blah blah, she thought it would really be best if they didn't see each other. The chocolatier work kept her really busy anyway, et cetera. Adamou smiled to himself. At least he'd been able to use her to fend off the Sadou madwoman.

Pascaline hadn't been half as bad as he'd been led to believe, but it was a good thing he was flying out already. He had the distinct impression that she routinely got everything she asked for and only limited access could keep her from having everything she wanted. Especially because he wasn't sure he would mind.

The stories those plant foremen had told about her. He could only shake his head. She was a pain, but she was right! Some of the longtime workers had pointed out former death traps which—at Pascaline's insistence—had been fixed. The Sadous didn't know her value.

Adamou had had those conversations with the workers and managers alone, so the chief wouldn't hear about it from the few staff that had been sent with him. The chief, head of the Endeley family, as well as of the Bakweri tribe, generally would need to be appeased about the wedding not going through, unless of course he could find a way to get Pascaline to seriously reconsider. Adamou empathized with Pascaline's need to occasionally give the family what they expected from her, but it didn't mean he didn't have the same issue.

He had a stepbrother who'd thought he'd pretend to be an orphan. After all his schooling was complete, he'd moved to France. Got a regular job and a bank account. Direct-deposited his pay only into his personal account. Family showed up on his doorstep, and he wouldn't put them up. Uncles called telling him to come home and explain himself, and he refused. Adamou shuddered at the idea. His stepbrother was about fifteen years older. They weren't close. But he'd had to hear the raging fights the family had had about what to do about him. They'd finally chosen to stop paying his new wife's student loans. The man had returned home deeply apologetic. That was ten years ago and the family still didn't trust him. He'd probably never get his spouse or children accepted as core members of the tribe and any time he ever needed a loan or expected a payment from family coffers he wouldn't be getting it.

Pascaline seemed like she might be the Sadous' rebel child. But she didn't hide or run away. She fought directly and they seemed to respect her for it for all that they wished she'd stop fighting and go live the life they wanted to pick out for her.

Her life was definitely missing something. He thought she really needed to have a nice mountain, preferably a volcanic one. He had one and it was a delight. Her volcano should probably be only figurative, but he still felt that she had a mountain-shaped hole in her life.

Fako, the mighty volcano which rumbled and spat unbreathable sulfur fumes but generally did no great damage, was quite peaceable for a volcano and quite unruly for a mountain. To say that his relationship to his study was complicated would be a vast understatement. Adamou was quite fully convinced that there were no spirit beings in, with, and under the matter that made up Earth's surface, but at the chief's insistence he'd stopped saying so out loud.

Adamou didn't particularly want to serve as the lead cat wrangler for his extended family during his generation's tenure at the tribal helm, but none of his extended cousins seemed particularly likely to do the job well. Some wanted the position, which in due course Adamou expected would make his life more difficult than he wanted it to be. The chief had pulled him aside privately to share that he hadn't wanted the chieftaincy either, but that not wanting the job was part of proving that you were suited for it. Anyone who wanted it for its own sake didn't understand how much work and how little reward the position involved.

Chiefship was rather like volcanology actually. Study the great craters in hot, dangerous environments. Get demands from neophytes to predict the far future with an impossible level of detail, and then get blamed no matter what happens.

Adamou arrived home just after the news of the arrival of the Sadous' latest contract. Corporate secrecy was no match for family gossip. One of the men traveling with him tapped Adamou on the shoulder and whispered it.

"The head of the Sadou family stopped by to see your uncle the chief. They want to use your mountain."

"Don't worry," another one said, "my brother got the Sadou grandfather's car for him, and he didn't leave happy. The chief sent him away, I'd bet."

The first man gave Adamou a sharp nod. "Thought you should know. My cousin brought in the coffee," he added by way of explanation.

Adamou and the chief had coffee themselves not much later. In fact, thanks to concerned extended family working at the landing strip and in the cab service, Adamou got from the airport to his uncle's home office faster than he ever had before.

Chief Endeley Bouba himself looked more bureaucratic than kingly. He usually wore old suits because they still fit, and had no beard because the scraggly tufts he still tried to coax out every now and then itched. If chieftaincy were chosen by beauty, his uncle wouldn't have ever gotten the job. The little bit of Chinese in their ancestry had skipped Adamou entirely, but it gave the chief both a flat nose and a height well under average.

His uncle's creased forehead wasn't the only sign of distress in the room. The chief had always preferred suits over the handwoven and embroidered robes sold mostly to tourists, but his uncle had one of the old-time outfits in dry cleaner's plastic hanging on the hook that normally took his suit coat.

That was chieftain business and nothing Adamou should comment on, but the mountain remained absolutely Adamou's responsibility. And also, he wouldn't mind giving Pascaline her favor immediately.

"Sir," he said, "I realize the engagement with the Sadou woman hasn't gone through, but are you sure about..."

"It didn't?" His uncle sat back, obviously relieved. "Thank Allah." Chiefs had shrunken power bases now compared to the days when they were either heads of state or high priests, or sometimes both depending on the size of the tribe and the nature of their family traditions, but they remained very important people. "I'm so glad I sent you," he said.

And yet even with the man's supposed reduced

power, most people Adamou knew tried very hard to do everything this chief asked.

As the Bakweri chieftain, Adamou's uncle kept offices down near the palm plantations for managing that business, and also at home for all the work of family and tribe. The Cameroonian government was staffed with representatives from most tribes including theirs and run by members of the most powerful families. Not every elected politician aligned neatly with one tribe or another, and some quite wealthy families had links to so many tribes that they no longer fit under any chief's influence and had become independent powers—like the Sadou with all their oil and gas interests.

The Sadou family had in the past also managed the nation's energy business and on occasion built other industries as needed to support their primary work. That family's patriarch, Sadou Moussa, had an excellent reputation for finding places for any younger-generation family member a tribal chief asked to see employed. He rarely asked for favors in return.

"I'm grateful." Endeley Bouba opened his hands to lift them up in a motion half prayer and half thanksgiving. "But how did you know to turn her down?"

"Pascaline, uh . . ." Adamou searched for words.

"Never mind. I've heard more about her since you left, and I completely understand."

"Um, sir." Adamou briefly considered telling the man the full truth about his conversation with Pascaline, but if he was willing to turn down a request from the Sadou patriarch, he wouldn't be inclined to support Adamou's continued interest in the man's granddaughter. "I'd like to hear about that contract. It might not be a bad idea to get involved."

"I didn't tell him no outright," his uncle allowed. "It was Sadou Moussa himself after all, but I read the papers his aide sent ahead. It was an offer to buy the mountain, and I can't permit that." He nodded at a picture on the wall of one of their ancestors in full priestly regalia. It was Endeley Issa, who was chief three generations back. The photographer had captured the light streaming through the rising fumes in a way that gave the simple mountain top an unearthly feel.

"Moussa is coming back in a few days." His uncle stood up and went to his own hanging regalia. He peeled the plastic covering back to more fully reveal the robes. "I need you to be the priest who tells him no."

His uncle sniffed at the robes and pulled back again in disgust. "They still haven't gotten the smell out."

Adamou smiled. "Don't worry. I'm used to our volcano god's incense. But are you sure about this?"

His uncle gave him a frank look much better suited to the man's usual demeanor than this talk of priests and their mountain. "Moussa will understand, or if he doesn't his staff will explain things to him."

"Not that." Adamou nodded at the other framed photo of family on his uncle's wall. The one that showed all Endeleys at a feast a few years back. There'd been other posed pictures taken, but this one showed Bouba's three sons presenting a great platter of roast antelope. They'd taken a hunting trip before the party specifically for that purpose and the cook had done a fantastic job with the meat they'd brought back. "There are other men who expect to be chief after you, and if I'm the one you have talking to people outside the family about what's good for the mountain, it'll be hard to make a change later and pick anyone else."

His uncle nodded. "Yes. And since none of them want to live here all the time, or want to spend time on the mountain, and especially don't want to be telling any man of Sadou Moussa's stature no, this is exactly the right thing. Let them see the real work of the job, and ten, fifteen years from now when I'm sick of it all, they'll thank you for taking it." He patted Adamou on the shoulder. "If there wasn't a nasty job like this to do, I'd have to invent one to set up a smooth transition. Keep it in mind when you take the job yourself and have to find your own replacement to train up."

The chief returned the robe to its hanger and fussed with getting the folds to drape neatly. "And on the business side, I could negotiate a land-use agreement instead of a sale, but whatever old Moussa wants it for, he's not the most capable business man out there."

He turned to give Adamou a knowing look. "There are some people who might come to you with a proposal and if you don't take it, you'll never hear anything like it again. But no. Whatever this plan is, someone else will come to us in a couple years and offer twice the amount if we just hold out."

"Not this time, sir." Adamou leaned in. "I know what this is all about, and we want the Sadous to owe us favors now more than ever." He paused, thinking about how to explain what he'd learned. He'd start with the source. "Have you heard of Moussa's Tchami relative who goes by Mami? She told me a few things I think you should know."

"Mami, as in Mami-Wata?" His uncle recoiled.

"Um, no." Adamou blinked. The spiritual talk had him for a moment actually thinking of the old woman as a little witchy and finding it fit. "She was married to a cousin of Moussa's. I think Tchami Magdalene is her legal name, and she has an amazing number of small business connections. It seems she and another Tchami relation are repaying a favor to the Sadou family."

"Yes, that's who I was afraid you meant." Endeley Bouba shook his head. "And yes, I know who their Aunt Mami is." He dropped back into the chair with his brow furrowed and indecision pressing his lips into a tight line. "Whatever craziness our family does, I don't want to ever hear of you pulling the ridiculous stunts that Aunt Mami does. Or if you do..." He shook a finger at Adamou. "I don't care if ancestor spirits turn out to be exactly as much a figment of our imaginations as I think they are, I'll still come back and haunt you for it!"

"Yes, sir," Adamou said.

But his uncle wasn't done. "Do you know what that woman did to start her whole mystical powers hoodoo nonsense?"

Adamou almost said, "No, sir," but he actually did know, and while he was fairly sure he didn't believe in ancestor spirits either, his uncle was alive and well and currently acting as both head of his family and chief of his tribe. So he answered honestly.

"Sir, I believe she had a near-death experience and her husband died trying to save her."

"Sadou Michel died trying to save Tchami Magdalene." Bouba made the statement with a tone of flat disbelief. "Pour me more coffee." He tapped his finger on the rim of his long-empty cup. "If you've got that history wrong, who knows many other things haven't been passed down accurately.

"Idiots in love don't walk in the bush country at night without a light. They'd been married—what, two or three months—and already he was slipping out at night? A reasonable woman would have gone straight for the divorce, and a few people thought she was actually out there with a machete and no flashlight because she intended to cut off something from his body and not to mangle any unfortunate snakes. But back then Aunt Mami was a sweet little thing, and she probably never intended to do more than threaten him.

"And as for the other woman having never come forward." He stopped to sip the coffee that Adamou provided. "That most certainly does not mean the other woman was Mami-Wata herself punishing the man for straying from her chosen path for him or some such nonsense. There wouldn't have been just one other woman. Michel was in the habit of hiring several, and since those women were, ah, in the profession, none of them would have wanted to be associated with a client being found out.

"That younger relative of hers, Fabrice, had a part-time job at the hospital where they brought her. I think he stocked shelves and such in the evenings after school. But anyway, he was there and a lot younger, so nobody wanted to tell him any of the stuff about how bad Magdalene's marriage into the great family was while it looked like she wasn't going to make it.

"And then later Michel got snake-bit too." The older Endeley rolled his eyes. "And that happened because he got shredded by his entire family for treating his new bride so badly. A natural genius, his first response was to get staggering drunk, and then his second brilliance was to going snake hunting in the dark the next night while still drunk. And the family was furious enough that they let him. What did they think would happen? The Sadous of this generation are much improved, but it is not, believe me, a perfect family."

Adamou said, "I, uh, had only heard that she nearly died from a snake bite and that her new husband went searching for the snake so they could give her the right antivenom, and he got bit too, but he didn't get treated in time."

"Ah." Bouba nodded. "I suppose that's all technically true. But it doesn't begin to properly explain who their Aunt Mami is now. You think she's involved in this project Sadou Moussa wants to use the mountain for?"

"Do we want her to be?"

"Yes!" The chief leaned forward. "If I made another offer, do you think you could tolerate the other young Sadou woman? Business ties are all very nice, but if this is a project with Tchami backing—either Aunt Mami or Fabrice—and they've finally gotten the full force of the Sadou family behind them too, we don't want to just be supporting it. We want to be in it." He snapped his fingers in a quick half dozen twitches of his hand, thinking. "There's that other girl. Kind of plain from what I hear, but they all like her better. I think her name is Martine or Marthe or something like that."

"Sadou Maurie," Adamou said.

"Yes, that's it." His uncle nodded firmly. "We'll have you meet her. You might suit better. She's probably less of a snake than Pascaline."

CHAPTER FIVE

"**M**AURIE!" THE TINY VOICE FROM HER COMM snapped at her. "Wake up already. Aren't you supposed to be the industrious one?"

Maurie retrieved her comm from a pouch in her luggage case and flicked on the screen in response to Great Aunt Mami.

The device still worked in spite of the heavy dust and not being charged for over a week. Great Aunt Mami didn't often give gifts, but when she did they were high quality. And they came with strings, like not getting a choice about accepting incoming calls from her.

Maurie's luggage bag hadn't fared as well. Every seam and decorative bit of edging was caked with reddish-orange dirt. Inside the bag, a fine grit covered all the formerly clean clothing, but Pascaline, true to form, had elected not to include Maurie's boots, because "they'd get everything else dirty."

"Good afternoon, Great Aunt," Maurie answered.

"It's morning," Great Aunt Mami said. But of course

Great Aunt Mami was inferring she'd been sleeping her life away. Maurie could see that assessment in the way her older relative's eyes crinkled with a mixture of bemusement and judgment. Clear video images had no chance of transmitting realism when the filter of memory distorted everything.

The full sun beat down on Maurie's head with her scarf providing little protection. A squint at the upper corner of the comm read 11:58 A.M. Great Aunt Mami looked tired, red-eyed and faded. She also had tied a headscarf on her tight curls, subduing her normal halo of silver-white hair.

"Yes, Great Aunt." It felt like it should be afternoon already. Maurie had woken early feeling great. No post-hospitalization weakness lingered. Her appetite had been back, her strength had returned, and she had been ready to get back to work.

But the new day had not erased the mess Pascaline had left for her. The price of that water truck would have left a massive hole in the clinic's operating budget, so, of course, she'd had to cover it. The village headman who had evicted a relative to give her a bed might have smiled and waved away any idea of one of those Sadous paying for the use of his guestroom, but he had nothing to do with the clinic. The man would, she would make sure, be repaid in some handsome way by her family later. The clinic's costs had been another matter entirely. They couldn't wait.

Though apparently neither could her family. The mass of messages in her comm from Uncle Benoit were easy enough to ignore. There was no way Grandpere had been draining all the family business funds and hiring back engineers and technicians they'd had to put on half pay. Nobody could afford to do that with the way the oil side of the energy industry had been slumping lately.

Maurie schooled her face into a polite smile for Great Aunt Mami. The video feed would continue while Maurie scrolled through the rest of the backlog of contact attempts in the comm.

Grandpere had sent a message telling her to meet him at some friend's coastal compound near Buea, a town which she'd had to look up. Her heart had raced just looking at the map. A blinking GPS location marked Buea as partially up Fako. The coastal mountain might only be fourth tallest on the African continent, but that was enough that it'd probably still make her feel queasy to go from this low-lying farm country up to a mountainside town.

Her comm's wiki said it was a touch over four thousand meters high at the taller of two peaks. That was more than high enough to make her doubt the number. A second wiki she checked had had it as thirteen thousand some feet, and she converted the number. It matched. She still doubted it. That was *really* tall.

The location was no backcountry area to be a utilities repair mission. So it had to be Sadou Corporation oil and gas business.

Nobody would want to drill through that much extra dirt and rock. She would get a surveyor to find a better, lower location. She was absolutely not going to drill through that massive mountain or even any of the lesser ones in the Cameroon line mountain range.

Great Aunt Mami made an irritated coughing noise. *Oh right*. She had better focus on the call. The video-connected light winked out. Maurie blinked. The call had dropped.

Great Aunt Mami never hung up. Certainly she had interruptions and would imperiously announce that you'd be on hold for some unknown period. Her host of vigorous small business owners did have their share of emergencies. And her investigator-accountant-spies on occasion gave her reports on less vigorous co-owners in need of some threatening supernatural wrath. She might leave the call going for an hour while she dealt with an emergent issue.

This was weird.

The Great Aunt Mami who had peered at her on the comm screen hadn't seemed herself either. Maurie tried to ignore it, but she had nothing else to do while waiting for her transport. The oddness itched at her need to find and solve problems.

But even before the call, the morning had felt strange. Maurie liked helping Grandpere, but she'd had to remind herself of that. His projects were always interesting. He gave her the tricky ones where something wasn't working right and he didn't have all the details even of what was wrong, let alone what it would take to fix it. She again had to remind herself that she did like these jobs and had to push herself to get moving to collect whatever medicines she ought to take to complete her recovery and get transportation out.

The sender's location for Grandpere's message was on the highway between Buea and the city of Douala. Her spam filter had a bunch of reply-all messages from her aunts and uncles in response to Uncle Benoit. She ignored them. Uncle Benoit also wanted to speak with her. She tried to reach her cousin Pascaline, but she didn't answer. Maurie left a message on the house phone system with her status. If her cousin didn't delete it, someone else in the extended family might call and help. She didn't explicitly ask for money, but she was sure any aunt or uncle who heard it would hear that part of the request.

"Money, money, mountain money, curses, curses, mountain curses." It was her imagination, Maurie was absolutely sure.

There couldn't have been a ghost snake sliding between vendor stalls in the open market and laughing. She saw tire tracks marking the snakeskin just before a teen huckster selling roast peanuts walked straight through the spirit.

It wasn't there. Snakes don't laugh. They don't have the mouths and throats for it. They certainly don't have goatskin hand drums accompanying their half hiss half chant.

The mostly unintelligible jumble ended in a refrain. "Curses of money and money of curses, yours, yours, yours!"

Maurie's comm vibrated to the beat of the spirit dance. The drumbeat syncopation to the snake hiss was only her comm's message notice ringtone. Grandpere wasn't one to deal with comm systems himself, but he had his aide resending her the same terse instructions to come. The woman seemed to have set it for a ten-second auto-repeat. Maurie blocked it, and switched over to a new incoming call from Great Aunt Mami.

"Where are you, child?" The alert in the corner of Maurie's screen warned her that her camera was being operated remotely. Maurie gritted her teeth and tolerated it.

"A village Pascaline found near our last work site. The place is named Wangai. They had a doctor." Maurie reconsidered the accuracy of her statement. "Or rather they had a clinic and some, well, not exactly nurses, but..." Maurie glanced around. The few locals she's spoken with thought very highly of the orderlies working at the "hospital," as they'd referred to the one-room cement clinic building. "I'm alive, and the care was just fine, okay?"

Great Aunt Mami's expression grew alarmed. She had personal experience with less than credentialed medical care, Maurie remembered.

"Where's your chart? Did you get a copy? Did they use medical charts at all?" The questions came rapid fire.

Maurie sent her great aunt the file. Ms. Oumarou had kept paper charts, and when Maurie'd gone back to the clinic first thing this morning, it had been easy to snap photos with her comm to make an electronic copy. And when she couldn't find that doctor Pascaline had mentioned, she'd found an administrator instead and worked to resolve the bill.

And Maurie had already sent her medical file along with all the symptoms she could recall and her current vitals to a very good doctor in Douala. The man had many years of medical experience. He'd been able to discreetly verify that her recovery was real. If he'd also implied that there may have been a fair amount of nonstandard aspects to her treatment and that she may experience a few long-term side effects from one of the medications whose timely use had most likely saved her life, Maurie had elected not to complain about it.

Great Aunt Mami made concerned noises. She likely was also forwarding Maurie's file to a doctor of her own. Great Aunt Mami started reading it to herself without letting Maurie end the call.

Maurie ate her sandwich. The baguette tasted slightly stale, but the roasted meat was good quality. It proved to be a tough cut of beef, not goat. She'd watched it being slow roasted on the open fire and shaved off the spit into her open bread. The spicy sauce ladled over top hinted of harissa and *chita* pepper. She chewed slowly to enjoy the perfect blend of flavor and heat. Here on the edge of the marketplace, Maurie could see several vendors walking the market selling food. There was a girl selling fresh *makala*. Maurie had a good spot under the mango tree nearest to the bus passenger pickup, but she might be able to get the girl's attention and call her over.

Great Aunt Mami kept reading.

Maurie didn't tell her great aunt that she'd already gotten her second opinion. Great Aunt Mami's fretting gave her time to eat, and Maurie felt like she could swallow an entire goat herself without being full. So after the sandwich she had three *makala*. The perfectly crisped outsides stuck out in spikes and bumps like cartoon asteroids and the soft chewy interiors filled her belly nicely.

Leaving the clinic building and checking out had proved to be two completely unassociated things here where on occasion the sick could outnumber the beds, and as a person with the connections to procure a bed of her own, Maurie didn't entirely fault Ms. Oumarou for denying her reentry as soon as she'd been able to walk as far as the outhouse and back on her own.

A friend of Grandpere's managed the government's health services. The Sadou family did energy work, mostly. If she'd died maybe they'd have branched into medical a little bit, but it wouldn't be polite to go around challenging the bush clinic's practices. Especially after they had, probably, saved her life.

And she did feel really good. The word in the village was that everyone associated with the clinic trusted Ms. Oumarou implicitly.

"She's a witch lady," Pascaline had whispered in her ear, not quietly enough. Pascaline had said it in English, which not everyone spoke, but it was hardly a mystery language. "Mami-Wata," she'd added, which just made it worse. Now Maurie could never come back here or Ms. Oumarou might poison her on general principle. Few people liked being referred to as having mystical curse powers even if excellence in healing and prosperity sometimes came with it in the folklore.

Great Aunt Mami was the obvious exception. The problem with claiming Mami-Wata's powers for yourself, besides the sheer creepiness factor, was the other side of the folk stories. Mami-Wata's favor might bring healing and incredible wealth, but, if offended, she withdrew her blessing. Easy come, easy go on steroids. Those cursed by the water spirit lost everything, and so did the cursed one's whole family, for a very broad definition of family.

Maurie watched the frown deepen as her great aunt scrolled further down her chart. Great Aunt Mami looked unwell.

That gray undertone to her older relative's normally glowing brown skin bothered her a lot more than her own brush with ill health. She'd been about to ask for a loan to cover the water truck and clinic costs. But, maybe, this wasn't the best time. Perhaps, Great Aunt Mami might be interested in supplying seed money for some business start-ups in Wangai? The townspeople acted like Pascaline's water truck delivery was an incredible gift from the uber-wealthy and gracious Sadou family instead of just the stopgap fix it was. There seemed to be a business case for either installing municipal water piping for a further upstream intake or building a more rigorous town water filtration system.

Great Aunt Mami finished reading. Her scowl broke abruptly. "You aren't going to die," she announced.

"Yes, Great Aunt," Maurie agreed.

Great Aunt Mami narrowed her eyes. "You little scamp. You've already checked with a doctor yourself, haven't you?"

"Yes, Great Aunt," she said again.

Great Aunt Mami harrumphed, but she was pleased. Maurie could tell from the way the corners of the woman's mouth kept pulling up while she tried to maintain a good scowl. Great Aunt Mami approved of competency.

"I'm having it checked by my doctor anyway. He's calling now. Stay on the line," she admonished and switched over, not including Maurie in the second conversation.

Maurie's comm had continued its drumbeat notifications but on a silent vibrate. Grandpere really wanted her now. Or his aide hated her. Both could be true.

She checked the message headers to see the time stamps and noticed something else. The very first one had been sent to both her and Pascaline, but all

the follow-up repeats were to her alone. So Pascaline
might already be there, or maybe she'd done something
and Grandpere had decided he only wanted Maurie
on whatever this new job was. Maurie would bet on
Pascaline having done something.

"I'm back," Great Aunt Mami announced. "And
you're going to die."

"Okay, Great Aunt," Maurie said.

Great Aunt Mami rolled her eyes. "Not even a
reaction. You're fine, of course, and I checked with a
folklore professor about some of the weird stuff. It's
just a basic blessing invocation and a request that your
recently dead ancestors petition any powerful spirits
nearby on your behalf. And there's not a single story
of that sort of thing getting anybody immortality.
Sorry, kid."

"How about incredible riches beyond human imagining? Can I have that?" Maurie suggested. *Or maybe
just a little loan so I can trade in my bus ticket and
rent the headman's car?*

"Are you out of money?" Her great aunt opened
her mouth and lifted a hand to cover it in feigned
surprise. A mean glint shone in the woman's eyes.
"Did the Sadou wonder child make a big mistake?"

Maurie tensed. Great Aunt Mami was more tight-
fisted than most, but there was an undertone of rage
there she hadn't expected.

"The clinic care wasn't something I budgeted for,
but I'll be fine," she said. And she would. She had a
bus ticket. What could possibly go wrong?

Other than Grandpere's assistant completely draining her comm's battery with nonstop demands for her
presence in Buea or any number of other indignities of

trying to pass for the sort of person who could safely travel by bus. Maurie changed the block to stop the calls from Grandpere's numbers entirely. She could change it back when she switched buses at N'goundéré.

"The other day your cousin used a helicopter service that belongs to me," Great Aunt Mami said. "Picked her right up at a hover because there isn't a maintained helipad there in Wangai. Do you know how hard it is to keep good pilots when they can make twice as much in Europe? Do you have any idea how hard it is to keep parts in stock and aircraft operating with the amount of heavy grit in the air during dry season?"

"Uh, Great Aunt? It's me, Maurie. If I can help, just tell me what you need." Great Aunt Mami did look at her, but then Mami's focus went distant.

"No," she said. Great Aunt Mami stared straight through Maurie, and the anger in her expression told Maurie she wasn't seeing her great niece. "I owe you Sadous nothing. And neither does Fabrice, not after what he's done. Oh fuck, what he's done." Great Aunt Mami blinked fast as though she were holding back tears of rage, or maybe helplessness. "Maurie. You will get your ass to Grandpere immediately and make damned sure Fabrice regrets nothing. I do owe Fabrice."

The call ended.

CHAPTER SIX

FABRICE TCHAMI, KNOWN COMPANY-WIDE AS Chummy to everyone but the CEO down the hall, flexed his fingers and prepared to work administrative magic. His tools of choice were a battered desk and a connection to the corporate network. He used the same monitor and keyboard devices all the entry-level employees got; he didn't need anything fancier.

He also didn't want them. The latest generation neural monitor DeeDee had attempted to use for a few weeks stuck out of the office trashcan. But she really did seem to like the newest VR-compatible gloves for large dataset analysis tasks.

The office had a few more generous touches, because Jeffy insisted on it. And Chummy did appreciate them, but he could have done without. The white-noise maker by the door, the deluxe office chair, and the combination air scrubber and freshener with the lemon grove scent pod were overkill. Or maybe they were Jeffy's way of making sure Chummy felt both appreciated and indebted to the company. In which case they were working perfectly.

Because Chummy felt like shit.

He clocked out for his lunch hour. He could at least do his cheating on his own time. Since on a slow week he typically logged around eighty hours and the minimum was thirty-five, it was a meaningless gesture, but he felt slightly better about it.

The contract had gone through. Ethan Schmidt-Li had signed off on it. Sadou Moussa's electronic signature had been applied. Legal had filed a copy. Finance had dumped a great pile of money into a new escrow account and a withdrawal for the first quarter awaited only the Sadou Corporation designating an authorized individual to make the transfer.

None of the amounts were significant compared to the cost of the elevator itself or TCG's annual operating budget, and, Chummy reminded himself, as long as Sadous could deliver on the contract it would be a good price for the service. But only if.

Chummy needed to do something or this golden ticket could transmute into a Midas curse. Aunt Mami would tell him he was incubating fine eggs without knowing if they'd hatch wild geese or cobras.

Geese. He intended it to be geese. A whole flock of them laying golden eggs that hatched other geese that laid golden eggs and the whole Sadou family and their children and children's children could spend their days employed in metaphorical geese tending. That and separating 24-karat eggshell bits from the dung and straw of old goose nests. He couldn't imagine any future without some amount of work. Chummy was too much of a realist for that.

Or he'd take the snake version instead if the snake's eggshells were also gold. Antivenom treatments were very well understood these days.

He hadn't, quite, betrayed Jeffy's trust by keeping Sadou Moussa's. If only enough people of the right skills could be found to support the Sadou patriarch, Jeffy could have his elevator and the Sadous could have this small assist into that new economy as well.

All Chummy had to do was bend his own scruples a little bit more.

TCG had so very many teams working on projects. No one cross-checked them all. Well, no one else. And Ethan might be one of Chummy's better finds, but he was new in his position. He certainly didn't have Chummy's expertise in leveraging the cracks between the corporate hierarchies.

He forwarded a message with a copied bit of this manager's report and a different copied bit of that manager's report and a few attachments to push them all in the direction he wanted them to go. It took a knowledge of the engineering teams, their interests, and their competitive attitudes, but Chummy could direct researchers to examine the launcher problem without looking like he'd started the work at all. In separate one-on-one messages, he let the managers he'd selected know he could help them find funding lines with available hours if their teams needed more charge codes. They thanked him effusively for the unexpected support and assured him that they appreciated their teams being remembered for work supporting Jeffy's top project.

A cartoon with blonde hair and bat wings waved from the lower right corner of Chummy's screen.

His assistant, DeeDee Nelson, should be asleep. He'd sent her home hours ago after discovering she'd pulled an all-nighter scouring employee files and recruiter candidate submissions for the perfect public relations specialist.

And he had his other assistant, Samson Young, traveling. If, later, this all fell apart and the cutthroats he'd put on the corporate ethics team came after him, they'd find the time stamps proved his assistants had nothing to do with it.

Ethan Schmidt-Li's interoffice employee thefts had continued to mount, so Chummy had sent Samson on personal visits to all of the offended managers' offices. Samson had a snaggletooth grin and legs that didn't work, but he had a motor chair with racing stripes and could achieve likeable faster than anyone else Chummy had ever hired. And that skill, of course, was why Chummy had kept the young man for himself. He'd have to give the kid up soon to let him grow into his full potential, but for now the Samson and DeeDee pair were perfect. Well, perfect when he wasn't trying to stop their efforts to assist him.

The cartoon waggled its wings again to get his attention.

If DeeDee were monitoring his work, she already knew he was scheming. He had hoped she was still too tired to have noticed, and he didn't want to draw her attention to the things neither assistant should be involved in. So he made no effort to hide anything. As long as he didn't hide his work, there was a good chance she'd not have time to look at it.

A tap on the touch screen acknowledged the little cartoon. A text bubble opened.

"Hi Boss!" it said. *"The interoffice calendar has you on personal time still. Want me to fix that?"*

"Go to sleep, DeeDee," Chummy typed back.

"I'm not DeeDee. I'm a construct she built to check for accurate time card alerts." The cartoon smiled and flapped its bat wings. *"Would you like me to wake her?"*

Meticulous DeeDee and her programs. He did vaguely remember explaining to her after the third time she'd neglected to submit her time report that company policy called for employee termination to be considered any time two inaccurate time reports were made within a six-month period by the same employee. And he'd said that he'd keep filing the manager's correction paperwork to keep her employed, but would she please do whatever was necessary to stop forgetting?

Her tendency as a new hire to not file reports wasn't the same as intentionally submitting inaccurate ones—even within the most draconian reading of that particular policy she hadn't been in any real danger of termination, but Chummy hadn't fully understood DeeDee back then.

Her meticulous attention to detail had been clear from the first, but he'd been less careful about his own words than he could have been. And there had been some junior vice president or another who'd wanted Chummy out and had needled him in a meeting about his newly hired assistant flouting policy.

She'd fixed the problem, and he'd never thought to ask how. DeeDee Nelson was a truly dedicated assistant who might be about to get him fired if, after she woke up, she had enough time to check her program's logs.

He was in too far to stop now. He'd find things to keep her busy.

"*Would you like me to wake DeeDee?*" the cartoon asked again.

"*No, thank you.*" Chummy watched the cartoon take a bow and vanish into the corner of his screen.

After a moment he pulled up his time card and marked himself as back from lunch. If he backdated the work time to start when he'd logged into the network, would DeeDee be less inclined to check what his actual work had been? He'd have to allocate the time toward a particular time-charging code, and she would want to check to make sure he'd picked the right one. Let it stay a lunch break.

Chummy selected "human resources general operations" as his charge code for the next couple hours. He'd be able to find plenty of things to pile up in DeeDee's inbox while he checked on the status of the company.

And he needed to check on Samson's work anyway. Ethan knew more North American employees than German or Chinese ones, so complaints were coming in from European and Asian engineering managers who hadn't been robbed of people. Samson did such good work convincing team leaders to feel honored about having their best people stolen for the elevator that they were bragging about it.

From Samson's notes, he needed a bit more funding for recruiting replacements. Some of the managers wanted to increase the workload on their remaining staff without new hires in order to claim efficiencies for their own evaluations. Chummy added assessments of those managers to DeeDee's to-do pile.

He sent Samson a reminder to drop a word in those

managers' ears about the company liking to see the same managerial staff achieve benchmark goals for at least a year post staff reduction. Gut a staff, claim enough corporate savings to gain a promotion out into a new part of the company, and leave the old team broken behind them? Not with Chummy on the job, they wouldn't. He expected they'd want their full teams.

Though some of them might truly be overstaffed for their workloads. He added a note to DeeDee's list to check on the team's workloads as well.

"Tell them we have special projects," he added. People got scared when senior management types asked questions that might imply some employees had been stretching a few hours of work across a whole week. He expanded the note to explain that. Chummy was capable of inventing make-work to distract her, but these were genuinely useful tasks that she'd enjoy doing.

Inspiration struck.

Ethan could use some cross-enterprise support, and Jeffy would back it if Chummy made it happen. And it'd also appease the engineering managers prideful enough to be upset instead of relieved that Ethan lacked the connections to steal away their most brilliant employees in addition to the ones he'd already been grabbing from North America.

Chummy flexed and started firing off emails. "No formal realignment, but certain key positions will be reassigned to this important project." That was a good line; he dropped it into a notes file to save for future reuse. "Please nominate your best and brightest for special projects in support of the elevator enterprise movement." He didn't like the phrasing of that last bit as much. Enterprise was such an archaic corporate term and movement sounded like he was channeling that old businessman-as-evangelist trope. Still, it got him thinking about Ethan's public relations blind spot.

He pulled up DeeDee's notes. As he'd hoped, she had compiled data on the employees Ethan had drafted so far and even started preliminary assessments of their team strengths.

They were light on managers. So, Ethan was planning on either large teams or a bunch of engineering collaborations. It could work either way. Unless he was afraid of management competition.

Was Ethan Schmidt-Li scared of losing his job?

Ethan had drafted lots of engineers and scientists but comparatively few project coordinators. Chummy glared at the data. He might be.

Chummy couldn't allow that. Ethan's managerial strengths wouldn't hold up properly under that type of stress. Hadn't Cindy Brooks documented that well enough in Chicago?

Chummy swore at himself. He was losing his touch. Focus too much on the Sadou problem and he'd let Ethan freaking Schmidt-Li go supernova. Sadou Moussa needed to find a way to make good on the contract himself. Chummy had his hands full.

He checked the time in Beijing and then shrugged and dialed anyway.

"Yes, I know what time it is," he said into the phone by way of greeting.

A groan was his only answer.

"Omer, I'm sending you to Kilimanjaro."

"What? Kilimanjaro! For me?" Omer hollered triumph.

Chummy had to pull the phone away from his ear.

The automatic sound dampening would probably prevent hearing damage, but that didn't mean it was comfortable.

"Yes, Omer, I do mean you. I'm giving you a bad boss to go with a great job. Good luck."

"You mean Ethan? I get to work for Ethan Schmidt-Li directly?" An awake, but not quite coherent Omer Ehrlich didn't believe him. But Chummy was confident the new Director of Sciences, Worldwide, would show enough spirit for the man to understand what Chummy'd meant once he got on site.

"Yes, Omer. And call me if you need anything."

"Right." Omer let out a laugh. "I need a flight. Do I get to bring my people?"

"Sure." If there was ever a project Jeffy wouldn't mind throwing extra workers at, this was it. "But there probably won't be much in the way of office facilities set up right away. Check with Ethan's aide, Jax. I'll have DeeDee send you his contact. Don't wake him up," Chummy added. "I think he's still on North American east coast time."

Omer babbled his agreement without challenging the instruction to respect Jax's sleep cycle. Ethan had found Jax himself. That man's hiring had been the turning point when Chummy had realized just how effective a man like Ethan Schmidt-Li could be under the right circumstances.

Now onto giving Ethan the rest of the support he needed. Ethan had not been the only person who Chummy could have used to head up the building of the space elevator. He might not even have been the best candidate. But he ought to be able to do it. And he'd been malleable enough for the side plan.

Chummy focused back on the situation at hand. It

was too late to go back and change things. If he had Ethan fired, the next person in the job would have a real reason to be afraid. Scared managers were almost always bad managers. And the complexity of the job required excellence.

Chummy moved on down his list finding gaps in Ethan's teams and filling them. Testing, quality assurance, operations evaluators—the elevator would have plenty of problem finders on the job. Now he needed to make sure Ethan could match them with problem solvers.

The air freshener squirted another lemon-scented plume, and Chummy sneezed.

"Bless you."

Chummy jerked up.

John-Philip Jeffy, chief executive officer of TCG, waved at him from the doorway. "Can I convince you to accept another couple staff members? You'll run your two assistants ragged and break all your own nonexempt employee rules." The brown-haired short man with an easy smile wagged a finger at him but beamed while he did it.

"I'd have come over if you needed me, Jeffy," Chummy said.

Jeffy shrugged and wandered all the way in through the outer office into Chummy's workspace. "I was thinking about the elevator. Just needed to bounce a few ideas around." He eased the door shut and bumped up the level of the white-noise maker. Jeffy liked the settings a little high. True quiet helped him think, he'd often said.

"Sure, Jeffy." Chummy sat back while his boss and friend wandered the room.

"You'd tell me if this were all a big mistake, right?"

Jeffy ran his fingers through his short, thinning hair. "Ethan." He shook his head. "I really don't get a good vibe from that guy. I keep wanting to rip the whole thing out of his hands and do it myself."

Chummy's mouth went dry.

Jeffy chuckled. "I'm not actually going to take direct control. You've made it quite clear. This is a moonshot. And if the rest of the company has a dip in profitability because I let my focus shift... Or, God help us, if that results in a drop in investor confidence enough to tank our corporate bond rating, I suppose I could spin off portions of TCG and sell them to fund the elevator long enough to complete the construction. But the sharks would see me bleeding and underbid everything's value... Fuck me, I might run cash dry too soon. And then it would be decades before anyone else is gutsy enough to try it."

"I didn't say the elevator wouldn't be profitable," Chummy said.

Jeffy rolled his eyes. "Yeah, yeah, Fabrice. Profit and loss isn't your thing, you always say. I'm just a little stressed. And I do hear you." Jeffy poked at the air unit, sniffed, and made a face. "I think I'm changing your office to a linen fresh scent pod next. Funny thing about you and profits, though. The things you get involved in. Really involved in. They work. We make money hand over fist. And—" he held up a finger—"it's not just because you can get people to work for almost nothing. I had an outside consultant check on you."

Chummy did his best not to look uneasy.

"Not like that." Jeffy chuckled. "I wanted to know if anyone else has that same magic touch."

"And?" Jeffy didn't have a lot of people who he

could talk to without massive unwanted changes being made to corporate policies, but Chummy did have work to get back to.

"And you are not special." Jeffy shook his head in mock sadness. "You're good, but there are other companies, even big ones, that manage to recruit some top-tier people, pay them a lot less than we do, and still keep them loyal enough not to quit."

"Do you want to cut pay?" Chummy asked. He suppressed the sigh. He was fairly certain TCG payroll was around five percent more generous than it needed to be. He pushed policies to keep the extras mostly in bonuses, so employees wouldn't bank on cash flow they might not be getting in leaner years. But . . .

"Nope." Jeffy snorted. "I talk to you because you don't jump to make drastic changes like that. Profits are good. We could fatten up even, but I'm thinking we'll need the war chest for our expansion into the space industries."

"Sounds good, Jeffy."

"Yeah, sure. You got me distracted. Where was I?"

"I'm good, not special." Chummy flashed the man a grin and added, "Just another HR guy."

"Yes!" Jeffy snapped his fingers. "That was it. And no. It's not the people you find, or the compensation levels you convince them to take. It's the way you put them together. I was going to come over to tell you to back up that asshole Ethan however he needed, but you already have, haven't you?"

Chummy spread his hands admitting culpability. "It's my job."

"Thought so." Jeffy nodded to himself. "Okay. I'll leave you to it." He walked through the outer office and paused with the door to the hall half open. "Oh, and did you hear Shen Kong had another payload splatter at their Gobi landing site? Parachute failure again. The super lightweight ones aren't working for them. Cory Aanderson told them we aren't ready to sell orbit-to-surface transport yet, but they don't want to take no for an answer."

"The standard parachute systems and reentry vehicles that they've been using all along still work, boss," Chummy said. "And our biggest market will be surface-to-orbit lift, don't you think?"

"Maybe, maybe," Jeffy said. "Shen Kong's had good success with their asteroid mining efforts, so there could soon be plenty of raw material and fuel for everybody already in orbit. That's straight up 'industrialized space for the new green China' or however you translate the *yuefu* folk song's refrain. Julie Zhu's getting some dividends rolling in for Shen Kong finally.

"The coming influx isn't slowing anyone down now, of course. Lots of companies are seeking to expand their in-orbit manufacturing. And every one of 'em wants to lock in the most economical way to transport finished products back down here." He grinned. "Tell Ethan no pressure next time you see him."

The doors to every one of the C-suite offices lining the hallway hung open. Rodney Johnson, Cory Aanderson's deputy, leaned halfway out his doorway attentive to anything the big boss might say involving his own boss. Jeffy waved cheerily, and Rodney scuttled back inside to report.

Jeffy smirked. He'd intended those last remarks for the corporate rumor mill.

DeeDee Nelson slouched down the hall in almost

professional attire and a serious case of bedhead. She blinked without speaking at the CEO but did give him a polite smile and made eye contact.

"Good afternoon, DeeDee," Jeffy said.

"Hi, Mr. Jeffy," she said.

He nodded without commenting on the sleep creases on her face. But he gave Chummy a look over his shoulder.

Chummy shrugged, and Jeffy went back to his own office without further shocks to the office gossip line.

DeeDee closed the outer office door to the hallway, readjusted the white-noise generator to Chummy's preferred level and collapsed in her chair.

"You could have slept longer," Chummy pointed out.

"Could have," she agreed. "But Mr. Schmidt-Li just got arrested."

"He did not!" Chummy did intend it as a question, but the shock overcame him.

DeeDee flapped a hand. "It wasn't so bad. Jax talked to the Kenyan police and then to the Tanzanian police and he didn't even have to stay in the jail overnight. But I think he needs some help with government and international agency collaboration." She checked her inbox for taskers and groaned. "Can we please call Samson back from his hand-holding trip? I'd really like to sleep again sometime this week."

Chummy nodded slowly. "Yes, I think we can do that."

DeeDee retrieved her interface gloves from her desk drawer and started in on the task at the top of her list without letting the display or chair adjust for ergonomic comfort. Her back was going to demand surgery in payback for that posture one day.

"How did you find out about the arrest?"

"Huh?" DeeDee's head came up. "Oh, one of my programs looks for that kind of thing. But Jax actually called me while I was on my way in. He should have called Samson; he's better at people stuff, but still." She made a plus-one sign in the air granting Ethan's assistant a point. "He called for backup. Didn't know the right amount for a police gratuity. Well, he did call it a bribe, but when I pointed out that corporate policy reimburses gifts and gratuities but not bribes, he made the self-correction quickly enough."

She poked at her assignment a bit more before adding, "Can you believe Ethan Schmidt-Li got into a brawl over office space?"

Chummy winced. Unfortunately, he could believe it. "I'm sorry, DeeDee. But I think we're going to have to go to Kilimanjaro too."

DeeDee nodded. "That's why I wore my pajamas to work under the suit jacket." When Chummy didn't say anything she added, "They're nice pajamas. And I put on shoes."

He glanced at her feet: one black shoe and one brown shoe both of a slip-on variety. She followed his look down.

"I can change. There's a store that delivers to..."

"Don't worry about it. Foreigners are expected to be eccentric."

"But the dress code says..."

"It's okay, DeeDee."

"I really don't like breaking rules."

Chummy nodded minutely. He did know. "It'll take a few hours to arrange transportation anyway. You can go home and grab a few things and change shoes. Or shoe at least."

CHAPTER SEVEN

SADOU MAURIE STUFFED HER COMM BACK INTO her bag and hefted it to her shoulder. So Great Aunt Mami was upset about something. Grandpere would probably know what to do about it. Or he'd continue to ignore it along with all the rest of the growing problems.

She suppressed the traitorous thought, but not quite firmly enough. Douala, Yaoundé, and even smaller N'goundéré could still pretend to possess a growing city's vibrancy. Once she could get on to the next job maybe she could pretend along politely again.

In this era, the country only had twenty or so family groups really trying to hold things together. And most had a leech or seven in each generation. Pascaline was the child of the single most notable wastrel from Uncle Benoit's generation, so of course everyone assumed she was worthless too.

But the little town of Wangai had Maurie wondering if being a leech might not be the reasonable choice. The village camped on the west side of a long blacktop road that had seen better days. Some buildings like the clinic had all cement-block construction, but most were only made of sunbaked clay. Few of the roofs had solar panels.

The administrator from the clinic had Pascaline's water truck backed up between two stalls in the open-air market. He was selling what remained of the clean water, and the line of his customers snaked around out of sight.

Dirt crusted Maurie's toes and the pack of belongings hung heavy on her shoulder. The red flip-flops with their simple plastic strap felt comfortable in the heat. She and Pascaline had both worked hard for Grandpere, propping up the oil and gas business and fixing what they could here and there in the countryside. And a lot of places looked like Wangai, with living conditions no better than they'd been a hundred or two years prior. If she became a leech, she'd help no one. But she'd also not have to watch all her efforts evaporate with no more lasting impact than that soon-to-be-empty water truck.

Their bus laid on the horn for a solid five minutes before pulling off the road. Children scampered out of the way, and a few vendors wandered over to see if passengers wanted to buy something on their way through.

Her ride was a newer model commercial passenger hauler with a boxy frame. Aftermarket railings had been welded to the roof, and a sturdy ladder ran up the side. She could take this bus or wait for one coming tomorrow. Nothing else had so much as slowed on the paved road in the last hour.

The bus's horn stopped. It pulled off the road

toward the wide empty lot under the big mango tree at a crawl. The vehicle edged forward and back over a dozen times in a tight parallel parking maneuver which would've been necessary if there were other vehicles squeezed together on either side. It was the only vehicle here. Automated drive systems did things like that when confronted with terrain outside their program designs like: dirt roads, large potholes, or children waving mango leaves and giggling.

The market stall vendor shooed away the kids, and the bus was finally able to come to a complete stop next to the bus sign.

"Let's go!" the operator called out in French. He hopped out of the vehicle and stationed himself at the front corner of the bus. The man's head swiveled back and forth watching the sides of the bus for any-one who might attempt to climb it and steal a ride without paying.

A few other passengers paid the man and trudged back to use the ladder to claim a spot among the rooftop baggage.

Maurie fished her comm back out again and changed the display to show her ticket. He scanned it and waved her into the packed interior. No one got off the bus at Wangai.

No one else new joined Maurie inside either, so she had her choice of where to sit. Or rather the rest of the passengers did.

They sized her up and rearranged themselves to give her a seat to herself in front of a quiet family squashed together on one bench seat. The toddler slept but the older kid watched her with interest. Both parents avoided eye contact.

No one was afraid of her exactly, but she had boarded from a middle-of-nowhere village where everyone else had taken the half-price option of a spot on the roof. They'd wait to see if she were sick before spreading out to share a seat bench with her.

In five or six hours, they'd get to N'goundéré where everyone could easily switch to another bus if she still seemed potentially dangerous.

Maurie had a comfortable bus ride until the third stop when another woman chose to jostle in next to her. The window by her seat was stuck in the up position and not enough of the other passengers had pried their own windows open. Sweat dribbled down her back and salt-welded her shirt to her skin.

At the fourth stop, they used a police station's paved parking lot for the pickup. She considered joining the rooftop passengers, but a man from above came down complaining loudly of the road grit rubbing his face raw.

"You slow down!" he said to the driver and continued a lengthier complaint in a pidgin mix of Fulani, English, and French that Maurie couldn't follow entirely. He seemed to be describing his face being sandpapered by the wind.

"I keep the schedule," the bus driver insisted. "You don't like it, you pay for ticket inside."

The father from the family behind Maurie called for the driver to get the bus moving again. The rooftop passenger didn't seem to have enough money for an interior passage.

The driver pointed up and said something in pidgin, which earned him a scowl from his rooftop passenger.

"We paid. You go slow."

The man spat on the ground and walked off without

even stopping to retrieve luggage. Maybe he wasn't traveling with any?

The driver called after him, but he didn't come back.

A few young men in worn uniform castoffs stopped repainting the police station walls to watch, but none of the other rooftop passengers came down to continue the argument.

The driver climbed back into the bus, slapped the door shut, and pushed the button to restart the route.

Maurie grabbed the back of the seat in front of her at the jerk of the bus's return to motion. Her seatmate sniffed and made a noise of disapproval.

She gave the woman a pleasant smile and tried to ignore the discomfort. She could leave at the next stop. That particular roadside town had looked barely twice the size of Wangai.

It might not have had any other buses coming through today, and she wanted a larger town with one of those travelers' kiosks with showers. At the Douala airport spa you could have a rainforest waterfall shower with adjustable temperatures or take a steam bath in a massive tub. Customer demand didn't support that sort of luxury in the bush county, but there'd be some options at the bigger towns. Even if the temperature controls had broken, a shower at whatever the water tower's ambient heat might be would be great.

And for her next bus, she'd really love one with a functional air-conditioning unit. Or better yet, perhaps she could end her bus-taking entirely and find a nice little airport with bush pilots willing to take on a passenger for the cost of fuel and a bit more for their trouble. Cost remained the problem.

After paying that water bill, Maurie's checking

account balance had hovered far too close to zero to afford a chartered flight. But the bus smelled more than she'd thought it would, and worse yet, Maurie realized her own body was contributing more than its fair share of the stink.

Maurie swallowed her pride and called Great Aunt Mami.

"Good afternoon, Great Aunt, I just wanted to apologize for my rudeness earlier," Maurie began.

"I don't care." The comm crackled a bit. The connection wasn't the best. Maurie switched to text-based and started typing.

"Great Aunt, I really am sorry. I don't know what I did, but you were clearly very upset, and..."

"Speak or don't speak. I have no time for staring at a comm." Great Aunt Mami switched on video which made the connection worse. She was using her admin controls again: not nice, but very great-auntish of her.

Maurie's seatmate squeezed closer to get a better look. Great Aunt Mami didn't appear to be lacking in time at all. The camera pointed at a ceiling like a comm does if a call is accepted with the device left flat on a table. Or like it would if a salon assistant pressed the button for a valued patron at Chez Angelique's in WuroMahobe. Maurie recognized the ceiling fan.

"Sorry to bother you, Great Aunt. I can reach out to someone else," she said.

"No, you can't."

"I'm sorry again." Maurie tried to squeeze further against the window to gain a bit more privacy. She ended the call and dialed Uncle Benoit.

Chez Angelique's reappeared, fan turning lazily. "I said, you can't," Great Aunt Mami's voice replied.

The corner of Maurie's comm showed the image she was transmitting to Great Aunt Mami. Maurie smoothed her expression back to neutral. She wished Grandpere had paid for the device. He never used the admin controls.

"Uh, Great Aunt. Is there something I can do?" Maurie tried a text-only message to Pascaline. It didn't go through. Great Aunt Mami again. Weren't older people supposed to be bad at technology?

"Oh probably," Great Aunt Mami answered. "If you try hard enough, I'm sure you'll think of something."

"Perhaps you could tell me what I did wrong?" Maurie felt snippy, but she was pretty sure none of it came out in her voice, because Angelique chimed in on the other side of the call.

"Maurie's a good girl, Ms. Mami." Angelique's elbow flashed in and out of the camera view. "Lean your head a bit more to the left please."

"Maurie never does anything wrong," Great Aunt Mami snapped. "But that doesn't make her less at fault."

Angelique's response was lost to static.

"Dirty child sent away," the older woman sharing Maurie's seat commented and shared a laugh with a few of the other passengers. The mother of the family behind her made up a few more embellishments. Maurie couldn't quite follow it all, but the gestures of smelliness made by the man with a bench seat on the opposite side were perfectly clear.

Maurie tried a message to Grandpere. It didn't go through either. She needed someone who'd actually have their comm with them, who might have cracked Great Aunt Mami's admin controls a while ago, and who would help if asked nicely enough.

She sent Uncle Benoit a message collect. *"Stuck on bus 38 headed to N'goundéré. Can u help?"* The device marked the text as pending. Well, that was something at least.

Angelique said something more. It sounded questioning.

"What do I care if he wants to go to Yaoundé and have a coup, he's got no right to go after me," Great Aunt Mami replied.

Maurie's seatmate grabbed her arm in a death grip, and the echoes of speedily translated rumor echoed through the bus as the words "coup d'état" were repeated up and down the seats.

"Not the government," Maurie corrected quickly. No one repeated her correction. Her seatmate eyed her with distrust and moved to a different seat far forward next to the exit.

A new seatmate crammed in next to her. A hint of gray roots hid under dark braided hair adorned with brilliant pink and yellow plastic beads. She poked Maurie in the ribs.

"Not the government?" she said.

"No, ma'am," Maurie agreed.

The woman began a series of rapid translations in several different languages.

"Great Aunt?" Maurie kept her voice down. "You mean Uncle Benoit is calling for a vote again to replace Grandpere, right?"

"What else?" Great Aunt Mami snapped. "And this time he decided to have me shunned first. I told Moussa the foreign bank situation was a mistake, but no, he was always convinced he'd have a smooth transition handing everything over to your dad. Over ten years later, and he still doesn't have another plan in place. Little Benoit can't begin to do the job. Nobody likes Pascaline, and you're too nice to do it."

"Also too stinky," the kid from the seat behind her suggested. "Chiefs can't be stinky."

She ignored him. "Uncle Jacques," Maurie suggested.

"Isn't family," Great Aunt Mami said. "He's not even a direct marry-in. He's a cousin of a marry-in who happens to be a decent manager."

Maurie glanced around the bus. She had a large audience now. Some of the bus riders were translating softly to their seatmates. The woman beside her had left out quite a few bits in her translation. There hadn't been any mention of banks or financial accounts in the French version and while Maurie with her off-continent English-only education didn't have a hope of following the other languages, most everyone else on the bus would be able to understand her seatmate. The multiple translations at volume weren't necessary; they were reassuring. She'd been trying to keep everyone calm.

But the woman's hands, out of direct line of sight for her audience, held a yellow leather handbag in her lap with a white-knuckled grip. Maurie swallowed, but her seatmate's voice maintained its calm, even tones. The woman seemed able to project peace without feeling it herself. The hair beads matched the purse exactly. The swirling print of the woman's blouse had an unusual pattern like something made with of child's fingerpaints and custom printed at a novelty fabric shop. Heaven help her, she'd just been joined by a proud grandmother.

"Ma'am," Maurie whispered, "it's really okay. Not the government at all. Just my family is having some difficulties. Our grandfather is older."

The woman set her chin, neither appearing to believe or disbelieve her just yet. But the bus passengers had calmed down.

"Great Aunt," Maurie held the comm close and kept the volume dialed down. "I'm on public transportation. So we've got an audience. Why don't we turn off video and switch to a text call?"

Angelique's response was soft and barely audible. "Ms. Mami, did she say public transportation? That isn't safe. Not for a Sadou."

Great Aunt Mami grabbed the comm and stared. She shook her head at Maurie.

The comm chose that moment to fritz. No signal, and not something Great Aunt Mami had done remotely.

The volume hadn't been quiet enough to avoid her closest neighbors overhearing. Her seatmate's eyes went wide, but mouth stayed clamped shut.

The father of the family behind coughed.

"I know electricity," he said with a careful lowered voice. "Any system, any house or office, run generators or fix." When Maurie didn't answer immediately he changed tactics. "My wife, she cooks. Good frugal meals for staff. No waste."

The wife gave her husband a frightened look, no doubt remembering that she'd laughed at Maurie not too long ago, before they'd realized who she was.

He tried another pitch. "And, and, I have cousins with degrees. Very bright. My one brother is top of his class. They work hard all day, every day."

He lowered his voice further and began to list off his marketable skills and those of his family members who might be able to find positions with her extended family's businesses. He had his son slip a business card to her in the narrow space between the side of the bus and the seat.

The grandmother beside her relaxed enough to dig out a refurbished comm, and beg a contact transfer from Maurie for a hiring manager in Douala that a certain grandson of hers might look up.

Maurie tried to shrink. They weren't repeating her name. They knew not enough good jobs existed for everyone to get one. She promised to give their names to Grandpere, and they relaxed their pressure, not mollified and not entirely believing her promise, but satisfied that they'd done their family duty.

The rest of the bus returned to other distractions. Maurie stayed quiet.

"Listen to your mother," the woman from the family behind Maurie finally spoke up, softly misidentifying Ms. Angelique as a relative instead of family staff. "One like you should not be here. Don't tempt a starving man."

Maurie's grandmotherly seatmate clucked a warning noise effectively silencing the soft outburst. "The roads are safe. We have a good gendarmerie."

"When she gets kidnapped for a really big ransom, do we fight for her? The other passengers that do that always get shot in the movies," the child said into the pause that should have included only an agreement about the effectiveness of the police. The kid missed the startled looks his parents exchanged and switched languages to beg his father for a sweet.

His mother shushed him. Without answering either of the child's questions, the father said, "His grandmother lets him watch too much television."

Maurie's seatmate and the boy's parents turned the conversation into a cheerful argument on the disgraceful state of young people in this day and age. When they agreed that kids these days were spoiled, Maurie suspected they were referring to her more than to their own children. But they didn't explicitly say so.

"No VR time for kids one expert says. Don't limit, another says, kids need to know how to use it for jobs. All these parenting rules are 'two crocodiles joined in the middle,' you know," the boy's mother quoted the truism, earning a nod of agreement from Maurie's grandmotherly seatmate. The rest of the proverb, of course, was that when the two-headed crocodile found food, the heads fought over it even though they shared a stomach.

Continuing on from that agreement, they also agreed it was harder these days to find good work. All three adults avoided looking at her. Maurie's grandmotherly seatmate quoted a proverb of her own: "Not everyone who chased the zebra caught it, but he who caught it, chased it."

"I don't watch the little children in my family much," the grandmother added, "but my sons and daughters-in-law all ask me who I saw on my travels and give me thanks for the positions I can find for them with my many friends." She shared a grin with the mother and father, and all three adults looked at her with the same pleased look in their eyes.

Apparently Maurie was the zebra today. She supposed it was better than being one of the heads on the self-destructive crocodile that represented a family quarreling with itself about how to raise the kids. She was beginning to suspect that the real reason other Sadous didn't use public transportation was that the general public would get far too good at zebra hunting. And considering Uncle Benoit's many messages, she probably didn't get to opt out of being a part of a single-stomached but multiheaded crocodile.

Maurie focused on trying to get her comm working again. With the connection itself unreliable, she might be able to use her local settings to get something through before admin resets either blocked it or redirected everything to Great Aunt Mami.

She dialed the numbers she could think of for Grandpere. The public number for his administrative office would reach a polite administrator, but she didn't bother with that one because with Uncle Benoit on offense, Grandpere would have made himself more difficult to reach. She tried the private number, theoretically for family and close friends only, and got a not-in-service message. That was her own fault.

She'd served as his assistant for several interim periods between hired aides and had implemented a policy of changing that number frequently to cut down on the unwelcome calls.

It seemed she didn't have the current one. There were other ways to do call screening which would have worked better for also maintaining connections with intermittently communicative relatives, but Maurie hadn't known about those simple programs at the time. And no one else in the family had bothered to enlighten her. One of the curses of being thought of as smart was that even people who should know better assumed she possessed uniformly deep knowledge rather than bits and pieces scattered over a broad range of topics—just like everyone else.

The bus driver sold her seatmate a candy bar. Maurie declined anything from his tray, and he turned to the opposite side of the aisle. The empty driver's seat had the seat belt buckled to fool the bus's autopilot into thinking the driver was still in the seat serving as backup. No one else had a seat belt, so the driver not using his showed a fatalistic sort of solidarity.

"Shouldn't you be up there?" Maurie asked.

"This is my job," the driver explained. He tapped on his chest where his shirt displayed the food service logo matching the emblem on his tray. "Regular driver sick, so"—he nodded with a confidence—"I do both today."

He continued on his way giving children their choice of the cheaper snacks for free.

Maurie's seatmate raised an eyebrow at her and whispered, "Do you know how to drive?"

She looked up from her search through the contacts to determine who was most likely to both have Grandpere's current number and be willing to share it with her. "Um, yes."

"Good," the grandmother said. "I tried it once. Too scary. I prefer the autodrive."

Maurie had been her father's shadow and then Grandpere's at countless new construction sites with unpaved access roads not yet programmed into autodrive systems. An out-of-control autodrive scared her a lot more than driving a vehicle did. But she understood why the grandmother and most of the public would hold that view. Learning to control a vehicle without autodrive was something the wealthy did in order to go extremely fast on a private racetrack. Here, and on most of the rest of planet, driving was a rich man's hobby.

Mauri tapped on Uncle Benoit's contact. He would have Grandpere's current contact even if Grandpere didn't want him to. Uncle Benoit used one of those more advanced screening tools and while the underlying number might change, she didn't have to manually update it. He'd answer or not as suited his whims, but she would reach his device. The call started to go through and then disconnected. She tried it again.

Maurie's seatmate squeaked a warning.

"Clear the aisle!" the driver bellowed from the far back of the bus, and the autodrive at the front of the vehicle let out a series of disturbing beeps. Then he took a deep breath and yelled even louder, "Does anyone on the bus know how to drive?"

The road was turning a gradual curve to the left, and the bus was not.

The bus driver called out in several other languages, somehow remaining calm. Maurie stood up.

Branches slapped the side of the bus. The right tires edged onto the ancient rumble strip and longer branches whipped into open windows.

She vaulted over her seatmate into the aisle. Her knee clipped against the old woman's cheek knocking her down. Maurie had to get forward, though, or they'd all get battered a lot worse.

Branches snapped against the right side of the bus and turned into whips when they found open windows. A man yelped and clipped Maurie's side, trying to avoid a long branch. She jumped over a couple who'd ducked into the aisle. She drew in a breath to yell for a clear path and was thrown against the side of a seat by another passenger's body.

"*A gauche!* Move left!" her old seatmate yelled over the sounds of panic. The full bus seemed to triple its passengers as they all crowded into the aisle away from windows on either side. Maurie gasped pleas for them get out of her way.

The driver tried another bellowed order for clearing the aisle and might've had some success except for the pounding drum of fists beating on the top of the bus. The rooftop passengers expressed their displeasure toward those within with a volume that drowned out even the shrieking metal-on-branches scream of the bus's side against the scrub brush lining the side of the road.

Maurie threw the last passenger out of her way and slammed into the driver's seat. She grabbed the steering wheel in a death grip to bleed out her panic and forced herself to calm.

Road ahead empty.

Two tires off the gravel berm.

Two still on the edge of the blacktop road.

She slapped the button to take manual control. She turned the wheels off the shoulder and back onto the road. Remembering the unbelted rooftop passengers, she very gently pressed down on the brake pedal to slow the bus to a crawl. Maurie eased the bus entirely off the road and parked.

Everyone quieted.

"Everything is fine," the driver announced. "Please get off the bus while we check quickly for damages. Come." He repeated himself in French while he scrambled up the aisle and quickly disembarked the bus.

"Free snacks!" he called from outside the bus door. Candy bars rustled and were held aloft and waved overhead where passengers could see them through the windows.

With this promise of normalcy, the front-seat passengers grabbed their bags and climbed down to claim first choice of candy.

The bus's center aisle immediately clogged with people as the passengers tried to boil out. No one thanked her, but her grandmotherly seatmate patted her on the shoulder as she hobbled out.

A spreading bruise marked the side of the woman's face, and she hadn't been hobbling earlier. The crush of panicked passengers in the aisle where Maurie had pushed her to get to the front of the bus had not been kind to her. The man from the family behind her helped the older woman.

Maurie couldn't bring herself to meet his eyes. Who hurts an old lady? She twisted sideways against the press of passengers and made her way back to her seat. His wife clutched her sleeve as she passed and said something, Maurie pretended not to feel the touch and freed her sleeve.

At her seat, Maurie gathered her few things. The boy from the family behind her tapped her on the shoulder. She turned. The child at least seemed well.

He presented her with her comm, miraculously unscuffed, and pointed out the bruises on his hands and arms, incurred while rescuing her device. Heat rose in Maurie's face, but she thanked him. His mother patted the boy on the head proudly. It was worth it to them, and it shouldn't have been.

A better autopilot system, something that didn't

glitch in whatever way this particular one had, that might—possibly—be worth some bruises.

Maurie searched for the family's card, couldn't find it, and mimed for the kid to enter the contact information directly into her comm.

He did with great pleasure and returned to his parents beaming. After a brief conversation the adults looked back at her with matching expressions of pleasure. She was going to try to find at least one of their extended family members a good job. Hopefully, some of the skills they'd claimed for the clan members were accurately represented.

She pulled up Uncle Benoit's contact again. It showed her last call had, finally, connected and stayed connected for several minutes. But now the thing said NO SERVICE. She powered it off and on. Still no service.

Her comm might be broken after all. The scrub brush trees lining the sides of the road lacked the height to hide an ultra-luxe night club of the type which might employ jammers. And also, no such party venue would ever launch out here so far from a customer base.

Departing passengers packed the front of the bus aisle still, so Maurie opened the back emergency exit and went down that way.

The child from the family behind her tried to turn to follow her, but his mother held him back. The free candy waited with the snack vendor at the front exit.

The long dusty road back the way they'd come shot straight for quite a ways before it twisted out of sight over rolling hills. In the other direction, a splotch of darker green announced a village or at least a farmhouse with a good well. That much clumped dark green in the bush country meant someone had watered mango tree saplings all dry season long for at least three years to allow the trees' root systems to grow deep enough to sustain themselves. Maurie walked around to the front of the bus to suggest they head for the town. It would be a more comfortable place to wait for a new bus or repair assistance.

She came up behind a group of five men who could easily have stepped out of a high-end club. Except for the machetes, that is. Tall, broad-shouldered, and dressed in desert chic, they wore loose clothing to account for the heat combined with very nice hiking boots and face-covering head scarves.

A sixth man in a white headscarf puffing behind the group lugged both a toolbox and a large backpack sporting antennas. She didn't recognize the gear, but the man headed straight for the bus. Communications jammer and maybe something that caused the autopilot to fail? She felt an urge to take a wrench from the man's toolbox and ring him over the head with it.

The driver with his open tray of candies cocked his head to the side and goggled at the six men.

"Aren't kidnappers supposed to wear ninja costumes?" the little boy asked.

"People only do that in the movies," Maurie said. They hadn't been on the bus. There was no reason for anyone else to be around, and they weren't dressed like local farmers who'd just happened by. Maurie glared at the men. "I think these robbers broke our bus." She'd never been robbed in person before. People sometimes broke into Sadou properties or stole from work sites, but this was a new—very unwelcome—experience. And in the movies, they definitely would've been in head-to-toe black costumes. Maybe these ones weren't very good at it? Their faces were completely covered just the same, though. But really, weren't there ways to get more money for less risk than robbing a public bus? What could make this worth it?

"Maybe they aren't very good robbers," she speculated out loud.

The comment earned her looks of horror from the closest passengers who were just beginning to recognize what was going on. A few drifted back along the side of the road. She hoped they'd break into a run soon. If everyone tried to go at once, a few would get away. Some people would certainly be able to hide in the roadside brush and make their way to a village for safer transport somewhere else.

Maurie stepped forward. "Everyone go!" she called out, trying to sound authoritative but not to show any of the growing fear that might induce panic. She could afford to be robbed and if everyone else ran, somebody could get a message back to her family. Of course, only the grandmother and family of three knew who she was. What if they decided to kidnap her and none of those four got away?

A snake-y hiss of laughter felt like it was going to come bubbling out of her mouth, but Maurie suppressed it. Now was not the time to be seeing things.

"Who's the driver?" the lead thief called out. His head covering was a Hermès scarf. Maurie winced at the choice of non-disguise. The specialty stores that sold that sort of antique clothing kept records of their customers. The other five wore plain head scarves in white, gray, red, green, and blue like they were some kind of children's action hero team. Did only the boss get fancy headgear?

The driver gaped at the robbers in horror and panic. He slapped down the lid of the candy tray as if that were the most valuable thing he could protect and held it tight to his chest, covering the logo on his breast pocket. The passengers looked to him for guidance anyway.

The driver turned to Maurie and held out a hand like he was about to ask her what to do.

Hermès snapped his fingers at a couple of the other thieves.

"Green. Gray. Go with her. Get this bus out of here." Hermès gestured at Maurie, and she was pulled out of the crowd by the two thieves with the green and gray headscarves.

This was too much for the candy vendor-turned-driver. He rushed forward.

Hermès transferred the machete to his left hand and threw a punch with his right fist. The man crumpled.

"Hey, that's not necessary." Maurie held up her hands in surrender when one of the other thieves with a blue scarf pointed a machete at her.

Green whispered quietly, "The boss is pissed off, but play along, and you'll still get your cut."

"Do what I say, and your passengers don't get hurt." The Hermès thief looked straight at her and spoke in a carrying voice, clearly not intended for just her.

Maurie kept her hands up and tried not to look confused. "I thought we'd lost control," she said. "The operator was in the back with the snacks tray, so I didn't want us to crash."

Hermès slapped her across the face while Gray

yanked her away. The loud crack his hand made slamming into his other hand shocked her so much that at first she didn't realize that she hadn't really been hit at all.

Gray pulled her to her feet and spun her toward the bus. He kept her unbruised face turned away from the passengers. She stumbled and Green grabbed her by the other arm to help her keep her feet.

They marched her together to the bus and pushed her into the driver's seat.

"You were supposed to stop right away." Green narrowed his eyes, the only part of his face visible. Then the corners of his eyes crinkled like this was all a ridiculous joke. "Don't worry. We'll get you through this." He pulled at the sweat-slick fabric of his robe. "Get that air-conditioning on. We had to jog almost a kilometer to get to this bus."

The windows were still down and some broken leaves and branch stems lay in the aisle.

"The AC is broken," Maurie said. "And I'm not..."

"Get out your wallets!" Hermès yelled at the crowd of passengers. "We can fix your bus and have you all back on your way, but there's a fee involved."

White had his large backpack off and hunched head down over his toolbox. He grunted in annoyance and, finding her feet in his way, he pushed past to crawl into the space beneath the steering wheel. An automatic screwdriver whirred on and off four times. He popped open a panel under the dashboard, connected a computer, and batted at her legs. "Give me space," he muttered.

She moved and stood uncertainly in the bus aisle. Green walked the bus checking for abandoned bags and poking under seats, confirming no one was hiding inside.

"Turn over your cash cards and electronics." She could hear the Hermès-scarfed thief's orders continue at top volume, easily audible through the bus's broken windows. "Make sure to wipe your accounts. If you lock the devices, we'll notice, and you'll get hurt. Don't be stupid."

"Which passenger is the Tchami woman?" Gray-scarf asked her, waving a hand toward the crowd outside. "She's offended somebody rich," he added. "We're supposed to break one of her legs or arms."

Maurie swallowed hard. Her comm was registered to Great Aunt Mami. On a phone network it would have an ID as belonging to Tchami Magdalene.

"Not now, Gray." White put his head into the space under the steering wheel where he could access the autodrive system. "Please go away, I need to focus on this," he said. "Splicing the interrupt device in here is easy. Getting it back out again without hurting the autodrive is hard. And I don't like leaving fingerprints. Go whine about the air-conditioning somewhere else."

Maurie kept her mouth shut as she was hauled by an arm back out of the bus again by Green and Gray. They halted in a shady spot under a large baobab tree. The bus was lucky to have hit only scrub trees and not one like that. It would've crashed the bus instead of just scratching metal while being torn out of the earth.

"Also, you can't call anybody," Hermès continued.

Several people in the back of the crowd tried to look like they hadn't been attempting just that.

"None of you have a signal," he pointed out, clearly

not caring that some had been trying to contact authorities. "None of you are going to have a signal until we are all well clear. This is a nice quiet fee collection. You keep wedding rings. For anything that's been in the family a couple generations, you get in a line here. You can explain to my man in the red scarf one at a time why you need to keep whatever it is. Let me tell you right now, if everything you've got is very important to you, you'll be giving it all up. Choose one thing to make a case for and volunteer up the rest. Be reasonable and you'll be on your way to wherever you want to go very quickly." After a pause he repeated everything he'd said in clear-carrying French.

Maurie's head was spinning, but she reached for the comm in her pocket.

"Not you," Green whispered. "You're part of the team, you don't get robbed. They said you were a little hesitant about this, but nobody said you were dumb. I was told it'd be your first time but didn't anybody explain the plan?"

The group of passengers formed a disorderly mob around Red and complied with Hermès' orders. One woman attempted the argument that her new release phone was from her grandmother. She got to keep it after another passenger suggested that perhaps she'd paid for it with a bequest from that grandmother. The proud phone owner did turn over a significant amount of cash. A small pile of loot grew at Red's feet, filling empty backpacks apparently brought for that purpose. Maurie reassessed her mental judgment of them as inept.

Hermès passed his machete back and forth between

his hands and circled the whole scene, stopping next to Gray under the baobab tree.

White scurried over to Hermès with his toolbox. "I fixed the bus, sir," he reported. Then he looked at Maurie, really looked at her. "Who's that?"

"The driver," Hermès said.

"No, it's not." He shook his head. "My sis..." He stopped. "I know the woman who was supposed to drive." He glared at her. "What are you, a temp or something?"

This caused Hermès to look at her more closely. "You aren't the regular driver." It was an accusation.

Maurie saw the actual driver/candy-seller in line with the other passengers, head down, and trying very hard to be invisible with one eye starting to swell shut. He saw her and avoided eye contact. No help there.

"You might have caught the wrong bus," Maurie suggested. "I don't know anything about a plan. Nobody does." She took care to avoid noticing that White's sister was supposed to have been the driver. "If the bus driver had known this would happen, he'd have been in the seat to take operator control when the autopilot failed. We almost crashed." She pointed at the scarred side of the bus. "Those are new," she said in an attempt to add evidence to her claim.

"The Tchami woman isn't here and neither is the special freight," Blue reported. "We went through all the luggage. It's just passenger junk. No special freight. Nothing high value." Blue gave Maurie a speculative glare. "You drop it off somewhere on the route? Trying to hold out for a bigger cut or blame us and keep it all to yourself?"

"I don't know what you are talking about." Maurie

kept her voice very calm. Those machetes looked sharp, and she didn't want them riled up enough to try them out on her. So far no one had been hurt very much, but that could change pretty fast especially since at least some of them thought she was a co-conspirator instead of another victim. She considered briefly trying to bluff and pretend to be a co-conspirator. But, if she failed at it, then they might think she was pulling some kind of double cross. And White knew she wasn't his sister.

Hermès sent a man back to look more closely at the bus. "White, double-check the bus. Make sure it's the one we're supposed to have."

The man returned quickly. "Vehicle numbers match up exactly."

"Explain that." Hermès poked her in the sternum with the dull flat end of his machete. Not a comfortable experience.

Maurie shook her head. "I can't. I'm just a passenger who jumped in to stop the bus when I thought we were going to crash."

The assembled thieves made expressions of disbelief.

"Why would you know how to drive?" Blue asked. "Who are you?"

"Sadou Maurie," she said.

Green took a step back. "Sadou. Oh shit."

"I'm sure this is all a mistake," she suggested.

"Oh yeah," White agreed.

Hermès snatched the front of Maurie's shirt and shook her. "The hell you're a Sadou. Those people don't ride on buses."

Maurie's comm trilled from her pocket.

Gray fished it out and showed it to Hermès. "It says

missed call from 'Sadou Benoit.'" He let the face of the phone show. In response to Hermès' continued glare White said, "The call blocker is out here with us; when Gray and Green took her inside the bus, the comm must have been shielded enough to make a connection. That's a really high-end comm device; those things are better at making and keeping a connection than what regular people have."

"I don't want trouble," Maurie said into the silence. "How about you give these people back their things and just go. Nobody needs to have any trouble." *I'm not one of the heads on the two-headed crocodile,* she thought, *I'm the meal the idiot carnivore is fighting over. How the hell did Uncle Benoit and Great Aunt Mami do this to me?*

"We should kill her," said someone behind her. She thought it was Blue.

"Fine," Maurie snapped back. "You go ahead and do that. Murder always makes everything better. Who the hell decided I was special freight? It's nowhere near April 1. They are not going to get to wave this off as a family joke."

Hermès said, "Hold her. I'm going to make a call."

CHAPTER EIGHT

CHUMMY GOT A CALL FROM JEFFY BEFORE HE could get to the airport. He couldn't go to Kilimanjaro.

"Fabrice," Jeffy said, "you were right. Again. That Ethan got his entire core team on airplanes yesterday. He even managed to get Kilimanjaro office space for them. I'd tell you to get me five more just like him, but unless you can replicate yourself too—don't."

"Got it, boss," Chummy said. He signaled DeeDee to wait a moment. Jeffy finished telling him what was going on, and Chummy ended the call with bigger problems than Ethan's brush with the law. And Jeffy thought there weren't problems at all, which, once again, did not make anything better. He turned to his assistant. "Change of plans. We're going to Hainan."

She nodded sleepily.

Her exhaustion gave him pause, and Chummy opened his messaging application to contact Samson instead of calling just in case his other assistant was asleep.

DeeDee handed over her comm with Samson's

cheerful face appearing on the screen. "He's awake."

"Hi, boss," Samson said. "DeeDee says you're rerouting. I'll handle things in East Africa." The face on the screen wore a few more fine lines than it had when Chummy had snatched him up out of the junior management track a couple years before, and his gray eyes had a steely look to them now rather than being merely bright. Samson was ready for a job that allowed him to do more than just smooth personnel problems, but a replacement assistant would take time to reach Samson's skill level. So Chummy needed him to de-thorn a few more briars before letting him go. And since this trouble was partly of Chummy's own making, if, as he suspected, Ethan's personality had caused it, it didn't seem right to dump things on Samson. But maybe the Kilimanjaro placements would be Samson's final project, and thus it could become reputation gold for him. If it went well, Samson might be remembered for it as he moved on up within TCG. Though if things went very wrong, the TCG name itself could become résumé kryptonite for not just Samson but every executive in the company. Yet another reason it had to be made to work.

"Are you sure?" Chummy searched for the records TCG had on Kilimanjaro. The combination of the politically complex site and the new chief of sciences might be all wrong. Maybe it wasn't too late to change ground stations. He could talk to Jeffy about it. Could they buy a private island with a decent-sized mountain or pay the extra cost in tether length and build a platform at sea to anchor the elevator?

"Hey, boss," Samson called his attention back to the call, "I got this. Jax is apologizing. Nairobi is apologizing. Dodoma is apologizing. Ethan is pissed, but give me another hour or two and I'll have him be graciously forgiving. I think it'll be fine. I'll grab some interpreters and go visit the appropriate offices to make sure, but really, I got it."

DeeDee fed him background data on the things Samson was saying. Jax's TCG employee ID appeared as a thumbnail pic in the corner of the screen, but just briefly for him to tap on if he'd forgotten who Ethan Schmidt-Li's assistant was. DeeDee also sent screen captures of the comments released by government representatives from the Kenyan and Tanzanian capitals. Samson paused, letting the other assistant do her thing, and calmly awaited Chummy's response.

"Kilimanjaro was historically Tanzanian," Chummy cautioned.

"Uh huh," Samson acknowledged, sounding bored. "And in some administrations the Kenyan government has claimed it too. But TCG owns it outright now, and our management of the park has been great for the growth of both Kenyan and Tanzanian tourism industries. Both countries want to assure Mr. Jeffy that they look forward to the speedy construction of the elevator on the site and that they are expanding rail, highway, and airstrips to support the needs of our commercial spaceport."

A little icon on Chummy's screen did a victory dance involving a merged cartoon of road construction and paper bills falling from the sky with masses of cheering stick figures waving Kenyan and Tanzanian flags. "DeeDee agrees with me," Samson pointed out.

"That better be an amazing public relations team."

"The best," Samson agreed. "DeeDee sent me profiles

for a few former diplomats looking for a second career. I got this. Good luck in China, boss."

Chummy let Samson go, promising himself that if it went wrong, he'd find a way to make it up to the young man somehow.

"Shen Kong is ready to make a deal," Jeffy had said. "Go back up Cory Aanderson. He thinks you can help. I'm the profit and loss guy, Fabrice. Trust me and trust Cory. Go do your thing. This is going to be big."

Big was exactly what Chummy was worried about. Cory Aanderson engaged in deals directly when companies were bought and sold. He'd heard nothing.

They landed in Hainan with no new details. He should have slept like DeeDee did, but he spent the hours fretting about the little Sadou support launcher instead. They'd need a mountain too. Ethan's near daily reports on the status of the elevator showed a frugality that disturbed him as much as it delighted Jeffy. Ethan showed no signs of contracting for anyone else to duplicate much of anything beyond station-side life support.

Clearing the space debris remained a major problem, and Ethan "welcomed advice and ideas from the board." Anything with enough mass to be the space-side anchor for the elevator could easily use some of that mass to armor against debris impacts, but the tether itself must absolutely be protected from even the chance of a glancing impact. And if they sustained injuries in space to employees while building out the anchor station, it would sow doubt about TCG's ability to protect the tether, which should absolutely not be allowed to be sheered through and whip down through the atmosphere and slam into eastern Africa. If the first attempt at an elevator failed not in early design or in funding, but in a catastrophic engineering casualty, a stronger driving force than John-Philip Jeffy would be required to convince humanity to try it again. "Advice and ideas welcome," indeed.

Chummy could almost see Ethan sweating over the words and mopping at his face with makeup coming off on the tissues. Ethan had gone with gratitude for assistance and offers of shared credit for success rather than attempting to spread blame. Not bad at all. He must have realized he was too close to the project to duck responsibility. Chummy grinned to himself. That part of his efforts were working perfectly. The man was applying himself.

The engineers he'd set to reviewing launcher plans to select a system for the West African Launcher had come back with only a slightly more refined mass of ideas. They needed constraints. Someone from the Sadou family needed to talk to them. Pascaline? No. He wanted them to be happy about the interactions, not eager to see whoever they talked to pulverized by a failed rocket launch. It should be Maurie. He sent Aunt Mami a note. She hadn't been talking to him recently, which, now that he thought about it, was odd.

He closed his eyes to think. The jet landed with a jerk and his eyes snapped open.

"Want some coffee, boss?" DeeDee had a cup ready for him.

He sipped. Rich and strong, it smelled like heaven. He took a wake-up pill and used the brew to wash it down.

DeeDee talked for a few moments about the weather in Hainan and the instructions Cory Aanderson and his deputy, Rodney Johnson, had sent.

"Oh," she said. "And Samson has a report on East Africa. I read it while you were sleeping and you'll want the details later, but everything is fine, and you can wait until after this visit to get to it."

Chummy held his coffee mug a moment more while they taxied and lined up with a jetway bridge. He marveled at how well his assistants worked together to support him. He'd selected them for that, of course. But at times like these with too little sleep and who knows what tasks ahead, he really, really appreciated them for it.

That's when it hit him. Pascaline had always loved space and hated having her engineering expertise constrained to the Earth-focus of the Sadou Corporation's oil and gas industry needs. Maurie's management skills smoothed out Pascaline's brusque nature. Sadou Moussa already had the manager he needed for the launcher. It was a pair: Maurie and Pascaline. They were young for the work, but more experienced than most since their family connections had caused them to be pushed into engineering management responsibilities far sooner than an employee at somewhere like TCG would have been. He considered the variety of side jobs they'd also handled for Grandpere and the kinds of support workers they could draft or that he might be able to push their way as collaborating TCG technical liaisons. It might...

"Okay. Let's go," DeeDee said.

"Just one moment." Chummy grabbed his comm. It wasn't the personal one, but he'd have to risk it. They needed the data. The engineering teams' discussion threads on the West Africa launcher project and their preliminary specs were still there in his most recently opened files. He compressed all of it and sent them to Pascaline and Maurie with the barest minimum of explanation. He didn't have time for more, and surely Aunt Mami would be there to help explain whatever their grandfather didn't.

He followed DeeDee out to find out just what Cory Aanderson had done.

Shen Kong skipped past the preliminaries of assistants meeting with assistants. The chief executive herself met Chummy just inside the jetway at Haikou Meilan International Airport. He'd heard that Zhu Zhang Li, who generally went by Julie or Julie Zhu, liked to keep tight control of the schedules of senior visitors to prevent side meetings with competitors, but this was extreme even for her.

The slender leader of China's most successful space-based state-owned enterprise brushed sleek black hair behind one ear and rose to greet Chummy. Age brushed only faint marks over her features as if her iron will wouldn't allow it. The woman reminded him of Jeffy, for all that physically they had little in common.

All the hyper-effective executives had a certain something in their eyes. Julie's deep brown eyes smiled at him even while her mouth barely twitched.

She directed a few waiting staff to assist DeeDee with setting up any equipment. DeeDee gave them polite bows which was not quite correct, but they bowed back as if it were. She kept her equipment components in their bags and settled on an empty chair without plugging anything in.

Cory Aanderson, already there as Jeffy had said, waggled his fingers in greeting at Chummy. He looked more tired than usual in a wheeled hospital bed propped up to be almost chair-like, but he let one hand hang down where the Shen Kong executive and her staff couldn't see and made a thumbs-up gesture. Coming from TCG's VP of Sales, that was promising—except for what it meant.

Understanding hit Chummy hard. Ethan's messages, Jeffy's reaction, and the things Jeffy had said—he got it now. Cory and Julie smiling politely at each other meant that TCG and Shen Kong had just made a space deal. And that meant they were both betting heavily on the space elevator. The construction should be about a decade from completion, but everyone was moving fast and assuming total success.

He really wished the senior executives would hedge their bets a bit more. Or at least enough to let him hedge his bets. DeeDee offered a polite smile to all the strangers and moved to stand out of the way behind Cory Aanderson's deputy.

The salesman himself sat up a bit and made introductions.

"Julie, meet Chummy. And Chummy, meet Julie." Cory Aanderson exchanged a knowing look with the Shen Kong staff members and added a comment in Mandarin to the effect of, "Nobody uses their original given names for international business anymore. I feel so left out—will someone please give me a Chinese nickname?"

Julie laughed and responded in flawless English, "Watch out Aanderson. You only think you're fluent. Give my people a few more taunts and you'll find yourself being called Dog Vomit for the rest of your life without knowing it."

"Better than some titles he could end up with," Chummy pointed out.

"Ha." Cory laid back his bed a bit more and pulled up his lap blankets. The blankets were a soft charcoal matching his thoroughly rumpled gray suit coat. "I've got to make my jokes to keep in practice. Making the doctors laugh now and then is the only reason they're still working so hard to keep me around." He shook his finger at DeeDee, easily the youngest person present, and said: "Remember that when you get old. It's important to be a good patient, so they'll work extra hard to keep you alive."

DeeDee flushed, which earned a laugh from their Shen Kong audience.

"Oh and Chummy?" Cory Aanderson put a hand on his forehead and emitted a dramatic sigh of feigned regret, which earned more titters. "I think I'm going to steal your jet."

DeeDee held her reaction to only a blink, so Chummy pretended to be shocked, which no one believed.

"Those doctors are always on me to come back for checkups," Cory Aanderson said quite truthfully. And to Julie he added, "Chummy is our magic man. Let him help with choosing your crew for the asteroid retrieval. Call it a contract finalization bonus from TCG for you."

Oh. Chummy hid his relief. They were just teaming with Shen Kong for the space elevator construction. This wasn't about selling elevator freight prematurely. He held his expression carefully constant.

"So you're saying I should have argued for a bigger

discount on transport fees in exchange for providing the rock for the orbital station?" Julie's eyes twinkled.

"Oh, probably," Cory agreed. "And Mr. Jeffy is sure to fire me for saying so. But won't it be great to have it all in operation sooner rather than later?"

A medical device attached to the old salesman's bed beeped at him.

Cory grimaced at it. "Yes, machine. I'm not allowed to get excited," he explained. "Raises my heart rate."

He signaled to Rodney Johnson, and the unassuming man, who'd be sales vice president himself one day all too soon, released the wheel locks and turned his boss toward the jetway.

Rodney was a soft-spoken American with a shock of red hair and very white teeth who could still fade into the shadows when he wanted to. If Cory Aanderson had just closed a billion-dollar deal with contract options for expansion into the multibillion dollar range, it would explain why Rodney had wanted and had needed to be present in the background for the conversation—especially if Rodney might have to be the one to talk Shen Kong into executing those options.

Chummy gave the deputy a nod, which the man returned with hard, smiling eyes. Chummy suppressed a sigh. Cory Aanderson couldn't be read that easily, but Rodney's happiness meant TCG had done something big. It had to be more than an agreement to pay Shen Kong for the asteroid to be the elevator's space-side tether point. They'd worked out some more complex deal, and... Chummy's gut twisted. In context, it did have to involve elevator freight arrangements.

Shen Kong's orbital manufacturing made top-of-the-line satellites, but that was only part of their business. They were also an asteroid resource-extraction company. The costs of getting out to the Belt and keeping the crews supplied kept competitors few. It was also why only a company backed by a big government could get started in the industry.

Rodney checked the readouts on the side of his boss's bed and silenced the beeping one. He waved at everyone and pushed his boss down the jetway and onto the aircraft. DeeDee helped with the luggage, but they didn't have much.

"Should I send a doctor with him or at least a nurse?" Julie asked.

Chummy shook his head. "Old Cory does this airplane-stealing trick all the time. There's a slew of medical equipment onboard, and Rodney will get one of his on-call physicians to review everything remotely."

"Hmm," she said. "An ambitious man would have the job for himself. They say you recommended your company promote that almost-gone peddler and then you gave him an acolyte and a nurse and a successor all in one package?"

Zhu Zhang Li's summary of Chummy as the chief architect of Cory and Rodney's situation didn't quite match the real history, but he was typically credited for the duo. "Mr. Jeffy hasn't fired me yet." Chummy lifted his shoulders in a slight shrug. "I guess I haven't set up too many bad video dramas with junior businessmen stabbing their bosses to take their jobs."

She glanced at DeeDee, who had returned and stood shifting from one foot to the other.

"Hmm." Julie walked over and took Chummy by the arm. "Let's go then."

DeeDee trailed after.

They walked through customs without stopping, which meant Julie at least didn't feel cheated by the latest Shen Kong–TCG business arrangement. Business and government relations in China remained fairly confusing to outsiders. TCG's corporate headquarters in Beijing mostly existed to facilitate subsidiary and vendor relationships with wholly Chinese companies. The potential for nationalization of corporate assets made even the extremely optimistic John-Philip Jeffy hesitant to engage in much direct competition with executives like Julie of Shen Kong. And she knew it.

"That rock you're buying, it's overpriced," Julie confided in him. "So you might want to tell Aanderson to count his fingers and toes again when he reaches international airspace."

Chummy shrugged. "I'm sure he'll get along some-how. He says his doctors have made him half bionic already, so he might look forward to trying out a few toe prosthetics." DeeDee was trailing behind. The turns of airport corridors hadn't quite lost her, but she wasn't close on their heels anymore. "Why did you really ask for me, Zhang Li?"

"Chummy, you remember my name." She suppressed a smile. "But stick with Julie or I'll start calling you Tchami and you'll have to deal with everyone man-gling the name in creative ways instead of with your preferred mispronunciation."

He held his peace, waiting.

"Come on." Julie shook her head. "You're going to make me ask? You know I can double your salary."

When he didn't speak, she added, "Triple it even. Or even give you something you actually want, because we both know you're better than some European-American workers' health and safety protector."

"Human resources management specialist," he corrected.

"Mmhmm." Julie lifted an eyebrow. "Shen Kong could have an office in Yaoundé. Or Douala if you like the rainforest climate better."

"There's no spaceport in either," Chummy pointed out.

Julie looked at him. "And why is that, do you suppose?"

DeeDee caught up, out of breath.

"Hello, little spy." Julie greeted her in Mandarin which earned only a blink from the young assistant. The hubbub of a busy airport had the young assistant twitchy and focused on her own feet. When she could slow enough for it, she'd steal comforting glances at her own comm screen.

A soft vibration alerted Chummy to a message on his comm: *She called me a spy, but if you take the job with Shen Kong, can I come with? I don't know any Chinese yet, but my programs have translator subroutines.*

Julie saw it.

"You win again," she said in English. "Want to hire me a few unbreakably loyal assistants while you go over our asteroid retrieval crew candidates?"

"If you recall," Chummy reminded her, "I did try to hire you not once but twice when you were at university."

Julie made a face. "You had no interest in hiring

me. John-Philip wanted to try exotic dating, and you came up with a scheme of getting me hired on by his father's company, so he'd have enough to time to work up the nerve to ask me out."

His comm vibrated again. DeeDee was trying desperately to disprove Julie's assertion. That sort of hiring motivation would break several of TCG's current Best Practices in Personnel Management directives.

They paused inside wide glass doors for an elegant vehicle to pull up.

"Please, Julie." Chummy gave the senior executive a polite bow of head and shoulders, deeper than he probably needed, but the relaxation of tension in her face showed she appreciated the formality. "You'd've been an amazing hire. But you'd've been wasted in what we were then. TCG was just another Earth-focused multinational company. We might've been building some aerospace engines, but most of the company was and is in consumer goods. Our highest grossing product is a whitening toothpaste. Yours is minerals from asteroid mining. Our scale was too small for someone like you."

Julie's mouth twitched. She was mollified. Chummy made a note to have a talk with Cory Aanderson later. Twenty-some years was a long time to nurse a grudge about not being offered a job for the right reasons.

"But Julie," Chummy continued, "I've met that corporate psychologist you have assessing those long-duration mission teams, and you don't need me."

"I do if you hire him away from me." Julie raised an eyebrow. "I've seen the signing bonus your people are offering for anyone with even a hint of space operational experience. Smart of you to just hire whole companies for much of the station design for the elevator's upper anchor point, though. It makes the whole industry eager to help you instead of viewing you as the interloper you are." Her eyes glinted with a smile that didn't show on her lips. "And even so, it doesn't take a futurist to predict TCG is planning to expand into at least the near-Earth service industry."

"Are you looking for a promise?" he asked.

Julie gave him a level stare. "Consider it a warning."

"Ethan tried to get him." DeeDee helpfully supplied to his comm. Chummy gave Julie a knowing look.

"You have two of his three kids working for Shen Kong. They're having the time of their lives on cramped little spaceships. We'll come up with another teaming agreement at some point and pair some of our better people with him to learn the process. No one is going to steal your people, Julie. We need Shen Kong too much. You're probably going to be our biggest customer for a long time! And I'll talk to Ethan about it. But you'd have been insulted if he hadn't made that play."

Julie didn't admit it, but she seemed mollified again. She knew all that, but she'd wanted to hear him say it.

Chummy definitely needed to get Cory Aanderson alone for a debrief. Something was going on.

"And as for hiring me?" Chummy gave her the wide-eyed look that generally drew laughs.

Julie raised an eyebrow. "Yes?"

"I don't see what I could offer as a Shen Kong employee besides unnecessary costs—which you are quite famous for not tolerating." He gave her an extra bow. China's business environment would have eviscerated a weaker executive.

"Maybe," she acknowledged. "Though I get nervous when you start buttering me up."

The sleek black vehicle pulled up. A vending machine next to the glass doors offered air pollution masks, and DeeDee tried to get it to accept her cash cards.

"But the offer stands." Julie smiled at him.

"I couldn't," Chummy declined. "Unless of course you wanted to date?" He batted his eyelashes at her and saw her finally relax into the normal cheerful mode he remembered from her college days.

Julie howled laughter. DeeDee turned from trying to make a mask selection to goggle at her boss. Chummy winked at them both.

"You aren't my type, and I'm not yours either." Julie finally recovered her breath enough to reply.

Taking mercy on DeeDee, she scanned a card under the vending machine's reader. "I generally hold my breath and do the Beijing dash. The car's got a fast-start filtration system. Though Hainan's air is better than a lot of industrial areas. And my industry partners are moving more and more manufacturing off planet, so the air quality really is getting better, but go with the one with the bendable nose clip if you want to fuss with a mask."

DeeDee listened and nodded along at Julie's explanation. She bobble-headed accidentally when she tried to make a thank you bow at the same time as nodding.

Julie suppressed her laughter. "If you get your boss to come work for me, we are absolutely hiring you too."

Chummy's comm vibrated a third time; the message had been sent while Julie had her focus on the vending machine. DeeDee's text scrolled across: *"No record of job offer for any Zhu Zhang Li or Zhang Li Zhu or Julie Zhu or any common misspellings of those names."* He tapped the comm to silence it. He'd explain later.

DeeDee selected a pink mask with a fluffy kitten print and fit it over her nose and mouth. She reached for the buttons to pick out one for him, and Chummy shook his head.

"How do we do this Beijing Dash?" he asked.

Julie pressed a button and the vehicle's nearest doors unlatched and slid open. "We send the assistant with the mask out with all the luggage while we wait. Then we run out, close the doors, and either turn purple or take a few breathes of nasty air while the assistant laughs at us."

"I won't laugh," DeeDee promised earnestly.

It worked about as well as Julie had said, though the cabin air filter truly was fast, and he had a hacking coughing fit. Julie showed no signs of turning purple and managed to hold her breath an extra thirty seconds.

The doors whisked shut and fresh air poured in from vents all around. Julie took in a deep breath and patted him on the back.

They were settled into the vehicle: an all-in-one spacious cabin with windows all around and no steering wheel. It was configured for four seats facing each other with one of the rear-facing seats removed to make space for luggage. DeeDee had taken the furthest rear-facing seat and plugged into a data port. Julie settled into the forward-facing seat furthest from the door and Chummy had joined her in the last one.

Julie got the vehicle moving with a few quick button presses on her armrest.

"All jokes aside, we're good, though, right?" Chummy smiled at her. A company like Shen Kong could be an extremely valuable partner for TCG if the space elevator succeeded. China more than any nation had embraced the goal of moving industrial processes off planet, but they still had a lot of heavy industry and its pollution left. They needed a cheaper way to move more Earth-sourced materials up and delicate finished products down.

"With Aanderson's deal?" Julie quirked an eyebrow at him. "I wouldn't have signed it if I weren't." Her eyes tracked over to DeeDee who sat quietly, head bowed over her plugged-in comm. She looked back at Chummy.

"Are you happy?" Julie asked. "You want something. And it doesn't involve a date. My company has data miners too, you know. And you haven't been standing behind your buddy Jeffy in several of the last quarterly video sessions with shareholders. They've got the usual chicken-entrails guesses about what that means, but if you aren't happy, just know that Shen Kong would be delighted to help you find a new home."

"Just busy," Chummy insisted. "You may have heard that there's a space elevator under construction."

Julie nodded. "Might've heard something like that."

"Speaking of space elevators," Chummy said, "let's talk about the asteroid retrieval. Give me info. How long is the crewed portion of the mission? What kinds of skills do the specialists need? And is there anyone you've already picked out as absolutely critical that we'll have to form the team around?"

DeeDee's eyes lit up as Julie linked the vehicle into corporate systems and provided a database full of past mission data and current space crew profiles. A large side window blanked the view of Haikou's streets and became a screen.

"The usual," Julie said. She highlighted a few of the major parts of the mission plan. "We've done this sort of thing before on a more distributed scale out in the Belt. The only significant difference is bringing an intact rock all the way back instead of pushing it to a convenient spot for shredding into more commercial components."

Chummy scrolled through the employee files on the prospective team and laughed. These were a well-matched team with long experience working together. "Julie, did you really only pull me halfway around the world only to make a job offer? You don't need any input on this team. They're repeat performers, and you've already got them in orbit."

Julie smiled. "Aanderson offered, and it didn't cost Shen Kong anything. Did you expect me to decline an advantage in the middle of negotiating a major business arrangement?" She folded her hands. "So. Your turn. Tell me about the teams my people are going to be working with. Our space crew selection might be final, but I wouldn't mind your thoughts on the shifts of ground support teams. And it'd be especially useful to us if you'd share how you plan to populate the elevator team."

DeeDee's head snapped up, eyes wide.

Chummy arched an inquisitive eyebrow at Julie. To DeeDee he tapped his comm once to repeat the last message he'd sent her: *"Later."*

"After the elevator's built," Julie expanded, "do you intend to use TCG employees to serve as station crew, or will there be, shall we say, leasing opportunities?"

Chummy tried to imagine Ethan Schmidt-Li working effectively with not just a multinational ground crew at Kilimanjaro but also a station crew supplied by a subsidiary which might have different financial motivations. It sounded horrific.

"I'm open to hearing your thoughts," he said.

Julie watched DeeDee, who hadn't even blinked. "No, you're not," she translated, and relaxed. "Good. You haven't gone insane on me. We added in plenty of clauses that allow fractional payment for fractional deliveries up and down, but I'm really hoping you and Jeffy don't make a total hash of this thing. Stick with one central authority running things. Please!"

She flipped out a compact and smoothed a touch of powder on her face. "Most of my futures planners thought you would, but I've got some oddballs who were absolutely convinced that there had to be some kind of side project going on." DeeDee did blink then, but Julie missed it. "And keep the governments out of it, or mine might need to go to war over it."

DeeDee lost all her color at that, which Julie did notice. "That'd be bad for business," Chummy agreed.

"Just kidding!" Julie broke into a broad grin. "Did you see your assistant's reaction?"

The set of Chummy's jaw tightened despite his efforts to keep up a calm front.

"Fine," Julie said, still smiling. "You don't like teasing the staff. I get it."

"I'd prefer not to threaten Armageddon prematurely," he agreed.

"I didn't see it at first because she seemed on edge, but I get it now." Julie nodded. "And you care deeply about your protégés. I learn something from Jeffy every time. He gives you people to help you and you give him loyalty."

DeeDee seemed on edge. Chummy's stomach dropped. His assistant was nervous, and she had been before the whole war-of-the-elevator idea had been brought up.

She was worried about something, and she hadn't said a word to him. He ran through his day in reverse and found the reason for her anxiety. He'd sent proprietary files to a non-company comm in front of her when he'd sleepily messaged Maurie and Pascaline about the western launcher. Shit.

Had she talked with Samson about it yet? With her tendency to use electronics for as much human conversation as she possibly could, there'd be records all over the place of her knowledge when it all came out. He didn't want her fired. He could get her a position with the Sadous, but she'd hate that.

Julie misread his discomfort. "You can't take a joke at all anymore, can you?" Julie rapped on the side of the vehicle and the doors swung open. "We're here. Try not to look like I just kicked your puppy."

The vehicle had circled back around and returned to the same airport terminal.

Chummy got out, nodded to Julie—who waved rather than speak in the smoggy air—and walked back inside. DeeDee followed a moment later with her gear and her mask.

"Our jet is still here," DeeDee volunteered. "Mr. Aanderson hasn't left yet."

"About the files . . ." he started to say.

"Yes, 'Later,'" DeeDee answered. "I got the message." She dropped her mask in a recycling bin. "Mr. Rodney Johnson says we've got a slot for takeoff soon, so we need to get moving."

"They'd've better air quality if they didn't take a drive just to have a conversation."

"Mmm," DeeDee agreed. She towed the luggage and led the way through the airport. Officials nodded at them and waved them past security checks as they headed to the private aircraft gates.

"Or we could have done it remotely and saved the trip." Chummy was feeling increasingly grumpy.

"They have a higher level of corporate security here," DeeDee said. "This all makes perfect sense. 'Later,' okay, boss?"

CHAPTER NINE

LATER, ON THE JET, CHUMMY SETTLED IN A CHAIR and pulled out his comm to recharge. DeeDee snatched it out of his hands, but the other passengers were faster to speak than she was.

"What's Zhang Li up to?" Cory Aanderson demanded.

The VP for Sales followed the question with a long coughing fit. They all waited out the rasping bout of hacking. It sounded painful. Rodney hovered with a box of apple juice fitted with a straw.

DeeDee used the jet's connection rather than her own comm and queued up a call to the doctor. Rodney waved her off. "The medicos already know about the cough."

"I'm not dead yet. See, even Rodney isn't worried." Cory Aanderson accepted the straw and sipped. In the air on a direct flight back to Berlin, the cabin lights should have been dimmed again to help them readjust to their new time zone. But corporate necessity didn't always align with biorhythms.

"Trying to hire you was a cover," Cory said. "Not

that any company would mind if you ever said 'yes.' But there it is. And wanting an external review of their team selection was real, but only a second check, since the rock we're buying is already in lunar orbit and they are actually sending that team out to get the replacement."

"In lunar orbit?" Chummy had missed that. "But that means..."

"Yep. We just shaved two years off the timeline for getting the elevator in operation. I think Jeffy might have me bronzed." He stretched, very pleased with himself.

Rodney smiled at his boss. "I get that Zhu Zhang Li is used to elaborate conspiracies, but sometimes I want to shake the woman to find out what's really going on in her head."

Cory Aanderson coughed again, but it was a better sound.

Chummy shrugged. "I've got no idea."

DeeDee made furtive eye contact and raised a hand.

"Ms. Nelson." Cory Aanderson saluted her with his apple juice box. "Speak. Or send us an emoji-laden text scrawl. It's really okay."

"I, um, can't." DeeDee lifted her chin and spoke up. "Spies. Shen Kong wanted a spy."

DeeDee hadn't plugged any of her paraphernalia into her seat's varied data ports. She also still held Chummy's comm tight in her hands as if someone might take it from her and plug it into something.

"Though maybe I could be wrong." She darted a longing glance at the closest data point. "I couldn't check."

"What about your backup comm?" Chummy said. His assistant loved the cutting-edge devices. But things in beta broke frequently, so she always traveled with a backup.

"I had it set to auto-sync, so I wouldn't lose any data." DeeDee stared mournfully at her shoes, which matched today.

"Is she okay?" Rodney looked to Chummy for reassurance and took half a step toward the young woman. She shrunk smaller into herself.

Chummy tapped DeeDee's hand like it were a comm. "What is it about spies, DeeDee?"

"There's a new virus in my system," she said. "It's collecting copies of everything."

Rodney groaned. "Again?"

"But that's the problem..." DeeDee trailed off.

"How much is compromised?" Cory leapt to the core issue.

"Nothing." DeeDee looked over at the foot of the old salesman's bed. "I didn't reconnect to the company network after accessing theirs."

"The automatic scans would block anything anyway. There's really no risk here," Rodney pointed out.

"Wouldn't block this one. It's custom," DeeDee said.

Rodney looked at his own comm recharging. "I've got mine set to auto-connect."

"Not a problem." Cory Aanderson gave Rodney a rueful look. "The security goons don't give sales people, any sales people, full proprietary access. They know we're easy targets. But..." He looked at Chummy. "You've got full access? And your staff does too?"

"And she knew that," Chummy admitted.

"DeeDee didn't connect." Rodney repeated, looking at her like he could see inside her head if he stared long enough.

Cory Aanderson met Chummy's eyes over DeeDee's still-bent blonde head. "It'd be against the network security policy to reconnect without turning over your devices for a thorough check first, so of course DeeDee hasn't plugged them in," he said.

"And also I noticed the spyware uploading," DeeDee muttered. "Explains why Ms. Zhu's goons kept offering me chargers and extension cords for the data port outlets at the airport."

"They did?" Rodney asked. Chummy hadn't noticed either, but if DeeDee said they had, then they had.

"DeeDee's a rule follower," Chummy explained for what seemed like the hundredth time. "We've got a policy against connecting corporation-owned devices to public nets."

"Which the airport was but the Shen Kong vehicle wasn't." DeeDee defended herself without noticing no one had accused her.

"I'm impressed." Cory Aanderson beckoned to Rodney. "Can you see if the drink machine can manage a decent cocoa? Give the woman something to sip on. Add in some of my peppermint schnapps." Cory Aanderson winked, and DeeDee looked up far enough to see it. "Good job." He nodded at her and gave Chummy a bigger smile. "And now we know why she was really so delighted to drag you around the globe."

"Ah, there's also a bit of personal history," Chummy felt compelled to add.

"I'd heard." Cory settled more easily back into his pillows.

DeeDee shook her head. "It's not true. She and Mr. Jeffy never dated."

"Those two?" Cory Aanderson snorted. "You've been

protecting our boss longer than I realized! I'd gotten the impression she thought of you as the one that got away, not our own John-Philip."

Chummy shrugged. "There's no accounting for taste."

The mingled scents of peppermint and chocolate wafted forward. Rodney presented DeeDee with the first mug and then offered a round to Chummy and his boss.

Cory Aanderson happily relinquished his apple juice for a spiked cocoa mug of his own, cooled to lukewarm with a generous splash of half and half. Chummy accepted his usual coffee and skipped all the offered additions. The hum of air ventilation played a soft white-noise background.

"So it's just a data grab?" Rodney asked after he'd finished serving. "They'd risk a major deal for this?" He rubbed his head and looked at Cory Aanderson. "Boss, they've already redirected their crew but we can cancel the contract."

"We could!" Cory Aanderson's eyes lit. "It isn't like the orbital station has to be a rock."

"But using their rock would be a really good idea," Chummy cautioned. "We should talk with Jeffy first before responding to Julie. It isn't like Shen Kong succeeded in getting anything."

"Eh. Maybe not. But when a CEO gets her hands dirty like that, I don't think we should trust her." Cory pulled up a general, very general, orbital station design on the cabin's main display. "TCG could build a crafted orbital station instead. Don't we have designers working on that for possible second and third elevators?"

"That would delay the whole project." Chummy

shook his head. "Maybe by years." Years in which the western launcher would be supplying the under-construction orbital station for months on end. Except that Sadou surely needed more time to get it built and then needed a gentle low number of competitors in the market to survive and prosper as a business. This wasn't the way Chummy had arranged things. They were supposed to use the Shen Kong rock.

"So what if it's delayed?" Cory Aanderson said. "No one else has the tether material to build a competing space elevator. We don't have to work with people who try to steal from us."

"They have people in space headed out to collect an asteroid for us. Think how that would look to the global business community if we canceled the contract with a human crew already up there," Rodney cautioned.

Cory Aanderson settled somewhat but his dignity remained offended. "Lunar orbit hardly counts. And it's a bitty baby as asteroids go even if it is a nice fat solid thing rather than the collection of gravel held together by gravitational forces that I'm told is the norm."

"Shen Kong is scared," Chummy realized. "We've been talking about expanding into orbital industry. If we do that with a monopoly on cost-efficient ground-to-orbit transit, we can knock anyone else out of business at will."

"That's not it," DeeDee interrupted. "The employee files Shen Kong shared—they still have people working on the new low-mass parachute tech. And they haven't cut back at all on their reentry shuttle people. They are hedging all bets in case there's still no elevator ten years from now." She stared at her feet and babbled fast to get all the words out without typing them. "Selling the asteroid might be a backup plan. If they keep it back the value of the metals in the asteroid are higher for being already in orbit, which ones on Earth are not. And also if they decide they can't trust TCG, they could fake having difficulties delivering the asteroid to extend the time before they have true competition from the space elevator."

"Sending things down to Earth surface is hardly the main business case for the elevator!" Rodney objected.

"Give me a moment," Cory Aanderson said, and Rodney snapped his mouth shut to give the man his full attention.

DeeDee fidgeted with her comm, turning it on and off as if repeated restarts could will the malicious code out of the device.

"This changes nothing," the old salesman finally decided. "Zhu Zhang Li tried to cover all the angles, and we caught her at it. I'll talk to Jeffy first, of course, but I expect to have a conference call with her and her people later and work out a few more concessions. But!" He held up a hand forestalling Rodney from speaking again. "She'll offer them, and we'll decline. Chummy is right about us having scared Shen Kong, and if an established deep space company is worried, we've probably freaked out all the ones working primarily in orbit. I'll talk with Jeffy. We need a plan to ensure we don't completely destabilize things."

"War with China," DeeDee muttered.

Rodney gave her a disturbed look.

"Just a joke Julie Zhu made," Chummy explained. "And we really ought to consider that the elevator project might not actually work."

Cory snorted and splattered cocoa and froth over all three of them.

"Goodness Chummy!" He hacked a healthy cough and blew his nose loudly on a tissue Rodney provided. "You need to give some kind of warning before jumping headlong into dark humor like that. Might not work!" He grabbed the corner of his lap blanket and wiped at Rodney's face.

Chummy handed DeeDee a few of the tissues. He hadn't been joking.

"I like your plan," Rodney said. "For your arguments when you go back at Julie, remember Ethan's got an engineering firm on contract to supply the orbital station indefinitely. We can afford to build a station from scratch if Shen Kong decides not to come through with the asteroid. Sure, they might get their new parachute system working well enough to do orbit-to-Earth without us for a while but cheap uplift is in their best interests too. We'll still be able to finish construction without their help, and when we do, there's nothing that says we have to have any space available to sell to Shen Kong or any other business Julie is affiliated with."

DeeDee's fingers twitched. She would be sending him private little messages if her comm were safe to connect or if he still had his also infected device.

"We'd need backups," Chummy tried to inject caution again. Jeffy really did listen to Cory's insights, and Chummy didn't dare try to caution Jeffy directly. He couldn't afford to be found out before the Sadous' West Africa launcher got up and running smoothly or it would have been for nothing.

"Won't be a problem." Rodney waived off his concerns,

but Cory looked at him with the wrinkles deepening between his eyebrows. The old salesman was trying to read him, and he hadn't gotten to his position by being bad at that.

DeeDee hunched in her seat and muttered, "Wish I could search on Shen Kong's parachutes. Could find something. Probably."

"What if we sold a parachute system ourselves?" Chummy asked, welcoming the chance to give Cory Aanderson a distraction.

Rodney blinked. "I didn't know we had one."

That would be because TCG doesn't have one. But he didn't say so immediately.

"We didn't know we had the makings of a space elevator a year ago," Chummy pointed out.

"Learned about it around seven months ago, myself," Cory Aanderson agreed.

"We agreed to support the resupply of their belt-mining operations as part of this deal," Rodney said. "So if we push them on this after Shen Kong has already allocated their rock budget, Julie will have to work with us."

"You'd let them die?" DeeDee pushed her cocoa away. "They've got whole crews of people out there, and they'd get abandoned up there because of some bullshit contract dispute?"

"Jeffy would not," Chummy said with absolute confidence. Rodney grimaced like it was a character flaw on their chief executive's part. "But," Chummy added, "we have no idea what Shen Kong will do. They could probably redirect our rock to one of their mining operations and get their deep space crews resupplied there as they usually do."

"It's dangerous up there," Cory Aanderson agreed. "And so this parachute system of ours...Is it cheaper to produce than Shen Kong's?"

"No, let's say it's not, but that Jeffy will be willing to sell it at a loss to take Shen Kong's market share for however long it takes to bring the space elevator into operation."

"And the reason they haven't seen us testing it?" Rodney asked.

"Is because it doesn't exist," Cory Aanderson filled in smoothly before Chummy needed to say it. "But we'll say we realigned funding after DiamondWire proved to be possible in industrial lengths."

"But the crews," DeeDee went back to it again.

"That's another lever we have." Cory Aanderson pulled his blankets up a bit more.

The cocoa splatter had dried to almost invisibility, but now that he knew the blankets were dirty, Chummy noticed the whole hospital bed had a musty unlaundered smell.

"Our goal," Cory Aanderson said, "is that they continue with the asteroid delivery like they planned, and we have some resupply ready and waiting for them. Ethan mentioned the other day that he's already locked in a contract for orbit-side supplier for consumables and the carbon tether build powder."

"He'll have backups, though," Chummy pointed out. If he had to move to Kilimanjaro to ensure it, he would. Chummy needed the space elevator to have layers upon layers of redundancy not just in the engineering itself but also in the supporting operations.

"Not Ethan," Cory Aanderson said. "That boy is always sweating the bottom-line costs for things. It's why he's great for the elevator. He's got a wide-open budget, but he'll be spending it like he has to account for every single penny. He'll do backups for life support because he has to, but stuff that can wait maybe three to five days like food, no way in hell he'll pay for redundancy."

Cory Aanderson beckoned Rodney for his closer attention. "Got any ideas for those salvage companies? Next on my list is finding a deal for the space trash."

"You're going to contract with a sole provider for clearing space debris?" Chummy knew he was outside his authority, but the concept was ridiculous. They should know better, they should all know better. And TCG was going to depend only on the Sadous' western launcher for the orbital station's resupply during the construction phase? And then they had the potential for an excessive delay in the setup of the orbit-side rig because they might use some fragile, easily holed construct instead of a solid asteroid? A rock might not be pretty but there was significant value in a thing able to sustain at least a few collisions with small space junk. His little favor to the family might not just risk money. It might cost lives.

Chummy felt sick.

He needed to get off this jet. He needed to go back to his quiet little apartment and call Aunt Mami to make a plan. A very, very detailed plan with lots of exceptional people on site to make it work. Forget local talent and hiring from within and a cross-training program to develop the skills of domestic employees. Forget all that. People could die.

DeeDee tapped him on the shoulder. "You okay, boss?"

He looked up, gray-faced and trying his best to be blank.

"I'm really sorry about getting the equipment virus-infected. I'll pay the company back for it. It's just—" She swallowed hard. "I need a few months, cause, uh, I've still got some student loans."

Chummy slowly realized what she was saying. "DeeDee, you aren't responsible for what Shen Kong chooses to do when you connected to their network. You did a great job here, truly."

"But I let it get trojaned!" She waved a hand over all her fine gear. "They'll probably have to quarantine all of this. It'll take months to figure out exactly what it did and by then it'll all be too outdated to be worth overwriting and reinstalling the apps and installing all the updates, patches, and fixes. It's all *mech* waste now!"

Chummy nodded. "But you didn't infect the system. And you didn't let us spill all our proprietary data back out for someone else to see, steal, and copy."

"That's it!" Cory Aanderson clapped his hands, which made only a muffled sound because one hand still held the mug. "Shen Kong is after the space elevator. They took this enormous risk of losing us as business partners because they want the secret of how to manufacture DiamondWire."

"Are our proposed transport rates that usurious?" Chummy asked.

DeeDee's fingers twitched.

"Expensive," Chummy translated the word she would have looked up.

Rodney shook his head. "I don't think that's it. It's that we've got no plans to build a second and third elevator on Earth. They aren't needed here, not after we have a first one in regular, sustained operation."

"What do you mean?" Chummy said.

"The Moon might have a business case for one," Cory Aanderson allowed. "I've mentioned it to Jeffy. It's just that it isn't our business case. Our lunar interests are pretty minimal at the moment. We might have been looking at obtaining some, but our war chest is all about funding the Kilimanjaro space elevator now. We aren't in the business of buying companies at least for a little while."

"I'm not going to the Moon," DeeDee said. Rodney and Cory both blinked.

"We were about to visit the elevator site when I got the call from Jeffy redirecting us here," Chummy explained. "Your predictions make it sound like the next major build site might be lunar, so..."

"It's not the risks," DeeDee added. "It's the connectivity. Horrible, horrible connectivity between lunar networks and Earth networks. They say you have to wait for downloads. Can you imagine?"

CHAPTER TEN

"**M**URDER ALWAYS MAKES EVERYTHING BETTER." The echoes of Maurie's rash comment hung in her own ears for what seemed like an eternity. But Hermès flinched. He punched numbers into his own comm a half dozen times with no connection.

Your jammer is still on, she considered telling him, but didn't.

She'd had an opportunity for closer inspection; the scarf was a knockoff. A good-quality one, but definitely fake. The silk's copyright-infringed classic Hermès *"brides de gala"* pattern was exactly correct in all details, but too crisply executed. Originals were created by silk screening, not by a modern fabric printer. Maybe the police would not find a numbered antiques invoice record and associated lifetime insurance coverage complete with customer name and address to go with that classic scarf. *They are going to get away with this,* Maurie thought.

Nobody made any death threats out loud now, not even Blue Scarf Man. But the criminals stared at her and held their machetes like they thought they might

need to use them. The passengers stilled as the news of
who she was and what had been said worked through
the group.

"Hey," Hermès summoned his group, and they all
stepped back away from the passengers. Something
about Hermès still bothered her, but it wasn't until
that moment that she realized what it was.

I know him. The too smooth English this far into
the normally French-speaking part of the country,
and the odd bandana choice were all wrong for a
reasonably competent bandit.

I know him. He was one of the bored rich kids
Pascaline had enjoyed fighting with.

Maurie's fists balled up tight enough to make her
arms shake. Trust-fund kids were known to do stupid
things. But to go rob middle-class passengers and
to risk their lives too by fucking with the autodrive
system on a public bus? They had thought there was
a fellow thief on the bus itself, which would've made
the heist safer, but they were also planning to break
her great aunt's arm? With the connections anyone
Pascaline bothered to fight with had, he certainly
didn't need the money. He wouldn't be as well off
as a Sadou, of course, but still!

Hermès met her eyes and looked worried. He called
out to his fellow thieves again more sharply. Red,
who'd been negotiating with the passengers about
what they'd give up, moved to grab the largest of the
three backpacks of loot.

"Leave it," Hermès snapped.

Rumblings were starting in the crowd now. Maurie
could see the father who'd had his son rescue her
comm moving together with a few of the larger male

passengers. They had no weapons and were older than the thieves, but the father made eye contact with her.

Something hissed behind her, whispering that she should stay silent, stay still, and nasty brutal luck would protect her. Maurie would've chopped that phantom snake to fish chum if she could see it.

These passengers were going to fight. Hermès saw it too and glanced uneasily back at his own people. Somewhere a snake was laughing. She could see the python with the tire tread marks winding through the crowd of passengers. She glared it away.

"The bus is fixed," Maurie called out, earning shocked looks from both the robbers and the passengers. "Driver gets on first. Then kids. You and you." She pointed at the closest passengers. "Take the stuff. Everyone goes. I'll stay." *Nobody dies for me. Not today.*

The candy seller turned bus operator bolted for the vehicle. None of the robbers moved. Hermès winced, and the others looked to him—clearly unused to taking command of the robbery.

"But we don't want her," Red said.

The rest of the passengers surged in afterwards with no particular care for the order Maurie had suggested, though the ones she'd pointed at did grab up the mass of stolen property. Everyone crammed inside. Only the luggage was riding on the roof for this leg of the trip.

"They are leaving and you are going to let them go," Maurie said. The blare of the bus horn announced the autodrive was on and that it had detected obstacles in the path in front of it.

The door to the bus slammed shut, and the driver

switched to reverse. Maurie scrambled to the side of the road.

Hermès and his men cleared the road too as the bus lurched into motion. The candy seller was in the driver's seat, and they'd just been messing with the autodrive. None of them wanted to be the live test of the collision-avoidance software.

The bus roared away at the autopilot's max speed.

"Do you realize you just kidnapped yourself?" White said, hefting his tool case.

"No shit," Hermès muttered under his breath. Their eyes met. He knew she recognized him. It hadn't been that many years ago.

"We don't want a Sadou," Hermès called out to the others. He motioned at the equipment. "Turn off the jammer."

The other thieves looked at him and each other uneasily. They were afraid, but not all for the same reasons.

"It might take the family a while to get cash together for a ransom if they decide to pay it," she pointed out. "Or you could always chop me up and leave my body in that ditch."

"Shut up," Hermès said under his breath but with too much force to keep Blue from hearing and raising his eyebrows.

"The ditch is an option." Maurie didn't bother keeping her voice down. Somewhere snakes were laughing at her. "You could throw my comm in with me. You can see it's made intermittent connections, so my family can trace my location. And then there are all those passengers to interview. And maybe none of them will recognize those two of you with the splatters on your shoes from when you were repainting the police station, so it could work."

"Is she having a mental breakdown?" Gray asked.

"You should not be allowed out on your own," Hermès declared.

White shouldered his heavy pack. The others were backing away. Murder seemed not to be their idea of a good time.

"What were you even doing on a bus?" Hermès demanded in exasperation.

Maurie shrugged. "I ran out of money."

That earned a laugh from the group.

"Rich people." Green shook his head.

"People like you don't ride buses," Gray insisted. "It was just supposed to be the witch woman. And we wouldn't've hurt her. She'd've paid us double to tell her about who ordered it."

"Has before," Blue agreed. "Same guy too. You think he'd stop paying." He gave Hermès a sidelong look and jerked his head back down the road.

Maurie sighed and sat down on her bag on the side of the road. "People like you shouldn't rob people. You don't need to."

White snorted. "You think anyone can live off painting jobs?"

"You think you're being paid enough for this?" she replied.

"No," said Blue. He turned and walked away. The others looked from her to Hermès and back and followed after him.

Hermès shook his head at her. "Fucking Sadous. You're all impossible." He threw her comm at the dirt next to her and hurried down the road after his crew.

"Next time you get bored, try alcoholism. It's more socially acceptable." Maurie picked up the comm. The screen was shattered, which destroyed it. The touch screen sensors couldn't read her thumbprint to unlock it with cracks running through the whole surface. It started buzzing anyway. Incoming call: Pascaline.

Maurie considered throwing it at the ground harder to turn off the annoying ringtone.

An old red compact car came zipping down the road far in excess of the authorized speed limit less than thirty minutes later.

Pascaline stuck her head out the front window as the car slowed to a stop. She flicked a switch to throw open the rear door revealing two back seats, both out of reach of the steering panel.

"Get in, brat."

"I love you too," Maurie replied. She shouldered her pack and got in.

"Yeah, yeah." Pascaline belted in and started the vehicle roaring down the road as soon as Maurie did the same. "I don't know what you did to Great Aunt Mami, but she's both furious at you and very worried, so stay away from the north country for a while."

Maurie buckled in, and Pascaline launched the vehicle back into motion. She was driving manually at top speed.

"You would not believe the shit Uncle Benoit has been saying." Pascaline flipped down the visor to block the sun, as she veered around a bend in the road with only one hand on the wheel. "Something about getting a call from some friend's kid who said you'd tried to kidnap yourself and that he refuses to be considered responsible for you."

"I did not!" Maurie wanted to hit something, but Pascaline wasn't paying attention. She was reading something while driving.

"Pay attention to the road!" Maurie snapped.

Pascaline flicked the vehicle over to autodrive. It engaged and slowed to the speed limit. "Someone rip your spirit out and soak it in vinegar overnight or something? I just picked you up from the side of the highway. How about a thank you?"

Maurie considered that. "Thank you," she said. "It was very kind of you to come get me."

Her cousin wrinkled her nose and thumbed up the level on the built-in air freshener. Maurie's unwashed scent had permeated.

"How did you get to me so fast?" Maurie asked. "And why are you using Great Aunt Mami's car?"

Pascaline shrugged. "Grandpere has a new project, and Great Aunt Mami has to prove she's more supportive of the family or Uncle Benoit will get her kicked out. But she only likes me."

"I, uh, noticed," Maurie said.

Pascaline actually looked up at her. "You don't look well. Should we stop for a doctor?"

"I'm fine. I just need a shower," Maurie replied.

Pascaline looked back at the road and grabbed control of the wheel. She slammed on the brakes. The tires squealed. A phantom snake slithered safely off the road without receiving another set of tire tracks.

Her cousin slowly reapplied the accelerator and restored autodrive. She arched an eyebrow at Maurie, daring her to comment.

"It was nice of you to avoid running over the snake," Maurie said.

"Yeah, whatever." Pascaline gave her a wary look and changed the subject. "Check your comm. Do you see this stuff from Uncle Chummy? It's all about Grandpere's project. You've got a lot of work to do."

Maurie held up the remains of her battered device. Pascaline handed over her own.

Maurie started reading. Uncle Chummy's message was addressed to both of them, but she didn't immediately argue with Pascaline's expectation that she'd be the one to do the work. Projects always started that way and then Pascaline showed up when the technical nuances got too complicated and forced people to work together until they were uncomplicated.

Maurie read aloud, "Sadou Corporation will deliver carbon additive manufacturing construction powders to TCG's elevator station in GEO using described spacecraft via a maglev-assist launcher, design specification attached. Payments to be made per objective completion points as outlined in design document. Maximum bonuses to be paid out if TCG initial DiamondWire™ tether reaches Kilimanjaro station by five-year stretch goal. Prorated bonus available through ten-year-goal delivery point. TCG recommends an east-west rail positioned on a mountain slope for least fuel cost per launch." She squinted at Pascaline. "Carbon, huh. This is DiamondWire goo, isn't it?"

"Yup, I think so." Pascaline nodded. "Lots of speculation in the press about how exactly the tether will get connected for the elevator. In theory you could launch something super massive and sort of spool the tether out as you thrust upwards, but there's a lot of really difficult problems with that which don't end with building the massive spaceship. They can also construct the tether material in orbit and lower it down. But carbon's pretty rare in near-Earth space. With the number of metric tons of carbon dust they want delivered, I'd say they picked option two. The first tether lowered won't be the massive lift cord that they'd replace it with later. But once they have a narrow, comparatively, tether in operation, they can do their own lift with it to bring up all the carbon dust they want and build that second tether line."

"Huh." Maurie grinned. "The big space elevator people need help from the little guy to get stuff into space. And that whole east-west rail line up a mountain thing?"

"Yup, it's easier to use the rotation of the Earth to give a launch the motion you want rather than to waste energy fighting against it. And let the slope of the ground help give you an angled launch instead of trying to build a line of ridiculously high skyscrapers to copy what the planet has already provided for us in the form of mountains. Energy from the maglev rail gets your lift vehicle through the first couple kilometers of densest atmosphere. You could use rocket fuel for all of it, but then you have to use more fuel to lift the fuel. Even with the maglev on a mountain slope, to lift twenty thousand or so metric tons, we are looking at around a dozen launches a day for several years in a row."

"Pity it has to be a mountain near the equator," Maurie said.

"And why would that be a pity? I read the notes too," Pascaline said. "Grandpere says he's already talking to somebody about getting access to build on the tallest peak in the Mandaras."

"Um, hmm," Maurie said. "That'd be Fako. Ancestral home of the Bakweri tribe and controlled by their chief's family, the Endeleys."

Pascaline gave a slow blink and Maurie knew she hit a nerve.

"Just how much does Endeley Adamou hate you?" she guessed.

Pascaline bit her lip. "Let's get back to the project. I was explaining why we're screwed and can't do it."

Maurie snorted. "You don't have to do your eternal pessimist routine on this one. It hardly matters that we could do it if given a chance as we'll never win a bid for this sort of thing. Some multinational company will buy a mountainside in Ecuador or Indonesia to win the contract and then they'll probably even subcontract back to TCG for all the work. This is ridiculously easy compared to most of the miracles you've worked in the bush. We need an enormous amount of electrical power to charge the launch rail. Fine. Where do we need it? Is it in the bush somewhere hellaciously far from the existing electrical grid system? Do we need to have Grandpere influence government officials to get new roads built and extend municipal power lines? No and no. We need it at a developed site where there's even some roadways already built. Oh, and it's also near a deepwater shipping port not far from one of our refineries. But we don't even have to fall back on that because the whole area is absolutely wonderful for geothermal. There're two geothermal plants within a hundred kilometers. Their output is needed for the regular power grid, but it's not exactly hard to build a few more. We need a maglev system. Can we do that? Oh, yeah, there's a high-speed train that uses maglev running between Yaoundé and Douala. All the folks who build and maintain that are still around. Is it exactly the same thing? Nope. But we can adjust and so can they. Think of it as a nice *dabare* project. The spacecraft, I admit," said Maurie, "scares the shit out of me."

Here Pascaline finally laughed. "I love the spacecraft."

"I thought you might," Maurie said. "So, Adamou. You like him."

Pascaline looked away.

"Really? That's very interesting," Maurie said. "Because Grandpere is suggesting that I should try spending some time with him. Aunt Julienne says much the same thing and expresses bafflement that he remained interested after meeting you when you had the bad grace to decline even a first date. From the photos, he looks..."

"Hot," Pascaline interrupted. "I know."

Maurie leaned her seat back more, feeling an unwelcome wave of exhaustion. She could feel hissing again. Or maybe smell them? Auditory hallucinations probably. She really needed time at Great Aunt Mami's favorite clinic. The letdown from the adrenaline of nearly being robbed and kidnapped was likely hitting her system too. "I'm exhausted, Pascaline. Just tell me why I should waste time reading the rest of the plum deal somebody else is getting."

"There's no bid," Pascaline said. "The contract is signed, final, done. The first payment hit Grandpere's general account already."

"Fuck." Maurie sat straight up. "How the hell did

that happen? We won the bid? You wrote up a proposal without me?"

"There was no proposal," Pascaline said. "Our Uncle Fabrice—who is insisting yet again that we need to call him Tchami, I mean Chummy, to not confuse his corporate minions and overlords—has gifted the family with a plum." She tilted her head to the side. "I think Uncle Chummy has very few overlords anymore and while he might have only a couple minions on TCG's printed org chart, I bet he's got many who owe him gratitude for one thing or another."

"Wow," Maurie breathed. "But the elevator itself doesn't get built if they don't get the carbon to spin into gold, or rather DiamondWire. We've got to try to do this. What's our real biggest sticking point?"

"The timeline and our own people getting in our way," Pascaline said. "TCG needs a hell of a lot of carbon lifted. I bet they'll contract with several companies to get the carbon delivered. Other places have spaceports already built after all. But we do seem to be the only ones contracted so far. It took humanity one hundred and fifty years to get the first twenty thousand metric tons of material, bodies, and gear into space. We've got five years to throw about that much in carbon dust at TCG's station in GEO, which they haven't even begun building yet, I note. I hate how project completion always seems to depend on the actions of people you can't even fire for screwing up."

"Should we try to buy a mountain in Ecuador or Indonesia and subcontract back to TCG?" Maurie asked.

"Fuck that," Pascaline said. "We succeed or fail on our own without giving away two thirds of the profits.

I'll marry Adamou if that's what it takes to get access to his mountain."

The prospect, Maurie noted, did not seem to bother Pascaline overmuch. The brush and grasses on the side of the road had given way to small farms and sun glinted on metal village roofs ahead. "Navigation says there's a traveler's kiosk up here. You're getting a shower."

"If you leave me here, I'm making you manage Grandpere's launcher thing on your own," Maurie threatened.

Pascaline rolled her eyes. They pulled into a well-appointed bus stop. Newish smooth blacktop paved the whole area and only about half of it had been claimed by vendors expanding an open-air market. Pascaline pointed at the small building which identified itself as the promised kiosk with pictograms for toilets, showers, and laundry.

"Those are pricey," Maurie complained. It felt ridiculous to complain about costs where she'd just seen the amounts TCG was ready to pay them. But she didn't have access to those accounts from here, and roadside showering was not what it was intended for—family tendencies to comingle all moneys be damned.

Her cousin handed over the key ring with the vehicle's fob on it. Great Aunt Mami's credit chip hung from the stylized snake circle along with a riot of cheerful bright jewelry charms.

Maurie flinched back. "I'll pay for it myself."

Her cousin shrugged. "Suit yourself." But when Pascaline started to pull her hand back, Maurie snatched it. Without the fob, her cousin couldn't drive off without her. Few people would dare rob Great Aunt Mami, but the woman still kept her vehicle settings highly secure just in case. Maurie wanted a long shower with plenty of time for a full lather and no chance of her ride being gone when she got out.

"You stay here," she admonished her cousin.

Pascaline looked heavenward. "Do you really think I'd leave the air-conditioning?"

Maurie accepted that nebulous promise and got out of the car. Street vendors outside called out offers of food and drink. Her belly rumbled, reminding her that her last meal had been quite a while ago. She'd get something on the way out.

The traveler's kiosk proved to be in decent repair. It had storage lockers with power outlets, basic autodoc test kits to help travelers figure out if they'd contracted something besides normal travel weariness, and—best of all—good showers with soap dispensers.

Some enterprising person had ripped out four of the lockers and installed a clothes printer. The model was a mass market style only able to produce acrylic blend fabric. Maurie plugged in Great Aunt Mami's account and bought a full set of clothing. She chose an ocean wave print pattern at random and started the fast-print option. Accessing her great aunt's account unfortunately meant the account autosets co-opted the unit speaker to play business summary updates. Maurie reluctantly listened.

She paid for an hour in the shower compartment. A deluge of sun-warmed water cleaned the grime from her body and she ran her fingers around her bedraggled braids to clean her scalp as well. The waterproof panel on the shower wall let her add in an order for a matching head scarf to keep her hair mostly out of sight until she had time to get the braids reworked.

Pascaline's hair had been flawless, of course. Maurie sighed to herself. She could get Grandpere to reimburse Great Aunt Mami for all these traveling expenses, she was pretty sure.

The rinse cycle started. She squeezed her eyes tightly closed and held her breath. It stopped too soon, and she had to authorize the upcharge for another rinse to get the rest of the soap out of her hair.

Soap stinging her eyes got her thinking about Pascaline. They were really fortunate to have her. The messages from Uncle Chummy ran to an end now. She'd study it in more detail later. The essence of it was that they were going to be paid to supply raw materials to the space side of the elevator while it was under construction. They were to use a specific launcher design and acquire land to build it on. They'd get paid some even if it never worked, but underneath the mound of details, Maurie was certain that it would be far more valuable to everyone if they found some way to succeed.

God alone knew how Uncle Chummy had gotten them this project, but it was complicated. This new business was no simple pumping of crude oil up from the ocean floor using long-established processes. There were files with design notes from research engineers that her message reader balked at attempting to transcribe. There were schematics too. A lot of them. She had to pause her shower for a few minutes to marvel at a visual display. The overall system looked brilliant, with a host of interlocking designs put together, and all of them had actually been built and tested before. Operation-ready, several of the systems-design people from TCG had called it in the summary, but Maurie knew with a bone-deep certainty that there would be challenges and complications when they actually built the thing. Without someone with a real engineering background for their technicians to talk to, she had doubts that even Uncle Chummy could pull it off. And they didn't have him.

Thankfully they had Pascaline for that. Maurie squelched some useless guilt about why her cousin lacked the spacecraft design, operation, or systems-integration experience she'd've gotten outside family industry. If Pascaline'd been allowed to do what she wanted, she'd have been on the Moon by now and be even less help. Pascaline would have to be the one to identify which of the Sadous' many petrochemical engineers had the chops for joining this project.

Maurie emerged from the kiosk refreshed and smelling vastly better.

Then her comm in "play all" mode started in on the messages from family members. What in the vilest corner of hell was Uncle Benoit thinking? The uncles and aunts wanted Grandpere to increase the quarterly payments to their trust funds . . . Well, yeah, they were always wanting that. Somebody always had a better boat, and the high life only got more and more expensive. But they were going to have a vote against him, now? How was that launcher contract structured? Who specifically was the contract awarded to? Maurie dried her hands as best she could and tried to find the answers.

She dressed in distraction and left the kiosk still searching.

Pascaline scoffed. "Did you have to go full on spirit woman on us?"

Maurie looked down. The clothes printer had been filled wrong last time someone replenished the color packs. Her wave design had been made with reds replacing all the cyan portions of the print. The double portion of red turned the cool wave print into a stylized fire-colored snakeskin pattern. "It's clean."

Pascaline shrugged. "Great Aunt Mami wants her car back. She's been pinging me through the in-vehicle systems. It seems that someone has hacked the comm she gifted you to override the admin codes in a way Great Aunt Mami didn't think was possible, is ignoring her calls, and now has used her account to buy overpriced clothes."

Maurie glared. Her cousin had clearly neglected to inform Great Aunt Mami about the state of Maurie's comm. She filed away the information that shattering the screen and being stomped on several times in a near bus crash sent back error codes even Great Aunt Mami didn't immediately understand.

"I'm dropping you at the airport, and I even got you a flight." Pascaline shook her head. "No one ever appreciates how much I do for the family."

"You are coming with me," Maurie insisted.

Pascaline winced. "I think the initial visit to the Endeleys might go better without me."

"We can't do it without you."

Pascaline looked away. "I'm returning Great Aunt Mami's car. I'm not crossing that woman."

"She can't do anything to you." Maurie shook her head. "Really, Pascaline. Great Aunt Mami is sweet."

"Uh huh. But Uncle Chummy is throwing a few billion dollars at the family just as our other uncle is deciding to cut her branch off the family tree. We really know how to get in our own way, don't we? Is she really sweet enough not to care about that?"

Maurie froze. She hadn't finished listening to the family messages. Of course the aunts and uncles would be turning against Great Aunt Mami. That was almost as constant as their complaints about low trust payments.

"You didn't know." Pascaline covered her face. "I don't know why no one else pays attention to anything going on. I've got someone in Buea who owes me a favor. They'll give us the mountain and we can at least get the first couple TCG payments. You go be a hero and earn us a billion or two."

"I am going to need you," Maurie said. "Your engineering background is really going to matter."

"I'm not that good." Pascaline started to say more but snapped her mouth shut.

Maurie blinked at her. "It won't be just you, but we need coordination."

"And I'm such a people person," Pascaline said.

"Fine, I'll try to get Uncle Benoit under control," Maurie said. "But stay out of camera range and don't say anything, okay?"

Pascaline settled into the driver's seat and rolled her shoulders in acceptance. "Good luck, cousin."

Maurie dialed up Uncle Benoit and blinked to see herself added to a family conference call. A half dozen boat decks and beach house porches filled her screen with relatives.

"Oh, good to see you, Maurie," Uncle Benoit said. "Whenever you're ready, I can take your vote proxy. We should have cash flowing again by the fifteenth, my man tells me."

"Excuse me, but does everyone here remember Tchami Fabrice?" she said.

"We cannot afford to support the hangers-on anymore!" Aunt Julienne said. "Really, Benoit. We don't need the proxies for the grandkids. Just call the vote now."

"Actually, Jacques had to sign off again to go deal with some foreman issue or other," Uncle Benoit said. "So if we just get the half vote shares from Maurie and your boy Reuben we can get this moving without waiting for him."

"Grandpere personally has signed a multibillion dollar contract with Uncle Fabrice," Maurie lied. She'd found the answer. It was Sadou Corporation, not Sadou Moussa personally. And that meant if the family trust replaced Sadou Moussa with Sadou Benoit or any of the rest of the clan, they could take that initial payment and drain it all away without attempting to lift so much as a shovel's worth of dirt toward performing the project. But they didn't know that.

Multibillion. The words struck them all like a spell. Every person on the screen stopped moving.

Uncle Benoit recovered first. "You're certain?"

"He's called me in to serve as one of the project managers," Maurie said. This time not quite lying.

Uncle Jacques in stained construction overalls blinked on in the video. "Sorry, I had myself muted. Let's all give Moussa at least six months here. He'll need free access to the petty cash, don't you think, Maurie?"

A murmur of agreement followed. "Six months." "Yeah, sounds good." "Six month's okay with me."

"My boy shouldn't have to wait another six months!" Aunt Julienne said. She was flushing and starting to slur her words from the drink on her table. Her usual wine had been replaced with something clear today.

Maurie winced, but she didn't have a solution to the Reuben problem.

"Six months," Uncle Benoit said definitively. "No one bother Moussa with stories about our discussions here, eh? We'll all talk again in six months." And with a click, he ended the call.

"And that is why you are the people person," Pascaline said.

CHAPTER ELEVEN

DEEDEE NELSON KNEW SHE WASN'T A PEOPLE person. That was one of the more obvious results of the self-knowledge assessments her boss, Mr. Chummy, had had her take right after she'd first started working for him. In the literature—and she always read the accompanying literature for such things—a person was supposed to retake such tests every few years to see how things had changed. She had reminders on her comm for the retakes. But she'd let her comm get hacked, and now she felt like a limb was missing.

Mr. Rodney Johnson allowed her to borrow his spare comm for the flight home to Germany. She supposed he thought she'd be checking her messages or playing games. Or maybe he thought she needed an electronic teddy bear. She didn't know. He laid his seat flat, pulled one of Mr. Aanderson's extra blankets over his head, and went to sleep.

Her boss had passed out in his own chair. Not a surprise to DeeDee, since he'd stayed awake through the entire flight over. She pressed the release on his chair back and eased it down flat as well. He half woke enough to slide back and accept the pillow and blanket she provided.

The aircraft was larger than they needed, so she went far forward where the glow from her screen wouldn't bother anyone.

The drawer above the one with the thin airline blankets had easy-heat meal packets. The labels declared them gourmet, but most things tasted a little funny at altitude. She checked the next drawer higher still and found the drink powders Rodney had used to make cocoa and a selection of packaged snack foods. She helped herself to the cheese puffs and grabbed a handful of moist towelettes to wipe her fingers on. It wouldn't be polite to return Rodney's comm with orange imitation cheese dust caught in all the device's crevices.

The familiar crunch soothed her and the aftertaste hinted of white cheddar and possibly a tiny bit of asiago. DeeDee would've preferred a faintly stale chemical imitation cheese flavor, but one couldn't have everything.

Her check of the equipment turned up no unwanted tracking software. She wormed out a few common bits of malicious code of the type any device acquired when occasionally used by the unwary for shopping or entertainment, but she left them alone. A totally clean device ought to raise concerns when next TCG's in-house techs made a service check. She didn't care to alarm anyone until she knew for absolute certain.

A check of her corporate messaging inbox would be expected, so she did that, and found the sales deputy's messages instead of her own. The senior salesman had turned off the device's faceprint security before handing it over to her, she noticed with a hiss of consternation.

A message had slipped through his spam filter from an IP address in either Nigeria or Cameroon with a vaguely threatening tone and some ranting about hijacking a public bus. DeeDee deleted that for him.

She logged Rodney Johnson out and herself in. She'd have liked to shake him awake and force him to click through a security training module on insider threats.

Her boss's steady efforts to get her to accept corporate social norms deterred her from actually doing it, but she added a note to Rodney's file so future HR assistants would know TCG's deputy VP of Sales had flawed cyber security instincts. Her fingers hit the combination of hot keys to flag the note for her boss's eyes as well. Rodney's device didn't have her settings, so it didn't do it.

Her fingers trembled and DeeDee didn't do it the long way either. She ran her searches and did inquiry after inquiry, making only a half-hearted effort to reply to the backlog in her inbox. She'd look like she were working past exhaustion and half asleep if anyone checked. But her boss had an overabundance of trust too. She wasn't sure he'd ever look.

DeeDee composed the message to Mr. Jeffy four times before giving up on herself in disgust. They'd land soon. She deleted all four drafts and logged herself out. She slipped the device back into the pocket of Rodney's satchel and walked back forward to start the coffee.

A little terminal next to the coffee machine had a chat app installed. She pinged Samson. He flashed her a sleepy emoji.

"If you see a robbery and don't call the police," she typed, *"are you a thief too? Does it make a difference*

*if the robber takes only small things? Or does it just
mean the robber is experienced and has been doing
it for a long, long time?"*

DeeDee could only find evidence of the one, but
it was so smoothly done that she wasn't quite sure it
really counted as stealing exactly. And yet something
that smooth had to have taken quite a lot of planning,
and he'd have passed by many other easier options.

Samson's cursor blinked and a text response rolled
across the screen interrupting her thoughts.

*"Ug. No brainteasers, please. Attempting to get up
to speed on conversational Bantu Swahili is making
my head hurt more than enough,"* Samson replied.

The coffee gurgled and splattered into the carafe.
Should she tell him it wasn't a rhetorical? DeeDee
prepped a mug sweetened with a half spoonful of
Chummy's favorite raw cane sugar.

"Okay, okay, what about this?" Samson typed
more. *"Check with the boss, but I say it means: (1)
hire the robber for a position where local business
culture prevents the company from putting a good
anti-graft system in place and adjust the annual
bonus to top off whatever is due after the missing
petty cash is tallied up & (2) hire a silent watcher
to do the tallying."*

DeeDee marveled at the screen.

"Did I get it right?" Samson asked.

"Is that coffee I smell?" Mr. Aanderson called out
from the back of the aircraft, sounding much improved
after his rest. "And if so, is there a kind soul who
might bring a poor old man a cup? With two non-
fat creams and a half packet of the pink non-sugar
sweetener stuff?"

"In a moment, Mr. Aanderson," DeeDee said. She filled Chummy's mug first, then the top salesman's coffee with the additions as requested, and made a guess about what Rodney might want.

To Samson, she typed back, *"IDKGTO."* Autocorrect sent, *"I don't know. Got to go."*

"Later," he acknowledged.

Chummy woke to Cory Aanderson singing his second assistant's praises and half seriously threatening to steal her from him.

"She doesn't have medical training, and I refuse to authorize tuition reimbursement for her to get any," Chummy said. He pushed the armrest buttons to turn his bed back into a chair and stood to shake some of the wrinkles out of the suit pants and shirt.

DeeDee closed his hands around a warm mug of coffee. Chummy lifted it in salute to her and drank down the hot bliss.

"I let my assistant get some sleep." Aanderson pointed at Rodney Johnson, still flat with his blanket pulled up over his head.

They could tell the deputy was awake from the harrumph he made in response, but the blanket didn't twitch. A mug with a firmly attached lid waited for him in the built-in cupholder near his seat.

"A deputy vice president is not an assistant," DeeDee said. She looked frazzled with her lank hair sticking out in side fluffs like it did when she pulled on it under stress. None of it had the matted flatness from even a short nap on the long flight. DeeDee had worked through the night again.

Chummy sipped more coffee, thinking about the

things that might have kept a driven rules-focused assistant up all night but not resulted in a cold shoulder from his fellow vice president on the flight. Cory Aanderson had his corporate comm at his elbow already, and he'd been awake long enough to go through his priority messages if he had the attention to needle Chummy about getting his coffee made for him.

DeeDee tried to smile, but she wouldn't meet anyone's eyes. The two salesmen didn't know her well enough to recognize her distress.

He stared into his coffee looking for insights that weren't there. His assistant came around with the carafe and poured a refill.

"It'll be alright, boss," she said.

If only it were that easy.

CHAPTER TWELVE

GRANDPERE'S CURRENT PERSONAL AIDE, FATIMA, met Maurie at one of the Limbe airstrips. The beach town at the base of the mountain wasn't far from Buea. From the scowl on her face, Maurie doubted Pascaline's travel arrangements for her had been to Fatima's liking. Her cousin was somewhere on the northern roads again returning Great Aunt Mami's car and possibly trying to further calm Uncle Benoit down. The idea of Pascaline as a peacemaker brought a smile to Maurie's lips; an expression not appreciated at all by Fatima.

"You should have landed in Douala," Fatima said, giving Maurie a pinch-lipped glare. No "Ms. Sadou, may I help you, ma'am?" pleasantries from this woman. Her contempt was almost refreshing after the flight. Not quite, though.

The all-amenities inclusive flight on a small jet part-leased and part-borrowed from a friend of Uncle Benoit's had involved a full staff. But in the typical state of things they were nervous part-time staff who desperately wanted to impress a Sadou dropped into their midst and perhaps earn a full-time place in her extended family's employ. She could maybe employ the ground crew who serviced the machine, but probably no one else. And of course the mechanics were the only ones she didn't meet.

"Thank you for picking me up," Maurie said instead of the things she might have.

She examined the woman for a moment. Fatima stopped to the talk with the charter crew for a moment before discovering Maurie had no luggage beyond what she was already holding and hurrying back.

Fatima had new breasts and something had been done to her ears. They were flattened against her skull a bit more. Fatima's straightened hair hung in a simple ponytail today without any blackest-black lowlights, and her eyeliner was mussed in a way that didn't look intentional. She noticed the inspection and didn't care for it.

"What do you have against beauty anyway?" Fatima said.

"You do know you've always been gorgeous," Maurie said, trying to be consolatory. It would have been a bit easier to do if she'd believed it. Maurie didn't remember what Fatima had looked like before the touchups started, so she'd probably been sort of average.

Fatima still looked pretty with her face screwed up like that. It was amazing really. The ears looked vaguely familiar. Was there a famous musician with that overly rounded shape?

Curiosity got the better of Maurie. "The ears are an interesting choice. What doctor are you using now?"

Fatima gave a long-suffering sigh. "Mr. Sadou is

waiting for you in the car. He is very busy. Do not waste his time." She turned on bleach-white tennis shoes and stomped off to the waiting vehicle. "Some of us have work to do."

Unlike a lot of others who'd tried cosmetic surgery, the aide's changes always worked for her. When Fatima had taken the nursing job, she had, Maurie was told, acted like it was a marriage audition. But Grandpere wasn't interested in remarrying, at least not to someone the approximate age of his grandchildren and had told Pascaline to explain the facts of life to her.

A realization dawned on Maurie as she looked at the back of Fatima's squat neck where the puffiness and red marks from a not quite healed touchup made the sleek ponytail seem painful rather than snobbish. She'd been present when Grandpere had told Pascaline to do it, but somehow Pascaline hadn't delivered the message. It had been Maurie who was talked into doing it in Pascaline's stead, and yet Maurie had no recollection of how that had come about.

Her cousin's knack for giving away trouble like that should have made Pascaline eminently unwelcome. But every family needed someone who remembered to order the toilet paper restocked and to double-check on the maintenance that kept the generators running. Or at least to make sure a senior staff member who did so stayed with them.

Maurie let her mind wander back to Chummy's project. There had to be other companies who'd be contracted to deliver carbon and other stuff up to TCG soon. She didn't expect Sadou Corporation to end up with even half a billion out of the multibillions it could be. The stuff about a supersonic engine with maglev assist for a heavy-use surface-to-orbit lift system meant the whole thing was complicated. But Uncle Chummy believed they could do it. And when he thought that, he was right.

What was his actual message again?

"Here's the work of a few specialists to help with the project. This is a one shot thing. I need you to put everything you've got into making this work."

Supplying the space elevator during its multiyear construction phase would have been such an elegant way to jump-start a space industry. She raised a hand to block the sun and peered upslope toward the peak of the mountain. Clouds obscured it from view. The Endeleys owned this mountain, and she had it from Great Aunt Mami herself that Pascaline had just recently personally insulted their favored son, Endeley Adamou.

Grandpere suggested that she would charm him enough that Pascaline would be no trouble. Fatima's eyerolls were not encouraging. Sometimes she wondered if the rest of the family were blind.

Probably just as well. A mountain in Ecuador would be nice. And then they'd have to hire out to someone else to do all the work. She imagined the opinions the legendary spirit of the mountain might have about being used as a spaceport and had to suppress a laugh. The Mami-Wata nightmares had turned her thoughts far too wild to be spoken aloud.

"Are you coming, Ms. Maurie?" Fatima stood next to a pearl gray van with her arms crossed.

"Your hair looks really nice," Maurie said, trying politeness again. "Grandpere suggested I come straight here. How is he doing today?"

"See for yourself." Fatima still hadn't forgiven her. The aide flung her car door open and climbed into the driver's seat.

The rear passenger door opened at a button press. Waves of approval from Grandpere washed over Maurie as he positively beamed at her. It was impossible not to smile back.

"Maurie, Maurie! So good to see you!" Grandpere beckoned her inside where the flush of air-conditioning hit her with an instant chill.

He closed the door behind her.

"Ms. Maurie, seat belt, please," Fatima said, and she nosed the car out of the parking lot.

Maurie rushed to comply, but Grandpere laughed at her hurry. Fatima drove slowly and carefully. Few vehicles joined them on the outer edge of Limbe, and Buea's streets weren't particularly crowded either. Some of the buildings lining the road looked like they might have been boarded up a decade or so ago, but since then trash pickers had found a better use for the plywood.

"Did Fatima tell you our big secret?" Grandpere's grin couldn't get any wider.

Fatima spoke up before Maurie could answer. "I saved it for you, Mr. Sadou." Fatima's mood change toward Maurie might be false, but the assistant did have genuine affection for the old man.

"Did you . . ." Maurie trailed off. She wished she'd paid more attention to Fatima's hands. If Grandpere had changed his mind and decided to marry his assistant after all, she might need to punch Pascaline. But no, Fatima seemed frazzled, not triumphant. "I give up. What's the big surprise?"

"Your Uncle Fabrice has done the most wonderful thing!" Grandpere had never looked so smug or so triumphant. Maurie was used to him looking old, but today his wrinkles were laugh lines and he sat straighter than she'd ever remembered seeing him. Had the signs she'd taken for age been exhaustion before? But he had a fat mug of coffee in the armrest and from the rumpled creases on his normally pristine clothes, he hadn't been resting or slowing down enough to let even Fatima maintain her own normally polished appearance. "Whatever you were doing for the next couple years," Grandpere continued, "cancel it. I've got things for you to do."

"Years," Maurie repeated, mystified. Did he really not see that they were going to have to pass this off to someone else? Indonesia, if not Ecuador. The Bakweri were not going to be selling them a mountain even if Pascaline hadn't just offended Adamou. The Bakweri hadn't even let the Germans, British, or French have the mountain itself in the 1800s or 1900s. The colonizers had been stuck on the shoreline and inland.

"Five years, I think," he said, "but at least two and maybe quite a bit more if we do it right. We've got a contract with the space elevator."

Maurie blinked; oh, poor man. Nobody had told him about Pascaline and Adamou. "Ah, yes, Grandpere. Do you want me to go to Ecuador or Indonesia first to see about backup-site options?" Surely he knew that the Bakweri people held their mountain sacred, and the other mountains nearby weren't tall enough. Their chief would never allow a bunch of outsiders to build something like Uncle Chummy's launcher up the side of it.

"No, no, we're doing it here." Grandpere slapped his armrest and the other hand generally in the direction of the mountain peak. "Mount Fako will make a wonderful spaceport."

"Have you talked to the Bakweri chief about it?" she said. Fatima gave her a minute shake of her head, but Maurie had to know.

"Yes!" Grandpere fairly bounced in his seat. "At first, I'll admit"—he pressed his hands together in a gesture of prayer toward the roof of the van—"I thought Fabrice's risks might all be for nothing. We could buy rockets and set up a launch pad somewhere in the savannah maybe, but that wouldn't make anyone a reasonable profit even with supplying our own fuel. It has to make money with a good-sized margin." He knocked his fist on the armrest again in emphasis. "Remember that. Margins."

"But the mountain," Maurie said.

"Oh, yes." Grandpere looked out the window at it with a pleased expression of ownership. "I offered to buy it."

"They said no," Fatima pointed out. Of course they did. Maurie nodded.

Grandpere made a face, not losing his grin. "But they asked me to come back and talk again. We get to negotiate." He rubbed his hands together in pure delight.

In Buea, Endeley Adamou waited for the Sadous at the Bakweri compound gate in full priestly regalia. A light wind flapped the blue tarp held down with rocks on the neighbor's roof. As a temporary roof repair turned semipermanent, it worked. His uncle's place showed no such disrepair. Good concrete and brightly painted walls as befitted a chief and, like the neighbors, the house had a two-story wall surrounding it. That also worked.

The wide gate stood open, as it usually did. The sounds of the open-air market down the street drifted back. Some street performers played folk songs about the mountain, and he did his best to repress his grin.

His uncle, the chief, had been quite clear on that. "Stand there and let people see you being all spiritual, but don't smirk. Pretend everyone isn't looking at you. Pretend you wear that getup all the time. Nobody, well, hardly anyone, actually believes this shit. But it'll be a construction site. There'll be injuries, maybe even some deaths if the Sadous are sloppy, and I don't want people deciding Fako is against it." Then his uncle, who clearly saw nothing wrong with a chief wearing a face-splitting grin, had bounced with delight at the sound of an approaching car. "I'll be waiting in the office. You stand here and give directions. Don't explain anything. Don't answer anything about our plans or make any agreements."

Dibussi, the cook's boy, a tall eight with a fluff of untamable hair, hung back in the wall's shadow on the inside of the gate. Adamou obediently pulled on a bland expression, and when his uncle's back turned, winked at the boy, who clapped his hands over his mouth in delight.

The whole tribe had plenty to celebrate if this deal could be made. The press had more news reports about Kilimanjaro. The presidents of Tanzania and Kenya both had eloquent things to say about their support of TCG and how precious and unique Mount

Kilimanjaro was with many mentions of its great height and how right it was for the space elevator to be built there, as opposed to the many other sites now being put forward by nations who hoped to convince TCG to change construction plans.

"We have a mountain too," his uncle had pointed out when they discussed the news and weighed various options for work with the Sadous.

The speculative look on the chief's face had turned to a grin when he'd noticed Adamou's concern. "Don't worry. I understand that I'm negotiating with Sadou Moussa and not with TCG directly. I won't make him promise to shift the whole elevator construction itself to our side of the continent. But, we do have the mountain. And he can't do it without us."

The window of the chief's office cracked open, and Adamou heard him whistling the tune to the ballad about a chief who traded volcanic rocks for treasure. Adamou sent Dibussi scrambling off to close the window. The Sadous might not take the sentiment well if they recognized the song.

Pascaline hadn't answered his phone calls, but the Bakweri chief's call to Sadou Moussa had resulted in an immediately scheduled meeting. And then it had been delayed. The Sadou patriarch's aide had said, "Mr. Sadou is picking up a grandchild who will also attend." The woman on the phone had muttered the word *grandchild* like it was a curse, so he was certain it had to be Pascaline.

Adamou amused himself planning the things he could say about favors to the sharp-tongued beautiful woman. Or maybe he'd suggest that she owed him the favor now?

His priestly robe with its layers and thick embroidery

itched, but they were part of the role. People would feel better about the chances of the big project with somebody dressed up fancy as if the enormous pile of rock and dirt had some kind of essence that could be consulted. And his uncle was right about the sulfur stink being thoroughly embedded in the cloth. He imagined Pascaline's wrinkled nose. Would she say something or pretend not to notice?

Dibussi headed back at a run when the van pulled in through the gate. He signaled the boy to close the gate. No need to risk a bored kid scratching the important visitor's car while Mr. Sadou and the chief had their very important discussion.

The visitor's van had the battered rims and deep-threaded tires of a vehicle routinely used on unpaved roads, but its polish gleamed. He thought it suited the head of the Sadou family rather well.

The woman who emerged first was not Pascaline. Startlingly gorgeous and wearing white nurse's shoes, she ignored him and rushed around to the passenger to hold out an arm for Sadou Moussa as he stepped carefully out. The second woman who emerged with the patriarch was also not Pascaline. She was just as startling in a garish red snakeskin-print outfit with hair that had to be intentional but managed to look like messy braids following camping for two weeks. And then they shut the doors with no one else coming out.

"Ms. Maurie," the first woman said with a scowl at the second woman, "I will help Mr. Sadou."

Dibussi slid up next to Adamou to whisper identifications. The man was Moussa, the Sadou patriarch. The stunner was his aide Fatima, and the last was Sadou Maurie, one of his grandchildren.

"Fatima knows the way." Sadou Moussa cast a knowing look at Adamou, smiling in a way that made him wonder what else his uncle might have discussed. "We'll go speak with the chief. Why don't you and young Adamou here get to know each other?"

Sadou Maurie looked just as annoyed to be left out as he was.

"Is there some kind of festival going on?" Maurie nodded at his robes. "Something smells very, um, mountain."

"Volcano," he agreed. "Let's follow them in. I can't let my uncle take everything your grandfather's got or you'll have nothing left to build this launcher system with."

Maurie gaped at him. The expression would have meant a lot more on Pascaline's face. "Wait. Is Mount Fako a very active volcano? I mean, I know it's had some lava flows sometimes, but surely that's only semi-active or something like that, technically, right?"

He arched an eyebrow. The ashen pallor of her face didn't do her any favors even with the off-putting witch-lady aura of her aggressively red outfit taken into consideration.

"The correct term is 'active,' even when an eruption is predicted to be a long time off," Adamou said. "It has microtremors every now and then and we've got gas venting often. If you want me to predict the end of days, you've come to the wrong place."

"But we can't build on an unstable surface!" Maurie looked like she wanted to run after her grandfather and pull him out of the house.

Adamou blocked her path. "We can work with it."

"There's got to be another option." Maurie dodged to the left like she was going to skip around him but crumpled. She caught herself, using his shoulder to hold herself up.

"Dibussi!" Adamou called out to the cook's son, "Bring us a chair."

The kid dashed off, wide-eyed.

Maurie removed her hand from his shoulder. "I'm fine," she said.

"Um, sure." Something of Pascaline's backbone showed up in the milder cousin too, it appeared. "But I'm overheating a bit in this thing," he lied smoothly in return, "so why don't we both get into the air-conditioning?"

He convinced her to take his arm, and she leaned heavily enough on it that it was clear she wasn't fine.

As they reached the front entry, Dibussi almost bumped into them. He had a sturdy wood armchair over his head and was knocking it into the door sill. The kid returned the chair to its seating arrangement, and Adamou dispatched him for water.

Adamou's uncle, Sadou Moussa, and Fatima had the door to the chief's office closed, so he couldn't listen in to the more interesting discussions that must be starting.

Maurie's comm chose that moment to ring. She slipped the device out of her pocket and set it on the table. The still-locked screen showed a video feed closeup of Pascaline's face. "I know you're there, Maurie. Fatima messaged me when you got to the Endeleys and told me she'd replaced your comm with this one. Turn on at least the audio. I want to hear what Grandpere has to say."

Adamou tapped the answer button and angled it so Pascaline could see both of them.

"You and me both," Maurie said. "Grandpere went off separately to go trade the family fortune for a handful of magic beans."

"Magic rocks and far more than a handful," Adamou corrected. "Also, expect it to be a more long-term partnership than a simple sales transaction."

"Adamou?" Pascaline said.

Her expression was quite delightfully surprised, and he wanted to see her work through disbelief and finally recognition. But, he was also mid-argument with her cousin, Maurie, who might cause troubles for his uncle's arrangements with the Sadou family, if he let her doubts about the suitability of Fako as a launch ground go unanswered. So he ignored Pascaline.

"I'm not saying it would be a good idea to build the space elevator on Fako, but we've had the town of Buea halfway up the mountain for many centuries without ever having a *National Geographic*–worthy disaster. Our Fako is a friendly sort of volcano. And, as I understand it, this is a launcher, not a lander. If there's a micro-tremor in progress, we'll just delay the launch, right?"

Maurie accepted a glass of water from Dibussi and drank it. She looked at her comm. "You're the engineer. What do you think, Pascaline?"

"Why are you even here?" Pascaline had ignored Maurie's question, he noted. "And what have you done to my cousin? She was fully healthy when I put her on the plane."

Maurie did seem wan. She more lay in the chair than sat in it. She used both hands to drink. "Just trying to keep everyone from going broke," she said.

"Mountain people are hard for you flatlanders to handle," Adamou said.

"Yeah, right." Pascaline made a face at him. "You break my cousin, you're going to owe me double. Maurie." Pascaline snapped her fingers right next to the microphone so it made a nasty crackling noise through the speakers on their side. "Send him the files from Uncle Chummy. He owes me. They've been on Fako and the other mountains in the Mandaras range for centuries. Tribe, not family, remember. He'll have more engineers of all types than we do and some of them might even have specialized in something useful for the people who never left home."

Maurie did not move to give him anything, so Adamou helped himself to the data transfer with directions from Pascaline about which ones to read first.

He didn't get very far in before Maurie rallied enough to protest. "That's private and if you share it around, my family will take you to court."

Adamou shot a disbelieving look at Pascaline. She merely rolled her eyes at her cousin.

"It is private," he noticed. "But it's marked 'TCG internal-only' with nothing at all about it belonging on your devices."

Maurie shifted uncomfortably.

"Some people have trouble adjusting to reality," Pascaline said. "You're an Endeley, and if the Bakweri chief has you there while he works out the details with Grandpere, you are far more involved in running things than Great Aunt Mami chose to mention in her little summaries."

Adamou gave her a shrug and a smile.

"Fuck reality." Maurie emptied her water glass. Then saw little Dibussi hovering and waiting to refill it. She blushed. "Sorry, kid."

"I bring out the worst in her," Pascaline said, not without pride.

Dibussi, who'd heard worse, winked.

"Hmm." Adamou skimmed through more of the files. "Do you realize TCG's aerospace subcontractors have documents in here warrantying this as a tested design?" He looked at Maurie since she was the one in the room. "What are you worried about?"

She accepted more water from Dibussi and thanked him most politely. He grinned back and scampered off to refill the pitcher.

"I don't want to talk about it outside the family," she said.

"Well, to summarize," Pascaline ignored her cousin's glare and continued, "we've got a major deal here, that might not work at all if your tribe decides to pitch a fit about old-time religion, and it's pretty clear that the most successful guy the extended family has ever managed to get related to us has risked everything he's got to give us this one chance. And oh, by the way, you may not follow oil futures, because, you know, it's just some other little family's thing and not one that's related to the cashflow for your tribe's elite, but the taxes from oil and natural gas fund a massive portion of that thing we mere families like to call a government. So unless the tribal leaders want to step up and start covering elementary school construction and police officers' pension plans, and, oh yeah, roads and infrastructure"—Pascaline batted her eyes at him—"you might want to use that goofy outfit to convince a certain chief to let us use a slice of a really tall mountain to make some money. Because if this doesn't work, I'm betting my rich uncle has enough personal savings set aside to let my little family live at his French villa in relative comfort for the rest of our lives, because unlike some people, we Sadous don't have whole tribes to watch out for."

"Nice rant." Adamou saluted the comm screen. "But I give you about six months confined in a villa with your relatives before you steal the silver spoons and start hitchhiking to freedom. If, that is, someone else hasn't stolen everything not nailed down first and used it to buy some random toy. Your aunts and uncles don't have much of a reputation for frugality."

"Are you sure you aren't related to us?" Maurie muttered.

"I'm working on that," he said.

Pascaline's mouth tightened.

Excellent. Adamou beckoned Dibussi in and presented Maurie with a plate of Hadjara's chocolates. They had little hearts drawn in milk chocolate swirls.

Maurie ate one. Adamou held another up to the screen. "If you'd come yourself, you'd be having chocolate too."

"He's no relation, Maurie," Pascaline said. "And I expect you to save me some of those chocolates if they're any good."

"They're horrible," her cousin answered, reaching for another.

"I want two, no, make it four," Pascaline said. "And you can find out where he gets them."

"We aren't related yet," Adamou said, "but Pascaline and I are engaged."

He smiled serenely as Pascaline opened her mouth and shut it again without saying anything.

"If you'd like to be, that is." Amadou gave the comm screen a bow followed by a slow wink.

Maurie just ate a third chocolate rather than interrupt.

"Hey," Pascaline snapped, "I think some congratulations are in order."

"Congratulations." Maurie nodded at Pascaline, but not as though she really meant it. To Adamou she said, "Are you sure that's a good idea? You have met her in person?"

Adamou removed the chocolates.

"Fine." Maurie held up her hands. "I withdraw the question. It just isn't often my cousin gets along with, uh, real live people."

"There's nothing wrong with needing a little space," he said, surprised at the growl of anger in his voice. "And of course it's purely business. We have our own little spaceport to build. Nothing like the elevator itself, but things will go more smoothly if your family has a few more ties to the stronger tribes. I can make some introductions for you too, if you want."

"She doesn't need any introductions," Pascaline interrupted. "Maurie's an old soul loved by all but too busy saving humanity for any real relationships. And besides, Great Aunt Mami's plans won't work if she's running around dating half the tribal princes in the country."

"That is way overstating it," Maurie said. "I'm just sick of dating right now. Again, tell Great Aunt Mami that I'm sorry again about letting the comm get broken, and I need the name of that clinic she said was good for bush diseases, like, yesterday..."

"Ignore her," Pascaline said to Adamou. "According to our Great Aunt Mami, our Little Maurie has been possessed by a water spirit and hasn't come to terms with it yet."

Maurie's jaw dropped. Pascaline added more softly, "Great Aunt Mami's doctor called several times. It's hard to reach someone who shattered her comm. He's got some concerns, and yeah, I did get Fatima to make you an appointment."

Adamou considered Maurie's outfit more carefully. She did look like some of those posters of the made-up water spirit Mami-Wata, if you left off the snake familiar.

"I think she needs to hiss a bit more if she expects that to be interpreted as a cobra face." Adamou raised an eyebrow at Pascaline. "Are you sure about this? My divine connection thing has been going on quite a while and is mostly about making people feel better about doing the things they were going to do anyway. So it's an easy sell. What's up with trying to channel a folklore spirit best known for drowning kids who play at the beach without supervision?"

"He's a coastal boy," Pascaline said. "You have to make allowances. He doesn't understand what stream-beds mean to people living closer to the desert edge."

"It's only been some fever dreams," Maurie protested.

Adamou gave her a sharp look and almost missed Pascaline's eyes widening.

"Right. Adamou has mentioned that certain members of our family aren't particularly known for their frugality. Well, Great Aunt Mami and Grandpere have had some discussions."

"Which you influenced by being right next to Great Aunt while I was stuck by myself on an aircraft that was supposed to have you on it too," Maurie accused.

Pascaline shrugged. "Uncle Chummy did say he needed us to give this everything we've got. I'm giving it you."

Maurie ate another chocolate. There weren't going to be four left for Pascaline. At this rate there might not be any.

"Anyway, fiancé"—Pascaline nodded at Adamou—"our Maurie has been made project treasurer. All purchases and expenses will have to go through her and her secretaries. And everyone knows Mami-Wata showers down riches on her devotees and snatches them back away again like a draining flood if you don't keep perfectly true to her. So, no dates for Maurie."

Dibussi ran back into the room and flashed him a double thumbs-up. "They did it. They agreed." He vanished again just as quickly off to spread the news.

Part II

Dabare—the engineering know-how to plan, implement, and follow through on a complex project

(Samson Young's note: Depending on context, "dabare" is sometimes applied to someone who only thinks they have this "dabare" skillset, but the resulting engineered object—also referred to as a "dabare"—proves the individual does not/did not.)

Definition from "Local Terms" in
The TCG Kilimanjaro Handbook

CHAPTER THIRTEEN

EIGHTY-FIVE DAYS AND A LOT OF WORK LATER, Pascaline heard other less welcome news. Endeley Bouba and Grandpere's joint influence had jump-started geothermal plant construction. Cement deliveries were running late again, and they need more earthmovers for the launcher line where the maglev system would go. Meanwhile there was this party to attend and that nasty rumor.

"What do you mean Great Aunt Mami is in the hospital?" She wanted to turn around and glare at Angelique, but the woman slapped her hand and growled a threat to have her strapped into the beautician's chair if Pascaline didn't stop moving. The hairstyle had been good enough at least a half hour ago, but Angelique was having a bout of nerves over the Parisienne émigré who was doing Aunt Julienne's hair.

"Who is doing up Maurie these days?" Angelique whispered. "I'll never tell if you give me the name."

"How the hell should I know?" Pascaline groaned. "Maurie's been having doctor visits every other day, it seems like, and spending the rest of the time on the mountain. If I didn't know better I'd say she was interested in Endeley Adamou. Now, tell me about Great Aunt Mami."

"Ah." Angelique went silent, which made Pascaline suspicious. Angelique always had something to say or some tidbit she wanted to hear confirmed or denied. The beautician hummed to herself for a moment, and completely ignored Pascaline's order. She gave a curt nod. "You're all done then. Enjoy the party. No, not quite. Wait." Angelique gave a side of the headpiece a minute tug. The dress was some bamboo-fiber-blend fabric or other from a Yaoundé-based designer Great Aunt Mami had sponsored. It itched. But it also flared and curved and held up quite flatteringly while repelling wine stains. The headpiece Angelique finished pinning in place complemented it.

"Angelique," Pascaline said. "Tell. Me. About. My. Great. Aunt."

"Oh," Angelique fluttered her fingers in apology. "She's checked into that nice clinic villa. You know the one with the really good spa?"

Pascaline did know the one. "Yeah, and with the hospice wing where you get to have your bed rolled out onto the veranda to die listening to the rainforest birds."

"Oh, well." Angelique flapped her hands in denial. "I doubt it's come to that. Though our Ms. Mami is getting on in years, and the spirits don't tend to let their blessed ones linger once they've moved on."

"What?" Pascaline shook her head which made Angelique hiss and flutter around checking the hair-style for any damage the extreme motion might have caused. "Great Aunt Mami is not allowed to die."

"Of course not," Angelique said soothingly as if the two of them would have any say in the matter. "But you might send her some flowers. It'd be the nice thing to do." Then she reconsidered. "Never mind. Forget I said anything. I'll just call Maurie."

Pascaline clenched her teeth and left for the party.

"I could be nice if I wanted to be." Pascaline scowled at her reflection in the mirrored elevator doors. There was nothing she could do for her great aunt. Great Aunt Mami hated cut flowers. Why did nobody else know that? The details of the elevator distracted. Beauty and elegance were blended seamlessly with functionality. One side was glass instead of mirror and a screen behind the transparent wall displayed a waist-height railing and the Douala skyline. It gave the rider the impression of standing in a lush rooftop garden instead of a tight elevator. Whoever had done the design work on this high-rise hotel complex should be hired away quickly by someone foreign who was willing to pay them a tremendous salary. But the sorts who had the means to offer that would probably never visit this hotel. Reality frequently sucked like that.

And yet, her reality was just going so smoothly now. Pascaline fought with the corners of her mouth. They kept wanting to twitch up into the most ridiculous grin. It was Adamou's fault.

Uncle Benoit had let slip that there was to be an engagement announced today. She ought to be mad about it; Adamou hadn't talked with her about formally announcing on behalf of the two families yet. Maurie knew and that kid Dibussi knew that she and Adamou had been considering wedding dates, but neither one had spilled. Maurie seemed to expect everything to fall apart, and Dibussi didn't consider it significant.

Also in the original deal Adamou owed her a favor which he hadn't exactly delivered. Sure, he'd given her use of a very nice mountainside, but she thought she could negotiate for more. And Maurie was right it might all still fall apart. But Adamou was getting more appealing over time instead of less, so perhaps she'd go ahead and see what it was like to be engaged for a while.

He spent a ton of time up on his mountaintop tweaking new sensor designs and mathematical prediction software. His large extended family liked to bother him about that and she was very skilled at frustrating interlopers enough that they quit their stupid shit. The first time she'd done it he'd been startled. The second time amazed. The fourth and fifth time his mouth had gone all soft, and he'd asked if she'd like to elope before someone else discovered her. It hadn't sounded like he was joking. Adamou sounded like he was falling in love. With her.

She might need to marry the man. He could always divorce her later, but he seemed to genuinely like her. For now anyway. The constant suggestions from her side of the family that Maurie would be the perfect bride for Adamou were fading into the background of the family's usual casual disdain for her.

Half the family had turned out today for this celebration feast. It was part corporate merger, part debutant ball, and all circus, but she had a certain image to maintain. Everyone expected her trademark scowl and a liberal smattering of sharp remarks. If she walked out of the elevator all gooey, Adamou would get far too much credit, and her new extended family would be in for far too much of a shock when her normal personality came back out. Far better to start out with a properly cranky attitude.

Besides, Adamou wasn't even here to enjoy her family's shock if she did come out smiling and chose to play the demure blushing bride. He had some mountaintop tradition to engage in. That sneaky Bakweri chief had made it sound like a deeply religious event involving dawn ceremonies in the upper mists and a humble request that the mountain accept the even more humble bridegroom's choice of bride and bless the tribe for another generation. Pascaline rather thought refurbishing sensors would be more useful than nebulous blessings. His accuracy for the timing of microtremors needed improvement. Adamou's past research had focused on when the major quakes and lava flows might happen. He'd gotten pretty good at issuing warnings and keeping tourists safe. He needed to do even better. Maurie now believed it would all work out somehow. Pascaline had spent less time with him going over the numbers, but she'd looked at the data. And she'd sent Uncle Chummy some messages to get a few math boffins some supercomputer time to check Adamou's work. Adamou claimed he already had a couple math boffins at the University of Yaoundé. She'd checked on the names. Both female and bookishly attractive, naturally. With an inner sigh, Pascaline mentioned their past assistance to Uncle Chummy and suggested they might only need the simulator time and not the extra nerds.

Unfortunately for Adamou, Pascaline had relatives who couldn't keep their mouths shut about the mountaintop celebration. Uncle Benoit even got himself invited somehow. He wasn't exactly the mountaineering type, but he did like a good party. Uncle Benoit had used words like *wildest bachelor party ever* and *so much partying to do that no one goes to sleep before dawn for three straight days*. There seemed to be a competition among the Bakweri tribe's homebrewers for which concoction provided the most ceremonial libations on the mountaintop—after passing through various celebrants' livers of course.

Adamou's latest messages on his comm implied he'd left the party going at one of the lodges partway up the mountain and skipped out to check on the launcher-route build crews. Such a useful thing to do it was hard to complain about it. And he wasn't even lying because his comm had shown a location track exactly matching his words.

It did remain that he wasn't *here*. Off up on his mountain working with the crews installing side roads next to the planned track line, he got to do useful things while she had the job of looking pretty. The unfairness helped set her face back into a more normal position. She looked for something else to think irritated thoughts at. Her mind skipped straight past Great Aunt Mami's hospitalization and Maurie's concerning recurrent health troubles. She needed anger, not fear.

The braids just over her left ear itched. Pascaline stood a bit straighter, relaxed her forehead, and the feeling vanished. Angelique, the overly competent hairdresser, ought be doing something else like working microminiature repairs. The glare returned and with it her posture slumped a bit, restoring the itch. A good scratch would fix it, but she couldn't mess with the braided art piece her head had become while looking in the mirror.

Pulling on it to loosen one or two loops called for a club bathroom with appropriately dim lighting. Destroying art in favor of comfort should only be done surrounded by drunks and where even the drunks couldn't see very well. These bright lights with two rich families competing to outdo each other while throwing a block party was not that place. The glamour lights strung inexplicably in a ring around the top of the hotel elevator threatened similarly bright lighting in the event spaces themselves. Pascaline kept her nails out of her hair.

The doors opened to a hallway buzzing with hotel staff and double doors across the way leading into a frigidly air-conditioned event space. Soft music and a babble of voices welcomed her in. Again, she banished a smile trying to flicker across her face.

Far too many chandeliers hung from the ceiling spilling brightness all over the room. Someone had used sea glass and thousands of tiny electric diodes to make fountains of light. The crowd of guests met the challenge with brilliant formal outfits in designs from Grandpere's pricey robes in handwoven cotton to the nouveau designs on his assistant. The woman's clothing consisted of ribbons seamed together to create a light breathable mesh with strategically placed solid patches. It was a clothing idea that had been done before, but on a certain sculpted body type it looked fantastic. So it would probably be cycled back into high fashion every thirty years or so.

"Good evening, Ms. Pascaline." The assistant bobbed a greeting at her. Her hair didn't look painful. She'd had it fluffed out gently and trimmed in a soft dark halo. The contrast of normal hair with wild dress looked good on her.

"I want to steal your hair," Pascaline said in passing and searched the room.

She spotted Uncle Jacques off in the corner. She needed to give him a piece of her mind about his concrete-delivery delays. WuroMahobe needed to be sending them a steady stream of shipments with nobody else getting priority. The foremen at the plant would do what she wanted, but Uncle Jacques' involvement could give her someone anticipating her needs instead of just complying with orders. Jacques, as plant manager, ought to be making sure there were no delays in supporting Grandpere's top project.

A fluff of hair moved in between her and the plant manager. Pascaline looked back down to see Grandpere's assistant brighten and smile widely.

"Thank you, Ms. Pascaline! I wanted something like your style, but I can't afford Angelique." The woman shivered with excitement and beamed goodwill. Also, her breasts jiggled out of sync with the woman's actual motion. It was mildly disturbing to Pascaline, but attracted all the male attention in the area.

Did the ribbon dress do that or was it something else? Oh. This was Fatima, right. She was the one who liked all the body modifications. So, no, it wasn't likely to be caused by any unusual tensile properties of a new fabric material. Standard old breast augmentation with some sort of cutting-edge implants explained it. Pascaline mentally dismissed the woman.

Uncle Benoit, an even less interesting person, made eye contact and headed her way. He likely wanted something she wouldn't enjoy hearing. The aide saw him coming too.

"Again, thank you so much for the compliment." The woman snatched at and pumped Pascaline's hand. "And congratulations on arranging the engagement! Even if it is only Ms. Maurie, the Bakweri should be so proud to marry a Sadou!"

Pascaline rolled her eyes. She didn't feel like explaining to another person that Maurie and Adamou were not interested in each other. Well, there'd be some toasting later and everyone would be set straight at once. The Bakweri were eager to have another connection with Great Aunt Mami and with Uncle Chummy. The powerful energy company family wasn't, or at least wasn't anymore, and even Grandpere knew it. She'd have thought his assistant would have the real details of the engagement, but self-denial in family staff wasn't unheard of.

Fatima nodded her farewell and swished away, trailing a flurry of ribbons. She'd chosen to ignore Pascaline's eye roll or might not have even seen it as the woman's head had bobbed back and forth as if trying to count all the male glances that turned her way as she moved. Some people didn't seem capable of being properly offended no matter what Pascaline did.

She shook her head and noticed Uncle Benoit's face among the many turning to track Fatima. He'd made it back from Adamou's party in time for this one. Was Adamou here? No. Another brief check on her comm showed him still up on the mountain. She shoved the comm back into her clutch.

Pascaline ducked behind the pile of fruit on the buffet table and pushed past a gaggle of servers working to refill it. She didn't care to chat with Uncle Benoit. He did too good of a job souring her mood for real, and she didn't want to have her engagement party spoiled quite so soon in the evening.

The catering staff bumped into each other to make room for her, apologized, and moved out of her way as she moved smoothly down the side of the room partially hidden by the displays of food. Serving as a second line of camouflage for her, the partygoers clumped along the other side of the tables intent on filling their plates.

"Sadou Maurie and Endeley Adamou," one guest said to another, "I never thought either one would settle down. Adamou, we love him of course, but he can get downright grumpy when torn away from his studies, and what woman would be happy to take second place to a mountain?"

Pascaline gritted her teeth. People had no respect. Adamou loved his work. As if any true partner would want to take a passion that defined a person and demand the work be abandoned. That wasn't love; it was slavery. Adamou wanted to give her a spaceport. On his mountain.

She did like Maurie, most of the time. But this was getting ridiculous.

"Our Maurie is so sweet." Pascaline caught Aunt Fatime chatting with a young Bakweri mother. "Why let me tell you about when she was just ten years old and all the boys at the schoolhouse brought her flowers," Aunt Fatime trotted out one of the favorite family stories.

Pascaline paused to check her comm. Adamou was definitely still on the mountain. Maurie was here...

No. She zoomed in the map. Maurie was at Great Aunt Mami's clinic.

Near the end of the two tables piled with savory delights Pascaline found the voice she'd been aiming for.

"Oh, uh, how am I related?" Uncle Jacques shifted uneasily back and forth on his feet as the pair of partygoers interrogating him looked on with less than tolerant expressions. One produced an image of the Sadou family tree on the comm removed from her purse with a miniature of Maurie's face on the bottom and the rest of the family connected by an array of spokes.

"It's, um, a somewhat distant connection," Uncle Jacques said.

"Not really," Pascaline said, deciding to rescue him. She gave the crowds a slow turn to ensure she had their attention. They knew who she was. "This is my Uncle Jacques."

Pascaline's favorite plant manager looked over with an expression of deep gratitude, but when he saw which relative had claimed him, confusion and wariness warred with thankfulness and won.

She favored the crowd with a flat smile and hit them with the truth. "My Uncle Jacques is married to the former second wife of my deceased dad's brother. He has accepted the Sadou name for business. My dad's brother later remarried and became the father of Sadou Maurie who you have at the bottom of that silly family tree app."

She favored him with an almost real smile, and the audience with a more predatory one. The two with the family tree slipped back into the crowd rather than engage with her. Pascaline rather doubted they were up to locking wits with her if their idea of a good time was sniffing around an engagement party looking for possible gate-crashers.

Uncle Jacques turned to another more mature woman Pascaline didn't recognize, likely an extended family relative on Adamou's side or a member of the broader Bakweri tribe with some clout. "I never did catch those ladies' names," he said, almost apologetic.

"No relation to our side that I'm aware of," the woman replied.

Pascaline snorted a suppressed laugh. She took it back. Only the best party-crashers made a game of outing other party-crashers. But she did have work to do and needed Uncle Jacques. She restored her scowl.

"Uncle Jacques—" Pascaline claimed his arm and pulled him away from the Bakweri relation who merely murmured a polite "Congratulations on fleeing another engagement, Ms. Pascaline," and let her have the man.

Pascaline gave the woman's back an exasperated glare.

"Ms. Pascaline," Uncle Jacques said, "before those rude people interrupted, I was having a conversation with Adamou's aunt. Remarkable woman. I was only halfway through explaining the mix proportions for our grades of cement powder."

"I'm sure she can ask her comm to give her the rest of the details if she really needs to know," she assured him. "But the main construction project on Bakweri property right now won't be having any more supply back-order issues from your plant again, now will it?"

"Ms. Pascaline, I'm sure you've misunderstood." The man looked around for someone else to rescue him. "This really isn't the time or the place?" he suggested.

"It's a perfect time. Thank you for your assurances. It means a lot to my fiancé's family to know that our family is fully behind supporting this very lucrative joint project." Pascaline lifted an eyebrow at him and dared him to disagree.

"There are other back orders," he pleaded. "And, who? You have a fiancé?"

"Endeley Adamou, of course." Pascaline patted his hand. "I'll speak with Grandpere on your behalf and make sure you get support in issuing rebates for those willing to take delayed shipments and support to increase overtime budgets so you can run the plant at top production for the duration."

"Um, I don't think so." Jacques' forehead wrinkled. "And I'm not sure he's going to be the person with the authority to make those calls for long."

"You all agreed on six months," Pascaline reminded him.

"Well, some time has been passing since then," he said. Her quasi step uncle looked around at the crowd in an uneasy way that drew the attention of several Endeley cousins and then leaned in way too close to whisper, "The quarterly trust payments were low again."

"So?" She didn't move back.

"They are saying this launcher thing has cash in the general fund. So we just replace him; the trust accounts can be filled back up." He raised his eyebrows and waggled them.

"It's not," Pascaline lied. "It's an escrowed account with funds disbursement tied to project-completion milestones." Well, that part wasn't a complete lie. Additional very large payments would be made at major milestones. But how the spending was allocated for the smaller project-completion points was entirely at Sadou discretion. "And Maurie won't be able to sweet-talk the TCG into paying early if there's even a whiff of the money going elsewhere. The concrete, Uncle Jacques. Get us the raw materials we need."

"Ah," Uncle Jacques nodded, his face still concerned. "I guess you can make it look like you are trying and get a few more of the payments before it becomes obvious that it won't work. It'll be hard on Maurie, though, when she has to tell her in-laws."

"Maurie isn't . . . Oh, never mind," Pascaline said.

Fatima sailed around the buffet tables and interrupted. "No business at the party, please," she chirped. "Chief Endeley sent me. They can't find Maurie anywhere and wondered if you could stand in for the announcement of her engagement to Adamou."

Uncle Jacques tilted his head peering around. "But Adamou's not here either. How can they announce the new couple when neither one showed up?"

Pascaline's face froze. She had initially rejected Adamou's suit and told the family so, but later the two of them had . . . Her eyes narrowed. *Family!* Uncle Jacques stepped neatly out of her way. Fatima squared her shoulders and looped an arm through Pascaline's elbow with a determined expression, ready to drag her across the room if she had to.

Grandpere and Chief Endeley stood on a little dais in the center of the room with the final pages of a lengthy contract in front of them. They had glasses charged and ready for toasts on a tray in a waiting server's hands at their elbows.

"If he thinks he prefers Maurie, you're better off

without him," Fatima said. "I had thought he was almost good enough for you. Of course that Maurie would try to steal him. If I'd known, I would've... I don't know, I would've something."

Pascaline was surprised enough at this unexpected support that she let the young aide lead her. "You do realize the rest of this crowd disagrees with you."

Fatima sniffed. "Only the family. And not even all of them. The marry-ins generally know better. And of course all the staff supports you. We can't afford to disbelieve our own eyes." She closed her perfectly colored lips tightly as a young Bakweri boy came scampering over.

Dibussi gave Pascaline an oblivious smile. The Endeley chief nodded at Uncle Jacques who'd trailed along after them. Close enough to hear, Pascaline realized, and he'd not chosen to disagree with a single word of Fatima's diatribe.

Endeley Bouba turned away from Grandpere and looked at Pascaline like a man might examine a particularly dirty puppy following a grandchild home. That reaction felt more like normal and gave Pascaline a bit of her own balance back. Dibussi trailed the chief with a platter-sized plate of party foods. "Hard at work organizing family business, I see." Chief Bouba favored both Pascaline and Uncle Jacques with a half bow and half nod greeting. "Finally, we get a classically trained engineer in the extended family. And just in time with this new venture."

Uncle Jacques opened his mouth as if to say something, but he decided to fill it with a bite from Dibussi's tray instead.

The chief shook Uncle Jacques' hand warmly and

encouraged him to take something more from Dibussi's tray. "The nieces got together and made some of their favorites. With so many options already on the buffet, they've bribed this little scamp with batches of his own to wander the room stuffing everyone with their creations. Skip the ones with the eggroll wraps," he advised. "It's an Indo-Congolese fusion recipe, and I don't think the fish paste and bitter-greens filling is going to win our budding chefs any awards." He looked at her and shook his head. "I still can't believe you turned down our Adamou."

"No, she didn't," Dibussi said. "They're engaged."

"What?" Grandpere said.

"What?" Chief Bouba repeated.

Pascaline looked at the two men. So, Adamou hadn't rejected her. This was just family being family again. She reached for a chocolate truffle, and Dibussi turned the tray to offer the fried plantains instead. She gave him a narrow-eyed stare, and he sheepishly turned the tray back to allow her access to the chocolates. Endeley Bouba's focus on her intensified.

"You don't have any engineers in the whole tribe?" she asked.

The Bakweri chief laughed. "Oh, we have some, but nobody else studied aerospace or space systems engineering, much less a double major in the two! And a perfect grade point average on top of all that."

"Grandpere has been bragging on you," Fatima whispered. "Congratulations on your engagement. He's still not good enough for you."

Uncle Jacques glanced at Pascaline, with a worried expression. "You'd have made the business arrangement for use of the mountain for the launcher construction in any case, though," he said. "It isn't as if you couldn't hire out for whatever training was needed, right?"

The chief laughed. "Of course not. Not if it was Adamou with Maurie either." He shook his head. "I can't believe I misunderstood which grandchild. Well, never mind all that." He beamed at Pascaline. "Aerospace types are almost impossible to hire these days. Anyone good has already moved East. Everyone except family. You are such a treasure. I hope you don't mind, we had already included a proviso in the contract that you'll be lead technical manager over the project as a whole and have hands-on involvement in the construction. Hired hands are all very well, but some things need a family member involved to make sure they go smoothly."

"There's our honored guest; Mr. Endeley Bouba, a pleasure to finally meet you," Uncle Benoit invited himself into the conversation as well. He eyed Dibussi's tray but refrained from taking anything.

With a deep nod to the Bakweri chief, he said, "I'm Benoit, one of dear Pascaline's uncles on the Sadou side, a pleasure. I am curious about the terms of that agreement. I'm the family's board member for the geothermal power plants which will be supplying power for the launches, at least initially. You'll find I have more experience than our Pascaline." He smiled as if there were no insult implied.

Grandpere chortled derisively. "Live long enough and you'll have more experience than anyone."

Chief Endeley put an arm around Grandpere's shoulders and joined him in the chuckle. "It hardly matters when it doesn't come with the right set of core knowledge. Tell me this, my friend, how many launch vehicles

did you study while getting your fine arts degree major-
ing in, what was it, the intersection of tourism and folk
art with a concentration in alcohol poisoning?"

Uncle Jacques choked on his next bite, and Uncle
Benoit shot him a scowl.

"The launcher project would be fine independent of
me," Pascaline attempted to rescue herself. A piece of
her heart still felt frozen. She'd nearly believed that
Adamou had rejected her. Could she stand to be on
the same mountain as him if he had intended to dump
her and was only faking for the purpose of building
a spaceport? Fuck it, yes, she could. She would. But
all determination aside, she wasn't sure she was really
capable of managing all of this. A perfect grade point
average for only one semester of an undergrad degree
meant nothing at all. And, it seemed someone had
failed to mention to the Bakweri chief that she'd
never completed that degree when a shortage in family
finances lined up disastrously with her tuition needs.
The fine college in question had objected to the idea
of providing financial aid to a foreign national from a
family with a claimed net worth in the multimillions.

"It seems so." Uncle Benoit gave her the tiniest
smile. He knew she had no completed degree. "Don't
disappoint the chief, Miss Engineer." Pascaline would've
liked to gut her uncle.

Chief Bouba gave another laugh and patted Uncle
Benoit on the back. "Don't worry, there'll be plenty of
work for us old men too. Once this thing is in operation, the international visitors are sure to be arriving
in hordes, both to see the spectacle and to shepherd
their valuable payloads. You might even want to get
your fine arts galleria network busy carving faux ivory

into launch craft miniatures and rebranding some night clubs for a volcanic spaceport theme."

"I might," Uncle Benoit agreed with a tone that implied he'd do nothing of the sort.

The chief raised his eyebrows at Pascaline. "Do you generally receive so little support from your extended family? I've a mind to use that ninety-day annulment clause on our land-use agreement if you aren't prepared to step up into the design role."

Uncle Benoit froze. "My understanding is that many of the launcher project materials had already been ordered."

"I'm sure they have," the chief agreed. "And the TCG contract might have been arranged by one of your own, but it did contain their standard clauses financially separating the larger company from any obligations to pay bills you incur while servicing their contract. That starter capital is something of an advance against the payments for payload deliveries. Provided, of course, you manage to make those deliveries. It might be a tiny bit more difficult to do so, if you have to find a much, much longer stretch of flat land for your launcher... And you'd need still more cash to buy the properties in the high-risk crash zone. Let's see. Add in the extra charges for transporting the payloads themselves inland from our convenient port system... You might really miss Mount Fako."

"None of that will be an issue," Grandpere informed the Endeley patriarch. "This is family work under family management like any other plant or project. Pascaline will pursue her doctoral studies some other time."

Uncle Benoit suppressed a laugh. Her college disaster hadn't been near the secret from everyone she thought it was. The contempt in the curl of Uncle Benoit's lip and the concern radiating from Uncle Jacques announced quite clearly that these men, at least, were well aware that she was in no graduate program whatever. Something about Uncle Benoit's expression and the way he looked at Grandpere as if the man were completely senile instead of woefully misinformed made Pascaline want to break him.

So what if this would be learning on the job at frantic pace with far too much riding on it? So what if Adamou might dump her any day? She'd been abandoned by closer relatives before. Screw him and his mountain. She'd build this spaceport, and Adamou'd have to hear the earsplitting booms of her launches all day every day for years. If he really wanted Maurie and not her, he was in for a rude shock. Maurie was not someone who'd appreciate his love for the mountain.

"Do you really think you can handle engineering management for a space launch construction project, Pascaline?" Uncle Benoit asked with that same sickly sweet smile.

You expect me to scuttle this project right now, don't you, Uncle? Chief Bouba expects us to try to build it no matter what. But if we have no mountain, we could do no building at all. All I've got to do is admit my non-degreed status and Uncle Benoit wins.

Instead of saying "I can't do it," instead of informing the Bakweri chief that her Grandpere had allowed the family to fail its younger generation in so many important ways over the years that she'd been kicked out of her prestigious undergrad program for nonpayment of tuition and fees, instead of feeding Uncle Benoit exactly the line he expected, she said: "Yep."

His jaw dropped, and it was all worth it.

Pascaline turned on her heel and walked out. The party could continue without her. She needed staff. Lots of very good staff. Lies like this one required it.

On her way out her comm chimed with a message from Adamou. *"My queen, everything okay?"*

"It's fine," she sent back, and surprising even herself, she meant it. Her heart was calloused enough that she could take this. She sent a few details from the party including the news of his engagement to Maurie.

He replied with a pleasant flurry of curses directed at his own family, her family, and pleas for forgiveness.

Oh. Her heart lifted. He hadn't meant to abandon her. A mist clouded her vision.

But, she did not tell him about her fake education.

Adamou sent a half dozen more messages not believing that "fine" could actually be "fine," and she was about to turn the comm off to stop the new message beeps when she saw one come in from Maurie.

"Great Aunt taking turn for worst. At clinic. Please come."

CHAPTER FOURTEEN

"**I** NEED YOUR ATTENTION HERE, PLEASE," THE LAND surveyor said and from his tone he intended none of the politeness his words implied. The middle-aged man with the perpetual annoyed expression gazed around a breathtaking vista of ocean, cultivated palm oil groves, mountainside wilds, and the higher frost-covered peak as if it were all no better than a crumbling parking lot.

Adamou had shed his ceremonial robes for more construction-area-appropriate attire, and he regretted it. If he hadn't matched the surveyor's rough pants and a cotton shirt, the man might be speaking with more respect or at least more... something. Adamou had a pullover in the car trunk for when they got further up the mountain and would need it. But it was the same brand of mountaineering gear as the one this man had tied around his waist. Adamou suppressed an urge to strangle the surveyor with it. The problem with the man's work wasn't respect exactly. It was that Adamou wasn't confident in the accuracy of the report, and every time he asked a question the man got surlier.

The surveyor lifted up a hand to beckon Maurie over. She ignored him to give the ocean a long stare. She stood statue-still in a fluttering red dress with a mass of gold and charcoal-black hair beads. They clattered like old bones when she finally turned her head.

"The spirits are not at rest here," she said.

The surveyor blinked and looked to Adamou.

"This doesn't look like the path the engineers recommended," Adamou said. He really wished Pascaline were here. The great aunt was important and all, but she'd gotten through that recent worrying spell. Pascaline could stop visiting her so much and get her butt up to the mountain. She was supposed to be the top technical expert to reign over all these specialists who kept trying to rearrange their component parts without consideration for how badly it would throw off their portion's connection to the larger project.

"Civil engineers," the surveyor snorted. "I bet they never even looked at the land. If you'd gone with the original route, it would cut through acres more of your uncle's palm plantations."

"While this cuts more wilds to bleed the countryside," Maurie said with a dreamy distracted tone. "Sacred bushlands beloved of the ancestor spirits who fought to hold this mountain when they lived."

"Uh, what?" The surveyor shook his head and focused on Adamou. "I'm sure you understand not wanting to give up good production land, not to mention the zebra wood groves. I managed to entirely avoid them with this change. Can't even see them from here. You're welcome for that. That artisan timber is not to be wasted for an odd rail system to nowhere that, let's be clear here, is probably not ever going to be finished."

"We will complete the project," Adamou said with a stiffness that was becoming way too necessary lately. Who the hell had convinced so many of their new subcontractors that they weren't serious about the project?

"Of course." The man made a gesture brushing aside his earlier comment. "You must get as many of the Objective Based Targets completed on or before schedule to cash out the payments and claim maximum bonuses. That was made clear to all of us when Benoit visited for his little encouragement talk. Thank him for that wine, by the way. I'm usually more of a beer man, but that ice wine from his Austrian villa? A very tasty vintage with quite the kick to it on the way down."

"Ashes. All are ashes," Maurie muttered.

The surveyor shifted away from her.

"I want the originally chosen site surveyed, not this random other path," Adamou said, gesturing vaguely off to the north where he thought the path was supposed to be.

"Bad idea," the surveyor said.

"It's not your choice." Adamou wasn't sure how he'd ended up losing this argument that he shouldn't have to be even having. He needed to be firm now to take advantage of the man's wariness of Maurie to press for what seemed to be the only sane choice. He didn't actually know if this alternate path would work or not, but he strongly suspected that the answer was not. And besides, the surveyor was supposed to be marking on the land the path selected on the map, not picking some other route and changing the map.

The growl of wheels on gravel announced a new vehicle arriving, and Adamou hoped Pascaline would be in it. They desperately needed their technical lead on hand for this nonsense to end.

"Benoit will explain it all to you," the surveyor said, also looking toward the car as if he expected the answers to come from its passenger as well.

"Benoit who?" Adamou said, exasperated. He knew a half dozen Benoits. None of them worked on the project.

Finally, the surveyor had the grace to look confused.

Pascaline pulled to a stop next to them in an open four-wheel-drive vehicle and hooked a finger at the three of them. "Uncle Benoit," she said, "is an interfering busybody without hiring authority. The surveyor we actually are paying is at the real site. See you there." She put the car in gear again.

"This is absurd!" The surveyor threw his notes on the ground and stormed off. His vehicle tore down the road after Pascaline's.

"I think we're still going to have to pay him," Adamou said. "Did you ever get that guy's name?"

Maurie shrugged. "No idea. My head is thumping, and I'm seeing auroras over everything again like it's all covered with shiny specks of gold or something."

"Uh, is that an expected side effect? Pascaline said you'd been sick. Of course she also said you always know everyone's names."

"Maybe. No. I know a lot of names, but usually people have them embroidered on their shirts, and when I can see straight, I can read." Maurie shook her head. "You better drive."

"Tell me about Benoit, and I will," he said, engaging the autodrive. He kept one hand on the wheel and foot over the brake, in case the system glitched on the rough roadway.

Maurie grunted. She did not explain anything. For several minutes Maurie pressed buttons on the vehicle's console seemingly at random, and then leaned back into her seat defeated. "It insists on staying audio-locked to your comm. Do you have Bible audio files? I prefer Old Testament, but anything helps. I'm running out of vaguely religious out-of-context things to murmur, and everything is riding on me playing spirit woman properly."

He gave her one lifted eyebrow and returned his focus to the road in time to brake for a two-foot-long snake. It slithered the rest of the way across the dirt track, and he let the autodrive continue on.

"You saw that? Wait, what did you see?" she said.

"There was a snake on the road."

"Oh, good," she said. "These meds are working."

Adamou shrugged. "We get a lot of snakes on new roads or whatever we want to call this particular raw path that we didn't need to spend time and effort—not to mention money—on clearing because it isn't even the right part of the mountain slope. I don't run over animals if I can help it. I don't care if it was too small to damage the undercarriage."

"Huh," Maurie said. "So that's why Pascaline likes you so much. You're a softie for poisonous creatures, but for humans wasting resources, you turn pricklier than a cactus. Good fit for my cousin."

"Pascaline would be delighted for the reincarnation of Saint Patrick to cast out all the snakes from Africa," Adamou said. "She's not a fan of poisonous creatures."

Maurie waved away his objections. "Eh. It's complicated. She respects them." She pointed at a bare patch of land ahead. "Turn here. Like I said, Benoit is our uncle. One of Sadou Moussa's younger half-sisters was his mom. He's a fairly decent guy most of the time. Not addicted to anything. He doesn't torture puppies. He probably even would still be married to his first wife if she hadn't died of cancer a decade ago."

"I'm waiting for the but," Adamou said, turning the vehicle.

"He likes to host and be hosted. Charities and art. He's endowed a few museums even. His life is about spending money."

"And the Sadou fortunes have been shrinking for much of his lifetime, I'm guessing?"

"Yeah." Maurie shrugged. "He and the others would've had to just learn to do with less eventually, but . . ."

"Your other uncle landed this project. So why's Benoit getting in the way?"

"The heirs, as they see themselves, the ones in Uncle Benoit's generation believe Grandpere has mismanaged the family oil trust. It's a sticky situation. Our family adopted some Western ideas for family money management, and it's not working out so well. Grandpere controls the trust now, but Uncle Benoit almost took control." She waved a hand to indicate a lot of other details and maybe some water under the bridge. "It's been more than six months since the last board meeting. So they could call another vote, but I think people must have realized it was stupid. I mean, the original idea wasn't. When they figured that if they cut off the more distant members . . ."

"Oh, fucking hell," Adamou said.

"Yeah. They figure the money would last longer. And they aren't entirely wrong," Maurie said. "But it'd be pretty misguided under the current situation to cut out Uncle Chummy."

"Wait, who?"

"Tchami Fabrice."

"I know who Tchami Fabrice is," Adamou said. "Everyone knows of him. They were going to cut him off?"

"Yeah, well. He doesn't use the Sadou name, which makes it easier for the heirs to see him as not really one of them. And also Uncle Tchami Fabrice has just accepted foreigners' trouble with pronunciation and been going by Chummy for his working life, which further makes him seem like not really one of us. He's told us to call him 'Chummy' too, because it confuses the TCGers if we use his real name. That, and we aren't to call him 'Uncle' either, because it looks bad to the Westerners."

"The launcher deal was a little sly gift for the family, was it?" Adamou said.

Maurie lifted her eyebrows. "Do you really have to ask?"

"What else don't I know?"

"Probably a lot. But the biggest thing is that my aunts and uncles can drain the seed capital for this launcher before we get even the proper track path cleared if we don't find a way to secure the bank account."

Adamou blinked.

"No. You can't get out of the agreement now. Great Aunt Mami called a lawyer in and went over it line by line with me in her hospital room."

"Why's she in the hospital?" Adamou said.

"Long-term health troubles related to snake bite

and the antivenom overdose. Don't be nosy," Maurie said and then she added more without him having to ask. "She gets these flares sometimes. She'll be okay. Probably. Anyway, her lawyers agree that you Endeleys are stuck with us and TCG might even be able to sue your family too if they can prove we didn't make a proper effort to build this launcher."

Adamou hissed his breath between his teeth.

"Who has access to the funds now?"

"Early on, Great Aunt Mami got through to Uncle Chummy and got it changed from a blanket 'Any Sadou of Sadou Corporation' authorization to just her."

"It's solved then," Adamou said.

"No." Maurie shook her head. "Great Aunt has been not well. Very not well. She signed over authority to Pascaline and me jointly. I've been avoiding the family and so has Pascaline. We also stay away from each other, because we have to both sign at once in person at the bank to release funds, and, well, family can be very convincing."

Adamou pressed his lips into a flat line. "You need someone else added to the account. Someone who you can blame for the refusal and not be unwelcome among your own kin after Sadou Moussa passes on. You need me. And that's why you're telling me. Not because you think Endeley lawyers can't find a way out of legalese written by Sadou lawyers."

Maurie flapped her hands this way and that. "Pretending to be the embodiment of a cursed water spirit known for tricksy sudden prosperity helps. I mean, her myth includes that she will shower evil curses on the newly wealthy and everyone around them if crossed. I am suddenly in charge of a project with extremely high funding and even higher potential future incomes. I'll make the legend work for us."

Adamou wasn't so sure. People with Austrian villas weren't known for superstitious qualms. But a more important detail had been revealed just now. "So that's why Pascaline is avoiding me. I thought she was holding a grudge about that mix-up where my uncle and your grandpere tried to make the two of us engaged."

"I'm not interested in polygamy," Maurie said. "Also, Pascaline would murder me, and I don't like you."

"Of course we can't be engaged. I'm marrying Pascaline whenever I can finally convince her I won't abandon her at the worst moment like your asshole family members have. If she got sick of me, I suppose we could pretend to have a thing, but I doubt it'd work. You're really annoying, and I'm not that good at pretending to like people I don't."

Maurie rolled her eyes. "You are far more annoying than I am. But we can't be engaged—not even for pretend to make the project look more stable—because the embodied vessels of Mami-Wata are always single and childless. Trying to marry or conceive twists the luck."

"Fine," Adamou said, "we can go with that reason, but you're still annoying."

"Says the guy who's infatuated with Pascaline and doesn't even know her."

"I know her better than you do," Adamou growled. None of the Sadous really knew Pascaline. And his feelings for her didn't fit into something as simple as only love. She was amazing and wonderful and wounded but still charging on to do the right thing no matter how little credit for it she usually received from those closest to her.

"Oh yeah, where did she graduate from college?" Maurie gave him a dead-eyed glare and Adamou was certain there was something off about that question. The detailed background supplied many months ago by Fatima on behalf of Sadou Moussa had listed somewhere impressive in the United States. He didn't actually remember which Ivy League school it had been. A more difficult question would have been to ask the year of graduation or the date. As a close cousin Maurie would have attended that event. Those sorts of universities made a spectacle of graduation with parties and galas to last a week at least. But Maurie hadn't asked for anything but the college name. And the much shorter summary on Pascaline from Great Aunt Mami before the first engagement offer had included that college name also, but now thinking back Adamou remembered it had mentioned no dates. He'd assumed back then that Pascaline was continuing on for a graduate or doctoral degree, maybe remotely. But her field should've required a lot of trips back for in-person laboratory studies.

"She never graduated," Adamou said.

Maurie flushed and looked away.

"Oh shit. She never graduated. Not just didn't finish a master's or doctoral program. She didn't enter one. She didn't complete her undergrad, did she?"

"I didn't tell you that!" Maurie said.

"We are so fucked."

"Oh yeah," Maurie agreed.

"Tell me the rest," Adamou said.

And Maurie did, ending with, "But Uncle Chummy thinks he's giving us enough support that Pascaline can do fine as our technical lead even so, and he's almost always right."

Almost always.

"We just need to keep her from quitting," Maurie said. "She keeps asking Uncle Chummy to replace her with some more experienced TCG hack. If that happens, I'm betting the flunky would move at least half the work to Ecuador or Indonesia or maybe both. And then if our build here slows down for any reason, like if we have to take more pauses than we hoped for, because maybe we need more rail realignments following bigger than usual tremors or whatever. We need her to stay."

"I want her to stay," Adamou agreed.

"So I think you should set date for the wedding," Maurie said. "How about next week?"

"No," Adamou ground out. "Not like this. Besides, I still owe her a favor."

CHAPTER FIFTEEN

ACROSS THE CONTINENT AT THE KILIMANJARO space elevator base station, Ethan had fixed everything. The scientists adored him, as well they should!

With all the work he had done increasing their reputations within the corporation and upping their salaries, he was just waiting for someone to start taking him for granted, so he could slap them down properly. But they didn't. They looked at him with shining eyes and sometimes he found himself checking the reflections of car doors and office windows to see if maybe one of TCG's most influential C-level officers was on a visit he hadn't known about and was standing behind him. Ethan kept his mouth shut and tried to pretend that success wasn't terrifying.

Just because he didn't care about money personally didn't mean he didn't value it. He knew the company showered love on its favorite sons and daughters through paycheck size and nothing else. And Ethan was also well aware that other people liked money quite a bit more than he did. It wasn't just useful for figuring out who was winning at life; you could also use the stuff to buy things.

One of the scientists was honestly considering an elephant. She'd fallen for a sob story about repatriating zoo animals and had gotten involved in nonprofit work on the side.

He preferred to buy more useful things, like loyalty. It paid higher dividends.

His hordes of scientific teams were working together to find a way to make this Herculean task of constructing Earth's first elevator a reality. That kid Samson Young with his self-designed motor chair had proven especially useful with team organization. Sumedha, with the orbital mechanics specialists, and Asim, the group lead for the design of the lift system to connect the tether to the orbital station, had clashed at first, and not in a useful pushing-each-other-to-greater-successes-for-the-company way. Ethan had been about to sack them both when Omer Ehrlich had arrived. Omer with all his unconscious sixty-something wrinkles and talent for understanding so much of what the engineers said might have been someone to fire too, except that Omer consistently forgot to mention his own contributions to any effort. The man really and truly only cared about the success of the projects he was assigned to.

Ethan decided he didn't mind having a modern saint around.

He stared again at the overall design document. TCG's DiamondWire™ tether ran from Kilimanjaro up to a station in geosynchronous orbit. He needed great, nearly unthinkable, metric tons of counter mass at GEO to make the overall dynamics of the system hold everything in place. No, not unthinkable. Omer had an exact number for him. And another exact number for the amount of carbon needed to build the initial tether. There were a half dozen designs for the climber units which would go up and down the completed tether. More designs scoped out defensive arrays for ensuring space junk had no chance of ever impacting with the tether. Ethan put a reminder note on that one. He had years to go before the tether could be put into place.

They should be starting the clearance part of the project now. He had the Sadou Corp, of course, for that. Cory Aanderson had been looking for some more space debris companies to partner with, but so far the other Earth-based ones were overpriced, and the in-orbit ones only wanted to pick up convenient or high-value debris.

Sumedha wanted a decision on power plants for supplying the growing city of the ground station. The project had at least dozens of months (hopefully not as much as a dozen years) to go before becoming operational. But adjacent land speculation was already spiking to insane levels.

Nuclear, geothermal, and solar provided much of Earth's baseload power. A scattering of hydro and wind farms did their part too. Ethan didn't want to make an extra decision.

"Ask HR for an expert on that," he sent to Sumedha.

There. Make Chummy's people finally do some useful work. And maybe they could involve the local governments a bit. Power grids seemed like the kind of thing a government would want to control and tax.

The launcher system in the works to supply his

elevator's orbital station would charge their maglev with power from geothermal, he'd heard. Whatever worked for them. He couldn't bring himself to care about other people's technical details. Except that he got a twinge. *What if they got it wrong?* Everything needed to function for the whole project to work. *Gah!* Why couldn't he be back in sales with other people responsible for delivery and follow-up?

There had been a note about that supply launcher in West Africa. Ethan looked it up. His technicians and their technicians were talking to coordinate details. They wanted forgiveness for having commenced coordination without prior approval. He granted it.

The sheer number of briefs and synopses on his plate now were staggering. His eyes glazed over at the business cases for asteroid-mining companies, and the profit and loss estimates his research teams had done on the private firms working in orbit. TCG would need some of them. He could identify which ones of them to target for corporate takeovers.

A smile finally lit Ethan's face. That part of this job could actually be fun! Most of them had shares they'd sold to friends and family to get their start-up capital. They weren't, most of them, big enough to be exchange-traded, and a lot of them probably hadn't done their legal paperwork properly, which meant the family members who'd supported the start-ups likely didn't really own anything at all. Buying out companies that badly managed was generally a nightmare, but he had people for the actual grunt work. First he'd find out who had gutted their employee ranks prior to offering up their intellectual property for TCG acquisition. And who had scammed the early backers who provided support by not following through on the legal transference of share ownership. Not every company had to get the same kind of offer.

Ethan had gotten his start in places like that. He'd spent fifteen years working for one space start-up after another before he'd decided it was all idiotic. The companies that were going to make it had to have government connections, not just bright ideas and a sufficient number of committed employees willing to work for nearly nothing. In the early days of the second space race it was enough to have grit and drive, but not in the boom that came after.

Now Ethan had the kind of work his younger self would not even have dared to dream of, and it pissed him off. He did not want to build a space elevator. He liked things the way they were. He did not want to have to figure out how this was going to change global commerce and what he'd need to do to reposition himself for the next step up the corporate ladder. The way the C-level officers were talking, they intended to silo him here forever.

Damned Chummy had impressed them with his stories, and Ethan knew those looks. They were scared of him. They'd gone from not knowing his name to considering him a threat. And because he was coming up sideways, none of them felt safe. He might potentially end up displacing any of the C-levels, so they were united against him. Ethan wanted to bang his head on the reclaimed hardwood desk. This was not how it was supposed to work. This was not how it was supposed to work at all.

Worst still, Chummy thought he was happy about it. Chummy was the sort of asshole who listened to what people said and believed them. So, when Ethan had shot out that line of bullshit the scientists loved so much about spreading humanity across the stars and building a better future, Chummy had taken him at his word.

The ass.

Still, still, Ethan breathed deeply.

He could work with this. Make the elevator work and make sure everyone knew it was his leadership that had made it happen, and he might not need to end up CEO to have the CEO's level of power.

Weren't football coaches still the best-paid university staff members across the board including college presidents and top professors? That sort of power disparity didn't usually exist out in industry. But chief of sciences hadn't existed until about six months ago when Chummy had started talking to the C-levels and spreading around those business-case proposals Ethan had written as a backdrop for his planned leap back into operations.

And now Chummy was coming to Kilimanjaro for a visit. Ethan had invited him. But the man had actually accepted as if he truly believed he was helpful when he dropped in and stuck his nose everywhere. Chummy must want something from him, and Ethan still waited to see what it was. Chummy could and had come up with some real stinker ideas. Ethan wasn't about to let Chummy talk him into something that would complicate this situation even more.

Ethan's mass of old plans was in disarray. He'd bloated everything here extravagantly when he was in his last position. Back then, he'd been certain someone else would have to deal with it. And now he should have been facing a need to lay off a solid third of the science staff, but instead the C-levels had doubled his personnel budget and encouraged him to take on whoever *else* he thought he'd need. Ethan would have liked to stab Chummy for that.

It was a trap, of course. Every employee had to provide about three times salary in return on investment to cover facility costs and pay and benefits and not be a drag on overall investor returns.

Take a low return team that lacked a matured profit strategy and then double the required returns he, as chief, needed to deliver? Yeah, Ethan knew exactly what those C-levels were doing. If he hadn't been the one they were doing it to, he could have sat back, taken notes, and expressed deep appreciation for their business tactics.

Ethan moved another one of his files out of the business cloud and into his personal encrypted file vault. That should be the last of his old plans for gutting the science labor rates. He couldn't afford to implement his previous plans now. If he fired that many people there would be no one left to build the elevator. Instead he was hiring. Still. He shivered.

He might not survive if anyone even learned about his original plans. Jax McAllister, his assistant, knew. Probably. Ethan was almost certain Jax knew. He'd overheard the tubby man make a comment about him always war-gaming worst-case scenarios and being the most foresightful man he'd ever known. Ethan would've ignored it as basic flattery designed to sound like loyalty if Jax hadn't also added something along the lines of, "So, of course, you'll see heartless research questions and really painful staffing plans in some of the files. He does these deep dives to push himself to make sure those things never happen."

Jax'd been chatting with DeeDee Nelson that time, not the more talkative Samson Young. Both of Chummy's aides were creepy in their own way, but DeeDee at least kept her mouth shut. Samson could ask the most deceptive little questions. As if anyone at the C-level should care whether or not the office building maintenance staff in Kilimanjaro had access to dentists who would accept TCG's health insurance!

Jax had managed those ridiculous questions.

And Ethan had actually found himself double-checking the corporate policy on benefits for sub-contractors and making quick changes to match the wide-eyed reply, "Oh no, of course, Mr. Schmidt-Li wouldn't let something like that happen!" that he'd heard Jax respond with.

His man was good. Jax had had the forms backdated when Ethan had gone to get them filed.

Ethan glared at a notice on his screen. Samson Young strikes again. *"Based on HR review, employee Jax McAllister routinely performs duties beyond administrative-assistant-aligned functions. The pay-level increase for employee Jax McAllister is attached. Titles of personnel in aide roles to senior executives vary. If a new job title for employee Jax McAllister is desired, HR suggests 'Executive Secretary' or 'Staff Liaison.'"*

Great. Already outsiders were spending his money. Ethan made a note to himself to tell Jax about the raise before the next pay period. He could spin it as his own idea, he supposed. If he even remembered without Jax doing the reminding. Ethan glared at the HR message.

"The boss doesn't care about money." He could hear Jax explaining it away to anyone who asked. Ethan suppressed a shudder. Of course, he cared.

The massive research funds they'd been promised had already hit his business accounts. He had a small army of accountants managing plenty of smaller trans-actions: buying materials and moving personnel around. The expected returns would begin being assessed against his teams immediately. Oh yeah, Ethan knew exactly what those C-level TCG executives were doing. Or at least what Ms. Garcia, the CIO, was doing. He couldn't read Mr. Jeffy at all, and Mr. Zhou, the CTO, had been either the best actor in the history of show business or he truly was enraptured by the prospective expansion of the space industry that the much cheaper transport to and from Earth orbit implied.

Ethan scheduled yet another meeting with Omer to work on his space elevator spiel. The scientists all knew he didn't understand one word in seven that they had to say about how everything worked, and they didn't expect him to. But everyone else in the world, including far too many news reporters and internal business associates in operations, expected him to be able to not only understand the science-speak but also translate it to their level. It was enough to make him want to pull out his newly planted hair treatments. Cameras now came with this job too. He'd had to drop the age-concealing makeup efforts altogether. No time to maintain it properly, and he had staff now who'd actually worked in China who wouldn't believe his claims about why he'd adopted the fad.

Chummy had a hell of a lot to answer for.

CHAPTER SIXTEEN

MORE MONTHS PASSED; ETHAN STOPPED KEEPING track of his mistakes. He didn't have time for that. It was all he could do to try to juggle the fixes. He added another public relations aide to his continually growing list of new positions. The one Chummy had given him worked fine, but he wanted a lower-level minion of his own in that office who'd call him up and tell him if he really needed to know something. He'd like a personally loyal headhunter too. He certainly wasn't going to just take the inter-directorate transfers of all the dead weight the other offices wanted to shift his way. The other parts of the company were starting to catch on to his methods. Nobody dared steal people back from him directly, but they were getting ruthless with each other. It was only a matter of time before someone tried to take back one of his top people. He needed to be ready.

Yet another just graduated propulsion systems engineer had cracked the TCG email system to send him a résumé directly. Ethan almost deleted it, but with a reluctant nod to the grit required to overcome his spam blockers, he sent Philip Chao's messages to HR. On his screen, DeeDee Nelson's neat organizer bot replied with a short thank-you and swept all the correspondence and résumé attachments into Samson Young's To Do pile.

Ethan groaned at the sheer magnitude of the elevator project's To Do pile. Nothing necessarily had his name on it, but he was in charge of putting names on all the tasks. If he was going to make this work, and Ethan always made things work, he'd get the best to do it. He was going to keep breaking every polite-handshake no-compete the conglomerate had ever made and rob anyone and everyone to get the strongest team possible. Certain rude people—Cindy Brooks formerly of Chicago Admin Support came to mind—might say he'd already done just that. But Ethan didn't feel like he'd done enough of it. Damn them all. He was stuck as chief of sciences. That meant he had to make the space elevator into his very own moon shot and steal all the superstars that the planet had to offer.

He was not going to be bloated into becoming too big to succeed. Ethan knew that trick, and it was not going to break him. They thought they'd given him rope to hang himself. Not going to happen. He'd be happy to garrote at least half the private trade deals the company had and cut the feet out from under key suppliers who'd been loyal partners for decades, if he needed to. Later on they'd write books about his bravery, and the other chiefs and vice presidents would have to repair the broken relationships. His bridges were already on fire, so Ethan would use this position to its fullest.

There would be an elevator, and Ethan would be its heart.

Presiding over yet another design review breakout session, Ethan had had five lead engineers and three top scientists sketching designs on actual paper while a dozen lesser project managers stood back against the walls taking notes and sending prototype orders to distributed teams to build and test mock-ups. Ethan had not the slightest idea what any of them were saying, but they believed each other and from the looks in those eyes, they had confidence they could and would complete the project successfully. Ethan hoped he didn't need to know what any of it meant. He could read the people instead...except for Chummy.

At that last visit, Ethan had hid his glare as Chummy himself, the original troublemaker, came in pushing a cart with a gurgling coffee machine and a soda dispenser loaded with Diet Coke. The project managers had swarmed the cart immediately and several distributed fresh cups to the core team which were taken but barely acknowledged.

"We don't have a beverage contract for this facility," Ethan remembered having said.

Chummy had given him one of those sparkling white-toothed smiles. "We own the facility. I talked to Cindy. She doesn't mind."

Ethan had hovered and watched while Chummy chatted with this and that low-level scientist about nothing at all important. No schemes were revealed, no accusations were made. Chummy had left again without anything more than a threat to come visit again soon.

He'd contained himself and not snorted publicly at Chummy's comment about Cindy's opinions. Ethan would have bet she'd support Chummy if he'd come in with kilos of cocaine for all the staff, never mind a few outside-budget Diet Cokes.

Cindy Brooks, current chief of administrative support, minded absolutely everything, except of course when Chummy asked for it. Ethan suppressed an eye-roll just thinking about it. Ms. Brooks was certainly not Cindy to him. Not since he'd cut secretarial support staff five years back at the Chicago office when she'd just transferred out to Beijing. He'd saved that division of the company a half million dollars and earned her enduring hatred.

The experience with Ms. Brooks made Ethan even more twitchy about Chummy. He'd had Ms. Brooks contained on all sides rather like a slowly decaying zombie. All her teeth were pulled, but he couldn't afford to properly bash her head in. Still, it took time and energy to make sure the people around her respected him and not her. It had once come back to him that she'd called him a monster at the Beijing holiday party. He could have, should have, gotten her fired for that, but the incident was now too far in the past. It would look petty now. And truly at the time he'd been afraid that if he spread word of the incident, too many others would agree with her.

His standard interview question response was to claim to be a tiger fiercely protective of his people. Internally he found the shark metaphor more appropriate, but the soft butt-sitters with no ambition who filled out most senior interview panels in advisor roles got scared if you spoke too much truth, so he stayed with tiger. But he never forgot that the company was really a shark tank and not some beautified field of wildflowers.

He was going to need to break Chummy to keep the power balance aligned right. The man had made him, and now he was the only one besides Mr. Jeffy who could fire him. Ethan wasn't sure how to get a handle on Chummy yet. Someone like Cindy Brooks was easy. Ms. Brooks had, still, hundreds of people scattered throughout the company's offices, and she cared for all of them deeply. With her, all he had to do was force her to fire a few and it brought her fury up to a peak where she couldn't think any more and became easy to predict.

Chummy had no real departments: no real people. By now Ethan had the man's job description nearly memorized. The CEO, Jeffy himself, had chosen to assign rather more than typical HR duties to Chummy. Strategic vision was in there, and he always had two assistant positions filled by young support staffers who worked like dogs for nearly nothing and who were frequently headhunted by other organizations. Chummy actually encouraged them to move on every two or three years. They generally stayed for five. Foolish besotted puppies. There was no weakness there, and at least right now, Chummy himself seemed flawlessly armored.

Ethan got up from his desk, locked his account accesses, and put on his people face. Chummy was visiting, yet again. He should be landing within the next half hour.

Ethan's own faithful assistant, Jax, was tracking all the senior-level arrivals for him. When Ethan had found and hired the much older man, in his sixties then with a bit of a paunch but with a meticulous attention to detail, it had been in a spurt of personal insecurity. Ethan thought back to that old interview. The man had smelled of desperation and reminded him of how he might have ended up if he hadn't learned to be ruthless. Ethan bestowed a smile on Jax in passing and the man levitated just a bit. Back then, Jax had been out of work for over two years, in the middle of a divorce, and about to lose his house. Ethan had saved him, and now Jax would do pretty much anything for him. Except, of course, anything that might even faintly harm Mrs. McAllister. That pending divorce had been called off as soon as Jax's paycheck started coming in. Ethan thought ill of the woman on general principle, but he didn't need an automaton, and as long as Mrs. McAllister stayed out of the way, he wouldn't try to break up Jax's marriage.

"Mr. Schmidt-Li," Jax called out as he arrived at Ethan's elbow with a tablet display. "Chummy's arrival is on schedule, and I've double-checked that the coffee at the airport lounge has been switched over to his brand. Chummy's assistants were very helpful."

Ethan let the slightest crease of a frown show.

Jax flinched back. "I didn't ask the assistants. You wanted us to surprise Chummy. My twins are the same age as DeeDee."

Twins? Ethan blinked. He hadn't known his assistant even had children.

"So I checked their profiles," Jax continued. "DeeDee Nelson had mostly just cat photos. But Samson Young had pictures of the three of them—Chummy, DeeDee and himself—and he wrote public posts about the coffee Chummy likes."

"Good," Ethan said, and watched Jax's anxiety level drop a few notches. It was pleasant to have a responsive executive secretary who could read him without Ethan needing to resort to overt critiques that might damage his personal brand as the lovable manager with the flawless long-term vision. One of the engineering team leads was waiting in the outer office, so Ethan added more loudly, "Keep up the good work, Jax."

Ethan reached out a hand and shook his lead engineer's hand firmly. "No major problems, I hope?"

"Not major," Omer Ehrlich agreed, "but I was hoping to get on your schedule to talk through our options for orbit debris clearance choices."

Ethan would have liked to let his eyes roll into the back of his head. These sorts of details were exactly the sort of thing he'd wanted to get away from with a transfer back into a sales-oriented profit center where someone else was in charge of delivering on the big promises.

"Sure, sure, but I'm confident your team can come up with a good solution for the company." Ethan patted the man on the shoulder. "Come on down to the airport with me, Omer. I'm meeting Chummy, who's in from Berlin for the week to have a look around. He might like to hear your ideas directly and you can fill him in on some of the recent wins your teams have had."

Ethan couldn't off the top of his head think of anything the engineers had been doing right. From his perspective they brought him nonstop problems.

If it weren't for some of his favorite scientists insisting that the engineering team was top-notch, he would have fired the lot of them and brought in a group more capable of filtering their communications

with him into a list of planned solutions instead of all
these nitnoid problems and their convoluted interrelated
fixes which caused other problems.

The engineers seemed to delight in pointing out
third- and fourth-order problems they'd identified but
not yet solved. It was a wonder any of them were still
employed. His scientists at least had learned not to
come to him with those sorts of things. They sent him
bad news by email instead. It wasn't much better, but
they did set up experiments to look for solutions without much prompting. And his executive secretary was
earning his pay increase with a carefully maintained
interconnected tracker of the ways the problems and
problematic fixes were developing.

Jax hopped into the driver's seat to plug in the
destination and adjust the car's main cabin to Ethan's
preferences. The part of Tanzania they were headed
to down the slope from the Kilimanjaro site was far
too hot for Ethan's preference, but he'd taken to
wearing linen-blend suits and drinking his coffee iced.
With a minion like the engineer in the car, Ethan's
temperature choice was mid-seventies with a healthy
air circulation. It supported the image of being frugal
with corporate resources and adapting to local conditions. Ethan hoped Chummy would ask for it to be
cooler on the return trip. Sixty-eight felt like heaven
these days, but he rarely got it. The high elevations
on Kilimanjaro where the temperatures were too cool
for comfort were reserved for construction, and early
on, Ethan had established the portion of the resort
altitudes where the temperatures were idyllic as a mix
of reserved wildlife refuge and an elite living space
for the on-site build crew.

Jax met Ethan's eyes through the rearview mirror. It would have been sixty-eight degrees Fahrenheit if only the two of them had been in the car. Once the autodrive engaged and the trip started safely, Jax's seat turned him around to angle conversationally toward the two back passenger seats. Jax offered up coffee and water. Ethan declined. He planned to drink with Chummy in a few minutes, but Omer gratefully downed bottles of icy cold water.

"His airplane just landed," Jax reported as the car parked itself at the drop-off spot in front of the airport concierge desk. The company lounge was three floors up with a view of the tarmac.

Ethan popped out of the vehicle with a practiced bounce. It hurt his knees but made him look fifteen years younger. The engineer followed more slowly. Jax waved them on. "I'll stay with the car to keep the airport valet program from burying it in the back of the auto lot. Ping me when you need it back, and I'll switch it back to autodrive."

Ethan felt the rush of blessedly cool air on the back of his neck as Jax ratcheted down the interior temperature before the doors fully closed. Ethan would bet it was going to be a fine icebox for Jax while he waited, but the man was dependable. He'd have it at seventy-five before Chummy stepped inside. Ethan gave his executive secretary a wave as the vehicle slid away from the curb to clear the spot for other travelers.

The plane waited on the tarmac about to taxi over to a skybridge. Omer tried to bring up a few more elevator design issues awaiting a decision as Ethan ushered him inside the terminal, but Ethan was able to distract him from too much detail with a few words about who Chummy was and his role in the conglomerate. It was all the bullshit position description stuff that didn't matter, but that sort of distinction wasn't always clear to the lower levels. Something in the way Omer's eyes glinted suggested that maybe Omer already knew Chummy fairly well.

But if not, it wouldn't hurt to make sure Omer was informed and could tell others. It should elevate Ethan's credibility a bit that someone titled Strategic Visionary had flown from Berlin special to see him.

"Oh, Chummy's just in awe of you, like everyone else," Omer said. He rubbed his head where he had more hair missing than present. "You could have him come to you on the mountain or reschedule if you're too busy."

Ethan's eyebrows rose. "He is a company VP."

"Oh yes, he's that." Omer shrugged. "But he's also Chummy. I think he might commit *seppuku* if anything he did harmed the elevator. Any of the VPs would. Or else"—Omer's face split with a grin—"Mr. Jeffy would gut them himself."

Omer looked through the airport's wide glass windows at the road they'd left which led back up the mountain. "I am so very happy to be part of this." When he turned back, there were tears glistening in his eyes.

Ethan looked away and suppressed a shudder. Adoring scientists were hard enough. Now he had adoring engineers too. At least Jax hadn't turned into a pure sycophant.

Jax had arranged for an airport map outline on Ethan's comm and used corporate comm access codes to track Chummy's progress through the terminal. The red dot should arrive any minute.

Omer's comments disturbed him. If Chummy had a drop of Japanese blood in his ancestry it certainly didn't show, but pseudo samurai doublespeak sounded exactly odd enough to be the next management-science fad, and Ethan hadn't been keeping up on the fads. So Ethan kept his mouth shut about the *seppuku* concept.

The only thing Ethan could remember doing lately was abusing the suppliers to get his teams the stuff they needed cheaply and ahead of schedule while robbing other parts of TCG for people. That shouldn't get him accolades, but Omer wasn't the only one prone to spontaneous bursts of gratitude.

He looked back at Omer Ehrlich, who, thankfully, no longer looked about to drip tears.

He briefly considered demanding the man explain his infatuation and dismissed the idea as counter-productive. Instead, Ethan took a longer moment to consider his own grim future if the project were less than successful. It was more than enough to get him to relent about avoiding Omer's true reasons for tagging along on the uncomfortable trip out to the airport and back.

"Tell me about those debris clearance ideas you have." If Chummy got there while they were still talking about it, maybe Ethan could twist the old personnel finder's arm into a pretzel until he magicked into existence another team able to debris-clear at other than insane prices.

Omer babbled for a while about the challenges of orbital dynamics for the in-orbit companies.

And Ethan started to wonder if maybe the sales guys hadn't been talking to the engineers. "You do realize those are only backups, right? We've got a subcontractor building a launcher in West Africa to toss up stuff to the orbital side as we build. You know, additive manufacturing powders and foodstuffs and such. Consumables. It's a rough launch for things that can take some force, but maybe we could get it smoothed out enough to send non-inert payloads. Cory Aanderson got them to put debris clearance gear in their contract a few months back. I guess it's a kinematics thing. They just play marble games with the sky and smash debris with a payload to deorbit it safely into either an atmospheric burn-up or an open sea splashdown, I guess?"

Omer winced. "Please don't say that in front of the Board, boss. I'd hate to have them repeat that and then the media say we are turning all the space junk into ocean junk just because they've got bad orbits. So much of it is still very reusable; with the right robotics we could realign some orbits... Hmm, yeah." He started to grin. "Let me get some people on that."

"Tell the Board?" He could hear the capital in Omer's emphasis. TCG's Board of Directors included only the highest of the C-level executives, a few key vice presidents, and a handful of shareholder representatives. They generally didn't involve themselves in TCG operations without a direct invite from Mr. Jeffy.

"Yeah, you've got a meeting with the Board as part of Chummy's surprise. You weren't supposed to know. Mr. Jeffy said it'd stress you and be a distraction, but your assistant found out." His comm beeped. "Yes, Jax, I'm going to tell him," he told it and muted the device. "But of course your people would leak. And, yeah, for the space junk, I'll have some folks see what else we can do. I didn't think the West African Launcher was in operation yet." He tapped on his comm a bit. "Looks like they've only taken the first two payments. But from satellite imagery, they've got the build line cleared well ahead of schedule. Wonder why they haven't claimed their next two milestone payments yet? From imagery, they've been eligible a while."

"Really? They're under budget?" Ethan failed to hide his surprise. "Now I've definitely got to offer them a contract expansion." He sent Jax a note to query the Sadou Corporation about how soon they could be ready to do orbital debris clearance work.

Omer shared a manager's grin with him. "It does happen sometimes. Looks like they're doing well for us." Then he saw something else on his comm's screen. "Of course they are. I didn't realize you'd signed off on them for us personally. Damn, sir, you're good. Whoa! They're building the maglev launcher system up the side of a volcano. That's..."

Absolutely insane, Ethan thought.

"Brilliant. Just brilliant," Omer continued. He held up a hand shaking with excitement and started ticking off the positives. "First, they're near the equator, so that saves launch energy. Second, they've avoided building skyscraper-sized pylons for the track by using the height of the mountainside for some of the elevation. Third, wow! I'd not've thought to hire an oil and natural gas company to build a spaceport. But, of course, it all makes sense. They are making the hydrogen fuel by methane pyrolysis. And they've got the maglev rail power coming from geothermal. They'll be dealing with microquakes somehow, but, oh, Endeley. Yeah, if anyone can do it, an Endeley volcanologist can... Oh, sorry, I babble. You're amazing to have found that team, sir."

"I what?" Ethan said.

Both their comms pinged at once. Chummy strolled across the concourse.

Ever cheerful, he shook Ethan's hand and gave Omer a bear hug. Samson Young hung back wearing a bland smile, seated, as always, in his motor chair.

"So sorry to rush you, Ethan," Chummy said. "But Jeffy and I were chatting in the air and he's hoping to join in on our little chat. He would've come in person but Cory had a turn for the worse, so he's visiting with him. Rodney's got everything set up for us all to virtual in, though, if we can get to a secure conference room."

Of course they could get to a secure conference room. They could have even used a reserved office space within the airport itself if Samson had bothered to give Jax a heads-up. And now that prearranged coffee was going to be wasted on people who'd have preferred the Kenyan blend they'd replaced.

Ethan pasted a smile on his face as Samson hurried them along. "Boss, Jax has a car waiting on the lower level. I'm setting up the call details with Cindy now."

Sweat ran down Ethan's spine from nerves, not heat. The air-conditioning in this Tanzania office suite purred at sixty-six degrees. Thank you, Cindy Brooks, for making him look like a spendthrift. The sweltering heat outside wasn't to blame for his unease. On the video call, Mr. Jeffy listened, face impassive, as Omer updated everyone on the elevator progress. Ethan should've been doing it, but he'd found his tongue sticking to the top of his mouth and back when it was only an update for Chummy, it had been Omer who was going to talk technical details on a driving tour with Ethan filling in the other bits as possible. Without a primary speaking role and not needing to tweak a vehicle's autodrive to go this way and that gave Ethan time to study the participants in this surprise meeting.

Rodney Johnson's bleached smile on the video conference call sparkled far too much for a modern high-level sales guy. How had that man managed to keep his position when he looked so much like an actor playing a used-car salesman? Rodney was still only deputy to Cory Aanderson's vice presidentship, but he was sitting in on more and more office calls. The background behind Rodney showed the nondescript beige walls and beeping machinery of a private hospital room. Cory's voice, weak but insistent, sometimes commented from off camera.

Ethan's jaw hurt from the effort it took to keep his face frozen in an attentive pose instead of grinding his teeth like he really wanted to.

Marketing had dumped millions into ore sales and low-gravity manufacture. Sales had killed it using the free promo all the elevator news had garnered. That should have been his bump, not Cory Aanderson's!

New names populated almost half the engineering management members who dialed in to listen to this "Update to the Board" call. This unplanned executive meeting turned town hall had Chummy's fingerprints on it, but even he didn't seem to have complete control. Mr. Jeffy welcomed the new promotees warmly, and Ethan realized there were a significant number of people on the call-in roster missing. Jax lit up his comm with a listing of folks who'd been moved out of his department by a new memo from the CEO's desk. No one else made mention of the massacre in the engineering management ranks. Ethan recognized the missing as the ones who'd stalled space development projects or run studies which found the return on investment to be insufficient for a business case. Most had been written quite a while ago. Ethan had been planning to use those other reports after he'd made the transition to sales to be the stalwart company insider who, with true humility and dedication to the good of the company, reported that the person taking over his former job couldn't actually execute any of the bold plans he'd been promoted out of the position for.

This was horrible. This was fantastic. Ethan didn't know what to think.

The setup he'd arranged had been thoroughly de-toothed by the very top echelon of the company. Nobody would dare now do to him what he'd planned to do to somebody else. But, heaven help him, the whole company could go under if the elevator failed to work. Not just a subsidiary would fail, the whole of TCG would be gutted and chopped to pieces for small-time competitors to bid over and then liquidate for assets.

Ethan wasn't sure if there even existed enough space business to make a decent profit with the cheap planet-side-to-orbit transport their new tether material seemed to make possible.

"There might be some time before we hit a positive return on investment," Ethan tried out as his most mild of all possible cautions. With the tone of the call, his comment now remained as the most critical of any of the things said.

Mr. Jeffy's answer, and also Cory Aanderson's, and God help them all, even the CFO's was the same. "You get the thing built, Ethan. We'll make sure the company keeps your teams well funded."

Ethan did the only thing he could under the circumstances. He nodded, as if none of this surprised him in the least, and signaled for more coffee.

The medium roast blend tasted the same to him as every other cup of coffee he'd ever had, but "Chummy's blend" Jax mouthed silently as he handed it to him. Ethan tried to notice the differences in order to say something nice about it later. It tasted like coffee. A note on his comm had the details about the family-owned coffee plantation in West Africa which supplied the beans. *"Partial stake in coffee company owned by Chummy's cousin. /jm,"* the note from Jax said.

The conference ended with more glowing words from Mr. Jeffy. "I trust everyone will give their full support to our Ethan here." Jeffy's grin couldn't have spread any wider. "You are our future. In case anyone doubts it," he added, to a murmur of laughter from the vice presidents who were the only ones allowed unmuted lines into this conference call, "the elevator is our future." He winked. "Don't fuck this up, Ethan."

Slight motion in Cory Aanderson's room brought Sales Deputy Rodney's face momentarily into the call focus as most active video feed. Samson Young had it shrunk down immediately, but Ethan's eye followed it.

"I'll do my best, boss," he said. Rodney's face was a study in envy. Ethan decided to ignore it. Rodney had been his prime competition after Cory Aanderson himself once upon a time. Now the man was about to be handed that plum top sales job without even having to really fight for it. Ethan ought to be the one twisted with raw covetous agony, but to his own surprise, he wasn't.

The call ended.

There was too much work to do, and Ethan was starting to actually believe it was really possible. That thought felt too much like hubris, so he distracted himself with an analysis of the things said on the call with an emphasis on his own words. Had he promised too much? What about that sign-off? Was calling Mr. Jeffy "boss" too standoffish? And Ethan couldn't quite bring himself to call the CEO "John-Philip" as he'd been encouraged to do, or even "Jeffy" like most of the vice presidents did.

"Back to work, everybody!" Omer announced and led the mob of employee spectators out of the conference room. "Nobody's going to be trying to undercut our Schmidt-Li after that," one build foreman said to another with a note of extreme satisfaction.

Ethan returned to his office and found his path blocked by Samson's chair. The young man was in it, facing the other way but backed into the alcove of a doorway. Ethan, standing on the other side of that same doorway, could see Chummy in conversation with Omer a little further down the hall. The spaces between rooms weren't particularly designed for privacy, but Ethan could see why a man might think he was having an unobserved chat with a colleague here in the quiet hall. The ventilation ducts carried the sounds clear enough.

"It's fine, Chummy," Omer said. "Nothing to worry

about. I just got the word on Aanderson's Shen Kong space rock deal being up in the air, too. But Ethan was ready for it. He's already got Jax ginning up a more detailed contract expansion with that Sadou group he has building a launcher to supply the orbital side for when we're ready to put people up there and need to keep them supplied with food and build materials."

Chummy's answer wasn't clear, but it was short.

"Sadou Corporation's great. They're under budget even," Omer said.

Chummy turned then, and Samson rolled his chair forward to bring several refilled cups of coffee. A look of concern briefly present was wiped off the man's face as he noticed his assistant approaching.

Ethan hadn't been seen yet, but this was his damn building. One of several. He opened the door and invited himself into the conversation.

"Hi, Chummy, Omer."

Samson offered him a coffee.

"No thanks, Samson." Ethan waved it away. "Why did I lose my space rock?"

Omer flapped his hands and looked at Chummy.

Samson answered. "Mr. Jeffy is pissed off at Julie of Shen Kong for trying to hack our system to get the DiamondWire manufacture technique. He wants to back out of Aanderson's deal, because it'd give them a major portion of the first five years of elevator lift mass. That means they wouldn't give us the rock, which is what he insists on calling that very solid, very expensive, and very conveniently already in lunar space nickel-iron asteroid. And that'd mean a whole lot of lower-kinetic-energy space debris becomes no longer low enough, and it'd have to be cleared, or it'll shoot bullet holes in the orbit-side station as our elevator gets built."

"That wouldn't be the real issue," Ethan said. "Up that far there's just not a lot of stuff and much of what is there is also in geosynchronous orbit, so relative to my site, it isn't moving at all."

"Collisions or explosions could happen to make some debris up there, especially if we were building from scratch," Omer said, ever the engineer, "but the boss is right, of course. It'd be slow relative to lower-orbit debris fields. The big issue is getting the pathway all the way to the surface cleared to protect the tether line. As long as we have full debris clearance before the tether goes out, it'll be okay."

"But I take on more schedule risk without that rock," Ethan said. "Building a station of sufficient mass to serve as a tether point will delay my timeline."

"And there's design risk too." Omer pressed his lips together without any apparent eagerness to add to the elevator's already complex build plans. "We shifted all our concept testing to builds including the rock after the Shen Kong deal came in. But as long as we've still got full debris clearance lined up..." Omer waved away his own concerns. "Thankfully you found us the Sadous for that, boss."

Ethan grunted acknowledgement, still focused on the rock. "Is Cory Aanderson okay with this?" He had difficulty imagining the salesman being pleased about his most recent big win being set aside.

"He doesn't know it fell through again," Samson said. "There was chatter right after the deal but he's been left under the impression it's still all a go." He gave a nod to Chummy. "DeeDee just confirmed. Rodney hasn't told him. And she's also confirmed that Rodney hasn't had any meetings with Mr. Jeffy since Mr. Jeffy told legal to hold on the Shen Kong contract."

"They shouldn't have tried to steal from us." Ethan was appalled.

"We need that rock," Chummy said.

"Fuck them," Ethan said. "I'll do without. Omer, get with Jax and whoever else you need to get the Sadous to agree to a contract expansion."

"How about a formal apology?" Chummy said. "I'll get Julie to apologize to Jeffy, and maybe they can still work together."

Ethan shrugged. "If you can manage it, okay. If not, he's the CEO. I'll make my fucking bricks without straw."

Omer blinked.

"Biblical reference. Hebrew slaves building Egyptian pyramids, um, not sure how it relates exactly," Samson said.

"Not that," Omer said. "You getting Julie to apologize. She doesn't exactly like you."

"He'll send me," Samson said. "Everybody likes me."

Ethan made a note to himself to just have Jax get a note to Cory Aanderson. Brave words aside, he wanted that rock, damn it. Sales wasn't allowed to fuck him over like this. That famous vice president wasn't dead yet, and Mr. Jeffy didn't seem the type to deny a loyal employee's last request. But it was fun to see Chummy scurrying around trying to solve problems on his behalf. So he didn't mention his own plan. They were right about the value of the rock. There was also the issue of how powerful countries might react if they were cut out of use of the elevator entirely. TCG was a non-state actor. Ethan didn't feel like building the world's first space elevator just to have some nation-state destroy it. There was somebody on his public relations staff who was a former ambassador. He'd have a meeting and see what the woman recommended to make the elevator into the sort of thing all the powerful nations saw as mutually beneficial. He so hadn't needed this. Fuck Rodney Johnson.

"Samson," he said, "bring me a rock."

"Of course, Mr. Schmidt-Li," Chummy's senior assistant said.

CHAPTER SEVENTEEN

DEEDEE NELSON DIDN'T USUALLY READ HER BOSS'S mail, and she hadn't intended to that morning either.

The corporate jet's faint thrum vibrated her seat with a deep mechanical growl heard more by her elbow on the armrest than her ears. Her travel supplies had grown, not shrunk, with the frequent trips to East Africa.

The security assessment team rated the local subsidiaries and political dignitaries they'd be meeting with as "high favorable" and corporate espionage on this trip "unlikely." None of which meant entities like Shen Kong or even less scrupulous companies wouldn't be present and posing as people they weren't. DeeDee really wished polite society would catch up with modern times and do retinal scans and fingerprint checks instead of handshakes or bows before beginning a business meeting.

The luggage jammed between her admittedly luxurious seat, and the interior wall of the corporate jet transmitted the thrum, but she wasn't letting them out of her sight. There were comms and backups in those bags. And she did have a few devices that might be able to remotely check biometrics of the non-TCG individuals they'd be meeting with. Chummy didn't need to know what she was doing and as long as it didn't interfere with his scrupulously polite meeting etiquette requirements, he probably wouldn't even mind. He had a lot to think about, so she'd been stepping in more and more.

Chummy, pacing the back of the aircraft on a call with Mr. Aanderson, hadn't gotten to his own messages in a while. With all the support efforts directed at Ethan's space elevator, he might not even look at them again for days.

Samson's device chimed at her. She'd been in the midst of a chat with Mr. Jeffy's night shift executive assistant, Wilbur, but that could wait. Stupid chitchat practice from her assigned career development plan: annoying at the best of times and pure agony at times like these when every minute wasted would cost her sleep instead of merely shortening her lunch.

"Oh, I'll let you go." Wilbur Fischer head-bobbed a seated bow at his desktop camera. "Have a good trip and let me know if I can help, DeeDee." He logged off before DeeDee had to reply. She was probably on Wilbur's career development plan too.

Sometimes their mutual bosses' arrangements weren't as stealthy as they thought they were. The man had let slip that he was sometimes chided for spending too much time on non-work-related chitchat. DeeDee could have helped him with that, if only she hadn't been required to do the opposite. She shook her head at her development plan one more time, and then banished the annoying thing from her mind to focus on problems she could solve.

The chat icon with Wilbur Fischer's corporate ID photo gained a light green available ring for only a fraction of a second before graying out again as he found someone else on the vast company network to talk with. No one needed to tell him to chat with people, so then again, maybe she wasn't on his daily work list at all.

She fished Samson's comm out of her bag and read the alert on the screen. It told her that usually Samson did a review of their boss's unopened messages every twelve hours or so with key word searches for important items and flags for important senders, and that the action hadn't been marked complete in thirty-six hours. Or more accurately, hadn't been done since he'd left the comm with her for his trip to China.

"Hey DeeDee," an unknown contact sent text scrolling across Samson's comm, *"been busy and forgot I couldn't do my work without the accesses…"* There was more there, but she'd have to tap to open the message or do a more involved workaround that made sure any malicious code that might be attached couldn't auto-start. Her fingers automatically began the workaround.

It was probably Samson, but DeeDee rubbed the back of her neck with nervous fingers. Everyone wanted a piece of the elevator, and she was not going to be the one that fell victim to a social engineering phishing attempt. And if it were Samson, she wanted to mess with him, just a little bit. He had been the one to say in her hearing, "I can't go yet, boss, you need a senior assistant." DeeDee glared at the comm as if it were Samson himself.

DeeDee muted Samson's comm. Her fellow assistant was off on a career development trip and hadn't checked in with her remotely in a couple days. After he finished patching up the deal for the rock—which it sounded like Cory Aanderson already had patched up on his own without anyone else's assistance needed—Samson was supposed to be assessing Shen Kong for a cultural fit to see if he'd be happy as TCG's management facilitator there for his next position. DeeDee didn't think he'd like them. He'd laughed off her hacking warnings, but he had at least left his super-connected comm and had taken a low-access one for the trip.

DeeDee tapped in a response she could use to test the sender's intent: *"This number is not receiving messages from non-address book senders. Please check your contact and send again."* It was a good automated-sounding response. But she didn't send it. Chummy would hate for her to be using call-screening code and would be even less approving if she were to pretend to be using call screening on Samson's comm.

She didn't have to answer the unknown number to reach to Samson. She checked the time difference on her own comm. If he'd followed his planned schedule, he should have been asleep for a while.

DeeDee steeled herself not to respond despite the temptation to demand more details from the sender. She turned his screen back on and read the rest of the message. The word choice sounded exactly like Samson. And the time stamp in the corner showed that the message had been written and given a delayed send instruction so it would arrive during her morning rather than in the night. It ended with a mention that he'd left his comm unlocked and would be using a cheap comm picked up at a Berlin airport kiosk if she needed him.

When she pressed her thumb over the scan button for his comm, all the accesses flared wide open. DeeDee sighed. That was such a Samson thing to do. How Chummy had gotten by when he was junior assistant, she had no idea. Maybe they'd played some elaborate Hansel and Gretel game with corporate data making a trail of sugary breadcrumbs while Chummy took notes on who collected what and how it got reported to their competitors. She doubted it. Probably the person in the senior assistant slot back when Samson was junior assistant had done what she did now and fixed his lapses.

Why couldn't he have set up a guest profile for her alone and used data on file for her fingerprints, face scan, and voice recognition like a normal person?

"Everything alright?" Chummy asked. She must have made a noise while grumbling to herself.

DeeDee went to cue her favorite avatar to send an all-clear message, but Samson's comm thought she was Samson, and her profile, which had reasonable security enabled, refused to allow her in. She hadn't built in a login method that allowed for her working under someone else's profile simultaneously. Her usual comm, which she'd set down to focus on Samson's, turned flat gray.

Her security settings had locked in. And she'd upped that response level after her Shen Kong visit. It wouldn't let her unlock it until she had the device plugged in at her desk in Germany.

"DeeDee?" Chummy said, looking more than a little concerned.

"Comms. Stupid comms," she said actually out loud. Then DeeDee remembered the rules of polite corporate communication, so she also looked up and made eye contact with her boss. "Samson better take that job with Shen Kong, or I'm going to have to kill him."

Chummy laughed. "Okay, then." He returned to his conference call.

She'd have to rebuild all her shortcuts and subroutines to do the things she'd planned to work on during this trip. DeeDee considered smashing Samson's comm on general principle. It wouldn't help anything. Instead she started doing his tasks. So now she held in her hand a comm logged in as Samson which had just told her the boss's messages were overdue for a review. Samson had built in a shortcut to mirror Chummy's messages, and he'd set up his device to give her full access just in case she needed one of his files.

DeeDee tapped OKAY and watched Chummy's whole backlog unfold. Keyword searches ran and a progress bar began a slow crawl across the bottom with a count of potentially important items ticking more slowly upward.

A new message popped in that should never have made it through the filters. Sender ID: Pascaline, no last name, no photo.

"Thanks Uncle," the last message read.

DeeDee fought herself to keep her eyes from bugging out. The filters should have screened out a chatbot. What kind of business contact didn't fill in a last name and at least use a placeholder logo if there wasn't a formal corporate identification photo? A spambot of course, or one of those social engineering hackers. For someone else it might be a new lover. But that name registered as 99.5% female, and a woman wasn't the boss's type.

DeeDee tapped on the comm and pulled up past communication threads with the Pascaline contact. Her hands shook as she read.

No. No. No. She would not allow this. Not Chummy. The rules were clear about what happened to someone if they fell for social engineering. Termination. Immediately.

Though, a hope-filled thought came flying up through her mass of fears: Chummy had pointed out on other occasions that bosses had wide latitude on following or not following corporate rules. HR always monitored to protect the company from lawsuits, but a strong boss could...

DeeDee's fingers found the chat connection for Wilbur Fischer. She needed Samson for this, but she didn't have him. She'd have to do her very best alone and try to imagine how Samson would sell it. How do you sell out your all-time favorite boss so completely that it saves him? Only someone who worked for Chummy would dare try, but then maybe also only someone who had worked for Chummy would have a chance at succeeding.

Wilbur Fischer's availability light remained gray and unavailable. She had to wait and had to think. Her fingers twitched, longing for a way to turn this problem into code and run test cases to find a non-awful solution.

CHAPTER EIGHTEEN

"**I** KNOW YOU'RE HIDING IN THERE," MAURIE SAID.

She banged on the metal work shed's siding. Pascaline gave her a glare through the glass door and returned her focus to the expanded comm screen. These modular offices fit on the back of a truck. Maurie had bought dozens of them. Their metal roofs shone in the morning light like spilled silver beads scattered all the way from the base station to the top of the construction zone. They even had their own, very low-capacity, solar and battery installation on top. Sadly, it was insufficient to run an air conditioner.

A long snake's hiss attempted to distract Maurie, but she didn't have time for Mami-Wata's nonsense today. The raging headache wasn't enough to make her eyes water, quite, so each less distracting symptom was going to be treated with the same ruthless contempt.

"Pascaline, you brat." Maurie raised her voice to make absolutely certain her cousin would hear it through any mild sound dampening the thin walls and door might provide. "I need you to approve the level-two build plans. We can't keep regrading the route indefinitely. At some point it has got to be good enough. And I need to order more concrete if you don't like the positioning for the pylons I went ahead and approved for you. We need decisions yesterday!"

A cough lodged in Maurie's throat, stopping her from continuing to yell. The morning fog encircled the mountain's upper slopes and seemed thicker in places. A whiff of it did make her eyes water. Even wet, half-dead snake shouldn't stink that badly. She might need to go back to the last medicine regime that had allowed a lot of auditory hallucinations but only infrequent visual waking fever dreams.

The car accidents from when she'd swerved off the roadway to avoid hitting massive snakes weren't that bad. Discovering that no one else at the scenes had seen the snakes had triggered her request to readjust her meds. But these side effects weren't better. That smell was foul. She could switch back and make Pascaline drive more often. *And really? A stink hallucination? The medication warning lists had not included phantom smells.*

Maurie concentrated and took another breath. The air stopped tasting quite so foul. *That's it. Mind over matter.* Maybe she could stay with these meds. She turned to glare at the fog. There weren't any coils in that thick gray mist. It was completely normal for the mountain's drop-offs to make some parts of the sky look like bands of blinding whiteness. The scrub bushes freckling the upper slopes moved in the wind like the scale-speckled skin of a giant boa sliding deeper under a boulder in search of the earth's heat on this cool mountain morning. *Just a trick of the eye*, she told herself.

"I said, 'I'm busy, and I'll get to it when I get to it,' Maurie." Pascaline slammed the metal-framed clear door for emphasis. "It would help if some people would stop interrupting me constantly." Pascaline scowled and failed to meet Maurie's eyes. The screen behind her displayed a solitaire game with a lot of new high scores. "Give me a few minutes to work in peace, and maybe I'd be done already?"

"Look," Maurie said, "I get that it's tough to be making these calls, but there's no one else. We can ask Uncle Chummy for some help, okay?"

"Right," Pascaline said. "Do you really think I haven't tried that?"

Maurie thought she could smell rotting snake roadkill mixed with freshly laid blacktop in the air now. *Not fair!* She hadn't even hit the ghost snake the second time. She'd swerved and had significant auto repair shop bills to show for it. *No, Mami-Wata, not today. Focus. This morning is about Uncle Chummy's project and Pascaline's need for someone to hold her hand and tell her it is okay to make some freaking decisions already.*

"I don't know," Maurie said with forced calm. "Did you ask Uncle Chummy?"

"Yes," Pascaline hissed. "I did. And I couldn't get through thanks to his assistants. His assistants. Can you believe that?"

The ground wiggled in the lift-and-drop feel of a snake writhing underfoot. Maurie ignored it.

"Assistants," Pascaline repeated. "I could only talk with his assistants! And you are not to call him 'Uncle' to the TCGers. Not ever. Just Chummy. Everyone in TCG is supposed to have no idea Chummy is related to us. One of the assistants figured out the family connection and read me the riot act for a single use of the title 'Uncle.' He thinks it's a big, big problem. But, I, unlike some people, am doing the extra work and am in the process of taking care of it."

"How?" Maurie tried to keep the suspicion out of her voice, but the clouds kept distracting her.

"I introduced him to Adamou, of course. The Bakweri have a special knack for handling foreigners. Did you know that this mountainside was never occupied by colonialists or cross-desert invaders? This despite other tribes trying to sell it a few times to undercut the Bakweri. And a particularly bold squadron of pirates sending up a ground force of slaver-sailors to try to take it."

"Living on the slopes of a volcano with a tendency to erupt on a timeline convenient to the Bakweri has nothing at all do to with that history, I'm sure."

"Fako looks out for his own." Pascaline smiled and made a bow toward the higher of the twin peaks not visible through the thickening fog. "Good Fako."

"Are we part of Fako's own now?" Maurie rubbed her eyes to wipe away the sense of the clouds thickening around them. "We might still be outsiders." *They are clouds, damn it. They are not coils.*

"We should be so lucky as to get swallowed up in magma," Pascaline said. "Chummy is going to get fired when this project fails. And it's going to fail, because the launcher pylons ... I just don't know. The numbers aren't right yet. So, fine, yell at me, it's really going to help." Pascaline reopened the shed's door as if she intended to go back inside and slam it in Maurie's face.

Maurie tried not to react when the mountainside gave a panicked death gasp and the ever-present clouds circled around like enormous boa coils.

Pascaline ran out of the shed. She tore the door off in her hurry and tossed the flimsy thing to the side. "Go!" she yelled. "What are you waiting for?"

Mami-Wata's wide-eyed face appeared in the mist. The spirit in her woman-snake guise waved panic-stricken coils and mouthed, "Run!"

Pascaline turned back. She grabbed Maurie's arm and dragged her over to the vehicle. She paused with a finger over the Jeep's power button and looked up the site's only access road. Pascaline's horror-filled face mirrored Mami-Wata's. The rough construction vehicle trail ran sharply upslope and wrapped out of sight around the mountain before, eventually, it met up with a turn down around a half kilometer further on.

Pascaline threw herself back out of the vehicle. Maurie followed. They dropped to the ground, and with the encouragement of another rumble, lay flat in the dirt and crawled under the vehicle.

"'Expect some rumbles,' Adamou said," Pascaline yelled. "'Some rumbles'! I'll some rumble him!"

"Oh, thank G—"

Pascaline pressed a dirty hand over Maurie's mouth. "Not on the mountain."

Oh, for Mami-Wata's sake! "That was going to be a prayer, not a curse," Maurie said.

"I don't care what it wasn't," Pascaline said, "I don't want to piss off the spirits while we are in the middle of an eruption."

The ground stopped moving.

The scent of, yes, sulfur, not burning snakes, hung heavy around the work site. Nothing fell from the sky. So, it wasn't going to be a big enough eruption to kill them all and put Pascaline out of Maurie's misery.

She took slow, deep breaths to control her rage. It was not appropriate to strangle the project's technical lead. Not appropriate.

"Adamou predicted this, you say?" Maurie asked.

"Yeah, of course. And I canceled all on-site work upslope of Buea's elevation to make sure nobody got hurt in the rumbles. You'd think that'd mean I'd get to be alone up at this site since it's above the line, but, no, you had to come pester me during the morning eruption event."

They both crawled out from under the Jeep. Pascaline dusted herself off and gave a distrustful glance up the mountain. "I don't know if he predicted all of that. We should go find out how much got destroyed."

"Maybe if we'd been building on schedule, we would have had some stuff in place to get only partially damaged instead of utterly destroyed in the warehouse. Better luck next time," Maurie said. "I'm sure it's slipped your mind that most of the lengths of maglev track and cement and rebar and all the rest are in downslope warehouses or still mounded in construction yards at the Limbe depot. All behind schedule, thanks to you. I'll let you tell the Bakweri and Adamou," she added.

"Every single one of our warehouses has a top-of-the-line mudslide barrier, and everything that needs to stay dry is either under a roof or heavy tarps. So, you could say, 'Thank you, Tech Lead, your requirements—those ones that all the foremen whined about—just saved us from a potential total loss of build materials.' But, sure, instead you can keep complaining about the maglev rail build timeline. Fine, whatever," Pascaline said. "I'll quit and go to work as a barista at Kilimanjaro. You can tell Adamou that."

Maurie blinked at her cousin. "You stood him up on a date again, didn't you? You got busy studying the project details again and forgot you had a date, didn't you?"

"I didn't say that." Pascaline would've made a very good snake woman. She had the hiss down to a science.

"Didn't deny it either," Maurie noted.

A familiar ringtone sounded from inside the shack. Pascaline looked the other way, so Maurie stalked inside and answered Adamou's call.

"Well, you didn't kill us with your pet volcano god yet, witchy priest man," she said.

Adamou squinted at her behind a thickly fogged helmet visor and replied with something unintelligible.

Maurie had a momentary pang of pity for him. "Pascaline is fine. She's avoiding you."

He made a gesture that Maurie had no trouble interpreting as *Put Pascaline on.* "I said she was avoiding you. And if she goes to extreme measures, I'm getting stranded at this work site. I have another migraine. I don't want to have to walk down to the next work site with all the sulfur smoke making my lungs feel super mystical and choked up."

Adamou made another unintelligible comment.

"She did stand you up, didn't she?" Maurie asked.

Adamou stopped moving.

"That'd be a 'yes,' then." She grinned at him. "Don't take it personally, she does it all the time. I bet she lost track of time and forgot you existed until the volcano reminded her of the existence of the parts of reality outside of launch equations."

Pascaline's hand descended from the top of the comm and shut the call off.

"I'm getting out of here," she said. "Adamou's weather

report for the day said, and I quote, 'Mild tremors for up to a half hour followed by a moderate chance of steam and toxic gases at upper reaches. Heavy rainfall and downslope flooding likely by afternoon.' If that was mild, I want to be far out of the way for moderate."

Pascaline drove. Maurie took slow, deep breaths. She ignored Mami-Wata's repeat appearances in the cloud line and urgent gestures to get down the mountain faster.

She needed to add breath masks to the list of gear they provided to the construction crews working on the upper slopes, and maybe some helmets. She'd been hoping to install the shorter of the TCG advisors' proposed rail line lengths. But with Pascaline being unwilling to make decisions quickly, Maurie—as project manager—needed to be ready for installation of the tech designs that used the whole of the mountainside for the maglev rail.

A longer rail meant more time for the vehicle to be thrown by forces energetically paid for with geothermal energy instead of from onboard fuel. She decided to continue the construction on all the additional geothermal plants. They were probably overbuilding, but better to have more power and not risk giving Douala rolling brownouts. As far as the launch was concerned, the more kinetic energy transfer that happened while on the ground (or the elevated rail) the better for their mass cost equation.

When the Jeep whipped around a curve, they broke through a cloud bank, and fat raindrops began falling on the dirt road.

Pascaline grunted irritation and picked up speed as if she could outrun the sky.

CHAPTER NINETEEN

ADAMOU, AT A MUCH HIGHER POINT ON THE MOUN-tain, did a victory dance around his data relay display. The tremors had been precisely as strong as he'd predicted. Precisely! Even the data from the downslope sensors was well within the new narrow error bar ranges he'd calculated.

"Praise Allah, I'm getting really good at this!" His voice through the mask sounded like a mumbled prayer spoken by someone who didn't speak English, but there wasn't anyone to hear him besides Old Fako, so he indulged himself. He whispered a fragment of an old prayer memorized during his childhood. "Praise be to the Lord of the Heavens and the Earth and all that is between them. Bless His holy name. By the work of our hands and our hearts, may we bring the people of the mountain to the heavens."

Fako gave a barely perceptible rumble of agreement as Adamou reached the end of the line. Adamou patted a stone outcropping in encouragement, and the mountain settled.

His comm pinged a reminder at him, and he, too, headed down the mountainside.

He had somebody he needed to see face-to-face. He expected to do a lot of yelling. Wearing a robe thick with volcano-stink and standing behind the chief's desk would help him get his points across without also needing to punch the officious TCG twit.

Adamou considered having one of the project foremen meet the TCG guy at the little Limbe airstrip which serviced the string of beach properties at the base of Fako. He could've had the unwelcome visitor brought all the way to the top of the mountain. But someone unused to mountain living would get altitude sickness from the speedy drive up and probably be too busy vomiting to absorb any other lesson. And, today, even Adamou wouldn't be able to breathe easily at Fako's peak without a mask.

The questions that the guy had been asking weren't rude in and of themselves, but the presumptive tone made Adamou inclined to strangle Mr. Samson Young, primary assistant to just-call-me-Chummy. The TCG minion should be landing in about a half hour and then be presented to him within an hour after arrival, provided that he didn't throw too many fits and waste time during customs inspections.

Dibussi called.

"Mr. Adamou, sir, I gotta call from my Auntie T. Um, she's really my oldest sister-in-law's cousin. But she called me from the Douala airport, and your visitor is, um, tricky."

"I already knew that," Adamou said. "That's why he's getting the mountain-chief treatment instead of the fellow businessman coffeeshop meetup."

"Oh, um, maybe do the coffeeshop anyway? I mean, Ms. Hadjara was working on new chocolates, right? You could feed him one of the ones with *chita*, if he's rude. But don't bring me back any of those. Wouldn't it be better to go to a coffeeshop right there in Limbe?"

"Dibussi, no." Adamou checked the stretch of dirt pathway in front of him and took a risk. The mists were clear enough that the vehicle's computer should be able to manage safe operation for at least a minute or two. He switched the Jeep to autodrive and turned on the video to give Dibussi his full attention. "If you want chocolate, we can get you chocolate without giving any to foreigner jerks."

"Oh"—Dibussi flapped his little hands in frustration—"it's not that. Or not just that. I do want chocolate. But he's not going to fit into the office."

"He's that fat?" Adamou dropped the comm and grabbed the wheel to jerk the car back onto the road. That rock hadn't been there in the middle of the lane on the way up. If rains were softening the earth up here enough for boulders to shift, he better be using operator drive mode. "Fako," he grumbled, "if you kill me off now, you won't have a replacement priest anytime soon. Maybe, not ever."

The road smoothed out again, but he didn't try to use autodrive again.

"You okay, Mr. Adamou?" Dibussi's thin voice rose up from the passenger side floorboards.

"Yeah," Adamou said. "How obese is Samson? Too much to walk, or what? How did he get onto the airplane, if he's that big? The little puddle jumper aircraft they use to go from Douala to Limbe usually doesn't have triple-width seats." Adamou jabbed a button on the dash to transfer the comm call to the vehicle's built-in screen.

"Um, not fat," Dibussi said. His young face scrunched with a childish concern for accuracy. "I don't know if his legs work at all or not, but they are really skinny in the photo Auntie T sent to explain the trouble. Mr. Samson has got a real nice motor chair with red racing stripes, and Auntie T said he's a very cheerful guy who had the whole flight crew laughing. But it was tricky figuring out how to get his chair secured well enough, so that it didn't get banged into other stuff on the flight.

"And he needed them to find the little skinny wheelchair thing. You know the ones that you can use for aisle races during the aircraft crew family days at the hangar? They get broke pretty easy, you know. When they couldn't find one that wasn't too banged up to hold a grown-up, he borrowed a kid's skateboard and tied his briefcase on top and somehow made that work."

"Oh," Adamou said. Samson Young's travel experience sounded anything but cheer inducing. It sounded closer to infuriating. "How badly did he curse them out?"

"What?" Dibussi's face wrinkled in confusion. "No, no, he was sweet. Told lots of jokes. Didn't let anybody feel bad about it."

Ah. So "very cheerful guy" hadn't been sarcasm at all.

"Okay, call Hadjara and ask her to reserve the coffee shop back room for a private party starting in thirty minutes."

"She won't be cheerful," Dibussi predicted.

"I know," Adamou said. "Remind her that my uncle put up the money to start her shop and tell her to fake 'cheerful' for my visitor." He thought for another couple minutes. "Warn her that the rainfall is going to be heavy." The town would probably see some more side street flooding in the parts of Limbe that didn't put in the drainage systems his uncle had recommended after the last moderate eruption eighteen years ago. "She might want to tell her employees to stay put for a while. Did your sister-in-law's cousin happen to notice if Samson can get into and out of a regular passenger car or not? And what are the dimensions for that fancy motor chair of his? Will it fit in the sedan?"

"Well, she didn't say exactly. But getting into seats oughta be okay. She said he hopped in and out of the airport assist carts real easy, but the chair will only fit in the chief's sedan if you don't put any people in it."

Adamou glanced at his rearview window where the many spares and tools lashed into their niches were reflected. The sheer number of them turned his work Jeep's spacious compartment into a warren of equipment. "Dibussi, transfer my call to Grandpere Sadou."

"Uh, okay, but you'll probably only get Fatima and she's still mad about Ms. Maurie's car accidents."

Adamou laughed. "Yeah, I'd heard about those. Try to get through anyway."

"Mr. Endeley, Fatima speaking. What would you like to discuss?"

"Thanks for taking my call, Fatima," Adamou said in his smoothest voice. "I was actually hoping to talk to you."

"I don't date engaged m—"

"Of course, Ms. Fatima," Adamou said, "though I suspect plenty wish you would."

A suspicious silence greeted his comment.

"So, anyway," he said, "is there any chance that in Ms. Maurie's adventures with wrapping cars around trees to avoid running over giant animals no one else can see, you might have any Jeeps stored away somewhere near Limbe?"

"I'm not giving that woman another Sadou vehicle until she finishes the safe-driver course." *That sounded like a "yes." Allah be praised.*

"I won't let her touch it," Adamou promised. "I need a vehicle to show a TCG rep around in. I'd planned on my uncle's sedan, but . . ."

"Oh, that won't do," Fatima said. "Mr. Young's legs are crippled, and his fancy motor chair won't fit. Did you know he built it himself?"

Adamou shook his head, listening as sounds of Fatima's typing filled the dead space. She came back on. "I'm willing to send it unoccupied as far as the launcher base station, but it's going to stay locked. You call me when you get there, and I'll give you—and only you—the entry code. Ms. Maurie is not, under any circumstances, to be allowed to operate the vehicle."

"Thank you, Ms. Fatima," Adamou said.

How did one intimidate into silence a man like Samson Young who'd already overcome so much? A man who had, somehow, so completely overcome the loss of his legs, that complete strangers knew him for his technical skill with his motor chair rather than for his limitations? Adamou increased his Jeep's speed, trying to find an answer in the fog.

Adamou reached the base station, transferred into the pristine new Jeep complete with a wheelchair loader ramp, and reached the Limbe airstrip before coming up with a plan.

The flight attendant and pilot waved a welcome at

Adamou and he was encouraged to drive directly up to the side of the small aircraft. Samson Young laughed off the pilot and co-pilot's offers to carry him down the steep stairs and hand-walked down the rail instead.

Samson paused with his eye level about four inches above Adamou's and gave him a knowing wink before continuing the rest of the way to perform an expert dismount into his motor chair. And, yes, it did have thick, red racing stripes painted on each side.

"Good morning. It's Endeley Adamou, isn't it?" Samson said with a wide grin. "I didn't expect airport service. Weren't we to meet up in Buea? I believe a chat in the chief's office was mentioned?"

Adamou let go of his plan to pummel the man and decided to try something else. "May I interest you in some lunch instead? There's a local place with artisan chocolates I've been meaning to visit."

"Some place around the corner that I can get to without using a vehicle, I suppose," Samson said. This time the man did not manage to keep a wry edge of tension out of his voice.

Adamou pressed a button on the Jeep's key fob. The rear door opened and the ramp descended. He chose not to mention the Sadou Grandpere's fading health and how Fatima made certain to have vehicles around that could accommodate him comfortably on days when the patriarch allowed his body a rest and let a chair do some of his walking.

Samson blinked.

Adamou glanced inside. "The wheel clamps are adjustable for whichever way you'd like to position the chair, or if you wish, it can be secured at the back of the compartment while you shift to one of the built-in seats. The trip'll take us about fifteen minutes routing around some of the more flooded streets."

Samson glanced up at the overcast sky.

It wasn't raining in this part of Limbe thanks to an ocean breeze, but that might change at any minute. Adamou didn't see any obvious umbrella attachments on Samson's fancy chair.

Thunder rumbled in the distance.

"Yeah, let's do lunch." Samson rolled his chair into the vehicle, latched it in, and gave Adamou an ear-to-ear grin. "I so love meeting up with competent people."

Adamou chose not to reveal that on this occasion it was Fatima's competence, Dibussi's family connections, and his own luck in knowing both of them that combined to make him appear more prepared than he really was. He punched in the address, set the autodrive options to route around flooding streets, and settled in across from Samson. "'Competent people,' huh?" he said.

Samson shrugged, still smiling. "Yes, I did know about your modeling and sims expertise, but a lot of people get really good at one thing and then aren't quite up to average at other stuff. From some of the communications coming into Mr. Chummy's inbox, I had some concerns about the space launcher. Nepotistic contract assignments aren't typically acceptable in some of the cultures TCG works in, you may realize."

Adamou gave Samson a long look. This conversation wasn't going in the direction he'd expected.

"Covert nepotism and cronyism are among the more successful methods of garnering support for business efforts that need political backing, as I understand it," he said dryly, "or I'm gravely misinformed about

Western world history with regards to your own company's growth and continued prosperity."

"Yeah, about that." Samson nodded his acknowledgement. "The key word there is covert. I like my boss. I like him a lot. And no senior vice president or above at TCG who was given a family tree for the Sadou oil dynasty would consider Chummy a close relative of Sadou Moussa. But here, Chummy is spoken of as the Sadou patriarch's nephew and the two people on the launcher contract as 'project manager' and 'technical lead' grew up calling him 'Uncle Chummy.' The TCG leadership might have a number of cross-cultural blind spots, but they won't stay unaware enough to miss this. Unless, of course, they never look, because the project smoothly meets and exceeds all the milestones." That familiar grin grew wider again.

"I'm here to join the conspiracy," Samson said.

A gush of water poured out between two buildings, and Adamou jumped forward to take back autodrive control of the Jeep.

"Um, excuse me, I better operate manually for a bit," he explained. "We are almost there anyway."

"Why is the road flooding?" Samson asked. The water only lapped at the wheels as Adamou turned onto a higher road with a more robust drainage and pumping system around it.

"Oh, it's a local microclimate thing. We used to have mudslide issues too before we built in some more robust civil engineering to redirect the runoff away from our towns. It's just life next to a volcano."

Samson lost his smile. "I saw the mountain range on the flight in. There was a lot of cloud cover, but the pilot made an announcement. He said the construction for the new spaceport launcher was just below our flightpath on the slopes of the largest mountain. I couldn't see a thing. How close is this volcano?"

Adamou pulled into the parking spot closest to the door of Hadjara's Café and Chocolaterie. "You already said you were joining the conspiracy. You don't get to back out that fast."

Samson piloted his motor chair out of the Jeep and followed Adamou in to a private table in the back of Hadjara's. Samson landed in the handwoven wicker chair with enough force that Adamou suppressed a wince. It hadn't broken, but he didn't think Hadjara had considered how hard stressed-out customers could be on the furniture, classic basketweave patterning or not.

"Do you really mean to tell me that some distant relatives of Chummy's conned him into handing them one of the elevator's critical path support projects and they threw the cash into an active volcano?"

Adamou tried not to—he really did—but he laughed in Samson's face.

"Oh thank God," Samson said, leaning back with deep relief. "You really got me there. I completely fell for it. I honestly thought the whole maglev sled-assist portion of the launch craft was going up the side of the volcano. I was picturing a full load of the carbon intended to become the core DiamondWire tether that finally gives humanity cheap uplift into orbit getting swallowed by great gouts of lava and then watching on a worldwide live broadcast feed as rocks bigger than your car out there dropped on what's left of the launcher rail line itself."

"Hmm," Adamou said, "I recommend the mini chocolate wafers with coconut paste dusted in *chita*. Local specialty. Hadjara called them 'coco lava melts.'"

Samson considered the menu. "I don't see those."

"They aren't on the menu." Hadjara herself came out to wait on them and set a loaded tray of mixed sandwiches and decorative chocolates. "And they aren't going to be. *Chita* is a pepper. A very hot one. It grows like a weed in the north near the desert, and the flavor doesn't blend well with coconut. I'm working a pomegranate-*chita* glaze that might go well with my sixty-percent-cocoa dark truffle. But it's not ready. And it's not for certain jokers to use on unsuspecting customers." She gave Adamou a glare. "I don't know what Pascaline sees in you, really I don't." Hadjara's face warmed with a grin as she turned toward Samson. "If Mr. Volcano gives you trouble, you call, and I'll kick him out of my shop."

"I'm his ride," Adamou pointed out.

"Then you'll have to wait outside in the rain for him like a good chauffer while he finishes his lunch. You could have told someone down here that Our Fako was having a rumble. I had two cartons of confectioners' sugar get soaked, because 'someone' didn't think to pick up the phone and let the local weatherman know there were Fako rains coming."

Adamou considered what response would be best.

"Don't tell me you didn't know ahead of time. I had half the launcher work crew stomp through here with muddy boots about a half hour before you arrived. They were all off-shift. Apparently the upper slope rail bed smoothing work was canceled for the morning due to a predicted eruption."

Samson's eyes flicked back and forth between them, and Adamou expected him to say something about the volcano. Instead, he asked, "Why were their boots muddy?"

Hadjara rolled her eyes. "Because the idiot builders all wanted to see what would happen. They'd all camped out at the highest elevation work site Ms. Pascaline permitted to remain staffed and watched with binoculars to see if there were any interesting mudslides or cracking of the cement footers for the rail line pylons."

"Were there?" Samson asked.

"I don't know. They were excited and happy, and chattering about Adamou's microtremor dampener thing, so I guess it was fine. Ask him." She pointed at Adamou. "He's the volcanologist."

Hadjara stomped off still muttering.

"It *is* a volcano. You weren't joking."

Adamou nodded.

"Shit," Samson said. "We're fucked."

Adamou reluctantly agreed. "Yes, but not because of the volcano. Fako's tame as volcanoes go. Now, it's the quiet mountains who don't do much who suddenly kill ten thousand people, black out the sky, and disrupt air travel for months. Our Fako grumbles, spits, and shakes from time to time, but he's not planning to rip open the whole side of his mountain anytime soon. He prefers to vent sulfuric gases and give us occasional minor quakes. Our real problem is that you are trying to steal my girl."

The door to their back room rattled open. Pascaline stalked in trailed by Maurie.

"Hey!" Maurie said. "That's a Sadou Jeep out there. Fatima told me that they were out. How'd you get one?"

Pascaline looked at Samson, looked at Adamou, whirled, and walked back outside. Adamou, ignoring Maurie, jumped up and chased Pascaline out.

The sound of a car starting and tires squealing

marked the rest of her exit. Adamou came back in, only a little damp, despite the now heavy rainfall pattering on the café's aluminum roof.

Maurie dragged a chair over with no concern for the bamboo cane legs scraping over the high-gloss cement floor. She sat heavily across from Samson, hair braids dripping.

"So. You're the TCG asshole who's trying to steal Pascaline from us. Tell me one good reason why I shouldn't have Hadjara put cobra venom in your chocolate."

"Hadjara would never stock snake venom," Adamou protested. "And besides, Pascaline is my fiancée. I'm the one who gets to fight with him over this."

Maurie rolled her eyes. "You might not even still be engaged. She just ran away rather than talk with you. That's typical of her," she added to Samson, "so you shouldn't want her for TCG. She belongs right here at home, as our tech lead for the launcher. And don't tell me about how you can pay her more over on Kilimanjaro and give her a bigger team to manage or some such horseshit. I've seen the full project details. Your man, Ethan, doesn't have any good backups for us. Sure that Luxembourg fly-by-night may be about to pick up some of the initial supply runs, but your debris clearance timeline is a mess without us." She poked a finger at Samson. "You need Pascaline to stay right here. So, you better stop trying to steal her. Right. Now."

Adamou sat back down. "He's not going to steal Pascaline."

"No?" Maurie's expression implied that she might be willing to murder him anyway.

"No," Samson confirmed.

Hadjara silently deposited a coffee mug in front of

Maurie's seat along with a little tray with a pitcher of milk and a bowl of sugar cubes. She topped off Samson's mug and left. Adamou lifted a hand in protest at Hadjara's retreating back. "I get no refill?"

Hadjara sniffed but did not bring him more coffee.

"She's an ex-girlfriend, sort of," Maurie explained. "Don't mind them."

"And now as the project's land-use stakeholder he's engaged in a tumultuous relationship with the project technical lead. I foresee no interpersonal risk factors with this at all," Samson said, absolutely deadpan.

Maurie allowed him a reluctant smile. She nodded to concede the point. "Adamou, are you going to give Pascaline hell about missing the date? I'm pretty sure she was up all night trying to make a decision about the spacing for the pylons. The TCG design reps disagree. I was just going with the more conservative closer spacing, but she thinks even that recommendation might not be conservative enough. There was a mumble about your mountain's microtremors again, but I didn't understand anything else."

"Oh good," Samson said, "finally a problem I can do something about. Are you familiar with the magic feather theory of personnel management?"

Maurie turned an interesting shade of purple and developed a coughing fit.

Adamou snorted. "For the last year she's been the divine embodiment of a luck-twisting snake spirit, and for most of my adulthood I've been the personification of a protective volcanic totem, but if you want to pretend we don't get the connections between mysticism and group dynamics in complex project management... then sure, go ahead and explain 'magic feather' to us."

Samson took a sip of coffee instead of speaking.

"I'd say he took that as a 'yes,'" Maurie said.

"Ah." Samson waggled his hand as if to wave away his earlier introduction. "I've got a wunderkind out of Dr. Ross' R&D lab. One of her protégés."

"Pascaline studied under her. But he's got more recent experience, I suppose?" Adamou asked.

Samson's lips quirked to begin to say something, and Maurie made a quick shushing gesture.

Shit. Adamou realized that Samson knew about Pascaline's unfinished formal education. *And I never actually told my uncle about it. But Hadjara probably will, if Samson mentions it directly.*

"Yeah, yeah," Maurie interrupted, "we're all proud of Pascaline, and yeah, we know your uncle the chief who owns the mountain itself and the lower slope land has insisted on Pascaline's *degreed* self's involvement in the project in order to allow the Sadous to use the mountain."

The woman was good. Adamou watched the realization of what Maurie had left out and growing understanding of how what she had said out loud related to it dawn on Samson's face. Samson's eyes focused on Adamou.

"I know," Adamou said. He changed the subject. "Why do you think this guy you've got in mind would be able to be a 'magic feather' for Pascaline? She might just immediately fire him if they can't work together easily. That would hardly boost her confidence."

"They'll work fine together," Samson said. "They've done it before. They were lab partners in college for a full semester of freshman weed-out courses designed to push the lower-achieving students into less demanding degree paths. They got excellent grades together too."

"Huh." Maurie gave an approving nod. "We could use a Pascaline veteran. Someone who can argue with her without becoming infatuated would be a nice change."

"Um." Samson stared at his coffee and gave it an unnecessary swirl with the spoon.

"What do you mean, 'um'?" Adamou said.

"Oh? Oh!" Maurie let out a quick burst of laughter.

Adamou's eyes narrowed.

"Oh, this will be great!" She beamed at Samson. "Yes, absolutely. I need to meet Philip Chao."

"You know his name?" Adamou asked.

Maurie stood up. "Well. You should be going now, don't you think? Can't let that airplane idle for too long or you'll miss the transoceanic flight back around to...Where was it?" She checked her comm. "Yeah, Fatima sent a message that DeeDee said, 'Haikou.' Come on, Adamou, time to get our visitor going."

Samson, eyes twinkling, wheeled out of the café and accepted the cover of carefully overlapped umbrellas held for him by Hadjara's staff as he entered the Jeep.

Maurie invited herself along for the trip back to the Limbe airstrip, where Fatima had arranged for an aircraft to be refueled and waiting to hop Samson over to Yaoundé Nsimalen International for his connecting flight. This plane had a pristine-condition aisle-width wheelchair and a smooth flat-floored lift to take Samson from the tarmac to even level with the plane interior.

On the drive back up to Buea, Adamou poked Maurie. "He's gone. He left without my Pascaline. Now spill."

Maurie grinned. "Let's wait and see if Samson can actually deliver Philip."

CHAPTER TWENTY

DEEDEE PUT HER COFFEE CUP DOWN ON THE table so hard that the rich black fluid splashed over the rim. She did not make eye contact.

Samson winced. This was the junior assistant's version of screaming at hospital orderlies and throwing non-fitting wheelchair repair parts at the wall. The young woman needed her caffeine to function and here she was so mad that she was spilling it. It was not a good sign.

"So, how was your visit to Shen Kong headquarters, Samson?" he said in a soft voice he'd learned from his own senior assistant back when he'd been the junior one. "Did you get us the rock back and smooth things over, so Rodney couldn't sabotage the elevator again? Like he did by telling Mr. Jeffy about the hacking attempt on your comm? Oh, you did? That's nice. Good job, Samson. What about saving the boss's job so it doesn't come out that he sabotaged the elevator too with that side contract to give his extended family money, did you manage that? Oh, yeah, you did? Okay

317

then, let's have a fight about something else then so we don't have to talk about any of that or how tired you are because you haven't had four hours of sleep in a row for three days."

DeeDee made eye contact now. She locked gazes with him like they were about to engage in magic mind meld straight out of an animated feature film. "You know," she said. "You should have told me."

Samson lifted his shoulders in an apologetic shrug. "I didn't really believe my own intuition until I made a side trip to visit the West African Launcher." He paused as another coffee shop customer passed by their outdoor table with a giant-sized to-go coffee and left the parking lot. "I haven't picked up my comm yet. You left yours behind too?"

"Yes, Agent Young." DeeDee glared at him. She was getting really good at doing face-to-face nonverbal communication. And that was even a sarcastic but workplace-appropriate dig to add in that fictitious agent title. Chummy would be so proud.

"Good. I know I usually suck at security stuff."

DeeDee laughed.

Samson tried not to take offense. "But at least I know that about myself, so I can take precautions when it really matters."

DeeDee allowed him a provisional nod. "Yes. Fine. You can do my job and your job both. But I'm still in the dark. How did visiting the West African Launcher site fix the fact that the boss has fallen for a social engineering scam, and been communicating with and sending company internal files to an outside contact named Pascaline?" She held up a hand. "And you don't get credit for fixing the rock. I helped Jax

McAllister get Mr. Ethan Schmidt-Li a direct line to Mr. Aanderson, and the two of them got Mr. Jeffy to talk with Ms. Zhu of Shen Kong. By my timeline they already had things mostly smoothed over before you even boarded your rescheduled flight to Hainan."

"A social engineering... That's not what it... Wait, what did you do?" Samson lost all the color in his already pale face. "Did you report it?"

"Not exactly," DeeDee said, staring into her coffee.

"Thank God," he said. "It's not social engineering, it's worse. Pascaline is his niece or first cousin once removed or something." He waved an arm dismissing the details. "Whatever the exact family tree, she is actually a valid business contact. Ethan Schmidt-Li was made Chief of Sciences, Worldwide, following extensive lobbying on his behalf by our boss, Chummy, the head of HR. Then within an hour of his accepting the position, I checked, and after a closed-door meeting with our Chummy, Mr. Schmidt-Li assigned the support launcher contract to a family-owned company with zero space business who happened to be the vice president of human resources' family."

DeeDee had her mug lifted to her face for another sip and her jaw dropped. She jerked her attention back to the coffee in enough time to spill it on the patio grass instead of her lap.

"Oh, it gets better," Samson said. "Better put the coffee on the table for this part. I was ready to put together a thin argument that the company had rights to the geographic location best suited for constructing the support launcher. But they didn't. That was owned by another party who his family subcontracted with afterwards."

"How the fuck is that fixable?" DeeDee said. So much for business-appropriate communication. Samson realized he'd never tell Chummy about this conversation anyway, so he could stop his automatic assessments of DeeDee's progress. She'd never be senior assistant to the vice president for human resources if the two of them couldn't fix Chummy's extremely flagrant misstep.

"It's not really," Samson admitted, "but it is forgivable." She blinked.

"Results. If it all works, the way that it all got there doesn't get critiqued. At worst there will be rosy retrospectives in twenty or fifty years with a lot of 'oh gosh and golly gee' and many reasonable choices will be spun to look edgy and unlikely to have worked, so even in that detailed analysis, this part will be hidden in the noise. And I think our boss knows that."

DeeDee nodded slowly. He could see her working through the chain of logic by the way her blinks slowed from a shocked flutter to normal. "So he's got it covered?" Her voice didn't lift at the end of the sentence, but Samson knew her better than to take it as a statement.

"He might think he does, but that family business could use some help. The contract is actually pretty well written for the situation and puts all the design and research on us with their company only on the hook for acquiring the site and getting it built. Their technical lead, that'd be Pascaline, is self-taught and doubts herself too much. I'm sending them an academic savant in space systems to be her deputy."

"You're giving them a Mr. Rodney Johnson? Don't you think we could try a new mistake?" DeeDee covered her face with her hands.

"I wasn't one of the assistants yet when that happened," Samson said. "Besides, Mr. Johnson has given us Cory Aanderson for a lot more years than we'd have had him without. And who knows? The thrill of still being able to work might be part of why Mr. Aanderson is still alive."

"Good repetition of the party line," DeeDee said. "And yes, I know we all pretend that it was Chummy's pick and when Mr. Jeffy gets invited to give talks at the business schools, he likes to trot it out as evidence of Chummy's genius. But Chummy was out with a really nasty flu the week Jeffy finalized the Aanderson-Rodney pairing out of a panel with five other more standard choices. Chummy's assistants back then put it together without Chummy's involvement, and the boss covered for them afterwards and you know it."

"And now I'm covering for Chummy," Samson said.

"We," DeeDee corrected. "Tell me about this savant you've found. If he's that good why doesn't he work for us yet?"

Samson told her.

"Got it," DeeDee said. "I'll make sure our résumé-screening systems keep him unemployed long enough for the launcher folks to pick him up."

"Okay." Samson started to disengage his wheel locks.

"Another thing," DeeDee said. "You need to get better at comm security."

Samson rolled his eyes.

"You have to," DeeDee insisted. "Our favorite deputy vice president has figured out somehow that he wasn't Chummy's top pick."

"Rodney knows?" Samson clamped the locks back down.

"I think Cory Aanderson told him a long time ago," DeeDee said. "The data breadcrumbs only make sense if he's known for ages. Most people would've let it go by now. But Rodney sticks to things."

"He does," Samson agreed. The man stuck to his boss Cory Aanderson and was instrumental in keeping him alive and relatively healthy for somebody with a terminal cancer. But in other areas that unwavering commitment could be less helpful.

"So he always follows up on any little comment. He's got an extensive file on Chummy on his personal comm."

"Networking 101," Samson suggested. "Personality details to review before meetings and such so a busy guy can correctly remember thousands of business contacts' names and their kids' names and birthdays."

"With a subheading titled 'Vulnerabilities,'" DeeDee said. "And a much more neutrally worded 'Efforts' which has the weirdest details recorded in the tagged documents. Some of it is obvious fantasyland conspiracy nonsense. His comm security is even worse than yours," she added.

"Does he know?" Samson asked. "No, he can't have known," he answered himself.

"Just let me talk," DeeDee said. "This is hard when I can't type it to you. Rodney seems convinced that he won't actually get to be Vice President of Sales if Chummy is still with the company when Cory Aanderson eventually leaves us."

Samson opened his mouth to respond and shut it at DeeDee's glare. Chummy would never go back on a promise like that, and Mr. Jeffy wouldn't stand for it even if Chummy had an alien body-snatch experience and suddenly became a person who'd do something like that. DeeDee knew that. He didn't have to say it. He focused again on what she was saying.

"There's a bizarre number of efforts that mostly didn't seem to do anything. He knows Chummy's got a bunch of relatives who could call on him for favors, and he's identified them as Chummy's primary weakness. He's done some minor talent poaching to try to get Chummy to voluntarily leave TCG and go back to help out the family business in a headhunter role. Turns out nobody in the family has even reached out, so Rodney gave up on that angle before doing some of the more elaborate stuff in there. Can you believe he had a scheme to pay a drug addict trust fund kid who'd been cut off from family funds to perform some sort of hijacking to abduct a Chummy relative? Obviously that one never happened. His stuff in West Africa seems to have been mostly notional because he lacked local contacts. But he did have private investigators based in Europe do some pretty thorough checks on people and used an anonymous tip to get a younger family member accused of securities fraud."

"What?"

"A young accountant named Reuben Sadou," DeeDee said. "He's been in jail with only a public defender. The lawyer wants him to turn state's witness but the guy doesn't actually know anything because he's not involved, so he can't."

"And Rodney expects Chummy to quit his job to go be a lawyer?" Samson was definitely not following the logic here and no amount of blinking was helping.

"No. I think he just got frustrated that nothing he did was getting back to Chummy, and it was an easy way to hurt him. If Chummy knew about it, he'd probably at least take out a loan to cover bail and fund a private defense attorney."

"You haven't told Chummy yet?"

"No," DeeDee said. "That would make Rodney happy. I don't want to do that. But I do want to stage a jailbreak."

"That won't play right into Rodney's hands at all," Samson said.

DeeDee grinned. "Trust me. I have an idea."

Samson winced. "Please promise you won't make it worse."

CHAPTER TWENTY-ONE

A FEW DAYS LATER, SADOU MAURIE PULLED THE car to the curb beside a shabby but overpriced chalet outside the Douala airport. The compound's doorman accepted a far too large tip from a gangly white guy in a badly fitting sport coat as he exited the air-conditioned gatehouse. The man's thick glasses fogged and he smeared them with the tail of his dress shirt to clear them. This chalet directly under the airport's primary flight path was owned by a cousin of the Douala Airport Information Services night shift desk clerk. Only the sort of person who didn't plan ahead at all would end up staying here.

Maurie checked her comm for the notes written out by Fatima: *"Philip Chao, of MIT, student of Dr. Ross (the two-time Hunsaker Award winner Ross), by-name hire recommendation from TCG. Ms. Maurie: DO NOT SCARE HIM OFF!!!"* She suppressed a snort and got out of the car to make sure the young man was the right nerd. Usually someone unaware enough to end up staying at this place would not be a great hire, but Uncle Chummy's assistant recommended him.

"Taxi? Taxi?" the man said, repeating himself louder and slowly. "I. Need. A. Taxi. Please?"

"Philip Chao?" she said and hoped it wouldn't be.

He beamed at her in obvious relief. "Oh, of course, thank you. I need to go to, um—" He fumbled through pages in a plastic briefcase.

"You're going for an interview with Sadou Moussa," she said. Samson Young appeared not to have Uncle Chummy's knack for choosing people. Grandpere could give this guy the bad news that they didn't really need anybody like him. It was hot, though, and she had some sympathy for his sweating body. "Why don't you get in the car?"

The remote-clicker thing to open the door didn't work. She should have known Fatima would give her the lemon of the family vehicle fleet. She pressed the button on the outside of the door to open it for him.

Philip gave her a grateful glance and slid in quickly to sit, not in the seat next to the driver, but in the rear one as if she were a chauffeur.

Maurie shook her head and closed the door behind him. Definitely not a prime candidate. She got back into the car and started it going on autodrive. Fatima initiated a text chat on the driver's console before she even turned around.

"*Did you pick him up?*" Fatima sent.

"*Y,*" Maurie replied.

"Um, thank you for the prompt pickup," Philip said. A pale hand appeared over Maurie's shoulder and dropped some crumpled bills.

Maurie checked the amount. "Is math not your forte?"

"*He got a perfect score on the math section of the*

ACT just like Pascaline did," Fatima typed. *"I can hear you, so don't think you can talk him into canceling the interview without anybody noticing."*

"Oh, it's not enough?" Another wad of bills appeared.

Maurie folded them and stuffed them into a cubby in the dash. A transcript featuring a lot of *A*'s scrolled across Maurie's screen along with a short résumé for a position called "Oil and Gas Production Manager's Deputy." That didn't look right.

"Hey, do you mind if I practice my interview answers with you?" Philip said. "The job services office at school said it'd be a good idea to do it at the hotel..."

"At MIT. He should be emphasizing that he went to MIT. 'At school'?!? He definitely needs to practice," Fatima wrote.

"...but I got in really late, or really early, whatever it was, and all the aircraft noise made it hard to sleep, so I snoozed my alarm too many times this morning to get it done there. My messed-up comm said we have a half-hour drive, so, hopefully, I've a little time now. And, it's okay, right?"

"Sure," she said. This would be interesting.

"God, I hate interviews," he said.

"Not the best start," Maurie told him.

"Shut up, he's practicing," Fatima wrote.

"Oh, yeah." Philip gulped. "Okay, thank you, sir, for the opportunity to talk to you about joining, uh, what company was it..."

Maurie let him flounder.

"Fuck, I hate this. These things always go horribly wrong. I mean, I get the internship or admission or whatever anyway because of course my test scores are good. I wish I could just hand somebody my transcript.

Or Dr. Ross could write me a recommendation letter."

"*We have his transcript,*" Fatima typed. "*And at least he knows to name-drop Dr. Ross. She was on his references list and responded *herself* to our messages. She says he has, 'my highest possible recommendation' with a triple underline for highest.*"

"What job are you applying for?" Maurie couldn't help herself.

"I don't remember," he said. "I just need something in Africa so I can use the Eurail to pop over to Kilimanjaro and get time talking to actual lab people. I'm an aerospace guy. I should be working on launch vehicles and shit. I like the tweaks of the final design phase best, but I guess people don't get to do much of that now that the elevator is going to be a thing. But maybe I can help out with the craft that they plan to use to lift the tether."

"What if they construct the DiamondWire at geosynch and lower it down instead?" Maurie said.

Philip laughed. "Geosynch, I love it, what a time to be alive! Even taxi drivers are keeping track of space developments. And, yeah, maybe they could. But there's not much carbon up there already. And we don't know if the nanotube construction process even works in low gravity."

"*Yes, we do,*" Fatima wrote. "*It actually works best in zero gee. One of the labs that verified the Kilimanjaro team's work was TCG's Luna One. That was in Uncle Chummy's whole project overview info packet. So, whatever TCG's super-secret manufacturing process is, it's either not gravity dependent or centrifugal forces can substitute for it. And I resent that 'even taxi drivers' comment.*"

"And if you have to lift it up anyway," Philip continued, "why not turn the carbon into nanotubes before sending it up? That way if something goes wrong, you can fix it on-planet. Cheaper that way. I haven't checked the math on the total uplift mass yet. I figure they must have a way to join segments of nanotube in low gravity or they'd be pouring research dollars into making a really fucking big rocket to lift the entire tether at once. Twenty-two thousand miles of the stuff, even if it is nano-thin, is going to be an impressive total payload. Say, have you ever seen a launch?"

"Wait, wait, I'm still stuck on his plan to use the Eurail to ditch us and go work on the elevator. What continent does he think this is?"

"I haven't seen a launch in person," Maurie said, ignoring Fatima.

"Oh, no, you wouldn't want to be that close. You'd get roasted, but at safe standoff distance with hearing protection and cameras to observe all the closer-in stuff, it's the best, the absolute best," he said with conviction.

"What an amazing deep vocabulary, our geographically challenged opportunist has. Such a poet. I take it back, you can drop him off at the airport instead. It's not like Grandpere doesn't have enough else on his schedule."

"So, launches are like poetry?" Maurie asked.

"Yeah, uh, no," he said. "Not like English-class poetry. You know the ones where you have to look up all the words, and the teacher says they've got other meanings still besides those, and you end up wondering if you even speak English? Definitely not like that. It's more like, um, the thrum of a rocket

takeoff and the heartbreak of the failed test... I
think *that* might really be 'a window into the soul of
human expression and the rawest hope for a better
future.'" Philip blushed deep red. "Or at least I think
so. That last bit was something Dr. Ross said once in
a speech, and I wrote it down, because that is how
it is, or how it should be."

"*She said that during her second Hunsaker Award
acceptance speech. He really ought to have name-
dropped the Hunsaker too.*" Fatima's next comment
bubbled an "in progress" symbol with a delete and
a renewed "in progress" bubble several times before
she sent: "*Okay, he's *maybe* okay.*"

"*Ask him to say that again in Swahili,*" Fatima
added. "*If he can, I'll put him back on Grandpere
Moussa's schedule. His résumé claims moderate flu-
ency in Swahili.*"

"Do you speak Swahili?" Maurie asked.

"Not really. I dropped that class. But I can say,
'Wapi bufuni ipo?' That means, 'Which way to the
bathroom, please?'"

"*What?!? He said, 'where bathroom exist.' The
word choice is all wrong, and the grammar is awful.
Nobody would say that. Seriously. Take him back to
the airport.*"

"We don't speak Swahili," Maurie typed back. "*Why
should we care if he's a bad fit for East Africa?*"

"If you always get the jobs anyway, why are you
interviewing now?" Maurie said out loud. "Shouldn't
you be getting ready to defend your third doctorate
or something?"

"Only the first doctorate, though I might have
defended two related thesis projects. I wasn't certain

which one I wanted to do and was considering just working on the research for both." Philip sighed. "But I failed the professional engineer's exam."

"No, he didn't. He missed a single question."

"The PE exam is usually this minor thing only relevant for folks who want to work in industry. The test score didn't even count toward a grade in any of my classes, but your percentile ranking on the test compared to other applicants is part of what they look at for formal admission into the doctoral program I wanted."

"There's informal admission?"

Maurie typed back, *"Sometimes profs let high-performing undergraduates take graduate courses. If some wunderkind appears to be headed toward becoming a lifelong academic but keeps failing a required language arts course needed for the bachelor's and his tuition checks keep coming in…"*

"Right," Fatima replied, *"they'll take the boy's money for as long as his family keeps handing it over."*

Philip groaned and laid his head back against the headrest. "I was such an idiot. I should've gone to the University of Florida for their space undergrad. They've got a decent enough program and then I could've gotten in to work with Dr. Ross for the PhD program as an outside applicant. But she only takes the top student from within the same school, and I didn't get the highest score this time. There was a key, you know."

"What key? The wunderkind has gone cryptic again."

"The test's answers type of key?" Maurie asked.

"Yeah, yeah, it was Lucas, my roommate and my lab partner for every year except freshman year. His mom works at the company that administers the exam.

He always gets intense test anxiety. So, she slipped him an early copy. I mean, he offered me a look and wanted me to double-check the answers the group of them had worked out over the course of the weeks they'd been practicing with it. But, eh, it's not like I thought I needed to, you know?"

"This, I did not have in his record," Fatima wrote. *"But I bet the TCG people knew it."*

"So, yeah, give me a time machine, and I'd definitely take Lucas up on it. *He* applied to five different graduate schools instead of just the one. If I'd just taken one look at it, I'm sure I'd have passed too. I memorized *pi* to two hundred places in elementary school just to see if I could do it. I can still remember out to fifty places now. Yeah, next time, I'm definitely going to do the right thing and cheat."

There's no one in the whole world who is this bad at interviewing, Fatima wrote.

"That sounds like exactly the sort of thing you should tell a future employer," Maurie said.

Philip made a noise between a snort and a laugh. "Oh yeah, I should get back to practicing. Ask me about where I see myself in five years."

"Working in a TCG lab," Maurie replied.

"Or dead in a ditch." Philip rubbed his face with his hands and groaned. "This sucks so much. Okay. What I should say is, that I hope to be ready to apply for whatever the next level up is at the company. Shit. I really need to figure out what the position I'm applying for is. My comm junked itself on the trip over here. I restarted the thing three times, and it insists I'm in West Africa. Everyone knows the Kilimanjaro site is on the east side of the continent."

"Sadou Corp will supply you with a company comm. Don't sweat that part," Maurie reassured him.

"Oh, that's right, I'm interviewing with Sadou Corporation! And the guy I'm interviewing with is Sadou Moussa. My lab partner freshman year was a Tchami-Sadou; I wonder if he knows her?"

"You should tell him," Fatima wrote. *"Really this taxi driver farce is letting him make too much of a fool of himself."*

Maurie considered telling him, but he was just sharing so much.

Philip turned bright red before she could speak and started talking fast. "I didn't mean that. I know. I know. It's a big continent, of course not everyone from some place in Africa knows everyone else on the continent. I did *not* fail the Ethics and Diversity Inclusion for Engineers class! Pascaline was the one who was getting a D in that before she dropped it to keep it off her transcript. She was supposed to retake it the next semester."

"You were Pascaline's lab partner?"

"Well, yeah, but just freshman year. I'd've stuck with her too, but that asshole family of hers—"

"Asshole?"

"Oh yeah, the biggest assholes ever. They stopped paying tuition and what with them being these oil gazillionaires the scholarships and financial assistance reps for the school wouldn't even talk to her." He blew out a breath and made an exasperated face. "Now if she'd taken the spot as Dr. Ross' next PhD candidate instead of Lucas, I'd've seen it coming. Pascaline was smart."

"Her family stopped paying tuition," Maurie repeated,

trying to hide her shock. *That can't be public.* "You're certain?"

"If he can't keep his mouth shut, I've got to put him on an airplane out of here," Maurie typed.

Fatima didn't reply.

"Yeah." Philip shook his head. "She showed up again for a summer internship we'd both gotten into at a Luxembourg satellite builder, and she took classes remotely whenever somebody could slip her a login code, but there's no substitute for being there for the lab work."

"Somebody, meaning you?" Maurie said.

Philip blushed again and shrugged.

"Does the university see that as cheating?"

"It's not like anyone else loses anything by someone who belongs in the class and was even formally admitted getting to keep learning." Philip hugged himself. "That's going to be me next, I'm just going to vanish."

"Don't you dare vanish him." Fatima typed, *"We'll keep him away from the Bakweri. Ms. Pascaline needs him."*

Maurie closed her eyes. Pascaline did have a lot more aerospace engineering education than she'd realized. But the Sadou family still did not have an aerospace engineer credential, and if they hired Philip, he might talk to the wrong person.

"Fatima, you will erase the transcript and any recordings of this interview."

"Yes, Ms. Maurie." Fatima typed back.

But Pascaline needed him.

"Philip," Maurie said, "you're hired."

"What?"

"And watch your mouth about Pascaline or you'll never work in any space-related industry ever again."

CHAPTER TWENTY-TWO

IN THE DAYS THAT FOLLOWED, PHILIP STUDIED the plans and made only a very few suggestions which he relayed quietly to Pascaline. The pale Chao boy wore floppy hats too large for him, far too much bug spray, and a general sense of desperation. He hadn't gotten any less intelligent than she'd remembered. Fortunately for her, he also hadn't gained even a cubic centimeter of street smarts either. She kept watching for signs that he was going to turn against her and intended to tell everyone about her lack of real credentials, but he said nothing. He didn't even ask for a raise.

But he helped!

Philip Chao seemed much the same quiet creature he'd been years ago when she'd seen him standing shocked inside the dorm room entryway when the resident assistant had chosen to inform Pascaline at full volume that she couldn't go up to her room because she wasn't enrolled anymore. No one in her fine extended family had bothered to pay her tuition that semester, and thus she didn't get to have a room in student housing.

The precious, naive boy had been—on paper—hired into an engineering management position, because she'd felt certain he'd want that for résumés later. But he had both no skill and no interest in directing people, so he now served exclusively as her engineering assistant.

She gave a slow sweeping glower to the build site and the work crews. The people moved the earth around along the path where they'd soon be putting the maglev rails in alignment. They'd been on schedule for all the early completion bonuses. But now, they were on schedule and she was confident her choices were the right ones. Everyone avoided catching her eye, except Adamou's little cousin Dibussi, of course, who responded with a brighter grin. Until the kid's gaze fell on her pale shadow and that smile turned distinctly superficial.

The Bakweri didn't care for Philip, which was absolutely for the best. Perhaps she shouldn't have implied that their history was other than professional, but sometimes the mass of prospective in-laws got too possessive. It was fun to rile them up a bit. And yet Adamou seemed utterly unaffected.

Not ideal. Not by any means, but she couldn't exactly tell her dear fiancé that half the reason his family had been delighted for their renewed engagement was a sham, and that she needed to have her old lab partner who, yes, she had gone on a date with once, trailing along because he had all the knowledge she should have had stored in his fat brain and his comm was packed full of the old course notes she desperately needed to maintain the facade.

Nothing else for it, Pascaline looked around for something to complain about. A bit of track where the rails would be out of alignment would do nicely.

The upper line foreman approached and gave her a greeting a touch deeper than a head nod.

"Ms. Pascaline, anything we can do for you today?"

"I need to see the specs for that curve." She pointed down the mountain a fair distance where someone had decided it would be a good idea to add a small kink for the in-ground stakes and then twist them back again to follow a walking trail's easier path rather than maintain the straight glide lines cleared through the lower mountain palm tree groves.

"Ha!" he said. "I knew you'd agree with me. It doesn't match the specs unless we clear a few more palm trees. The Bakweri workers didn't want to clear that spot, because it's where the first palm tree in the whole grove was planted. History." He waved a dismissive hand. "I told them you'd want it straight," he added with some pride and handed over the relevant section of the design document.

"The first tree's still there?" Philip asked.

"No," the foreman said. "There's a plaque. Historians care about it, I guess."

"Move it," Pascaline said. "Or embed it in the side of the pylon. Do whatever you need to do to build this thing correctly." She turned to point at one of the closer stakes where a cage of rebar had been set up in preparation for the addition of concrete. "That height's wrong."

"No. We got that one right. Matches the numbers." He pointed at the spray-painted numerals at the base of the structure. "It's just this angle makes it look short." The man grinned. One of the crew yelled over a question about where the gravel needed to go, and the man hustled off to do his job.

She looked through the plastic-protected site-build instructions. The measured height was written on the ground next to the tower of rebar. They matched the launcher build specifications. He was right. Worse, she checked it against her master on the comm, and it was still right.

Pascaline glared. It didn't look right.

She snapped her fingers at the closest crewman and got him to take the foreman's plastic-covered build spec sheets back to him. She waved farewell at the crew generally with the noise of the newly started-up gravel spreader too loud for speech. The crewman took the pages from her with a quick little bow and jogged down the line to return them to the supervisor.

Pascaline grabbed Philip by the elbow and dragged him up the mountain far enough for them to hear themselves think. Another rise gave them a better view of the whole down-track line. She could almost see how the rail would run smooth and straight up the mountain with those perfectly crafted lift vehicles on the track and their precious payloads safely stored within.

A distracting shriek rang out below. The flash of machetes reflected the brilliant sunlight, and a large snake lay across the open earth, dead.

"They shouldn't just do that," Philip objected.

"You'd think snakes would know better by now," Pascaline agreed, even though she was sure he meant the snake might not have been poisonous and even if so might have passed through the construction site without biting anyone if they'd all stopped work and stepped away.

Philip did his typical open-mouthed blinking as he tried to come up with a way to explain, but he was getting better. He shut his mouth again without saying anything else. His comm angled just enough that she could see him write: *look up local snakes poisonous.*

"Try snakebite death rates and average cost of antivenom treatments instead. I'm giving that foreman a bonus."

Pascaline turned her attention back to the track line. The wiggle in the staked-out route height was clearly still there. It hadn't been an illusion from the spot where she'd been standing before.

"They better not build that section yet." She pointed Philip at it. She had to snap her fingers to get him to focus on what she was gesturing at instead of the edge of the cleared area where a couple of the crew had started to poke at the brush with the tips of their machetes. "You see that?"

"It's not scheduled for a couple days yet," Philip agreed, and put his head down to focus at his comm instead of looking up at the actual site she was pointing at. "Though, this particular team is with the access road installation, not the rail line bed just yet, so they're just running an access road."

"Because an access need not have, oh, I don't know, actual access for the line being maintained?" Pascaline waved her hand in front of his comm. "I said. Look. At. That." She pointed at the wiggle again.

"Oh." Philip somehow managed to pale, which was impressive with his skin tone. "Sh—"

Pascaline clamped a hand over his mouth. "No curses

on the mountain. We don't want it thinking ill of us."

He jerked his face away to get his lips free, as she'd expect he would, but he also didn't repeat himself. "But Adamou doesn't..."

She silenced him with a glare.

Philip shook his head and turned back to the engineering issues he had the capacity to understand. Pascaline looked down the line at the little ants of people working further down. Most had machinery of one kind or another tearing into the mountain here and building it up there. Piles of materials with rough tarps thrown over top them dotted along the emerging build path. Above them, going up the mountain, the line's route was less obvious as fewer tall things in need of clearing grew and the upslope cloud cover hid this nearer peak of the mountain.

Adamou spent part of almost every day up there in those sulfurous clouds, sometimes remembering to bring breathing gear, and more often forgetting. The Bakweri chief had found occasion to discreetly inform her that long-term lung damage from sulfur fume inhalation at the levels typically found around the peak were not extraordinarily damaging, but that there were always extra masks stocked at the little shacks around the peak which held other supplies for the volcanic sensor equipment. So if she should wish to call Adamou, perhaps every morning after he'd left, she might make him promise to put on a mask?

Pascaline had met that suggestion with the scowl it deserved, and the chief had dropped the subject. Annoyingly it was morning, and she had an urge to call Adamou. Just to check on things, she assured herself, not because she was the sort of person who enjoyed his presence. Pascaline brushed off the distraction, checked her surroundings to ensure no one else had approached, and snapped her fingers again to regain Philip's attention.

"Well? You've had time to review the whole launch system. Are we screwed or what?"

He made a face at her. It took a few moments and Pascaline realized that "screwed" might be considered not the politest of terms if a mountain spirit felt like being picky about such things. She brushed that off too.

"Well?"

"The specifications for the line are based on original plans to launch water and manufacturing pellets. The course will be fine for that."

"But?" Pascaline considered shaking her assistant to make him spill the details faster, but his head was down with the glow of his comm reflecting that shade of blue that went with the engineering computations software. His lips moved soundlessly.

"Smoothing the path a little more," he muttered, "yeah, narrower tolerances for optimal launch instead of just acceptable range. That'd be a lot better." His eyes flicked away from the screen barely long enough to take in a look at the actual terrain before returning to his calculations again.

That look of intense concentration was the one she wanted. Yes. Pascaline waited. It was the expression that meant he'd seen something that his training had taught him was important and his brain was forming it into words for her. She silently crossed her fingers.

"I wonder if we could do something about the vertical bend too?" Philip murmured.

He poked at his comm for several more minutes

without bothering to elaborate while Pascaline waited with growing annoyance. He was very lucky she needed him or he'd be assigned to a muggy desk with only intermittent air-conditioning and she'd be up here on the cooler part of the mountain slopes doing the project surveys on her own.

"Yeah, updated specs're good." Finally Philip looked up.

"You aren't speaking in complete sentences yet," she informed him.

"Oh." Philip's face did the confused wrinkle thing.

Pascaline sighed. She'd have to spell it out to him. "Tell me what needs to change with the track route and why or I'll make you personally be the first payload for the test launch."

Philip's face managed to go completely colorless. "This is not rated for human transport. Not even close. Even foodstuff like the freeze-dried meats that get sent to the Moon crews for special events would be pulverized before they left this track."

"So the track as currently laid out needs to be smoothed," Pascaline translated. "But I already knew that. So we get the line fixed along the ground route here, but what about the vertical rise for the slope?"

"I don't know," Philip said immediately.

"So I should put you on a flight home and hire someone else who's competent then?" Pascaline hid her slight smile. He'd gotten nervous about overstating his expertise recently when he realized how quickly his suggestions repeated through her mouth got implemented. Uncle Chummy had some particularly helpful and, more important, experienced engineers that he'd connected her to through TCG's network. She'd taken to running

Philip's suggestions past them before implementing major changes, but she felt no need to tell Philip that. Let him earn his paycheck. Especially if he remained serious about dropping them the moment he got a job offer elsewhere, she felt no need to coddle his feelings.

"Seriously," Philip said, inadvertently echoing her thoughts. "It isn't rated for human spaceflight and probably never will be. There are so many extra tests and checks for that. We couldn't possibly get it approved."

"I don't care about other people's approvals." Pascaline thought he should have realized that at least by now. "And didn't military jets start using rail launch assists over a century ago, on your country's aircraft carriers no less?" She knew very well that they had. Part of her midnight research from the previous weeks had uncovered quite a lot of other financially successful, well-tested uses for rail launch systems even if no one had poured the amount of money and time into making one quite like theirs. There remained some comfort in seeing that TCG's engineers had pieced together old, well-understood tech instead of handing them a bunch of barely ready ideas strung together with bits of string and entirely too much hope.

She'd seen the records of the prototype designs extensively modeled and sim-tested by top researchers at TCG. She reminded herself: *We are merely installing Uncle Chummy's design and operating it for a fat payoff. And continually telling his designers about little things they seem to have forgotten, like to check that material properties remain within acceptable limits for the temperature changes from near sea level tropics to four thousand plus meters.*

She briefly considered explaining to those engineers

that they could stop arguing back and forth about the cost to value trade-off for an enclosed track line. Maurie didn't even pretend at engineering know-how, but even she had agreed with Pascaline that they'd be installing the partially enclosed version no matter how many centuries the management analysts said it'd take to have a positive return on investment from increased machinery preservation. Some people didn't understand that the plants and animals who thrived near the equator conspired at every turn to bury machinery in green tombs and then the critters would lay in wait to eat, bite, or sting unsuspecting repair techs.

"Gah." Philip shook his head. "I need to do more calculations."

"So I'll be telling the build crews to expect that some of the rail line supports might need to be higher than current schematics indicate," Pascaline said.

"Um, I guess," he agreed, "but whichever the lowest ones are can still be pretty close to ground level."

"Nope," Pascaline said. "None of them will be directly on ground level. We've got far too many creepy crawlies that would love to get themselves smeared across the full length of the line and mess up our tolerances."

"Come on, Pascaline"—the whine in Philip's tone was getting really annoying—"can we please go back to a nice air-conditioned building to finish this up? We don't really need to go the whole length of the build line, right?"

She hadn't considered checking the full length today actually, but now that he mentioned it, she realized that that would be exactly what an on-site engineering management executive should do.

"Of course we do."

"Then can I go back?" Philip begged.

"No. You come with me everywhere. Where I go, my assistant goes."

"Except for the parties." He shook his head.

Pascaline raised an eyebrow. "You hate parties, and you can't speak anything but English."

"A lot of people speak English!" Philip protested. "It's the language of business."

"Except you don't speak business English either because you're only fluent in North American accents and can't seem to get your head untwisted enough to understand anything else." Needling him was entirely too much fun.

"But I don't need to talk to anyone back at the office," Philip protested. "And my comm is overheating, so I'll need to get it into air-conditioning before it can do the calculations you need to check the slope adjustments for the rail line anyway!"

Pascaline pointed up the line. "Walk."

He scowled, turned, and started trudging upward.

She passed him easily and after a few moments he jogged up after to trudge alongside her.

"We could take a vehicle," he suggested. "It would be faster, and I could put my comm under the vents to chill it faster. Seriously. It may have battery-life damage."

"Yup," Pascaline agreed evenly.

"What?"

"Most electronics have shorter life in hot climates. Fact of life. There's a stock of spare batteries in the supply closet if it gets truly dire."

"You should not be just living with that!" Philip objected.

"See anybody with the facilities to do warm-weather battery-life testing for the current models around here?" she asked.

"After the line starts up..." Philip began.

"Exactly," Pascaline agreed. "We get this thing up and running and maybe somebody with a design shop decides to rent a little space and do some lab work on site. Maybe some of the corporations with the bigger research departments kick in a little grant money for our engineering colleges and some of those brainiacs will be able to buy the tools to try out the pet theories they have about fixing that problem."

"Uh, I was thinking more of just building some more air-conditioned facilities at key points along the line."

"It will always be necessary to inspect the line," Pascaline spoke with absolute confidence.

"Cameras are really good," Philip argued.

Something slithered in the shadow of a scrubby bush ahead, and she grabbed his arm by reflex, holding him back until the full length of the snake could cross the open ground of the cleared track and disappear back among the rocks on the other side.

"How did you even see that?" he asked.

Pascaline shrugged. "I live here."

"But not here, here. You're from up north somewhere; all the Bakweri people are very clear about you being not from around here."

Pascaline rolled her eyes. "I've moved around a lot."

"Huh," Philip said, "maybe you'll end up like the Wright brothers and when this launcher is finished, every state you spent an overnight in will claim to be your hometown."

"We have provinces, not states." Pascaline looked

side-eyed at him. He continued to scan through design documents unaware.

A roar of an engine overtook them, and Adamou pulled a battered but well-maintained utility vehicle to the side of the rough-cut dirt road. He hopped out and sauntered around the hood of the car to open the passenger side door for Pascaline.

"Drive you the rest of the way up?" Adamou suggested.

It wasn't a two-seater, but the back had been stacked with equipment and parts. Philip would be able to wedge himself in, barely. Pascaline almost turned down the offer in favor of continuing on foot the couple kilometers more she'd planned to see today.

But Philip was drawn like a magnet by the rush of air-conditioning and crammed himself into the backseat. He looked back from among the parts boxes, blinking.

Adamou gestured at the front seat. "I don't want to disturb your work," he said. The passenger side seat was pristine. The drink holder held a fresh iced coffee with chilled beads of condensation running down the side. "It's caramel mocha on ice." He nodded at the drink.

She got in. This looked a lot like "I love you," or even better, "I respect you and want to help you succeed."

"Go slow," she ordered. "I need to get a good view of all of this."

Adamou preened.

That wasn't what she'd meant. Pretty men should never be allowed to know they look good. It wasn't good for them. But she winked at him, and the corners of his mouth twitched as if she'd said, "I love you too."

Adamou took the back-and-forth cornering on the single-lane road quickly. The boxes in the back shifted, and Philip yelped.

"Careful with my stuff!" Adamou instructed when a small avalanche of the foam-packed instruments nearly buried Philip.

"If you break my assistant, I'll make you find me three more," Pascaline warned.

"I'm sure I can find you some excellent engineering grad students to help out," Adamou said. "In fact I'll send you a list."

"I'm not interested in hiring all your ex-girlfriends."

"It'd be only fair," he observed.

"I'm not interested in fair," she said, enjoying the banter. But she didn't add the follow-on thought out loud: *I require someone with Philip's skills because I don't have them.*

"What sort of pathetic creature takes an assistant position with an ex-girlfriend anyway?" Adamou inquired with raised eyebrows directed at Philip through the rearview mirror.

Philip, wisely, didn't answer. But Pascaline wasn't quite sure if it was because he was tongue-tied or because he hadn't quite understood all the words. Philip could be remarkably bad at understanding normal spoken language at times. And Adamou hadn't bothered to imitate a North American accent like she had to when communicating with the man.

"I'm worth it," Pascaline replied instead. "And slow down more, or I'll get back out and walk."

"You are," he agreed. Adamou dropped the speed down to a crawl not much faster than a jog. "What are you looking for?"

"Anything," she said, because she didn't know. And she rather hoped Philip was able to see enough with the distraction of the constantly shifting piles. She could feel them jamming into the back of her seat with every jolt and bump in the road, so he was probably buried up to his knees at least in the backseat with all of the stuff piled around him.

"You get a lot of wildlife up here?" She decided to pump Adamou for information. They might not need the full mesh enclosure along the full fifteen-kilometer length of the maglev if wildlife was rare at these heights.

"Eh, some. Not really my interest. I can tell you more about the rocks," he replied.

"Did you refine that idea you had for the micro-quake compensator?" Philip asked.

"Yup." Adamou nodded. "Already passed that onto Maurie and the ground crew. It's basic earthquake-resistant construction techniques. No need to reinvent anything on that account. Though whenever we get a big rumble, you'll want to recalibrate the rail line adjusters."

"What size are these rail line adjusters?" Philip asked.

Adamou shrugged. "I can get Maurie to send you the specs."

"Please," he said, "might need to adjust the heights of the rail pylons for them to integrate right in the whole system."

"Oh yeah," Adamou said, "I had that pier right next to where I picked you up lowered to put up a test one on it tomorrow."

Pascaline punched the emergency stop button on the vehicle and hurled herself out of the car seeing red.

As she slammed the door behind her, Adamou said, "What's wrong with her?"

"You tried to break her space launcher," Philip said in a far more reasonable tone than Pascaline would've been able to manage. She decided to give the boy a raise without waiting for him to ask for it. Pascaline made herself take deep breaths in and out. She was not going to hit Adamou. She was not going to tear open the instruments in the back of his car and shatter them on the path to help him understand what he'd done. No matter how much she wanted to, she was going to keep her calm and go back downslope to fix that screw-up.

"I didn't do that!" Adamou said. "I only had the pier height changed so that . . . Oh shit." He hit his forehead. "I'm sorry," he said. "I'm an idiot."

"Have. All. Design. Changes. Sent. Through. Me. Please." Pascaline said breathing between each word. She was going to have to have him watched. Very, very carefully.

"Of course," Adamou said. "I'm sorry."

Pascaline shook her head. Philip was looking at his comm, scrolling through design documents trying to figure out how Adamou could have accidentally been granted the authority to change a design, and Pascaline knew he'd find nothing. The workers had done it, because Endeley Adamou had asked. The workers hadn't told the foreman or made a note on the earth beside the structure or warned anyone, because it wouldn't have occurred to them that Adamou might make a mistake.

An odd thought reminded her of her pleas to Uncle Chummy for an experienced TCG replacement. A foreigner might have caught this. Possibly even without crashing a launch craft in a hypersonic derailment casualty. But a foreigner would not be able to see what had allowed the error.

"Don't do it again." She rubbed her head. "And I need to talk with your uncle, Endeley Bouba, about a plaque."

She began listing in her head the respected people she'd needed to have banned from build site. Or no, that wouldn't work. Ah. She'd use honor guards instead. "Welcome, welcome, Chief Endeley. Oh you don't want to bother our Maurie or our Pascaline. Here, let me give you a coffee and record some notes. No trouble at all. How many sugars, sir?" Yes, she could see the solution clearly. That'd work quite well.

Part III

Dabare—early texts using this term can be understood to mean some combination of the following: (1) scheming, (2) the practice of magic, (3) the application of knowledge in an attempt to force a result, not always successfully

Source: University of Yaoundé, *Fulani Folklore Wiki*

CHAPTER TWENTY-THREE

PASCALINE GAVE THE PANICKY ASHEN-FACED Fatima a discreet wave as she found a chair for herself in the back of the worn family conference room. It was fun to have a secret, but maybe not so kind to the help. Grandpere, good old Sadou Moussa, blinked on his throne of an old office chair and asked querulously for another cup of coffee, expressing his usual obliviousness. She wasn't sure if he was just that tired or if he no longer respected the people on the call enough to project any vitality he didn't feel. He took the coffee steaming with plenty of sugar despite both the heat and his only semi-controlled type 2 diabetes. The air-conditioning in the family villa had gone out again, but they did have electricity. A backup generator rumbled a steady hum against the back wall. City power hadn't had brownouts in a couple weeks, but for this meeting they needed to be prepared. Uncle Benoit was fucking everything up. Again.

Personally somewhat clear of his influence, Pascaline did sympathize. It was fun to be the one with the

power to break things. She hid a smile at the remembered rage-filled phone call from the City of Yaoundé
public electric utilities assistant director. They'd hired
away a lot of very good electrical engineering techs
for the new geothermal plants. That included the
former director, who'd previously been both severely
underpaid and severely overworked. Naturally as the
new foreman for launcher electrical construction, he
was even more overworked now, but he was no longer
underpaid. The mayor had called shortly after and
apologized to "Sadou Moussa's granddaughter" for his
subordinate's rude language and asked about buying
profit shares in the launcher.

Maurie landed in the chair next to Pascaline only
bare seconds before the screens flickered on to display
Uncle Benoit's face. Their comfortably middle-aged
uncle radiated confidence, and even had a wineglass
filled with something bubbly positioned just on
the desk in front of him so the camera angle would
include it in the livestream but not block his face. His
silk suit suggested the air-conditioning was working
just fine in his home office.

"We are completely screwed, aren't we?" Maurie
whispered into her ear.

Fatima hissed a shushing sound and angled the feed
to focus on Grandpere and to leave the two of them
tiny in the large screen's background. It made them
look as if they were at a kids' table for a family meal
and not the two people running the most valuable
project their family had ever seen. On the screen
against the wall, aunts and uncles started to fill in
squares on the family call. Maurie craned her neck
to try to see. Pascaline chose the more comfortable

option and joined the meeting on her own comm with no outgoing audio or video.

A lot of people were present today. Almost all of them. Uncle Jacques was looking tired and wearing working coveralls instead of the pristine suit he usually favored for Sadou events. Aunt Julienne appeared triumphant, but she still had worry wrinkles forming a permanent fold between her eyebrows. More second cousins and extended family with half-share votes joined. Many members were appearing actually live on camera as required in the bylaws for their votes to be counted instead of using the more common unmoving photo profile. They were older than their pictures and a handful had the too wide pupils of narcotic indulgence. The bylaws made no limitation on how sober a voting member had to be.

Pascaline snapped her fingers once below the table to draw Maurie's attention to a side chat she'd started.

Great Aunt Mami appeared on Pascaline's comm in the one-to-one call. The woman sat propped up on pillows in her clinic bed, looking exhausted and defeated. She was speaking instead of typing, but Pascaline made the program text-caption the words while Fatima worked on setting up the room's audio levels to Grandpere's liking.

"I tried, Pascaline. It's over. I even paid old debts with some of the narc suppliers to see if our family addicts would get high and miss this vote, but Benoit has enough of their household staffs on his side that it made no difference." Great Aunt Mami hugged herself tight, pulling an IV line and wincing at the pinch. *"I hope no one overdoses."*

Pascaline started typing a response. *"Great Aunt, it's all fine..."*

But before she could send, her great aunt shook her head. *"I can't watch this."* The old woman ended her participation in the call. *Shit. But, it was still fine.* Pascaline pulled up a messaging app to tell Great Aunt Mami the details of why she was sure it would work out.

A bang of the conference room door earned a squeak and a glare from Fatima. Philip Chao stuck his head in and then was pulled right back out again. Endeley Adamou stepped inside alone and shut the door, soundlessly, behind him. He was looking very fine. Pascaline stopped to admire him. But for the brief moment when he met her eyes, he looked embarrassed and a little bit belligerent. It was as if he'd done the wrong thing but didn't want to admit it yet. He paused to compliment Fatima on something and then seated himself, not in the empty chair next to her, but closer to the exit on the far side of Maurie.

Fatima adjusted the room video feed to refocus on Sadou Moussa and leave off all the back-wall chairs entirely.

Maurie let out a low groan and rubbed her temples.

"Side effects turning bad again?" Adamou asked in a whisper. He put a hand on her forehead.

Maurie flicked off his hand. He looked at the empty side tables and jerked his chin at Fatima, miming for her to bring over some drinks.

"I have a screaming headache, and I'd like to kill you for slamming that door," Maurie grumbled. "Yes, it is a known side effect of a drug regimen that's finally letting me not have raging vision-inducing fever spikes. But since I can't function, I'm going to have to go back to babbling at fuzzy nightmares that aren't there. Happy, jerk?"

He leaned over Maurie to grin at her. "Her snakes have fur now? Should we be concerned?"

"I meant the way the things waver in and out of focus like heat shimmers over asphalt on a muggy day." She shook her head. "Never mind. Not important." Maurie stared straight ahead at the screen.

Pascaline winced at Grandpere's slumped posture in the director's chair. He should've been either relaxed as a proud king of the lion pride or growling in fury about to destroy Benoit and the cowards who'd enabled him. Instead he was blinking sleepily at his coffee as if Uncle Benoit were right to be taking over the family. Pascaline reminded herself that she didn't care. She'd protected the launcher. She didn't have to have a solution for protecting the family too.

Adamou nestled closer to Maurie. Pascaline's eyes narrowed. The man was trying to pick a fight with her. What had he done now that made him feel guilty enough to try to get her to verbally throw the first punch? He hadn't given build-site workers orders again without permission. She'd made sure of that.

He leaned even nearer to Maurie. Her cousin twitched like she wanted to elbow Adamou in the gut, but at the final moment decided it would be too rude and pulled her whole arm and shoulder back in. Her move left Adamou gaping at a female cringing away from his touch. It was likely a first-time experience for the man, Pascaline judged.

She muffled her laugh and it came out as a snort.

Fatima bustled over with a drinks cart. She shook a finger at Adamou and then proffered a drink to Pascaline. She sipped. It was a perfect fancy iced coffee. Someone had used fresh roasted beans to make a delicious brew and then mixed it with melted chocolate and just the right amount of cane sugar before pouring it all over a mound of shaved ice. The double-layer metal travel mug would keep it chilled for her through the whole meeting.

"He doesn't deserve you," Fatima said, "even if he did message ahead and ask me to make that drink for you." Pascaline was inclined to agree, but he did apologize nicely. The updated microtremor-predictor model delivered after the screw-up with the launcher build interference was nice. That he'd also included three dozen white roses showed that the man had promise.

"Hey, I'm a catch," Adamou insisted.

Fatima sniffed, and deposited drinks for Maurie and Adamou. "You have some sort of plan?" She looked to Pascaline and sounded hesitant and scared.

"You'll be okay even if I have to pay your salary myself," Pascaline said, "but, Uncle Benoit does have the votes."

Maurie grimaced.

"What?" Adamou asked.

Of course he didn't get it. The way the Sadou family operated wasn't obvious to outsiders. They were the wealthy on their way back to poverty if Uncle Benoit took control. Pascaline let Adamou talk rather, attempting to explain.

He said, "Look, I just stopped by briefly to tell you..."

Fatima cut Adamou off. "Uncle Benoit has the vote to take control of the family funds. To distribute out the launcher moneys in quarterly dividends, including all the working cash, not just the profits," she said.

She handed Pascaline a street vendor's bakery bag heavy with *makala*. Maurie received nothing for a beat. Then, following ingrained manners Fatima clearly would've rather have ignored, she pushed a bottle of water and some ibuprofen tablets at Maurie.

"I can't take these," Maurie said. "They interact badly with what I'm already on."

"Then drink the water," Fatima snapped.

On screen Uncle Benoit took an early sip of his celebratory champagne, and an off-camera staffer topped it off.

"Spending the launcher capital would be stupid of him, but he'd do it," Maurie added.

"I'll take that as, 'Thank you, Fatima.' And 'I appreciate your help, Fatima,'" the young woman said with a scowl.

"Good coffee," Pascaline said.

That was not a thank-you, but Fatima gave a sharp nod as if it were. "Yes, it is. Anytime, Ms. Pascaline."

Maurie groaned some more, continuing to rub her temples.

While the formal conference was getting set up by people like Fatima at family compounds and boats around the world, a lively text chat had sprung up. Several were attempting to plan parties and events with the anticipated money Benoit was expected to forward to their respective trust accounts, but Aunt Julienne had her keyboard stuck in all-caps mode and was ranting about Reuben. Again. It seemed she hadn't been able to have her weekly phone call with her boy yesterday and thought everyone should be writing complaints to the jailhouse on her behalf.

"We'll be fine because of Adamou," Maurie said.

The cold water seemed to clear her head enough to process details. And unlike Pascaline, she had the social conditioning to try to explain it all. "Adamou won't sign off on emptying the TCG-funded accounts for our launcher build prematurely. We should still be protected."

"Uh, about that . . ." Adamou said.

Pascaline speared him with a glare.

"So I told him about the family strife," Maurie said, misinterpreting the focus of Pascaline's look. "Not like he wasn't going to figure it out, and besides he needed to know why he had to be added to the accounts as the 'signatures required' person."

"I can't be that guy," Adamou said. "But I've got a solution."

"Of course you can be that guy," Pascaline ground out. "You've already accepted. I sat next to you at the bank and watched you become 'that guy.'"

"Well, about that," he said again. This time both of them kept silent, demanding he finish. "So Chief Endeley found out. He's not pleased. The lawyers told him that it really would open up the Bakweri for possible legal entanglements. So I went to the bank to put Philip Chao on the accounts instead."

Maurie covered her face with her hands.

"He's not remotely qualified to stand up to this sort of pressure," Pascaline leaned over Maurie to hiss at Adamou.

"I, ah, didn't realize there'd be quite so much pressure this soon. And he's not actually on the accounts right now."

"Good." Pascaline sat back. "And he won't be. You stay on it, and do it like I told you."

"But I'm not on the accounts either. The bank manager let me withdraw myself, but I couldn't put Chao on without your two co-signatures. Well, my signature isn't needed at all now since I'm off it."

"We're getting tossed out of the family," Maurie said. "There's no other way. We have to say 'no' to the fund transfers, and we will get kicked out."

"Thank you so much, Adamou," Pascaline said. "I suppose you can also tell your beloved uncle and chief—"

Fatima grabbed Grandpere's comm from the table and ran from the room. The door slammed. Grandpere sighed and leaned over himself to turn up the speakers and key on his microphone. "Is everyone hearing me okay?" he asked.

"No," Uncle Benoit said. "Not okay." His voice was loud and crackly. "But none of that is yours to trouble about anymore, Uncle Moussa. I have the votes," he said. The call formally began. No chitchat. No inquiries into everyone's health or even a more thorough check to see if everyone could see and hear. "Moussa is out, and I'm in."

A clamor of cheers and lifted alcoholic beverages in the various screens confirmed that most did have audio at least.

The door banged open again, and Philip Chao ran in. "She said I have to tell everyone to wait!" he said.

Even Adamou winced. Nobody on the conference call paid Philip's outburst any attention.

Philip's brows pinched together, inexperienced with being ignored. He turned, where else, to Pascaline. "What do I do?"

She shrugged. "Quit? Go job hunting somewhere else? Try to sell a tell-all to the tabloids?"

"Ignore that last suggestion," Adamou advised. "The tabloids in Europe and North America don't know enough about Sadous to care and the African tabloids are owned by friends of Sadou Moussa and wouldn't print it."

"Wait. Is my job gone? I thought I was doing a good job." Philip paled with genuine shock. "I'm fired?"

Adamou turned back to Pascaline. "We go straight to the bank. Maybe we can get me back on the accounts again before any funds-transfer requests go through. If anyone asks, we just don't mention that I was ever off the accounts."

"No," Maurie said. "We go up to the work site and prepay for as much work as we possibly can. Buy some time to get close to another payment milestone and try to talk Uncle Benoit into giving the launcher a chance."

"He only got the votes because he promised them immediate cash," Pascaline said. "If we spend it before they can get it, he'll lose his support, but that won't mean support will go back to Grandpere."

The door slammed open again, and Reuben marched into the room. Grandpere grinned, absolutely unsurprised.

"Little Benoit," Sadou Moussa said. "You have to actually take that formal voice vote. Reuben can go first."

Aunt Julienne's eyes widened as her son sat down next to his grandfather. "Hello, family," he said. "You're all assholes. And I'm voting for our Grandpere, who is the only one of you to ever visit me in person. Uncle Benoit, hi there. Thanks for blocking my trust access when I tried to get a lump sum out for bail and blocking it again when I tried to get a retainer for a decent lawyer. Very, very much appreciated. I hate every one of you very, very much."

Silence followed his announcement. The chat room went wild with accusation and counteraccusation.

"So how'd you get out?" Maurie called from the back of the room. "This is Sadou Maurie, by the way. Hi, family." She walked up and stuck her head next to Grandpere's on the other side of Reuben to give a quick wave. "Our Uncle Tchami Fabrice, as you may have heard, has arranged a generously funded project for the business to expand into a new industry. But if the working capital is drained and redistributed as dividends, I won't be able to deliver and earn us the delivery payments."

"Multimillions in delivery payments," Pascaline called out.

"It's more complicated than that, as I've explained," Uncle Benoit said.

"Like you explained that Reuben would never get out of jail without your help?" Aunt Julienne asked. "Like that sort of complicated? I vote for Grandpere. With all of my voting shares and the fifteen proxy votes I hold from the folks who've already signed off to go party."

"That was not their intent," Benoit growled.

"Then call another vote in six months." Aunt Julienne smiled, white lipped. "Son." She nodded at Reuben. She signed off.

Reuben turned to Pascaline. "Tell DeeDee I said thanks."

Fatima returned with a tray of champagne glasses, and Uncle Benoit ended the call with a cut-off expletive.

CHAPTER TWENTY-FOUR

MAURIE PINCHED THE NECKLACE BY THE THROAT just behind the jaws. Water lapped at her feet in the dawn light. Sunshine finally clawed over Fako's double peaks to brighten the dark shoreline.

"Okay, snake woman," she said. "It's time to talk terms."

No one answered.

This cove of the Wouri estuary had been used hundreds of times for baptisms. She'd checked. The first pastor from Fako South Presbytery of Limbe had launched unasked into a doctrinal defense of clergy from an affusion baptism denomination using full immersion for refugees who intended to someday return to a baptism by full immersion home church, with a digression into his thoughts on sins against the Holy Spirit. She'd had to cut him off to escape additional theology. The second pastor merely confirmed the site and encouraged her to attend services at his building on Sunday, adding that they had fresh roast coffee and *makala* in the community center after each service.

She'd almost decided not to come down to the sea-side at all. But when she'd been in town for another thing and paused to buy *makala*—the street seller next to the two big churches had the best ones in town—the second pastor had greeted her on the road. Then the first clergyman stopped by for a snack and started to razz the second one about having repeated dreams of the Virgin Mary calling on her people to build a sky ark. The two churches were diagonally across from each other. It wasn't surprising that the two men knew each other.

"I'm not even Catholic!" The second man had laughed it off and then given her a rather suspicious look. "Sadou Maurie and her space launcher. Saint Mary, the Mother of God, and a sky ark. It's probably too much late-night television."

Maurie had found the discussion interesting, so she'd had a few more talks. She'd discussed options with her doctor for stopping the migraine-inducing pills. He'd suggested meditation and talk therapy with a stress reduction specialist to help manage her ongoing symptoms, but Maurie had decided this was a better idea.

She pulled out her handheld thermometer and checked her own temperature: 99.9 degrees Fahrenheit. Early morning fever coming on as expected. Time to do things her way. She shook out the finely worked snake-shaped necklace to its full length and tossed the entire eighty grams of 24-karat gold into the surf.

Mami-Wata coiled up from the waves immediately before her and rubbed sleep out of thick lashes. "Don't you think that it's a little heretical to be calling on evil spirits?"

Maurie sniffed. "It would be if you were a demon. You're not, though. Even the really old stories about you are decidedly mixed about your good-versus-evil alignment."

Mami-Wata hissed in a manner that managed to display disdain. "Even now, you aren't certain of that."

"You," Maurie said, "are a convert. Not angelic originally, but you're on their side now. What I want to know is why."

"How is that any business of yours?" Mami-Wata demanded. Her snake familiar twisted out of the waves and curled around her, spitting cobra venom this time and hissing at the waves. The snake woman trailed wet fingers along the reptile's head to calm it.

Maurie refused to allow herself to be distracted. "If I'm supposed to be preaching to the volcano spirit, it'd be really helpful to know how it was the water spirit had her conversion experience."

"Ah." Mami-Wata wiggled her neck and shoulders back and forth sinuously. "I can see how you might have a point. But I'm not allowed to tell. Mary was involved and since the martyred weren't technically supposed to be leaving Heaven and all, it was all rather a no-no."

"She what?" Maurie gaped. "You mean to tell me the Virgin Mother was part of your conversion experience?"

"You think Paul did it all on his own?" The snake blurred down from Mami-Wata's shoulders in a lightning strike, defying the friction the surface of the water should have supplied. The tail vanished beneath the next crashing wave.

"And now you're blaming the Apostle Paul."

"Oh no, not that one. He didn't get this far west

and south. Didn't get much farther than Egypt on this
continent, from what I'm told, and the Egyptians were
very protective of the Nile. I rarely got to manifest
anywhere north of Kush." She sighed and then her
lashes fluttered with delight as she crouched into the
water and lifted out Maurie's gold necklace. She held
it gently and the heavy gold slithered up her arm to
loop around Mami-Wata's neck and grasp its own tail
in the clever jeweler's clasp.

"So, Paul?" Maurie prompted.

"Yes, Paul," Mami-Wata agreed, petting her necklace.
"He was born with another name, but after he converted,
he took the new name of Paul and preached Christianity
to, oh, a few dozen Bantu-descended tribes before he
was martyred. Then he started witnessing to me."

Maurie gave a slow blink.

"You have a Bible, right? And you have read it?"
Mami-Wata gave Maurie a long look. "You do know
about the blood of the martyrs crying out for vengeance and God promising them justice, but only
later, because He holds back the End to let more of
humanity go ahead and have lives? He has this interest
in Redemption, you know. Seems to think a lot more
of you can be gathered into the Peace that Surpasses
Human Understanding. Sound familiar?"

"Um, yeah."

"Well, around here the martyrs have more on their
minds than eternal justice. That whole tradition of
ancestral overwatch doesn't vanish just because the
souls in question are Redeemed by the Blood. Some of
'em come from matrilineal tribal groups too. That might
not have mattered much since the Holy Spirit is super
tough, and She's got no trouble answering prayers with

'not only no but unholy hells no' when She considers a lot of prayers to be shortsighted and stupid.'"

"Uh, who?"

"God the Holy Spirit. Third part of the Trinity?" Mami-Wata rolled her eyes. "The ignorance of humanity these days."

"The Holy Spirit is female?"

Mami-Wata gave a deep sigh. "And I quote, 'God created humanity in his image. Male and female God created them.' Sure implies a certain amount of female, doesn't it?"

"I'm not so sure," Maurie said.

"Fine." Mami-Wata shrugged. "I'm just the far-more-knowledgeable-than-you spirit creature you're coming to for advice. Go ahead and doubt everything I say. I'm probably unreliable and going to lead you to your inevitable doom anyway."

"Uh, yeah. You were saying something about the ancestors."

Mami-Wata gave a deep sigh. "The brats went to Mary. Yes, that Mary. And she listened to them!" Mami-Wata threw up her hands in exasperation. "You do know whose mother she is, right? They can't go talk to their descendants directly. That's not allowed. But that *Blessed* Mother." Mami-Wata gritted her snake fangs as though she really wanted to use some other term rather than "blessed." "Yes, that Blessed Mother arranged for them to be allowed to talk to me."

"Purgatory!" Maurie snapped her fingers. "That's what's going on. You're in purgatory." She paused, processing the thought out loud. "But in some techno-spiritual way also able to interact with Earth while making amends."

Mami-Wata made a grumpy noise. "I liked you better when you accepted that I was delusion made manifest as a result of declining mental health."

"I've decided you're a product of my overstressed psyche instead, and talking with you will help me process. So spill," Maurie said. "What do the ancestors want you to tell me?"

Mami-Wata groaned. "It's not that simple. I can't just be a messenger. There are centuries and centuries of these people. They accumulate. I have to translate and interpolate."

"Yeah, yeah, but they aren't interested in justice, so what's their thing?"

"Not what I said," Mami-Wata snapped. "They love justice. Not only eternal justice, though. They want social justice."

Maurie snorted at the archaic term. "What? Are they all from the twenty-first century?"

"The idea is hardly that chronologically constrained. They heard about Abram who became Abraham and his people numbering the stars. They want to be numbered among the stars."

"Do you mean the spirits want their descendants to go into space?" Maurie said.

"Yup. And the Blessed Mother does too. She's got a thing for stars. Ever since Bethlehem apparently it's been a special interest for her."

Maurie nodded. "Okay."

Mami-Wata stared, mouth open, and fangs dripping venom into the surf. "That's it?"

"Yup," Maurie said. "Because we were going anyway."

The snake woman shrank into her own coils under the water. She turned half away, looking at the waves as if she didn't care at all what Maurie said next. "I saw that fire priest has been installing slivers of volcanic rock onto the tail of each launch vehicle. Telling his Fako that parts of himself are soaring higher into the heavens than any eruption in the history of the world, and all the volcano spirit needs to do to see it continue is to rest quiet with only the small rumbles necessary for pressure release." Mami-Wata ran light fingers on the crest of a wave, lifting with it and crashing back into the sea surface. Very softly, almost inaudible over the surf, she said, "Do you think someday I could go, too?"

"I'll see what I can do," Maurie replied. "Tell the ancestor spirits that they will rest in power, and I will put their children in the stars."

"I'll swallow your soul if you don't," Mami-Wata promised.

Maurie's lips twitched into a smile. "I'm betting even with the Blessed Mother on your side that'd be considered a mortal sin."

Mami-Wata hissed and sunk beneath the waves. "I so wanted Pascaline," the water whispered with a ghostly voice.

"And that concludes my brief on how my engine system will put your people into the stars with less fuel and more payload per launch in my energetically cheaper variant of the A-HRV." The young academic presenter from MIT, Lucas Brown, grinned broadly.

Maurie's eyes narrowed in recognition of the name. A faint hiss in the background was probably from the overworked air conditioner. She avoided turning her head to look for snakes.

The hiss came again with a mountainous rumble, and Pascaline's comm also chirped with Adamou's ringtone. Just her comm, that was all.

Lucas, on the screen, glanced at Pascaline who'd flipped to the back of the packet. "A-HRV is..."

"Aerodynamic Highly Reusable Vehicle, we know," Philip said. "This is the forty-third time you've used the acronym, so somebody here would've asked if anyone hadn't understood it."

Lucas looked back from Pascaline to Philip and was smart enough not to say that he'd known Philip knew what he was talking about. It was Sadou Pascaline, the decision maker, who he'd assumed was an idiot.

"And," Philip continued, "it was spelled out on the cover slide, again in the reference appendix background slides, and it also is the exact same acronym used by the legacy design you are arguing for replacing."

From her angle Maurie could see that Pascaline was looking at the equations, not the glossary of terms. Well, if Pascaline wasn't irritated then Maurie could let it go too.

"It's man-rated?" Maurie perked up. "You said your people? And all the way to the stars, not just high orbit?"

"Uh, no, um, only a figure of speech." Lucas flushed. "And nobody says man-rated anymore. Um, not considered polite. 'Human-rating' or 'crew-rating' for vehicles safe enough to have a pilot or pilot and passengers."

"But 'your people' does imply some folks don't deserve the full due diligence for live cargo then?" Maurie poked back.

Lucas flushed brighter red. "I didn't mean..."

"Not important," Pascaline said.

She glanced at Philip. He gave a firm nod.

"We'll buy it," she said. "Get the components that your prototype changes from our base model shipped here soonest for on-track testing." The Adamou ringtone chimed several more times. Pascaline silenced her comm and turned back to the MIT presenter. "Acknowledged. Briefing received. I'll go through your data again later. Right now you are over your allotted time." She stood. "Let's go, Maurie. Adamou's waiting for us to get the quarterlies out to the suppliers."

Maurie followed Pascaline to the door when a wave of nausea hit. "You go on," she said.

"Need some water?" Pascaline asked.

Maurie shrugged. "I'd rather have coffee."

"I'll get us some. Meet you at the car."

Maurie leaned her back against the cool concrete wall next to the door and waited for the hiss to fade from her hearing.

Philip flipped again back to the proof of concept numbers.

The door shut. The line stayed open with Philip the only person the presenting group could still see.

"Oh good," Dr. Ross said. "I'd hoped we could speak privately to finish supplying any admin details Lucas might need to get the prototype delivered. And your company will need to send over formal contracts to legally finalize funding."

Maurie could see the scribbled marks on Pascaline's presentation copy left behind on the desk. It showed that she'd started to work some flight equations in the margin and left them unfinished. She always drew a large rectangle around her final result if she solved something. No rectangles were on that page. Philip

Chao had the same equations on his papers with more numbers written out and several rectangles. He'd turned to some appendix slides and circled another number with the same units behind it. They didn't match.

On camera, Lucas Brown held up his fists and punched the air in delight. He turned and high-fived someone off camera. "Sold! I am the best presenter ever!" Lucas crowed. "We've got a test site finally!"

"Let's get some beers!" a voice Maurie didn't recognize from among the presentation speakers said. Lucas earned a dismissing nod from his supervising professor, Dr. Ross, and he left the screen.

Dr. Ross watched Philip, eyes narrowing.

Something had just happened with those numbers. Philip shifted his sheet up so that it was clearly captured by the camera, and the famous research professor stared at it.

Dr. Ross gave a polite cough as Philip scratched down the rest of the math with a worn pencil on the margin of the printed copy. Maurie continued to be grateful that Grandpere hadn't pushed them to try to do this launcher project as a paperless office and had authorized massive budgets for printing.

"Good to see that you landed well, Philip," Dr. Ross said.

He nodded and said, "Yes, thank you," without lifting his head from the numbers. Philip's pencil tip traced along the neat line of calculations working backwards now from the number in the printed appendix until he got to a point in the middle of the dense page and wrote, "Units mismatch."

Dr. Ross winced.

Ross beat Philip to getting the flight simulator

program opened and entering the correct numbers into the algorithm to let it run. An error blatted out.

Dr. Ross' expression turned blank. "We will get that fixed," she said.

Philip grimaced at the problem and adjusted a few details. Maurie squinted to make out what he was doing. "If we increased the fuel tank size a bit..." he said. "Yes, that does it. The prototype can still fly and fly pretty well." He looked straight at his former mentor and added, "What it doesn't do is provide revolutionary fuel cost savings. It's still better, but it's only another incremental improvement. Solid grad-student level work. Not ground-break professorial award-winning achievement.

"And you took him on instead of me?" Philip said.

Dr. Ross flipped one hand as if discarding past history. "The other candidates looked better on paper. Say, um..." A look flitted across her face. The corner of her mouth twitched with something Maurie thought might be self-revulsion, her gaze darted away for a fraction of a second, and she looked straight at the camera again calm and self-assured.

"Can you make this prototype testing still go through for us?" she said.

"Maybe," Philip hedged. "I remember the loads of rocket grants you had available to you for research funding, though. Why? Let your doctoral candidate pick another research line and spend an extra year to get his PhD. I do know Lucas, you remember. His family pays his bills and they aren't going to cut him off if he takes even more time getting credentialed."

Dr. Ross nodded fractionally. "Grant options are down. Way down. With the elevator construction going so well, the R&D funds are being redirected toward deep space propulsion, prospecting robotics, and low-gravity manufacturing methods. Earth-to-orbit technologies aren't high interest anymore. Not even excellent single-stage-to-GEO ones."

"This one's not excellent, only good. And it's a stretch, if a small one, to call it single stage when it needs a rail launcher to throw the vehicle and pay-load through the thickest atmosphere next to Earth's surface and into the region of the atmosphere where the engine performs optimally."

"But it's still an improvement over the engine you have on the A-HRV model you've got now," she pointed out.

"A cautious project manager would select the engine with the longer history of proven performance instead of the new one which was presented with flawed data, unless the local subject-matter expert argued for the change, that is."

She considered him carefully. "If you wanted back into academia, I could put in a good word."

"You could create a doctoral candidate position just for me," Philip countered. "You have before, and you could do it again."

"I could have an opening at the end of the term if a prototype could be corrected and have a successful test launch. I'll send him to defend his dissertation early."

"No good," Philip said. "He might fail his defense. I want my spot either way."

"My candidates always pass," Dr. Ross said. "And you get your spot either way."

"Deal," Philip said.

"Deal," she agreed.

Maurie let herself silently out of the room as the conference call connection ended. *He promised he'd cheat next time*, Mami-Wata whispered in her ear. *Did you really expect him not to?*

"Of course I knew he wanted to be a cheater," she muttered under her breath, "but we gave him a job when nobody else would; I thought he'd find a way to cheat on our behalf. That little rat. Screw his deals. I'm telling Pascaline what I saw. She can decide which vehicle is the better one for us to buy."

She thinks she needs the credentialed magic white boy to bless all her engineering decisions, Mami-Wata said. *He's her magic feather. Do you really want to steal her confidence now?*

"Hell, no," Maurie whispered to herself. "I should hex him."

He doesn't believe in hexes, Mami-Wata reminded her.

"We'll just see about that," Maurie replied.

And if you believe in hexes now, do you want one near that launcher?

Maurie shivered, and Mami-Wata's snake familiar laughed.

CHAPTER TWENTY-FIVE

THINKING ABOUT HEXES AND HOW HE MIGHT BE about to have his entire blessed lifetime's worth of luck recoil into a massive bout of ill chance, Chummy tried not let his dread show. *You made your choice. If this fails, it's on you,* he reminded himself. *It was hard work to get to the point where I could pay back Grandpere. And I did that. It was the right thing, really,* he tried to reassure himself. The churn in his gut wasn't easing any, so he tried for stoicism instead. *It'll be what it will be.*

That wasn't working either. He didn't feel any calmer.

"Launch day! Launch day! Launch day!" DeeDee's bat-winged avatar chittered and chattered at him from the rental car's screen while he let the autodrive take him along a newly paved access road running up the side of Mount Fako.

Chummy forced his face back into a wide smile. DeeDee's programming used the device's facial recognition software to take the cue. The avatar did a backflip and muted.

Since he was taking this ill-considered side trip, Chummy reminded himself that he was in public and he had to fake confidence. Every other time in his career that things had gone sideways, it had been when he didn't show up. So he was here. That meant the launch had to be a success, right?

The Sadous' work had grown beyond his control and past his ability to positively influence it. But, he could, unfortunately, make bystanders believe he'd put a jinx on the whole launch.

No less than six strangers at the Yaoundé Nsimalen airport had recognized him. Chummy didn't know whether to blame his occasional background appearance in newscasts about the elevator or his locally well-known connection to *those* Sadous. The ones who had spoken to him directly had wished him and the family luck for today's launch. A lot more had watched him with oppressive interest. His faked confidence all the way through the public terminal had, hopefully, made its way back to the family and friends of all the team members out doing final checks. *All those people inspecting the rail, the sled attachment, the A-HRV, and the payload need to be focused and not jumping at shadows because somebody texted them that I looked scared...*

Stop thinking like that, fool, he told himself. *None of that spirit nonsense is real. It's just Aunt Mami's gimmick to help people do what they could already do. Besides, she's going to be here herself to grin and give everyone all the confidence they need.*

The car beeped to announce his arrival at the programmed destination. Chummy craned his neck around to see if he'd missed a turn.

"Local news drone has you live, boss." DeeDee's avatar flapped bat wings and winked at him before vanishing from the screen again. The level rise had only one other vehicle parked between the scrawny bushes growing on the side of the road. But Chief Endeley Bouba himself opened the door of Chummy's rental vehicle, and welcomed him into the icy morning air.

"Don't worry," Endeley said, "I won't ask after everyone in your family, not in front of the drones. Though I had hoped..." He searched the back of Chummy's vehicle and his smile faltered to find it empty.

"Where is everyone?" Chummy said.

Endeley's head-turn followed his own to check the road beyond them. No one else was on their way to join them here on this turnoff. Endeley nudged Chummy's shoulder and pointed with his chin at the news drone circling in the clear sky.

The chief stood very straight and grinned directly at that drone. Lifting his right hand high in a big wave to the onboard camera, he turned his head so his mouth was covered by his arm. "We're live," he said, "and yeah, it's just us. My people actually listened to me and stayed away for once. I don't care for risking anyone else."

Chummy fixed his own smile firmly in place.

The view from the West African mountainside was clear on this bright blue–skyed day. *Great launch weather.* The launcher's base station squatted in a former palm grove. The mass of new buildings lay on flat near-beachfront land before even the first rise of the foothills. Their crammed parking lots showed no movement at all outside the massive hangar.

Endeley followed his gaze. He tilted his head down

to say, "The folks down there should be safe enough, no matter how it goes on the rail."

"Come on." Endeley Bouba motioned toward a line of three folding chairs. "Let's look like we aren't worried and expect this to be a picnic. The drone will circle around again soon, and the team ought to be almost ready now."

"Really?" Chummy checked the sky. The drone was making a pass over the hangar parking lot. He couldn't help also looking at the top of the mountain. He hoped to soon see the bright streak of a launch, and not some horrible twisted wreckage along the rail line or mountainside from a crash.

"Yes, everything's almost done with the preflights," Endeley said. "Launch vehicle. Sled. Maglev rail. That stuff. Almost finished with it."

Chummy stuffed his comm into his suit-jacket pocket and followed the Bakweri chief.

"That's for Aunt Mami?" Chummy nodded to the third chair and kept his face pointed down. Aunt Mami's chair was the only one with cushions, a folded lap blanket, and some discreet ties along the armrests and backrest for securing oxygen and saline-drip tubing.

Endeley bent his face down too, trying to appear as if he were looking down at the launch hangar instead of hiding from the drone's cameras and studio lip-readers. "Yes, I'd hoped she'd change her mind and arrive with you." Endeley grimaced. "Couldn't make it. Her health. Would've been nice to have Aunt Mami herself on-site to bless this, as it were. But, eh, maybe for the best not to be riling Fako on his home turf. And also not something to try to explain to the foreign news services."

"Ah, right." Chummy fell into silence, watching. With Endeley Bouba at his elbow, and Aunt Mami a no-show, he tried to look hopeful. Endeley waited until the drone passed by and then moved the extra chair into the trunk of his sedan with the throw blanket tossed over it.

They sat on a clammy mountainside and faked smiles together when the drone came by again. Too far up the launch path to actually see anything at the beginning of the rail line but not far enough up to be endangered by the sonic boom if all went according to plan. By Chummy's increasingly threadbare official claim that he had no strong connection to the Sadous, he shouldn't have been here at all, but he couldn't convince himself not to come.

Sounds in his earbud crackled with the babble of the primary day-shift crew verifying final details before the Sadous' first live launch. Sweat trickled down his back.

His comm pinged. He pulled it out to look. *"Aren't they supposed to be sending up carbon pellets as the payload for Test Launch One? It should be impact resistant if it all goes splat,"* DeeDee sent him.

What the hell, DeeDee? This was his actual second assistant texting and not the programmed avatar. She should still be back at the TCG Berlin office. She shouldn't be involved! He'd taken this time as personal leave and paid for the trip to Douala himself and then accepted Bakweri help to get up the mountain to join Chief Endeley's party for the launch.

"'Goes splat,'" the chief read off Chummy's comm. "Ha! It better not. It's going to be a bunch of little sat-killers for this payload. They'd go boom instead, not that anything with the kinetic energy to reach orbit wouldn't be a nice-sized bomb all on its lonesome..."

"The final coordination with overflight nations go okay?" Chummy asked. "I can put in a few last-minute calls if you think..." He pointed with his chin to indicate the whole of the continent on the other side of the mountain and lifted his eyebrows.

Endeley shook his head. "Sadou Moussa might be aging, but he remains tremendously well connected."

"And the presidents of Tanzania and Kenya worked °together° to beat into submission any of those middle-of-the-continent countries—COUGH South Sudan COUGH—who wanted to be paid double what everyone else was getting and then also tried to put the tax squeeze on their own newly-employed-by-TCG citizens," DeeDee's avatar supplied in a scrawl of text across his screen.

"Your comm is listening to us, and you're okay with that?" Endeley gave Chummy a lifted eyebrow that suggested strongly that he should not be okay with it.

"DeeDee has it as securely fire-walled as it could possibly be." He also added, "And her little avatar is excellent at finding and sharing time-critical information."

"Why waste a launch on DiamondWire's carbon bits if your TCG orbit-side astrogeeks aren't ready to use the material yet?" Endeley elbowed Chummy in the ribs. "You will make certain that Ethan takes all proper precautions when it comes to installing that tether, right?"

"Absolutely," Chummy said. *If I have any position in TCG at all after today, that is.*

"Sat-killers?" DeeDee's voice squeaked. "Excuse me,

sir," she said to someone out of camera view, "what's the payload for this launch?"

"*BOSS!!!*" she typed. "*No confirmation yet, but I'm not getting ANY denials. They're saying debris removers, not sat-killer, but any devices that can maneuver enough after launch to align with different debris objects has to have onboard fuel systems. That means extra boomy-boom-BOOM stuff in the payload!1!!11*"

Chief Endeley leaned over Chummy's shoulder and snorted.

Chummy checked his contact list quickly to see if he had some non-obvious way to delay the launch while he found a polite way to get Grandpere to beat Maurie's and Pascaline's heads together for picking a tough payload for their first launch.

Chief Endeley patted Chummy on the shoulder. "The pelletized carbon we had failed initial launch tests. The stuff sloshes around, which messes with the center of mass mid-flight. Pascaline mumbled something about tweaking the simulations they were using to train the flight software with higher-fidelity payload density models, but Philip Chao got way too wide-eyed, so Maurie vetoed it . . ." He gave Chummy the knowing grin of a man who was far less naive about the launcher than he was pretending to be.

"No wobbles allowed," Chummy agreed. "DeeDee, where are you?"

"Besides," Endeley said, "you need the debris field cleared before you could drop down a tether anyway. The anti-satellite mini-rockets were ready. They'll be used mostly to give some larger pieces of junk gentle taps to make their orbits easier for reclamation corps to grab them up. The reclaimers are paying for that assist, of course. And the companies that lost teleme-try control of things up there are paying to no longer be responsible for any future collisions. Why send up something to be in-orbit-warehoused for five years, when you can instead send payload for immediate use and get paid triple?"

A snort from DeeDee came from Chummy's comm.

Chief Endeley waved a hand. "Immediately useful in launch terms. So, likely about eleven hours after launch for the payload to get up that far and then more hours or days for the various trajectory shifts to match with their intended targets."

"I'm at the Sadou hangar, boss," DeeDee texted. *"I took the same flight as you did. Samson was right that I'd fade into the background crowd better than he would. I just had to make sure my shoes matched."*

Chummy folded his hands with grim determina-tion that if he couldn't do anything to fix last-minute problems, at least he wouldn't bother the people who would be handling the crisis should any emerging issues prove to be big ones. His gut roiled.

"Why the nerves?" Endeley Bouba couldn't seem to resist needling him. "It's a test. If it all goes wrong, they can just rebuild and do it better the next time."

"Depends on how badly wrong and if it kills too many critical people," DeeDee's voice replied.

Chummy gave his assistant a sharp look through the screen.

She blinked back at him. "What? I really thought everyone knew that."

"They do; we do." Endeley nodded. "In fact, I'd go so far as to say, 'my thoughts exactly.'"

"Boss," Chummy's comm sounded in Samson Young's

voice, "you aren't standing right next to that experimental maglev launcher, are you?"

They were a long way from touching range with the closest part of the launch rail on the raised struts that allowed it to start near sea-level and continue in a straight, sharply angled line to the final lift point near Fako's highest peak. The curving hillocks and valleys of the mountain's slopes rose and fell beneath that bright line of railway.

They weren't directly beneath the powerfully charged rail. Chief Endeley had selected a parallel rise on Fako's broad slopes. But, neither were they in a bunker.

Chief Endeley laughed and leaned close to lift up Chummy's comm and pan around with the camera. "Of course, he's close! If this thing derails at supersonic speed and takes off part of the mountain with us down in Limbe or hiding halfway around the base of the mountain in Douala, how would any of us be able to look a bereaved mother in the eye to tell her we had no idea that would happen?"

"If it takes off part of the mountain, it could take you with it and then I might be the one talking to bereaved mothers," Samson countered.

"Now you've got the idea, lad," Chief Endeley said with a mischievous grin.

"Inaccurate statement!" DeeDee's avatar objected with a flurry of wings. *"If A-HRV leaves sled or A-HRV & sled leave rail before accumulated kinematic forces are sufficient to arc it over the peak, it will have INSUFFICIENT force to remove any significant portion of the bedrock. If somehow all onboard vehicle fuel and all fuel in the orbital debris repositioner devices currently in payload*

detonate simultaneously . . . click here for full calculation details . . . *Final Assessment: The mountain
would remain. Humans at the crash site would
not. The fireball on impact would be equivalent to
approximately 158 tons of TNT. Recommend new
location.*" The comm began blinking a bold red MOVE
TO SAFETY warning.

Chummy didn't click for details. He definitely did
not want to know. He told the avatar program: "I'm
on PTO." It stopped blinking the warning. "That's Paid
Time Off,'" Chummy added with a glance at the chief.

Endeley made a sniff that seemed to convey equally
a disdain for the concept of time off and amusement
that Chummy had felt it necessary to spell out what
PTO stood for.

"So," Chummy said, "Samson and DeeDee, neither
of you two need to be checking in on me. Don't you
both have other things to be doing?"

"Nothing more important than this, boss," Samson
said. "I'm here at Kilimanjaro sitting next to our
buddy, Jax." Through the comm screen, Samson gave
the Bakweri chief a grin and said to him, "Jax is Mr.
Ethan Schmidt-Li's right-hand man—"

"Assistant," Jax said.

"—but we don't hold that against him," Samson
continued smoothly. "He's the one who found us the
dive we've taken over as our local TCG watering hole."

Jax leaned into the comm's camera view and lifted
a full mug of beer. "Hello, Mr. Chummy! We've all
got glasses charged and ready to toast!"

"Don't you dare steal a sip, Jax! We're watching
you," voices yelled over the background bar chatter.
"Nobody better jinx this by drinking early!"

"But, of course, Western scientists aren't superstitious at all," Chief Endeley murmured in Chummy's ear and winked.

"Yup! Keeping toes and fingers crossed over here." Samson's grinning face returned. "We're all waiting to find out if Sadou Corp is getting that early completion bonus or not. There might be some friendly betting going on." He winked broadly. "I'm not digging for early intel or anything sneaky like that, of course not, boss." A chorus of laughter from the crowd glimpsed behind Samson's motor chair included calls for revoking Samson's bets.

"I'm taking paid time off too," DeeDee sent.

Chief Endeley bumped Chummy's shoulder to turn his attention back to the mountainside. A multitude of camera views appeared on Chummy's comm sent by both assistants.

Close-ups of the maglev track at various points appeared. On the thickly forested lower slopes a tube enclosed the track. In the middle stretch, the track rose on high struts over the rolls of the mountain terrain. Beyond the peak, the track continued for the sled alone to decelerate. It was as if an enormous pale serpent had stretched out to sun itself on the side of the mountain, and the very land had cleared a path for it to slide gently down the other side, if it proved that even ghost snakes weren't meant to fly.

One of the cameras caught movement. In the slice of track cutting through the palm groves, a riot of natural brush had grown up. A blue lizard with a red head skittered up the concrete between the rail. Its tongue flicked out at the massive tube wall surrounding the track. Louder rustling in the brush announced other creatures reacting to the thrumming noise coming from the charged rail.

"Ha! The wildlife wants to see too!" Jax chortled over Samson's shoulder. "Good thing they've got a barrier installed. That'd be a very flat lizard if it could reach the track."

Chummy and Endeley both leaned closer and watched the thicket where the planted palms gave way to natural forest. A ninety-kilogram-plus red river hog pushed his warted nose against one of the launcher struts and gave a testing shove. The structure stood as unmoving as any jungle trunk supporting the top of a triple canopy.

"Ha!" DeeDee sent, *"Nice try, piggy. They planned for that."*

"What's an alignment error autocorrection?" someone called from Samson's crowd.

"Actually we planned for volcanic microtremors," Endeley said, and took a sip from a hip flask. "This is called getting lucky."

He punched a call into his own comm. "Yeah, I saw it. What are we going to do if something bigger decides to head-butt a support while a vehicle-loaded sled is on the rail?"

"What could they possibly have out there bigger than that?" someone from Samson's side called out. A flurry of suggestions followed. "Ocean sea monsters!" "Salt water hippos?" "Ooo, maybe they've got train-sized snakes; I saw a Congo documentary once where—" Samson gave an apologetic grin and muted the sound from his end.

"That was weird," DeeDee sent. *"Another of the struts jiggled a tiny bit all by itself, but it looks like... Huh. Well, it's fine now."*

Chummy had visions of a derailed sled with vehicle attached spiraling off the middle slope track to crash into one of the meadows and maybe hit one of those wild hogs in return.

"Yes," Endeley said into his comm, "Call every animal warden you can reach and make sure none of the elephant herd comes wandering over this way. No, I don't care. Yes, I know they are wild. Make it happen. If you expect another *centime* of Bakweri funding for ecosystem restoration... Good. Good. Pascaline? Good. Do everything she said. You better make sure you do." He ended his comm call.

"*Huh,*" DeeDee typed. "*Look what my avatar found.*" Batwing avatar DeeDee reappeared on Chummy's screen. "*A herd of around 150 African forest elephants live in the meadows and foothills around—*"

"Not now, DeeDee," Chummy said.

"Of course," she said with a squeal of excitement, "here we go!" A tight close-up view showed the vehicle-loaded sled elevating a dozen-some millimeters above the charged maglev rail. "Whoa!"

Chummy tilted his head to the side and glanced at Endeley.

"She's not seen a maglev before?" the chief asked.

Chummy's mouth fell open when DeeDee sent another view. He'd only seen the vehicle and sled before in photographs and diagrams. The many-kilometer-long rail going up the side of the mountain was a narrow line shrunk by distance. The aerodynamic reusable vehicle stretched over ten meters wide from wingtip to wingtip and held a center core of payload filled with a half ton of tiny debris catchers.

DeeDee sent a graphic with the spots along the

launch path where the vehicle would be scattering its payload in waves before dropping back down to Earth. In the image, the smaller devices would starburst out in dozens of new trajectories to impact with space debris in orbits fouling the tether's eventual line.

"That's a lot of orbits," Chummy said.

"Yeah," Endeley agreed. "Almost like some of the smartest people on the planet worked together to take out the unwanted shell of trash around our planet, created by a couple centuries of executives ignoring their smartest people."

Chummy twitched at the implied insult to TCG and its predecessors. The wide tube around the lower rail frosted with dew as the dropping internal pressure lowered the temperature.

"They just sealed the tube and depressurized the whole thing to match the air pressure at the outlet altitude," Endeley said, "You know my boy, Adamou? He said something complicated about reduced drag on the vehicle lowering the total power needs, but Fako gives us all the power we could want. Say, can I interest TCG in a tour of our geothermal plants, there are some new—"

"Excuse me," Chummy said, and he leaned to the side to vomit.

"Maybe later," Chief Endeley patted him on the back. "After the launch at least." He took another sip from his flask.

Chummy's comm kept working while he tried to get his stomach to stop heaving.

"Hey DeeDee," Samson said, "are they calling it *Dabare* One or Black Mamba One? Who buys the first round is depending on this. What's the final call?"

"Oh, that's what they were saying! This one's the *'dabare mamba noir'* or the DMN. I thought they were pranking me," DeeDee said. "It seems like they are working down the list of scary local wildlife starting with all the snakes and also tacking *'dabare'* onto the beginning, which, I guess, means machine or something like that?"

"Um—" Chummy said.

"Something like that," Chief Endeley agreed.

"It's short for 'machine that works really well, we hope,'" Samson said.

"So it's a *dabare* snake launcher, then?" DeeDee said. She added in text, *"We better make sure the press releases say 'space launcher' and probably skip the 'I hope' part of the definition when the European and North American press corps want to know what 'dabare' means, yeah?"*

DeeDee sent camera views from inside the tunnel.

A ten-meter wingspan A-HRV clamped onto the launch sled lifted just over a dozen millimeters above the track by the force of the electrical current. The charged coils lining the full length of the ground path discharged one after another as the vehicle shot forward with increasing acceleration until a rumble emanated from the entire tube.

The brilliant streak exploded out of the very end of the tunnel and roared over the remaining stretch of open rail and into the sky.

"Yes! Yes! Yes!" DeeDee sent another camera view from a few moments earlier with a time counter at the bottom showing the slow-motion video. At liftoff, sled clamps released and pure kinetic motion hurled the already supersonic vehicle into the sky. The fuel injectors just below the knife-thin nose pumped hydrogen into the air compressed beneath the vehicle by the shape of its fuselage. The air-fuel mix ignited and, ducted through the engines on its belly, flames shot the vehicle upwards.

"Microquake compensators worked," Chief Endeley said, and he leaned over to vomit blood next to Chummy. "Ulcers," he said and grimaced.

They looked up at the sky, and Fako's ever-present steam cloud allowed only a glimpse of red streaking upwards.

"Fako is getting to erupt all the way into orbit," Chief Endeley said.

"Maybe we don't mention that in the press releases either," DeeDee texted. *"But doesn't that launch trail look a lot like shedding snake skin?"*

Samson provided a wide-angle view taken from an aerial remote. The A-HRV, free of the sled assembly, and with the full geothermal power charge of the volcano's warmed earth behind it, soared.

Between one blink and the next the crystalizing mists in the jet trail flared out into a cobra's hood and then folded back into disturbed water vapor.

"Shit! Shit! Sh—" Chummy's comm squealed with DeeDee's high-pitched curses, and Chief Endeley tried to wrestle it out of his hands to silence it.

"No foul language on the mountain!" he said.

Chummy kept hold of the comm. Ignoring the returning buzz of the news drone, he asked urgently, "DeeDee! What happened! We didn't see anything up here?"

Chummy could see nothing at all alarming. The rail line had emptied with the sled somewhere on the slowdown tracks. From the videos, the A-HRV seemed on course at the top of a red heaven-bound streak.

"All fine, boss," Samson sent. He shared a new twinned video feed. LIVE blinked in a red banner beneath the left-side panel which showed the sky and a tiny upwards-streaking speck. The other video read "5 minutes time-delayed feed" and showed a digital remastered view of the underside of the vehicle. The combusting fuel in a wave of fire beneath the fuselage lifted the vehicle ever upwards.

"What's failed?" Chummy asked.

Endeley glanced up at the drone and threw his arm over Chummy's shoulder. He was short, a lot shorter, but the chief had the muscle to tilt Chummy's head down.

"All the shows have lip-readers, dolt," Endeley muttered in his ear. "Pretend you have a little sense. There's no signs of any trouble. All my people are reporting a flawless launch so far. And it'll be at least a good ten more hours before we will find out if the payload release works out right. Don't be caught panicking on international news, man!"

Chummy closed his eyes.

"International?" Samson said.

DeeDee's voice came back on. "Yeah, boss. You and the chief are on all the local coverage, and turns out this is today's global interest news story. They're all talking about you for the in-depth background."

Fuck. It's over. Chummy lifted up the comm and typed out a response choosing his words carefully: "Has there been an official acknowledgement from Kilimanjaro?"

"Begin the toast!" Jax's voice roared. "Mr. Schmidt-Li confirms launch success!"

Chief Endeley threw back his head and cheered.

No less than three news drones turned and hovered in a swarm, clearly angling to capture a close-up of the Bakweri chieftain's face with the still rising streak of the launch beyond Fako's peak.

"Cheer. Or at least smile," Endeley said without moving his lips.

Chummy gave up. If Jeffy wasn't watching this live, he would be told within a day or two anyway. Chummy gave a fist bump to the air in the direction of the mountain's peak, another toward the sea and the launch hangar crew, and then wrapped Endeley in a bearhug lifting him off his feet.

Endeley grunted and patted him back with enough vigor that Chummy was laughing too by the time the hug was over. Laughing with pain, with exhaustion, and looking at what his people had built: with pride.

The drones did a few more circles and left to go capture the crowds converging on the launch hangar. The crews were pouring out of the building and Samson sent video clips of the streets in Buea, Limbe, Yaoundé and Douala. The president of Cameroon had a live press announcement with Sadou Moussa smiling at his side, and the newscasters covered congratulatory messages from Tanzanian and Kenyan politicians without even pausing to include a continental map to mark who was who for viewers from other continents. The elevator's primary supply and debris clearance spaceport was ready for full operation. That was what mattered now.

He said into Endeley's ear, "I need to get off this mountain to some place where I can do a lot of swearing without offending anybody who can call up lava on a whim, and go get thoroughly drunk."

"What? It worked," the Bakweri chief said. "So what if the reporters all know you have ulcers now. Everyone gets stress injuries at some point."

Chummy searched the sky. The drones were all circling the hangar now. He couldn't make out the tiny figures down there but a feed supplied by Samson showed Maurie giving a thank-you speech outside the hangar doors while all the cameras tried to catch a close-up of Pascaline and Adamou. Ah, they noticed the reporters and moved their celebratory embrace back out of sight of the cameras.

Endeley Bouba offered his friend the flask.

Chummy took a big gulp. Fire blended with a thick chalky aftertaste. He choked it down.

"Sugarcane rum mixed with prescription-strength ulcer meds. An acquired taste," Endeley said. "Your Aunt Mami gave me a case of the stuff."

"I just got fired," Chummy said.

CHAPTER TWENTY-SIX

DIBUSSI RAN AROUND THE SIDE OF THE A-HRV and shouted to Pascaline, "Your cousin is squirting water on the nose cones again where Adamou said I wasn't allowed to kick it or the aero-dimdim-ics would get ruined!"

"Should've told him Fako would drop fire and rocks on his head, or that we'd beat him ourselves if it didn't quit it," a foreman grumbled, not very quietly.

"You kicked what?" Pascaline's head came up fast.

Dibussi giggled. "I didn't kick nothing," he said. But he ran off under the glare of her scowl before admitting to more.

A small crowd of building foremen stood politely to the side of the hangar waiting for her attention. Philip sat on the cement floor, back leaning against the hangar wall, reading through design documents. Pascaline snapped her fingers and collected construction reports and requests to start the next maintenance items. Maurie's initials in the corners showed that she'd checked them over. That meant the work that had to be completed before these items started had been reported done and personally checked as done by Maurie. It also meant that the supplies needed to do it had arrived. *Oh good*, the substation for geo-thermal plant four was ready for electrical testing. *The high-voltage cable shipment must have finally come in. It'll be good to have more power-station backups for when we start night launches.*

Her cousin Reuben hovered, watching.

She'd been interrupted, again, while thinking. Her finger on the smart-paper schematic tacked to the hangar's wall tapped on the dotted lines marking the MIT changes for the fuel tank sizing and a few inches away Philip's secondary lines re-expanded the fuel tank volume to a point closer to the original volume. She had the schematic in layered-changes mode, which generally made it unintelligible, but it let her see this shift. And it shouldn't have existed. She returned the schematic setting to show the current approved A-HRV design specs.

The reports and requests had Philip Chao's initials in the corners. But Pascaline checked them very, very thoroughly. The workers reclaimed their forms and hur-ried back out of the hangar, giving Maurie a wide berth.

"What do you need, ex-con?" Pascaline said to Reuben.

"Nothing," he answered. "Just seeing if I can help."

"You don't have to worry about becoming the family black sheep, you know," she said. "Everyone knows you didn't actually do it. If you'd really done what the prosecution said and embezzled or shared insider information in exchange for gifts or whatever nonsense they claimed in those charges, you'd have done a better job and gotten away with it."

"Thanks, I think," Reuben said.

"Or you'd've at least done a cost-benefit assessment and made sure you got paid enough to afford a truly impressive legal team of the kind that'd've had you staying in a penthouse with an ankle monitor instead of sitting in a dirty jailhouse without bail awaiting trial."

Reuben snorted.

"Yeah. Besides, I'm the forever black sheep."

"About that," Maurie said, walking around from the shadow of the new A-HRV's wing, "when are you going to come clean about not finishing school at MIT?"

Philip's head came up. His eyes were wide and utterly failing to keep secrets, but he was behind both Maurie and Reuben. He slunk out of the hangar, and Pascaline decided he was the rat. But she might still try to brazen it out.

"There's no time to do a doctoral dissertation while getting this launcher running," Pascaline said, eyes hard.

Reuben waggled his hands back and forth. "If I were on a jury and you said it like that on the stand, I'd believe you. But . . ." He shrugged. "It's your under-graduate degree that you didn't finish. We're your family. I've known since my deposit check on my first apartment bounced that there were troubles. And I think Maurie figured it out—when, exactly?" he said.

"Around the same year it happened. Not too long after Uncle Benoit deleted your graduation party from the all-family shared calendar," Maurie said. "Fatima was upset about it, and Uncle Benoit said you'd failed out, which Fatima refused to believe— she really likes you, God knows why—and eventually Uncle Benoit said it was that your tuition costs had been cut from the budget to make sure the 'higher tier' family members got their full quarterly stipends that January. Grandpere didn't always pay the closest attention to spending recommendations and back then he still trusted Uncle Benoit."

Pascaline blinked. "So who doesn't already know?" *And if you knew, why didn't you use your good-child influence to get my tuition restored?*

"Pretty much just Grandpere," Reuben said, "and Uncle Chummy. And maybe Great Aunt Mami, but maybe not. I'm never quite sure how much she knows. And, of course, nobody outside the family is aware. They told me I needed to pay back the family for my own schooling and that it'd go to a fund for you and the other younger ones, but somehow that fund never seemed to get established. Anyway, nobody outside the family knows."

"Except the Endeleys," Maurie said. "I sort of had to tell Adamou so he didn't fire Philip, and I think he told his uncle."

"Adamou doesn't know how to keep his mouth shut, does he?" Reuben said.

That made Pascaline grin finally, because he'd met Adamou only a handful of times, but he was exactly right. She added. "Adamou ratted you out too, you know. And Maurie did. You find anything in that secret accounts audit you did with all your newfound expertise in matters illegal and financial?"

Reuben shrugged. "The oil and gas side has some comptrollers with stickier fingers than they should have. It's the usual level for a business of that size. Your project, though, is incredibly smooth. I found one supplier who'd padded expenses and then reimbursed the padding. That just doesn't happen."

"I blame the witchy girl," Pascaline said pointing at Maurie. "And what are you doing with that spray bottle, really?"

Maurie shrugged. "I don't really know. But I did check with some TCG materials scientists, and any water vapor that hasn't evaporated off before a launch will be blown off by air pressure and not cause any trouble."

Reuben and Pascaline exchanged a look. "She didn't answer," Reuben said.

"Is this related to your visions?"

"She has visions now?" Reuben said. He dropped his voice low and stepped closer. "Is it a psychosis? A lot of those are not just treatable but actually curable, you know." He turned to Pascaline. "One of the foremen mentioned her, saying, 'The mountains shall be melted as with their blood.' I thought he was teasing the new guy. He did also say everything was back on schedule."

"It's a farce," Pascaline reassured him. "Well, mostly. I've never been entirely sure with Great Aunt Mami. But Maurie's just her normal self but turned grumpy from all the discomfort. She caught something out in the bush that's one of those completely curable things. And she has been visiting Great Aunt Mami."

Maurie waggled a hand back and forth. "I'm getting morning fevers again and usually seeing things when my temp spikes, but playing it up some does seem to encourage the staff. And, yeah, Great Aunt Mami likes having visitors and has a lot of suggestions about using long-term illness to your advantage. That bit about melted mountains was straight from Isaiah chapter 34. I dreamed this morning that we'd have a baptism by fire if we f—um, messed up. And we really could. So I begged some holy water from these two clergymen I know and I'm spraying it on the new A-HRV while I do a walk-around."

"The holy water does seem to make a snaky hiss when it splashes on the nose cones," Reuben said.

"That's all in your head. Don't give it too much attention," Maurie said. "Don't deny it in front of anyone, though. Great Aunt Mami warned me that one of the track-layer foremen got a double major in civil engineering and folklore and, even worse, there's a really popular 'Legends of Mami-Wata' course in the University of Yaoundé online curriculum that lots of engineering students have taken to satisfy their humanities requirement. Great Aunt Mami's got the foreman under control for us. For now at least. She's convinced him to consider my Mami-Wata spiritualism a useful fiction for group cohesion like the World War II gremlins."

"Yeah, well, we've got a different problem," Pascaline said. And she explained what she'd figured out about the new A-HRV engine modifications being not quite as much of an improvement for the payload mass fraction as that MIT PhD candidate Lucas Brown had promised.

"Wait, what? No, that's not a problem," Reuben said. "You were going to do the extra launches to get all the payload up there when you had the starter A-HRV design. You might not have quite as few launches as you thought, but you'll still need fewer total launches. And isn't TCG paying per launch anyway?"

"No, they pay for mass delivery and there have been interim payments each step of the way on construction since they are funding the track system too. There's a very significant bonus, though, if we can get them enough material up there so that they can have an initial DiamondWire line dropped from the orbital side down to the Kilimanjaro ground station in five years. It's prorated after that, down to no bonus at ten years."

"It's partially dependent on their orbit-side team," Pascaline pointed out. "I hate that we can be penalized for other people's mistakes."

Maurie laughed. "Yes, yes, we know."

A gleam shone in Reuben's eyes. "The sooner you can start sending the carbon launches, the sooner they can get their secretive DiamondWire processing started up there."

"But, uh," Maurie said, "Philip signed off on the Lucas Brown engine improvement."

"Yeah," Pascaline said, "he lied."

"Fire him," Reuben said at the same time as Maurie asked, "But do you still need him?"

"Not if he's lying," Reuben countered. "And Pascaline can do it just fine herself; she caught the error."

"But what was really wrong?" Maurie asked. "Is it still a better A-HRV than the other one?"

"No, a math thing, yes, and nobody's firing him." Pascaline answered their babble. "I have a better idea. Did you know that Adamou has finally paid me back that favor he owes me?"

Both her relatives responded with a pleasingly increased degree of panic about her leaving the project. They interrupted each other again in an urgent babble that ended in a joint plea of, "But you can't leave!"

"I'm not firing myself," she assured them. "Did you

know that TCG offers a number of academic institutions research grants and has lately set up a board specifically for Earth-to-orbit initiatives? I suppose planetary surface-to-orbit initiatives is more accurate. They'd like the option of building a space elevator on Mars, rather than being forced into it right away. So they want relevant research to continue. The board will review proposals and select who should actually receive the cash. It's a small-time-commitment position with very high pay in keeping with the high value of my expertise. They asked Adamou to serve on it, and he recommended me. He'll be on it too, but I'm to be the chair. I look forward to reviewing MIT's grant proposals in the future. If my deputy tech lead chooses to abandon this project before completion, I shall judge his applications accordingly."

Reuben twitched.

Maurie scuffed a shoe on the floor.

"What?"

"Will you have that job after Philip Chao tells them you don't have any degrees?" Maurie whispered.

Pascaline blinked. "Actually, they won't care." She shook her head. "Oh, that's it! So that's why Adamou couched it to TCG that way. I've been selected for the board based on my engineering management experience. The biography submitted calls me a philanthropist. Ridiculous, I know, but he cited all those backcountry well repairs and electrical grid installs and solar power upgrades which we really did legitimately do. My experience with the launcher was just a bonus."

Adamou, himself, entered the hangar and greeted Pascaline with a long kiss. "That board position was

an early wedding gift, not actually my favor repayment. I've got an even better one for you for that."
He waited a beat with an inviting grin.

Pascaline lifted her chin in challenge and said only, "Well?"

Adamou pointed to her comm. "If he took me seriously, you should be getting some messages there very soon."

Pascaline lifted her comm and blinked.

"Thank you, my dear," Great Aunt Mami sent, *"I should've known it would all work out. This is the most excellent hex of my life."*

"He?"

Her comm pinged with the arrival of a long message. And Maurie's comm pinged. And Reuben's pinged.

Reuben read it first and started laughing.

Maurie's eyes went wide.

Pascaline finally looked.

"I had a chat with your grandpere," Adamou explained. "Great Aunt Mami, or rather Tchami Magdalene since the appointment names her by her given name, is now the Sadou Director for Arts and Culture. All art gala support funding, major family philanthropic donation approvals, and so forth will go through her from now on. Your Uncle Benoit is eager to convey his deepest apologies. Since she's not inclined to see him right now, he's apologizing to everyone she's still willing to see."

CHAPTER TWENTY-SEVEN

A MOB OF REPORTERS AMBUSHED ETHAN, JAX, AND that lead publicist person whose name Ethan kept forgetting. They pointed videography gear at them, blinded each other with flashes, and shouted out questions.

"How proud are you to be making this a reality?"

"What do you say to detractors who claim space elevator technology shouldn't be owned by a single company?"

Ethan's project press rep pushed him toward the office door as the reporters yelled questions after them as if increasing the volume would make him more likely to answer.

"Sorry about that, boss," Jax said. "I thought we'd cleared them all out but a new group slipped in after your car. I think they were following you."

Ethan kept his face smiling. He snarled at a volume he hoped the microphones couldn't pick up, "Don't let it happen again."

Pale, the press rep assured him it wouldn't. Jax

didn't react. Ethan noted that, and the crease between his eyebrows deepened. His executive assistant was confident now? When had that happened? The doors closed on the mob of reporters.

Jax patted the press rep on the back. "Send me your statement before releasing anything. The boss might have a fifteen-minute block to review it tomorrow. Or leave them all in the dark. You should consider blacklisting the rudest ones. That might help."

"Right." The press rep visibly regained his composure at this suggestion of a way forward. "I can give our updates only to the ones who respond reasonably."

Ethan growled an affirmative and found a lidded cup of coffee pressed into his hands. He sipped. It was heavily sweetened and topped with a dash of vanilla and cream just the way he liked it best. And with the lid, no one could see it wasn't straight black the way he claimed to drink it.

He sipped again.

Jax gave him a faint smile. Only that in acknowledgement that he'd provided good coffee, and he knew he'd done it precisely right.

Ethan let the executive assistant keep his smile until he saw the page on his desk. An actual newspaper, printed in full color at a who knows what cost, lay across the desk surface, unfolded to show the full article with the worst headline in the history of newspapers blaring across the top. He meant to throw just the page, but his hands spasmed.

The coffee, the paper, and one of the random desk ornaments he'd chosen in hopes that it showed intellectual curiosity went flying. Jax jumped out of the way, pushed the publicist out the office door, and clicked the latch shut.

"Um, not what you were expecting, boss?"

"Man of the Year?" Ethan felt the pressure in his ears rising. Was it possible for a brain to explode in a gooey mess inside his head like happened in cartoons? Could he have a stress-induced aneurysm at least and never have to deal with disasters like this ever again? "Man of the Year." He forced himself to project a calm he didn't feel. "I take it you don't see how horrible this is."

It wasn't a question but his executive assistant answered it anyway. "We'd hoped you'd be pleased, boss."

"We?" Ethan dropped himself into the chair.

"For the profile, they did interview a lot of the staff. We signed nondisclosures," he assured him, "and checked with Chummy of course to make sure it was all okay with corporate policies."

"Chummy." Ethan considered strangling that HR man. Chummy would have understood instantly just how bad this was.

"Uh. What's the problem? They do print it as Woman of the Year when the recipient is female, so it shouldn't be a gender rights thing, and..."

"Mr. Jeffy," Ethan interrupted, "John-Philip Jeffy should be the one they choose. Anybody else, anyone at all, even the guy who invented the industrial-length carbon-nanotube fiber connector and named it after his sainted grandmother should rank no more than a sidebar mention."

"A team developed the space elevator's tether fiber production process," Jax said. "It was cross-functional development and no one has named it after anyone, but some members of the team are grandmothers themselves." His brow was furrowed deeper in confusion.

Ethan buried his head in his hands. "Just get me another coffee. I'll deal with it."

He started the letter three times with: *"I'm so sorry . . ."* And couldn't find the right words. He changed it and changed it again. In the end he sent all of TCG's leadership a single message with only two sentences. The first was: *"I learned today about a planned article."* He appended the horrible newspaper clipping in a scanned electronic form. No need to let other vice presidents or senior executives know there had been a full color-printed version made. He concluded with: *"Maybe the marketing people can do something with this."*

The wave of congratulatory responses crashed into his inbox with the loudest voice from Mr. Jeffy himself. Ethan read that one through carefully five times and couldn't find any hints in the word choice or tone that might indicate a personal vendetta against him had been triggered by this slight. Mr. Jeffy's public persona was one of never needing the credit for anything, as long as the job got done right.

Ethan wasn't dumb enough to believe that could be the reality. Mr. Jeffy got a lot of awards. Could even someone like Chummy pretend that that had happened without John-Philip Jeffy quietly campaigning in the background to make sure his name was floated about as a candidate?

The West African Launcher continued to earn completion bonuses, Ethan noted. They'd expanded into night launches, and now news media in Eastern Africa time zones were enjoying seeing the results live on the morning news. Of course the best view of all was in the control room at TCG Kilimanjaro.

Jax and the managerial team he'd assembled watched the screens and *ooh*ed at the payloads smacking space debris in a choreographed dance. White cursor marks smacked into red hazard bits and spiraled them off into other orbits. The dots changed to light blue indicating successful course changes to match the range of new orbits reclamation companies had requested. Some few changed to yellow indicating the objects no one wanted to reuse were now in orbits safely collision free for the next several years. A few turned green for new orbits that wouldn't threaten the elevator again ever.

Jax bent to whisper something to a technician and the display's legend updated to label green objects as "next intercept >100 years" instead of "no intercept." They weren't being given enough force to break outwards from Earth orbit, and the lawyers had argued strongly against deorbiting anything that might not burn up in atmosphere. It was vaguely possible that some few of them would have other mutual chain reaction collisions and eventually be problematic.

Ethan watched Chummy. The man was walking around almost in a fog. Ethan was almost certain that Chummy was living in a continual state of surprise. The Sadou launcher had been contracted based on his recommendation, yet the man was amazed to see it working and working well. Why was that?

Ethan didn't like people doing things he didn't expect. He especially didn't like that from Chummy.

"Jax." Ethan's executive assistant sprang away

immediately. Diligent and attentive, he tore himself away from the screens with obvious regret, but patiently waited for Ethan to tell him what he wanted.

Ethan suppressed a desire to shake the man to wipe that expression of adoration off his face.

Jax blinked, still patient, and awaiting instructions.

Ethan twitched his head sidewise just a bit toward his office with its soundproof door.

His executive assistant entered immediately. Ethan followed and closed the door behind him.

Jax had a fresh cup of coffee waiting for him.

"Congratulations, boss!" The man's smile was infectious. "Another great step."

"Yeah. About that." Ethan drummed his fingers on the surface of his desk without bothering to go around it and take a seat. "Did you notice anything odd about Chummy today? Anything going on with his staff I should know about?"

"With Chummy?" Jax blinked at the change in topic. "I did hear that he was trying to get his senior aide, Samson Young, to accept another position in the company, and he didn't want to go." He looked at Ethan with questions all over his face, but didn't ask for an explanation.

When Ethan didn't say anything more, his assistant moved directly on. "There are press releases about the successful orbit-clearing maneuvers ready for release. Did you want to review them?"

Ethan thought about that for a moment. "No, let's hold off on that." An insight occurred to him. "Or rather, forward them to Chummy. Ask him to sign off on them. Maybe even release them himself to the press. He has connections with the company we partnered with for ground-side launch. Check with his assistant, the junior one: DeeDee. We should support his efforts to get Samson to take that new job, don't you think?"

Jax nodded and started making notes. The directions would go out exactly as Ethan had asked. Ethan made a few notes of his own and pulled up some records to check names and contract details.

"Get me some more details on the Sadou Corporation too. We need to make sure no one can do a corporate takeover or anything like that on them. They are critical for us now."

"Sure, boss. But you don't need to sweat that. It's a family-owned company."

"Is it?" Ethan said.

Jax hurried out at his normal, breath-stealing pace, but his head swiveled to admire the replay of the flawless orbital collisions as he passed the screens.

Ethan let himself be drawn in as well. A video feed with the latest on the West Africa Launcher arrived in his comm soon after.

Maurie, the Sadou Corporation subcontractor lead for the launcher, spoke with one of his TCG staff about plans for future launches. Seeing her face expanded on the screen and watching how she moved as she spoke, she reminded him of Chummy, but corporate's racial-understanding training warned him not to ever say that aloud. One was not supposed to acknowledge how racial similarities could make oneself face-blind. He was going to need to have side-by-side photos of her and other dark-skinned subcontractors prepared for him to study before meetings. He'd really thought he was better at facial recognition than that. But

Maurie's nose and her ears really did look very much like Chummy's. Delight shone in her face combined with a raw confidence he envied. Those expressions reminded him of the human resources executive too.

A ping informed him that Jax had delivered the details on their relationship with the launcher corporation.

He checked the contract terms and suppressed a growl. No wonder she was delighted. The Sadou Corporation was on track to make a small fortune supplying their space rock before the tether cable came down. And those payments would grow toward a large fortune in time, because TCG would keep them well funded for their support in clearing low Earth orbit of space junk from now until eternity. Of course, they'd help TCG make an even larger fortune.

He approved a bonus payment on top of the contracted amount.

And he sent a demand to the lawyers. Review the contract. Find out what we can do to protect this supplier. And, also do another search for what TCG could legally do to create some competitors that he could use if he had to. He considered the word supplier for a moment and deleted it. Service provider. Pressed send.

Message replies blinked into his inbox within minutes. It was good to be in charge.

The protections weren't needed. And the competitor options were severely limited unless the Sadous breached the contract, which, one of the lawyers pointed out, TCG needed them not to do because it would seriously delay the elevator construction. That one suggested a check with logistical analysis if the company wanted to prepare alternative plans for debris clearance.

Ethan reviewed those alternative plans again, and this time he did let himself growl. Those other options were tiny specialty companies with limited capacity and slow response options to urgent issues. Or they were governments, which were worse. Ethan did not want to owe a government for the safety of the elevator. Governments were filled with people who wanted to control things, tax things, and transfer money from TCG to inefficient projects designed to please voters rather than customers and corporate shareholders.

He tuned back into the discussion between his staff and Maurie, sliding the chrono bar back to catch the discussion from the beginning and then hopping forward over pleasantries when each side wasted time expressing mutual respect and appreciation and so forth. Small talk in international business was annoying enough without the translators; he was glad to see the whole discussion conducted in English.

The team on his side was effusive. Far too effusive. He'd have to have a word with them. Yes, yes, the launcher team had done what they'd been contracted to do and come in ahead of schedule, but they were being paid for it. His staff didn't have to act like it was a vital part of the work or like they were in any way part of the elevator construction team.

"About supplies," his rep was saying, "do you think you could make those adjustments in the specs we sent over and increase supply deliveries to our tether-point station?"

"Ah, yes," Maurie replied, "our techs have gone

through your packet. Thank you for that and the technician-to-technician connections, by the way."

"No problem at all. Whatever we need to do to make the project a success."

"I understand," Maurie acknowledged. "And I do think we can do it. I want us to start with some more stable supplies, not just water, but maybe special parts packed in additive manufacturing dust. It'll be carbons, of course."

"Right. A useful delivery with a proof-of-concept test built in to see if the forces are gentle enough for more fragile payloads."

Maurie nodded. "Yes, exactly our thoughts. We've got the test set for the second launch if you can confirm the station side is ready to receive."

"Absolutely. We'll make that happen."

Ethan stared at his display in horror. This was a recorded discussion. He keyed his screen over, and confirmed. Yes. That station supply launch was already in the air.

Cheers and thumping of feet resounded from down the hall. So much for soundproofing. And he'd take that to mean his carbon dust supplier and sole effective debris cleaner company had also just become a finished parts and edibles supplier as well.

Ethan didn't want to like that. But...it was working, and the contract terms didn't allow the supplier to spike up the prices they charged him. The Sadou Corporation, the lawyers noted, did have the strongest negotiating position now, when they'd proved they could deliver and while TCG needed them most. But they'd asked for no increases.

It was downright honorable. It was as if these

people thought the world was actually like the rosy reality Chummy pretended existed all the time. And that thought triggered the cascade of deductions which let Ethan Schmidt-Li finally figure out how he'd been used.

"So, you gave your cousin's family a sweetheart deal, Chummy?" Ethan said to himself. "What do you suppose Mr. Jeffy is going to think of that?"

CHAPTER TWENTY-EIGHT

ETHAN DRANK BLACK COFFEE AT THE PARTY IN the most isolated corner he could find. The bride, Pascaline, seemed to be trying her hardest to scowl but her groom, Adamou, kept making her laugh. The joy radiating out from the pair marked the center of the celebration's crush. Other more self-interested partygoers paid homage to the Sadou grandfather and to TCG's CEO.

John-Philip Jeffy had the presidents of Tanzania and Kenya arm in arm with him on the dance floor. They were toasting the couple, the elevator's success, and their countries' future international prominence. The president of Cameroon had his arm over the Sadou patriarch's shoulder, having just taken a turn dancing with the bride's cousin. Mr. Jeffy released the two dignitaries and attempted to demonstrate something called breakdancing. He'd had either too much alcohol or not quite enough. Ethan's public relations queen, the former ambassador, and her assistants took turns engaging in more sedate dances with the three presidents and kept the CEO from overcommitting to or offending the favored dignitaries.

The new Vice President of Sales, Rodney Johnson, slid onto an empty barstool next to Ethan, holding a flask that'd been emptied more than once. He smelled like he might have spilled some of the contents on himself, and it hadn't been a weak alcohol. "Hey," he said in greeting.

"Congratulations on your promotion," Ethan said, raising his coffee mug in salute. Congratulating some-one else didn't come easy to him even now, but at least he could see the headaches Rodney had coming. And, he, Ethan, couldn't be blamed for them. "Vice President of Sales. Well done."

Rodney snorted. "Sure. I do well, and everyone'll say the elevator cargo sold itself. I fuck it up, and contract for more than your technicians can actually deliver, and I get the black eye. Nice thankless job there. Hooray for me."

It sounded so much like himself that Ethan only barely got the mug to his face in time to hide his smile. "Accurate," he said, "and I'm sorry for your loss."

"Thanks," Rodney said. "Cory's funeral is going to be in three months or so. He's getting cremated tomorrow, but his will specified a wake. They are saying they need at least two months to get all the specialty alcohols on his drinks list ordered in. Some of his sons want to do it at Kilimanjaro even though it's a long trip for most of the Aanderson family. One of them actually works for us and got invited to this shindig."

Rodney waved a hand at the large wedding crowd. "It seems the Bakweri take open hospitality to a whole new level, and they invited almost everyone. Shit, they invited me. So, even a young Aanderson kid got to come to this wedding. And he's talking about Limbe being the event location instead of Kilimanjaro, because the funeral attendees could watch launches and maybe send up some of Cory's ashes. I'll probably be fired by the time the wake happens. Invite me anyway if I'm gone by then, won't you?"

Ethan set down his mug with a clunk.

Rodney took another slug from his flask. "Or don't."

"You will be invited," Ethan promised. "You will also still be employed. Who the hell would dare fire you? You and Cory Aanderson are, well, were, you know what I mean. You're the surviving core of Chummy's dream team." And Ethan's mind ran on with the rest of the unspoken thought, *everyone knows Chummy walks on water in Mr. Jeffy's opinion... Except that I told Mr. Jeffy about the family connection to the Sadous... But could that really tarnish all Chummy's successes back to the earliest ones?*

Rodney squinted at Ethan. "I always thought you were smarter than that. Chummy had nothing to do with my hiring. Not really. He let me slip into the short list, but he was out with the flu the whole week of the final decision. Yes, Cory Aanderson had shared with him his cancer diagnosis and wish that he could somehow continue working before he said anything to Jeffy, but it was Chummy's two assistants back then who put together the Cory Aanderson and Rodney Johnson workshare plan. I always knew Chummy wouldn't follow through on promoting me into Cory's position. I kept Cory going way past what all the doctors predicted, and damn we were good together, but I always knew that'd be as much as I'd get. Chummy thinks I'm an asshole, and Jeffy doesn't like to work with assholes or with people Chummy considers to be assholes."

He took another sip.

"I tried everything. Absolutely everything to get a handle of my own on Chummy. And nothing ever worked. The man's a paragon." He peered blearily at Ethan. "How the hell did you manage? He thinks you're an asshole, yet somehow you got Chief of Sciences, Worldwide. Who did you bribe?"

Chummy's entire family, Ethan realized. *I bribed the entire Sadou clan.*

"Fine. Keep your secrets," Rodney said. He stood with the exaggerated steadiness of the extremely drunk and stalked toward the bar. Samson Young rolled up next to Rodney as he started to stumble and after a low-voiced conversation helped the man toward the door.

Ethan turned back to his own mug as DeeDee joined him with a new carafe of coffee. She pushed a tray with cream and sweeteners at him. "Drink something you actually like," she said. "We need to talk."

He considered Chummy's spy for a moment and then doctored his coffee. "You're too late," he said. "I told Mr. Jeffy in person three hours ago. I gather you had Wilbur Fischer primed to alert you if I requested any private one-on-one meetings with the man, but your sneaky little digital tendrils couldn't do a thing for you when I had Omer Ehrlich make the appointment and walked myself down the hall to use his comm line to do it."

DeeDee shut her eyes. "Damn," she whispered. "Rodney won."

"He's Vice President Johnson to you," Ethan corrected. "But he's at least at zero point one zero blood alcohol level now, and he thinks he's getting fired. Hell of a win."

DeeDee took in a deep breath and let it out again. "At least the elevator will be fine," she said. She made eye contact with him in a focused glare that seemed unnatural and practiced, if still heartfelt. "Do not let them fire Vice President Johnson. He's an asshole, but he's our asshole. The company needs him to sell advance cargo space on the elevator, so we can stay in the black over the next five years. He'll need a deputy, though. Someone way too friendly. Like Samson. He'd balance him out perfectly. But Samson and me will both get fired with the boss. So find him someone, promise!"

She turned her head down to a comm screen and scurried off without looking up again.

Ethan considered the second demanded promise of the night. He didn't have the authority to invite anyone to Cory's funeral or to hire anyone as Rodney's deputy. Strange that everyone seemed to think he was the mastermind with all the strings. Chummy was the one with the magic touch. It had always been Chummy. And Chummy hadn't come to the party tonight. Ethan rather suspected the man was sitting at home with his own intoxicant waiting for a termination call from Mr. Jeffy. Omer Ehrlich would've made a courtesy call to him after Ethan left.

John-Philip Jeffy sported a bruised elbow and a rip on the left knee of his tuxedo pants, but both the Kenyan and Tanzanian presidents had left his side laughing. He had Wilbur make appointments for Rodney to meet with each of them in the next week and gift their nations a certain—small—percentage of elevator cargo space in exchange for a commitment to defend TCG's continued claim of Kilimanjaro as a land parcel with no nation-state affiliation.

Rodney would need a deputy. He paused. He did not ask Chummy. But his eyes lingered on Samson Young as the man used his motor chair to carry an intoxicated Rodney Johnson out the ballroom's glass doors to a waiting autodrive taxi. Samson would be perfect for the job. Perhaps he wouldn't be a good future Vice President of Sales himself like Rodney would be—was. But Rodney was young. In three or four decades, even Samson might be roughened up enough for the job. Unless Samson needed to stay on to assist a new vice president of human resources in learning Chummy's particular style of magic.

Zhu Zhang Li appeared before him in a stunning *qipao* dress with a glitter of sunlit asteroids on the dark gray silk instead of flowers. "You never did give me the apology in person that I was promised in exchange for my very fine space rock," she said.

"My deepest apologies for trying to date you inexpertly," Jeffy said immediately, "and you never apologized either."

"My deepest apologies for trying to steal your corporate secrets inexpertly," Zhang Li replied.

Jeffy nodded. "You look gorgeous. Are you going to be getting in trouble with party officials for wearing that?"

Zhang Li shrugged and flashed a smile. "They won't dare. I've got most of their mistresses wearing copies of this dress, and the woman singing 'The March of the Volunteers' at the Olympics this year will be wearing this style as well. Besides, our rocks have earned us prime elevator cargo space on the first hundred lifts." She held up a crystal champagne glass. "Cheers." After a slight pause she added, "And our scientists have just reported that the notes I delivered them on DiamondWire are both complete and accurate. They did stop at twenty kilometers of the nanofiber, though. That's a hell of a lot of carbon, you know."

"I do know," Jeffy said. "Did Chummy give it to you?"

"No," Zhang Li said.

Jeffy leaned back, very pleased. "Rodney."

Zhang Li nodded. "And you told him to do it after I'd already agreed to give you back the rock," she accused, "because you wanted to make sure he had the chops to make tough sales bargains when he didn't have all the advantages."

"So, did he really wait?" Jeffy asked.

"Yeah," she said, "and his comm was ridiculously data-safed, costing my best hackers complete burnout during the three days he was on the ground with us. Then the data turns out to have been in an unattached flash drive in the clasp of the lanyard for his hospital visitor badge. Very tricksy. I approve."

"Let me ask you something," Jeffy said.

She raised her eyebrows and waited.

"If Chummy were available, really available, but were, let's say, somewhat in disgrace, would you hire him?"

"Of course," she said.

"It wouldn't depend on the disgrace?" Jeffy asked.

Zhang Li waved a hand. "No."

"Why?"

"I'd rather be lucky than good," she said. She gave him a nod. "And so would you. He's not really going to be available, is he?"

Jeffy considered the host of people celebrating. "I'm keeping him," he decided. "But he's not getting his annual bonus this year. Or rather not a second one," he amended. "He's already been paid."

Maurie lay on the Wouri beach on a woven straw mat stargazing at the few bright planets still visible in the dawn light when Mami-Wata appeared early the next morning. The spirit's snake familiar slid off her shoulders into the waves. It was the boa again this time, with the tire track death marks beginning to blur away.

"Well?" Maurie said.

"Well, what, you brat?" Mami-Wata watched the streak of the A-HRV vanish into cloud cover as the rail thrummed again with electric power from the mountainside's op-test of rapid back-to-back launches.

"I've been thinking about how to get you up there. Astronauts are supposed to be obscenely healthy, you know. So whatever microbes or viruses you've converted to your cause as demon possession co-conspirators would be most unwelcome in a thorough preflight fitness assessment."

Mami-Wata hissed. Her hair flared in a cobra's hood behind her and her eye gazed down with growing menace.

Maurie glared back despite having no expectation of winning. Snakes had an unfair advantage in staring contests. A lack of eyelids was definitely cheating. And yet, Maurie lifted herself onto an elbow to peer more closely. The snake spirit woman's eyes were fogged. Mami-Wata shrunk down to more human proportions as Maurie's fear failed to materialize.

"Are you getting ready to shed or something?"

"That's an incredibly rude question," Mami-Wata replied.

"I've been reading up on snakes," Maurie said. "You're nearly blind while that layer of the brilles— those clear little eye-scales things—that you use instead of eyelids get ready to come off."

"The future is always in a state of shedding or near shedding," Mami-Wata snapped back. "Why do you think this's taken me so long? I can hardly ever see anything!"

"So, what do you see?" Maurie asked.

Mami-Wata tilted her head up at the sky. Her finger extended toward a bright planet. "I see." She whipped her head around to look toward Douala as if she could see straight across the whole bay and through the jutting peninsula sandbars and scattered islands blocking a normal human's view of the city. "Not again!" She dove under the water and came up hissing with her hands around the boa constrictor's jaws.

"How many times have I told you to leave that woman alone!"

Maurie looked back and forth from the hissing spirit woman to the equally hissing snake.

"We are with this one now." Mami-Wata threw the snake at Maurie.

It wrapped massive coils around her, squeezed, and passed through Maurie's body. The snake hissed irritation and tried again with no more success.

"Last days or not," Mami-Wata continued to the

snake, "you aren't allowed to hug Our Magdalene anymore."

"Is Great Aunt Mami dying?" Maurie demanded.

"Didn't I just tell you I can't see very well?" Mami-Wata replied. "How should I know?" The spirit woman beckoned and the snake returned from its angry coil to glide over the water onto her shoulders. Mami-Wata smiled at the snake. "We got ourselves a Maurie now, whether we have to lead her by the nose or not." She turned back to Maurie. "You were asking about my last human. So, let's talk about her."

"About Great Aunt Mami?" Maurie said.

"Yes, of course. Keep up," Mami-Wata said.

"But I don't think Great Aunt Mami ever believed you were real," Maurie objected.

"Just because she never believed in me, doesn't mean I don't believe in her," Mami-Wata snapped back. The snake hissed angry agreement.

A wave slid over Mami-Wata and the spirit woman changed to a soft wheedling tone. "Do you know some of my people used to put their ancestors' bones in the most lovely pots and tie them to the branches of the highest tree in the savanna within three days' travel of the village in any direction?"

"Great Aunt Mami plans to be cremated," Maurie said. "And you can get anywhere on the planet in way less than three days now. I imagine the residents living near the world's tallest-standing redwood would have some objections to having its branches turned into a mausoleum."

"Yes," Mami-Wata said in time with the snake's pleased hiss. She was floating with her snake in the water now and calm as the slow-moving inlet waves.

Maurie shook her head. "I don't think Great Aunt Mami would like to have her ashes scattered in a redwood forest."

"But there's to be a new tree," Mami-Wata said. "If Our Magdalene can last just five or so more years, the tree will even have its taproot connected to my land."

"The space elevator as an ancestor tree?" Maurie stood bolt upright. "Well, I guess it's sort of like a tree. But even if TCG let us, I don't know if Great Aunt Mami would like that."

"Then perhaps someone ought to offer it to her," Mami-Wata said. "It was always only the most revered who had their bones so treated anyway. Besides, the foreigners are already planning to do it for one of theirs. You can't tell me Our Magdalene is less deserving."

"Cory Aanderson's ashes," Maurie said.

"Just so," Mami-Wata agreed. "As if my Tchami Magdalene deserves any less reverence for all her years of faithful service than his long-suffering bones do."

"If we send up Great Aunt Mami's ashes, do you go with her?" Maurie asked.

Mami-Wata smiled. "I might," she replied, and she vanished back into the waves.

Author Bio

Joelle Presby is an American writer who spent twelve years of her childhood in West Africa living in N'goundéré, Tchamba, Poli, Garoua-Mboulaï, and Meiganga. Small-town life in Cameroon gave her a fear of venomous snakes, a wary respect for folklore, and a fascination with the way people can make things work without actually having all the expected parts.

After high school in Ohio, Joelle gained admission to the United States Naval Academy, where even the math majors take twenty-four credit hours of engineering coursework. Robert A. Heinlein had gone there, so it seemed like an interesting place for a would-be storyteller to learn her craft.

Following graduation and commissioning, she studied how to find and kill submarines at Naval Postgraduate School and began dating a submarine officer. During her six and a half years of naval service, nations with significant submarine fleets stubbornly refused to go to war with the United

States. But even though she was neither a war hero nor cannon fodder, she did still get the guy.

Joelle's book collection has survived seventeen household moves, one earthquake, three hurricane-induced floods, and zero volcanic eruptions.

In previous bios, she lied about being unwilling to move again. But seriously, what science fiction writer whose faithful first-reader husband got a job offer from NASA would say no? Her husband, the former submarine officer who now works for NASA, might point out that his wife is a storyteller who shouldn't be trusted, but he enjoys being happily married.

Joelle Presby lives in Ohio with her husband and two daughters. She demonstrates a continued suspicion of Earth's motives by maintaining both earthquake and flood insurance. (No one credible will sell her volcano insurance.) She prefers to keep as many books as possible in easily portable e-book form, because, one day, we might need to evacuate the planet.

Acknowledgements

Thank you to those who helped with research and technological accuracy: Ron Nelson, David Mann, Pam Mann, Dave Gast, and Jesse Nice. Thank you to Gena Smith and Meriah Crawford who provided first-reader feedback and polishing insights. Thank you to Toni Weisskopf for extremely helpful editorial direction and to all the folks at Baen Books for giving me the opportunity to share this story with readers.

And thank you especially to Andy Presby for invaluable support throughout.

Ashes of Victory pb • 978-0-6713-1977-9 • $7.99

Honor has escaped from the prison planet called Hell and returned to the Manticoran Alliance, to the heart of a furnace of new weapons, new strategies, new tactics, spies, diplomacy, and assassination.

War of Honor hc • 978-0-7434-3545-1 • $26.00
pb • 978-0-7434-7167-9 • $7.99

No one wanted another war. Neither the Republic of Haven, nor Manticore—and certainly not Honor Harrington. Unfortunately, what they wanted didn't matter.

At All Costs hc • 978-1-4165-0911-0 • $26.00

The war with the Republic of Haven has resumed . . . disastrously for the Star Kingdom of Manticore. The alternative to victory is total defeat, yet this time the cost of victory will be agonizingly high.

Mission of Honor hc • 978-1-4391-3361-3 • $27.00

The unstoppable juggernaut of the mighty Solarian League is on a collision course with Manticore. But if everything Honor Harrington loves is going down to destruction, it won't be going alone.

A Rising Thunder tpb • 978-1-4516-3871-4 • $15.00

Shadow of Freedom hc • 978-1-4516-3869-1 • $25.00
pb • 978-1-4767-8048-1 • $8.99

The survival of Manticore is at stake as Honor must battle not only the powerful Solarian League, but also the secret puppetmasters who plan to pick up all the pieces after galactic civilization is shattered.

Uncompromising Honor hc • 978-1-4814-8350-6 • $28.00
pb • 978-1-9821-2413-7 • $10.99

When the Manticoran Star Kingdom goes to war against the Solarian Empire, Honor Harrington leads the way. She'll take the fight to the enemy and end its menace forever.

HONORVERSE VOLUMES

Crown of Slaves pb • 978-0-7434-9899-9 • $7.99
(with Eric Flint)

Torch of Freedom hc • 978-1-4391-3305-7 • $26.00
(with Eric Flint)

Cauldron of Ghosts tpb • 978-1-4767-8038-2 • $15.00
(with Eric Flint)

To End in Fire hc • 978-1-9821-2564-6 • $27.00
(with Eric Flint)
Sent on a mission to keep Erewhon from breaking with Manticore, the Star Kingdom's most able agent and the Queen's niece may not even be able to escape with their lives . . .

House of Steel tpb • 978-1-4516-3893-6 • $15.00
(with Bu9) pb • 978-1-4767-3643-3 • $7.99

The Shadow of Saganami hc • 978-0-7434-8852-0 • $26.00

Storm From the Shadows hc • 978-1-4165-9147-4 • $27.00
 pb • 978-1-4391-3354-5 • $8.99
As war erupts, a new generation of officers, trained by Honor Harrington, are ready to hit the front lines.

A Beautiful Friendship hc • 978-1-4516-3747-2 • $18.99
 YA tpb • 978-1-4516-3826-4 • $9.00
"A stellar introduction to a new YA science-fiction series."
—*Booklist*, starred review

Fire Season hc • 978-1-4516-3840-0 • $18.99
(with Jane Lindskold)

Treecat Wars hc • 978-1-4516-3933-9 • $18.99
(with Jane Lindskold)

A Call to Duty hc • 978-1-4767-3684-6 • $25.00
(with Timothy Zahn) tpb • 978-1-4767-8081-8 • $15.00

A Call to Arms hc • 978-1-4767-8085-6 • $26.00
(with Timothy Zahn & Thomas Pope) pb • 978-1-4767-8156-3 • $9.99

A Call to Vengeance hc • 978-1-4767-8210-2 • $26.00
(with Timothy Zahn & Thomas Pope)

| **A Call to Insurrection** | hc • 978-1-9821-2589-9 • $27.00 |
| (with Timothy Zahn & Thomas Pope) | pb • 978-1-9821-9237-2 • $9.99 |

The Royal Manticoran Navy rises as a new hero of the Honorverse answers the call!

ANTHOLOGIES EDITED BY WEBER

More Than Honor	hc • 978-1-9821-9288-4 • $26.00
Worlds of Honor	pb • 978-0-6715-7855-8 • $7.99
Changer of Worlds	pb • 978-0-7434-3520-8 • $7.99
The Service of the Sword	pb • 978-0-7434-8836-5 • $7.99
In Fire Forged	pb • 978-1-4516-3803-5 • $7.99
Beginnings	hc • 978-1-4516-3903-2 • $25.00

THE DAHAK SERIES

| *Mutineers' Moon* | pb • 978-0-6717-2085-8 • $7.99 |

| *Empire From the Ashes* | tpb • 978-1-4165-0993-2 • $16.00 |

Contains *Mutineers' Moon*, *The Armageddon Inheritance*, and *Heirs of Empire* in one volume.

THE BAHZELL SAGA

Oath of Swords	tpb • 978-1-4165-2086-3 • $15.00
	pb • 978-0-6718-7642-5 • $7.99
The War God's Own	hc • 978-0-6718-7873-3 • $22.00
	pb • 978-0-6715-7792-6 • $7.99
Wind Rider's Oath	pb • 978-1-4165-0895-3 • $7.99
War Maid's Choice	pb • 978-1-4516-3901-8 • $7.99
The Sword of the South	hc • 978-1-4767-8084-9 • $27.00
	tpb • 978-1-4767-8127-3 • $18.00
	pb • 978-1-4814-8236-3 • $8.99

Bahzell Bahnakson of the hradani is no knight in shining armor and doesn't want to deal with anybody else's problems, let alone the War God's. The War God thinks otherwise.

OTHER NOVELS

The Excalibur Alternative   pb • 978-0-7434-3584-2 • $7.99
An English knight and an alien dragon join forces to overthrow the alien slavers who captured them. Set in the world of David Drake's Ranks of Bronze.

In Fury Born   tpb • 978-1-9821-2573-8 • $18.00
A greatly expanded new version of *Path of the Fury*, with almost twice the original wordage.

1633   pb • 978-0-7434-7155-8 • $7.99
(with Eric Flint)

1634: The Baltic War   pb • 978-1-4165-5588-9 • $7.99
(with Eric Flint)
American freedom and justice versus the tyrannies of the 17th century. Set in Flint's 1632 universe.

The Apocalypse Troll   tpb • 978-1-9821-2512-7 • $16.00
After UFOs attack, a crippled alien lifeboat drifts down and homes in on Richard Ashton's sailboat, leaving Navy man Ashton responsible for an unconscious, critically wounded, and impossibly human alien warrior—who also happens to be a gorgeous female.

THE STARFIRE SERIES WITH STEVE WHITE

The Stars at War   hc • 978-0-7434-8841-5 • $25.00
Rewritten *Insurrection* and *In Death Ground* in one massive volume.

The Stars at War II   hc • 978-0-7434-9912-5 • $27.00
The Shiva Option and *Crusade* in one massive volume.

PRINCE ROGER NOVELS WITH JOHN RINGO

"This is as good as military sf gets."   —*Booklist*

March Upcountry   pb • 978-0-7434-3538-3 • $7.99

March to the Sea   pb • 978-0-7434-3580-2 • $7.99

March to the Stars   pb • 978-0-7434-8818-1 • $7.99

| **Throne of Stars** | omni tpb • 978-1-4767-3666-2 • $14.00 |

March to the Stars and *We Few* in one massive volume.

GORDIAN DIVISION SERIES WITH JACOB HOLO

The Gordian Protocol pb • 978-1-9821-2459-5 • $8.99

The Valkyrie Protocol hc • 978-1-9821-2490-8 • $27.00
Untangling the complex web of the multiverse is not a job for the faint of heart. Navigating the paradoxes of time can be a killer task. But Agent Raibert Kaminski and the crew of the Transtemporal Vehicle *Kleio* won't go down without a fight, no matter where—or *when*—the threat to the multiverse arises!

The Janus File pb • 978-1-9821-9296-9 • $9.99
Detective Isaac Cho is stuck with an untested partner, whose notion of proper "law enforcement" involves blowing up criminals first and skipping questions entirely, on a case that increasingly reeks of murder and conspiracy. As they work to unravel the mystery, they may discover their unique combination of skills might just provide the edge they need.

The Weltall File hc • 978-1-9821-9265-5 • $28.00
The Weltall Tournament's professional VR games were supposed to be a symbol of cooperation between SysGov and its militaristic neighbor, the Admin. Then a star Admin play received a death threat, written in blood. Now Detective Cho and Special Agent Cantrell have taken charge of the investigation and must bring the situation under control as they race against time to solve the mystery before the tournament ends.

And don't miss
The Dyson File by Jacob Holo!
tpb • 978-1-9821-9301-0 • $18.00

Available in bookstores everywhere.
Order ebooks online at www.baen.com.

THE SCARAB MISSION
TPB: 978-1-9821-9239-6 • $18.00 US / $23.00 CAN

When a raven, a cyborg, and a dinosaur board the derelict colony Safdaghar hoping to score some loot before the colony is catapulted into the outer reaches of the Solar System they come face-to-face with a gang of vicious pirates. But there's an even more dangerous threat lurking in the dark passages and ruined buildings of Safdaghar . . .

And don't miss:

ARKAD'S WORLD
HC: 978-1-4814-8370-4 • $24.00 US / $33.00 CAN

Arkad, a young boy struggling to survive on an inhospitable planet, was the only human in his world. Then three more humans arrived from space, seeking a treasure that might free Earth from alien domination. With both his life and the human race at risk, Arkad guides the visitors across the planet, braving a slew of dangers—and betrayals—while searching for the mysterious artifact.

THE INITIATE
HC: 978-1-9821-2435-9 • $25.00 US / $34.00 CAN
PB: 978-1-9821-2533-2 • $8.99 US / $11.99 CAN

If magic users are so powerful, why don't they rule the world? Answer: They do. And one man is going to take them down.

The Wellstone
TPB: 978-1-9821-2477-9 • $16.00 US / $22.00 CAN
MM: 978-1-9821-2588-2 • $8.99 US / $11.99 CAN

Humanity has conquered the Solar System, going so far as to vanquish death itself. But for the children of immortal parents, life remains a constant state of arrested development. With his complaints being treated as teenage whining, and his ability to inherit the throne, Prince Bascal Edward de Towaji Lutui and his fellow malcontents take to the far reaches of colonized space. The goal: to prove themselves a force to be reckoned with.

Lost in Transmission
TPB: 978-1-9821-2503-5 • $16.00 US / $22.00 CAN

Banished to the starship *Newhope*, now King Bascal and his fellow exiles face a bold future: to settle the worlds of Barnard's Star. The voyage will last a century, but with Queendom technology it's no problem to step into a fax machine and "print" a fresh, youthful version of yourself. But the paradise they seek is far from what they find, and death has returned with a vengeance.

To Crush the Moon
TPB: 978-1-9821-2524-0 • $16.00 US / $22.00 CAN
MM: 978-1-9821-9200-6 • $8.99 US / $11.99 CAN

Once the Queendom of Sol was a glowing monument to humankind's loftiest dreams. Ageless and immortal, its citizens lived in peaceful splendor. But as Sol buckled under the swell of an "immorbid" population, space itself literally ran out. Now a desperate mission has been launched: to literally crush the moon. Success will save billions, but failure will strand humanity between death and something unimaginably worse . . .

Antediluvian
HC: 978-1-4814-8431-2 • $25.00 US / $34.00 CAN
MM: 978-1-9821-2499-1 • $8.99 US / $11.99 CAN

What if all our Stone Age legends are true and older than we ever thought? It was a time when men and women struggled and innovated in a world of savage contrasts, preserved only in the oldest stories with no way to actually visit it. Until a daring inventor's discovery cracks the code embedded in the human genome.

Modern Hard SF + Military SF =
PATRICK CHILES